"This hefty novel spews intrigue, drama, and horror like blood a bayonet wound in the aorta. Maniacal survivalists, a traumatized psychotic, and more guns than a National Guard armory provide the flawless moving parts for this unrelenting body-horror thriller that holds its own against the likes of Ketchum, Slade, and Vachss. With *The Old Lady*, Triana maintains his seat at the very top of horror's most relevant scribes."
—Edward Lee, author of *The Bighead* and
The Television

"This old lady is definitely not a Golden Girl! Triana goes all out with the carnage and bloodshed in his newest offering, *The Old Lady*. This book reads like an '80s action movie but is pure Triana, full of rich characters, a detailed plot, and enough gore for the most seasoned horror fan."
—Daniel J. Volpe, Splatterpunk Award-winning
author of *Plastic Monsters.*

"Kristopher Triana writes beautiful nightmares, horrific fairytales, and intoxicating horrors, and however depraved and damaged his characters, you get to know them well … whether you want to or not."
—Tim Lebbon, author of *The Last Storm*

"Triana's masterful, gripping storytelling will not let go … I'm blown away with what Triana can do and will read just about anything he puts out."
—*Scream Magazine*

"Kristopher Triana's work is a volatile mixture of visceral noir and twistedly disturbing passion play that invades the reader's psyche and exposes the raw and throbbing nerve hidden within. His prose is unapologetic and totally without restraint or mercy. There's no denying it. Triana is the Master of Extreme Horror!"
—Ronald Kelly, author of *Fear, The Saga of Dead-Eye,*
and *Southern Fried & Horrified*

"Kristopher Triana is without question one of the very best of the new breed of horror writers."
—Bryan Smith, author of *Depraved*

"Whatever style or mode Triana is writing in, the voice matches it unfailingly."
—Cemetery Dance Magazine

"One of the most exciting and disturbing voices in extreme horror in quite some time. His stuff hurts so good."
—Brian Keene, author of *The Rising*

"Kristopher Triana pens the most violent, depraved tales with the craft of a poet describing a sunset, only the sunset has been eviscerated, and dismembered, and it is screaming."
—Wrath James White, author of *The Resurrectionist*

THE OLD LADY

KRISTOPHER TRIANA

The Old Lady Copyright © 2023 Kristopher Triana. All rights reserved.

ISBN: 978-1-961758-08-7

Cover Art and Design by George Cotronis © 2023

Interior Layout and Design by C.V. Hunt

Edited by 360 Editing (a division of Uncomfortably Dark). Editors: Candace Nola & Mort Stone.

This is a work of fiction. All characters and events portrayed in this book are fictitious and any resemblance to real people or events is purely coincidental.

No part of this book may be reproduced, stored in a retrieval system, or transmitted in any form or by any means, including mechanical, electric, photocopying, recording, or otherwise, without the prior written permission of the publisher or author.

Bad Dream Books
P.O. Box 447
Hope, RI 02831

**For signed Kristopher Triana books and merchandise, visit:
TRIANAHORROR.COM**

for my Chandra

"Be polite. Be professional. But have a plan to kill everybody you meet."

—James Mattis, retired Marine Corps general
and the 26th U.S. secretary of defense

PART ONE
HOMECOMING

ONE

HAVING BEEN TORTURED THERE FOR the better part of a decade, Tracey never imagined she would return to her father's cabin. All those years she'd longed to escape these mountains, and when she finally had, she'd endured terrible living conditions to avoid coming back.

Now she felt she had no choice but to return.

She was alone and had fewer resources than ever. A life of hardship had taught her many valuable lessons, one of which was to take what she needed when she could get it, pride be damned. Tracey couldn't afford to be proud.

The White Mountains were bright in the sunshine, the snowy hills justifying the range's namesake. Tracey had taken highway 91 up, bypassing rusted silos and barnyards, watching smoke billow from chimney tops to blend with the morning fog. She passed by ranches where highland bulls congregated, their orange fur fluttering on the gentle breeze. Horses in coats slurped from heated buckets. Western New Hampshire consisted of towering mountains of igneous bedrock decorated with snow-covered evergreens and moose crossing signs. The countryside offered the most majestic vistas in the state,

THE OLD LADY

beset by the woodlands of Vermont and Maine, with the Canadian border less than a hundred miles away. The small towns that populated the area relied on the money of tourist skiers, with many businesses only being seasonal, and ski resorts and lodges being at the center of everything. Though there were more signs of civilization now than when Tracey had grown up here, the towns remained sparse and thin, and disappeared completely once she drove high enough into the mountainside, going deeper into the vast and unforgiving wilderness.

Even with the snow tires on, the old Ford pickup struggled on the dirt road. Water from the brook had bled over the pathway and froze, leaving vicious patches of ice. The leather of her fingerless gloves cracked as she tightened her grip on the wheel. It was a delicate balance of driving slower as a precaution yet having to build up speed when approaching a steep incline so she would gain enough momentum to make it up the mountain. Her ears popped from the elevation, shoulders tense as the Ford pushed onward.

Though the boards had gone gray with age, the covered bridge was still standing. Tracey gritted her teeth, her mind quaking with memories of having to climb on the outside walls of the bridge when she was in her early teens. Now she drove through it, over the freezing brook and its myriad of black rocks, and under the truck's weight, the bridge groaned like a ship at sea.

Making it to the other side, Tracey bit her lip, realizing how close she was getting to the cabin. Thinking about coming here was one thing, but doing it was something else. The familiar, tight ball of anxiety centered in her chest like a lodged grenade, then seemed to expand with a dangerous heat, threatening an eruption. The last thing she needed was a panic attack, but it was impossible for her to come home without one. She just hoped she could hold in her angst until she'd parked the truck. She bit what was left of her thumbnail, feeling the sting as she peeled away a protective layer of flesh. As always, she ignored the pain, just as she'd been taught to. Sucking the blood away, Tracey noticed some new trails had been carved through the wilderness. Some were big enough for ATVs, others so thin they wouldn't even be noticed by those who hadn't been trained in bushcraft.

The dirt road ended in a parking lot of muddy snow. Clouds had gathered, and a sky the color of gravestones cast gray light upon a forest of Red Spruce and Eastern Hemlock. Tracey stared at the alpine peaks and steadied her breathing, summoning the nerve to get out of the truck. Though this was bear country, it wasn't the wildlife she feared, nor the treacherous nature of the journey ahead. Her memories were always a legion of frothing demons, but here, in the very place they'd been forged, the demons grew louder, their fangs sharper.

"You can do this," she said to herself. "C'mon, you bitch."

She put one hand on the door handle but couldn't move beyond that initial step. Deciding she needed some help with her nerves, she checked her wristwatch to see if it was too soon to take another Xanax and, of course, it was. Cursing, she reached into her coat for her Marlboros and lit one with her Zippo.

Tracey growled to herself in the mirror. "I said *move*."

By the time she realized she was quoting her father, the words had already come out. It was like that sometimes. She often talked to herself without realizing it and gave voice to the thoughts Dad had cemented into her subconscious. When she tried not to talk to herself, she only heard his gravelly voice circle through her head.

"*I said move, Tracey!*" he barked in her memory. "*Don't just squirm there like a maggot. That's how you get fucking shot!*"

She opened the door—not so much to obey the ghost of her old man as to escape from it. Breathing deep of the fresh air, she zipped up her puffer coat and strapped her ice cleats to her hiking boots. She moved the blanket and small toolbox she kept on the passenger seat to the rear of the cab, grabbed her duffle bag, and locked the door. She opened the cover to the truck bed, revealing the milk crates full of tools and supplies. Tracey always had them on hand but knew she wouldn't need them in the cabin. Still, she snatched her backpack BOB—code for "bug out bag" but she preferred "bail out bag"—from the bed and slung it over her shoulders while carrying the duffle bag in one hand.

She hadn't bothered bringing any Duraflame logs. She used synthetics because it was unlawful to bring firewood from outside the area. Even in the winter, the forests were threatened by nonnative insects that destroyed trees in large numbers. But logs would just be one more thing to haul. Tracey doubted she would be building any campfires and had no need for the fireplace. Dad had always heated the cabin with propane. There was a large tank at the edge of the property. He wouldn't have made changes to that, and even in death Tracey knew her old man would never leave the tank—or anything in his sanctuary—on empty.

THE OLD LADY

Looking to the trail ahead, she saw a lateral path covered in ice, but knew that would only last about a hundred yards before the mile and a half trek uphill. With the truck secured, Tracey began the hike. As a teenager, this path had taken her about an hour to climb in good weather, with an added half hour in the snow or during extremely hot days. But at age fifty-five, she figured it would take her at least two hours, despite how she worked to stay in shape.

"Let's go, old girl," she told herself.

She flicked her cigarette butt into a pile of gray snow and pressed on.

The BOB on her shoulders was the same one she carried everywhere, a large hiking backpack with a water bladder pouch and multiple hidden compartments. In it were all the things she needed to survive, but to lighten her load on this trip, she'd emptied some items and left them in the truck, knowing the cabin would be well-stocked even though she hadn't been there in over three decades.

This high up, the winter breeze grew heavier, steadier, and she switched out her beanie for her balaclava, tucking her salt-and-pepper hair beneath it. She opted not to bother with the goggles unless conditions worsened. The air was thick with moisture, promising more snow or freezing rain. She would have to check the weather stats upon arrival and evaluate the necessary precautions. Tracey wasn't sure how long she was going to stay at the cabin but always wanted to be prepared. Her compulsions wouldn't allow her to rest until she'd covered all bases. Neither would her father's voice.

"*If you want to make it home,*" he echoed in Tracey's skull, "*then you'd better quit crying and get climbing.*"

Marching up the jagged rocks, she reflected on her thirteenth birthday, and how her father celebrated it by having her crawl up this mountainside in the rain with her belly low to the ground and a .22 rifle strapped to her back. It wasn't her first experience with combat training, but it had been the most grueling. At the time, she'd thought it was the worst thing he could have done to her. In the years that followed, Tracey would learn just how wrong she'd been.

The frozen woodland was silent, without so much as the whispered footfalls of another living thing. During her years here, Tracey had seen bald eagles, moose, white-tailed deer, minx, coyotes, peregrine falcons, foxes, Canadian lynx, and porcupines. She'd also eaten many of them, along with the regular servings of white-tailed hares, squirrels, and insects. Dad had hillbilly recipes for anything that moved, and by the time she was eleven, Tracey had been burdened with the chore of building, baiting, and checking on wildlife traps. Some were simple snares and cages. Others were far more brutal.

But brutality was simply the nature of these mountains—at least in her experience. Other people came here to enjoy the twelve hundred miles of hiking trails stretched across the beautiful landscape, but they also had the good sense to leave after a few days, and never stayed out at night the way Tracey had been forced to. They slept in rental cabins with all the amenities while she'd toiled in the dirt and defecated in a compost toilet. There had been no vacations, only long days of work, no matter the weather conditions. For Tracey, hikes hadn't been for enjoyment. They'd been grueling exercises and terrifying drills. And while her dad had thought of the remote cabin as his sanctuary, for Tracey, it had always been a torture chamber.

And now she was going back.

"It's a place to stay," she huffed.

She couldn't argue with that. Despite her reservations about coming here, she wasn't foolish enough to turn down free shelter and a chunk of land to call her own. It wasn't much, but it was more than she'd ever had. Though she lived in the poorest part of the city, her last shithole apartment in shithole Pittsburg had been more than she could afford. Every month she'd flirted with eviction, hopping from one hard labor job to another. It'd been that way since she'd been released. Bosses were hesitant to hire convicted felons, leaving all the worst jobs for them and illegal immigrants. Landlords were equally hesitant to sign on ex-cons as their tenants, even when they were females, who were generally considered less dangerous. Tracey spent a lot of time sleeping in her truck and always kept a blanket in the cab. By inheriting her father's cabin, she had found a solution to two of her biggest problems, but somehow coming back seemed like a bigger problem than all the others put together, which was why she planned to sell the place.

But first, she had to see what she was dealing with, and transform the property to be more hospitable to normal human beings. As it was right now, even her father's lawyer refused to go there.

Dad had made it very clear in his will. The cabin was left to Tracey, for only she knew how to get in and out of it safely.

TWO

ALICIA GAZED UPON THE LOOMING mountains, watching the mist make ethereal rivers through their crags. Her breaths were clouds of vapor as she took in the majesty of the Northern Appalachian trailways. She reached for Dylan's hand, but her boyfriend was busy snapping pictures with his phone, his gloves tucked in his armpit.

"Babe," she said, "live it, don't document it."

He smirked at her, his boyish face turning devilish. They'd had this discussion before. Rather than enjoy the moment, Dylan always whipped out his phone to take pictures and videos for social media, as if their adventures together didn't count without the applause of others. Alicia reached for him, and he stuffed his phone in his pocket as if she might snatch it away and hurl it into the creek below. When she took his hands, she could feel their coldness even through her wool mittens.

"Put your gloves back on," she said.

"Quit bossin' me," he teased.

Alicia playfully smacked his belly. "Stop being stupid, and maybe I will."

Her boyfriend pulled her into him then, the way he knew she liked. She looked up at Dylan, noting the pinkness of his nose and cheeks. He reminded her of carolers in a Christmas cartoon. All he needed was a sheet of lyrics to hold. His cuteness was irresistible, and Alicia went on her tiptoes and gave him a little kiss. He repaid her with a bigger, deeper kiss, and she flung her arms around his neck, wishing they'd come up here alone. It would have been nice to get cozy in the cabin without Marcus and Nori around. Even now, Alicia could feel their eyes on them.

"You guys ready to keep going?" Nori asked.

It was her way of separating Alicia from her brother. Dylan's little sister was pleasant enough, but became uncomfortable whenever Alicia and Dylan were intimate, even with something as innocent as this mountaintop kiss.

"She's right," Marcus said, adjusting the straps of his backpack. "We've still got a long way to go, and we want to make it to the cabin before nightfall."

Dylan turned to his best friend. "Calm down, dude. We're coming, we're coming."

Alicia giggled but resisted the urge to make a dirty joke out of it. At sixteen, Nori was only two years younger than she was, but seemed far less comfortable with her sexuality, and even less comfortable with the sexuality of her brother and his girlfriend. Dylan was her half-brother by blood, but they'd lived together Nori's entire life and had a powerful sibling bond. She seemed not so much protective of Dylan but disgusted by the idea of him getting laid, and therefore a little unhappy with him dating. It made Alicia wonder why he'd invited Nori along in the first place.

Bringing Marcus at least made sense. Without his influence, Dylan may never have agreed to something like this. Marcus was training to become a forest ranger and knew more about the wilderness than anyone Alicia had ever met. Even though they were sticking to popular trails and had a comfortable cabin awaiting them, it was reassuring to be with someone who knew where they were going and could teach them the best practices to get there safely. The trails were obscured by snow and debris, and without Marcus, they would be impossible to follow. He'd already had to redirect the others when they'd unwittingly started to stray from the trail.

Alicia could figure out subway systems in any city in the world, but had no sense of direction when it came to the woods. She relied

THE OLD LADY

on her GPS, not knowing how to read a paper map, and having never had use for a compass. And Dylan, despite being best friends with Marcus, couldn't have been more different from him, and not just because Marcus was black while Dylan was half white and half Japanese. Their bond came from having grown up together since kindergarten because they lived next door to each other. Where Marcus pursued physical challenges, Dylan preferred the challenge of video games and role-playing cards. Marcus was a weightlifter and rock climber, whereas Dylan was a skinny skateboarder who enjoyed comic books. Marcus was not without his love of playing *Call of Duty* and he adored the *Black Panther* films, but there was a maturity to him that Dylan often lacked. Marcus was a nineteen-year-old *man*. Dylan was a *boy* nearing eighteen. Though Alicia loved him, it was impossible to ignore these realities. But she'd never been attracted to traditional masculinity, anyway. She was an athlete like Marcus, but that's where their similarities ended. She was much happier being with someone who enjoyed PlayStation and Anime as much as she did.

"Can we at least have a snack while we walk?" Alicia asked Marcus.

"Best to leave them alone right now," he said. "The trail gets difficult around the bend here. You'll want to have your hands free so you can grab on to trees for balance."

Alicia glanced at Marcus' metal hiking stick. He'd tried to convince the others to buy some for the trip, but they'd not wanted to spend the money. Now Alicia wished she'd sprung for one but would never admit it.

The group continued through the slush, following Marcus around the bend to an incline. His muscular body propelled him with relative ease while the others struggled to keep up. Used to running track, Alicia was still feeling good, but Dylan and Nori were breathing heavily. The siblings hunched over as they trekked uphill, staring at their boots instead of taking in the scenic surroundings the way Alicia did. She looked all around, absorbing the imagery, savoring the moment. That was the whole reason they'd come here, wasn't it? To experience the beauty of untouched wilderness and put themselves to a test—albeit a relatively simple one. This was physically tiring but not emotionally draining. Being here didn't feel reckless or dangerous. The cabin they were going to had electricity provided by a generator, as well as propane heat and running well water. This was "glamping," as her grandfather called it—the wussy version of camping out, featuring all the comforts of home. While being this deep into the middle of nowhere was an adventure of sorts, the trip was also basic and, more importantly, it was safe.

The wind picked up, whipping Alicia's blonde hair across her face. She brushed it from her cheeks and pulled her beanie down over her ears.

A sudden sound like a lawnmower turned her head. The others looked toward the distant noise, too.

"Sounds like a dirt bike," Dylan said.

"An ATV more likely," Marcus said, "or a snowmobile."

Alicia grinned. "Oh, man. That's what we should have done. Snowmobiles are dope."

"Yeah," Dylan said. "Screw all this walking."

Marcus looked back at him. "Not everything up here is accessible by vehicle."

Dylan peered through the trees, still looking for the source of the noise. "Yeah, okay. But that does sound like a lot of fun."

"Maybe next time, babe," Alicia said, patting him.

It was an empty notion. With the cost of college, they couldn't afford hiking sticks, let alone snowmobile rentals. Part of what made this weekend trip worth doing was its cost effectiveness. This time of year, cabin rentals on the mountain dropped in price considerably because no one wanted to hike through snow and ice just to stay in a small cabin. This area was too wooded for skiing or snowboarding, so the cost of the cabin rental was within their vacation budget when they split the cost four ways (though Nori had only contributed her leftover Christmas money of fifty bucks). Luckily, Marcus had been kind enough to drive them all here without asking for gas money.

They walked for another half hour, the conversation dwindling as they focused on the terrain. Thin channels of icy water ran across the trail, and mounds of dead leaves made for hidden pitfalls. The group hiked carefully, Marcus advising them.

"Avoid the smooth rock surfaces," he said, pointing one out. "I know they look sturdy, but the ice makes them way too slick."

Alicia paused, bracing herself before jumping over a thin stream. Her toes were already numb. The last thing she needed was to flood her boots with freezing water. The soggy earth sucked her feet, as if trying to pull her down like quicksand, but her thighs were strong from those three years on the high school track team. Now in her first year of college, she kept up running for regular exercise. Alicia

THE OLD LADY

and Marcus had to help the others out of the muddy spot.

Nori groaned. "This sucks. Where's the cabin?"

"Almost there," Marcus told her.

Nori grumbled under her breath. Marcus asked her to repeat what she'd said, but she only stared at the ground, not acknowledging him. Sometimes it was hard to tell if she was being rude or if it was just her hearing loss that caused her to ignore people. Dylan had told Alicia about the Fourth of July accident. Nori was just four years old when the family set off fireworks in the driveway, and a bottle rocket had made an unexpected, misdirected launch, and soared directly into the little girl's right ear before exploding, leaving it almost completely deaf. She had a hearing aid but often didn't wear it out of embarrassment. She was even more embarrassed by the heavy scar tissue, which had left her ear looking like pink cauliflower, as if she were a retired boxer. Nori always wore her hair down to cover it. At sixteen, nothing was more important to her than fitting in, especially after she'd worked so hard with a speech therapist to get rid of her stutter.

Alicia slipped on a patch of black ice she hadn't noticed, and instinctually reached out for Marcus for balance. He caught her before she could fall. Dylan only stood there watching. Though concerned for his girlfriend, he just didn't have the same reflexes.

"You okay?" Dylan asked her.

"Yeah." She looked to Marcus. "Thanks."

Marcus nodded, then exchanged a glance with Dylan. Alicia sensed a mild discomfort between the best friends, as if Marcus had been wrong to touch Alicia even to save her from breaking a leg. She'd never known Dylan to be hostile, but he did tend to pout when unhappy. When Marcus started hiking again, Dylan stepped closer to Alicia and took her hand. She would have preferred to keep her hands free for balance, but held on to her boyfriend anyway, just to reassure him. Though Dylan was a modern young man and didn't subscribe to traditional gender roles, he still had a male ego, and Alicia knew how fragile those could be.

"Hey, um," he said to her, "just stay close to me, okay? I got you."

"Okay."

Alicia allowed him the delusion of being her protector. Dylan meant well, and he treated her like a queen, so although Alicia believed she was more equipped to deal with the challenges of this mountain than he was, she saw no need to point that out. They'd been dating for almost three months, but already she didn't doubt he would do anything for her—anything within his capabilities.

Nori gasped. "Oh shit!"

The group stopped, the others following Nori's gaze. She stared at something in the woods, but Alicia didn't see anything.

"What is it?" Dylan asked his sister.

Nori shushed him and pointed. The others looked into the woods again. Still, Alicia saw nothing.

"I think I saw a bear," Nori whispered.

Marcus moved his hand to the can of bear mace clipped to his belt and peered into the thicket. "I don't see anything."

Nori shook her head. "I *saw it*, Marcus."

Having known one another most of their lives, Nori's relationship with Marcus was almost like that of siblings, and she snapped at him the same way Alicia's younger sister always snapped at her.

"I know what I saw," Nori told him. "And it was way too big to be a bunny."

"Look," Marcus said, "I believe you saw something, but it might not have been a bear. They're usually hibernating by now."

"Well, maybe one came out to find food."

"It's possible, but..."

"Well, I don't know," she said, furrowing her brow. "But what if it's, like, hunting us?"

Marcus smiled. "Even if a black bear was up and about, it's not likely it would be hunting humans. You're thinking of grizzly bears."

"Well, maybe that's what it was."

"Girl, there aren't any grizzlies in New Hampshire."

"He's right," Alicia said.

Nori huffed and crossed her arms. "Fine. Then what was it?"

Marcus shrugged. "Could've been anything. Might've been nothing. This area is loaded with wildlife. It's their home—we're just visitors. And they're way more scared of us than we are of them." He flashed his charming smile. "Anyway, it's gone now. Relax. We're not being hunted. Nothing is watching us."

THREE

TRACEY WATCHED THEM FROM HER cover. Hearing the group coming up the trail, she'd quickly darted into the forest but knew the young brunette had spotted her before she'd crouched behind a fallen tree. Hearing a running motor nearby only heightened her alertness, but the sound quickly faded away. *A snowmobile*, she thought, *or maybe an ATV*. Her binoculars gave her a better look at the hikers, and when the group turned their faces her way, she saw they were only teenagers. The irrational fear that had shot through her began to fade as her heartbeat slowed back to normal. Her grip on her serrated hunting knife loosened, and Tracey put it back into the leather sheath and exhaled the breath she'd been holding.

"*You've gotten slow in your old age*," she thought in her father's voice. "*Slow and soft*."

But she knew that wasn't true. She was stronger now than she'd been before going to prison. Being locked up had cut her off from all the drugs, booze, and excessive junk food that had once damaged her mind and body. She'd also learned that when you were locked up, the most important thing was to pass the time, so she'd volunteered for whatever labor was available, and had started working out regularly.

Upon her release, despite her age, she was healthier than she'd been in decades.

"*But that girl still saw you,*" her dad's voice scolded.

"Fuck you," she whispered aloud. "So what if she did? They're just kids hiking. They're not…"

She didn't want to say it. The closer view through her binoculars had not just revealed the ages of the kids, but also their races. The white girl and black boy hadn't fazed Tracey, but the girl who had spotted her was Asian, and the other boy had Asian features. Over the years, Tracey had come to understand just how difficult it was to unlearn the racial prejudices a person's parents instilled in them. After spending the first eighteen years of her life believing they were the enemy, she'd had to put serious effort into not seeing Asian people as a threat. Regarding her everyday life, Tracey believed she'd succeeded in that, but being back on this mountain oiled the trigger of that dormant phobia. She shook her head, embarrassed of herself.

"This ain't Da Nang, Dad," she said.

She waited for the hikers to move on and checked her watch to see if it was Xanax time. There were still forty-five minutes to go.

"To hell with it," she said.

Tracey slung off her BOB to fish out the prescription bottle—one of several. The psychiatric drugs had been a huge benefit in prison, but now that she was on the outside, she had to pay for them out of her own pocket, which was the main reason she was always broke. She was a single American woman with no health insurance—a one-way ticket to the poorhouse. She'd weened herself off the Zoloft but needed her other meds to keep her in a mental state that, while not ideal, was more tolerable than the alternative. Even just going off the Zoloft had been a rollercoaster, with her depression slowly deepening, and her sex drive—which had lowered as a side effect of the drug—coming back as a snarling beast, causing her to masturbate several times a day to keep from regressing to her younger days as a promiscuous bar tramp. Eventually, that lust had leveled out as her body adjusted to the absence of the Zoloft, but menopause wreaked havoc on her hormones, anyway. Tracey often longed for a man, but as soon as she would satisfy herself physically, the craving would disappear again, which was for the best. She didn't want to be close to anyone. Honestly, she couldn't be. The psychiatric drugs helped, but not enough for her to maintain a healthy relationship. She'd learned that lesson already with Gavin.

THE OLD LADY

And with Olivia.

The blonde girl she'd just seen in the woods was close to Olivia's age and even looked somewhat like her. But the closest Tracey had to go on was the photograph Gavin had mailed to her while she was still in prison. In it, Tracey's daughter was a cute teenager smiling for her yearbook photo. Looking at it wrenched something inside Tracey, so she'd torn the picture to pieces and tossed them in the trash. But the memory of her daughter looking so much older than when Tracey had last seen her in person made a lasting impression.

Popping a Xanax, Tracey sipped from the hose of her BOB's water bladder.

"It's pathetic to need pills to steady those shaky hands," she thought in her father's voice. *"You used to be steady as a rock. Look at you now."*

"And whose fault is that?" she said aloud. "Don't talk to me. Just stay down in Hell where you belong."

But she knew no way to stop him. Her mind was not entirely her own. It never had been. In that sense, she'd never gotten away from her father. Coming back to the mountain had only made him more vocal. She could only imagine how loud he would be once she reached the cabin.

Tracey gritted her teeth and pressed on, but now she stayed off the trail, not wanting to be noticed by anyone, even though she had no reason to hide other than being generally antisocial. She moved through the woods stealthily, using a craggy path alongside a granite wall, ignoring the aches in her aging bones as the cold sunk into them, and making mental notes of potential landmarks. As she marched uphill, she kept her hand close to her hunting knife without realizing it.

~

The cedar tiles covering the cabin's exterior walls had gone gray with age, streaked with water stains and spots of wood rot. At first glance, Tracey was shocked her father would allow this amount of deterioration, but then she remembered how old he'd grown. Maintaining the necessities of rural living would be difficult enough for a man in his late seventies, so it only made sense that he would let the aesthetics slide. This place was about function, not fashion, and no matter how old her father had gotten, Tracey knew the cabin would be fully operational. If anything, allowing its shabby appearance might have been on purpose as a sort of camouflaging, to make the place look like just another mountaintop shack when really it was anything but normal.

Tracey crouched as she scanned the land surrounding the cabin. No trespassing signs lined the perimeter, and a worn Gadsden flag waved from a ten-foot pole, the coiled snake seeming to hiss at potential visitors. While there were some patches of ice and mud, most of the property was covered in snow, with a pathway carved from the front door to the start of the nearest trail. Tracey doubted the old man had shoveled it, and she wondered if he still had that special snow remover she'd used as a teenager, if he'd been able to maintain something so dangerous at his age. That such things were even legal amazed her. She wondered what the legality of her owning one would be but decided it didn't really matter, given everything else that came with this place.

She squinted as she searched for tripwires. They had made so many over the years, her father teaching her how to make mousetrap alarms, tin can alarms, and keychain tripwires. He'd also taught her to make spring spear traps and whip traps like the bamboo ones made by the North Vietnamese Army. During the war, the Viet Cong had targeted U.S. troops with these deadly booby-traps. Using springy green bamboo sticks about three to ten feet wide, the insurgents affixed barbed-spike metal plates to the end of the stick, which was tied to a tree along a pathway and cocked like a horizontal catapult, with a tripwire attached to the trap. Once triggered, the spiked end of the pole would whip forward and impale the victim through the torso, arms, or legs.

Though Dad had taught Tracey how to build the deadly whip traps, they didn't set them up on the property, opting to use non-fatal tripwire alarms instead. They'd always used braided fishing line tied to the trees because it was both sturdy and nearly invisible. Eventually Dad settled on lines attached to an alarm inside the cabin that was just loud enough for them to hear without outside intruders being able to hear it through the insulated and armored walls. So there wasn't much for Tracey to worry about if she hit one now, but she didn't want to get off to a bad start. To her surprise, her memory served her well, and she found the first tripwire was in the same place she'd set it up thirty years ago. Normally she had trouble even remembering what she had walked into a room for, but the memories of her training were hard-wired, and returning to the cabin brought them to the forefront of her mind with stunning clarity.

Stepping over the wire, Tracey moved cautiously, bracing herself for more traps. With there being so much snow and ice, it would be

THE OLD LADY

harder for her to spot them. She put down her duffle bag to free both hands, picked up a fallen tree branch, and brought it to the spot she remembered. Tracey pressed the tip of the branch into the ground. The ground bowed, and the stick went through it. She withdrew the branch. If she stepped forward, the hidden net would give, and she and the dead leaves would drop ten feet into the pitfall trap. She and her father had made it decades ago. Unless the old man had changed things, there were no punji stakes to impale the trap's victim on, but the pit was too deep for the average person to climb out of on their own.

Tracey shook her head. Filling the hole in again was going to be a serious chore.

Going around the pitfall, she drew closer to the cabin, and the motion sensor lights came on. They were bright even in the daytime, but she remembered them being blinding at night. She spotted a new security camera attached to the underside of the roof's overhang. It seemed Dad had entered the computer age.

When she reached the two steps of the porch, she skipped the second one with the pressure sensor that would set off the airhorn alarm. The front entrance was a solid core door reinforced on the inside with an inch-thick layer of steel. The only other ways in and out of the cabin were through a secret escape hatch with a hidden trapdoor. The windows were braced with security window film, which made them harder to penetrate and would keep the glass shards in place if they broke. Dad had always been against putting bars on them. He'd had enough of living in cages. Now that Tracey had spent time behind bars, she better understood the old man's aversion to them.

It wasn't until she was looking at the door's lock that she realized she didn't have the code.

"Shit."

If Dad's lawyer had given it to her, Tracey had forgotten it. He'd handed her so much paperwork to go through that she'd only grazed. Through her childhood, her father changed the four-digit lock code once a month, but always cycled through the same three combinations. She closed her eyes tight, trying to free the codes from the cobwebs of her mind. She tried one before she could doubt the order of the numbers. It didn't work. She tried another but wasn't sure she had it right either. Again, the lock refused to open. Her muscles tightened, sweat forming within her balaclava. She pulled it off to breathe better and bit her bottom lip against her rattled nerves. These moments of frustration were like seizures to Tracey. They made her curse uncontrollably and sometimes even scream. Her body would go tight, jaw clenched, fists balled. Even though she'd taken a Xanax, anxiety coursed through her like an electric shock, throwing fuel on her anger. It was incredible how an inanimate object could push her into such an intense fit of rage.

She entered the final code: *7-7-67*.

Her birthday—and just a few weeks before Dad was deployed to Vietnam.

The lock opened.

One down.

The lawyer had given her the other keys, which were spares given to him by her father. Tracey opened the latches in descending order until all four were undone. She breathed deep. The locks had annoyed her, but opening the door had the potential to launch her into a full panic attack. Just touching the handle made her short of breath.

"You can do this," she told herself.

She bit her bottom lip harder, hoping the pain would distract her mind, preventing it from unearthing all its pitch-black memories of this awful place.

"*Welcome home*," her father said from within her skull.

"Fuck you," she replied.

Tracey opened the door.

The cabin was dark, but she could make out the metal shelves that lined the walls. They were fully stocked. She almost flicked the light switch on the wall but hesitated when she imagined her father rigging an explosive to the electrical board. She used her flashlight instead. It was a sturdy halogen light with a steel ring on the end strong enough to bash through a windshield in an emergency. She spotted the lanterns on a shelf beside bags of MREs—Meals Ready-to-Eat. Just looking at them nearly made her gag, remembering the horrible taste. Tracey opened two of the lanterns, filling the cabin with a sickly, pale light. Then she opened the blackout curtains.

The cabin was revealed in full. There was a set of wooden bunk beds on the back wall, the bottom one lined with a sleeping bag and an inflatable mat. The top one—Tracey's old bed—was now used for random food storage. Huge bulk bags of brown rice, lentils, pasta noodles, and oats. Boxes of powdered eggs and cans of ham. Above the beds was a map marking all the sources of fresh water within five

THE OLD LADY

miles of the cabin. Tracey stared at the old wood-burning stove, then looked at the standing cabinet that served as one of many armories. Shelving was stacked with canned goods, paper products, over-the-counter medicines, batteries, and other doomsday supplies. Stacks of crates held gallon jugs of distilled water. There was a small corkboard stocked with tools, supplementing the larger supply in the shed out back. There had always been two sheds—one full of tools, gear, and weapons, the other a smoke shack for curing meats.

"Home sweet home," Tracey grumbled.

She went to the sink to wash her face, and when she leaned over it, she was struck by the memory of her father installing the system while Tracey, being only eight years old, held the flashlight. In addition to the 210-gallon water tanker he'd installed to collect rainwater off the cabin's roof, he'd hooked a supply line from the drilled well and outfitted it with a submersible pump to push water into the cabin's pressure tank. The process had frustrated him, and he'd taken out his anger on Tracey, yelling at her to hold the light better, though she'd had no idea what that was supposed to mean.

Patting herself dry with a dishrag, she caught a glimpse of herself reflected in the small window above the sink. The gray in her hair was more apparent in the natural light. The lines in her face appeared deeper, as if she'd been forged from cracked leather, but it made the thick scar on her throat less noticeable. She looked away, disgusted by what she'd become, as if there'd ever been a better version of herself, one that wasn't stained and shattered.

"You done got old, you crazy bitch," she mumbled.

Dropping her bags, Tracey placed one lantern on the table under the light switch and drew her knife to unscrew the plate. After inspecting the wiring, she confirmed it was safe, and turned the lights on. The bulb in the ceiling fan gave the cabin a warm, amber glow that would have felt cozy anywhere else. Here it was only a spotlight on Hell. But it seemed the old man had taken good care of the cabin right up until his fatal heart attack. Once it was de-weaponized, this place would be worth a small fortune to the right buyer, money Tracey could survive off for a long time.

"Live on the cheap," she mumbled, thinking out loud. "Make everything stretch. Every dollar, every dime."

She rambled quietly as she looked about the cabin, cursing and flinching at the memories.

Taking the deepest breath of the day, Tracey stepped to the

armory cabinet and popped the latch. The doors came open, their opposite sides cradling a litany of handguns. The back of the cabinet was where the shotgun and .22 rifle were stashed. The rifle was the same one she'd grown up using—the old "survivor's best friend" as her dad called it. Though not the most powerful firearm, it was best for target practice and small game hunting, with its ammo being cheap and lightweight.

Dad had upgraded the shotgun since Tracey had last been here. The old double-barrel had been swapped out for a pump-action 12-gauge. Many of the handguns were new to her as well. She didn't know all the calibers, makes, and models. With her criminal record, she wasn't allowed to own guns. But she knew enough to recognize a Glock 19, a .38 snub nose revolver, and a .380 ACP, and knew how to use them. There were knives of all shapes and sizes, three different stun guns, and a set of brass knuckles. Boxes of ammunition took up the rest of the space.

And this was only the cabin's arsenal. Dad kept additional weapons in the shed out back, including the heavy artillery, much of it illegal for civilians to own. Dad had never cared about legality. After the war, his loathing for the U.S. government became absolute, and he feared death more than imprisonment.

She remembered what he'd always said: "Worry about the six that will kill you, not the twelve that will put you away." It wasn't until she was older that Tracey realized this referred to bullets and jurors.

Closing the cabinet, she wondered how she would go about selling all these weapons, and if it was possible for an ex-con to do so legally. Tracey had no connections with criminals. She had no connections with anyone. Perhaps the lawyer Dad had hired to handle his estate could help her unload the legal firearms. The rest would likely have to be turned over to law enforcement, though she preferred to avoid dealing with the police. Some weapons she could bury—maybe even use the pitfall as a grave for them—but others were too dangerous. Ammo and other explosives couldn't just go in the ground. That would be an invitation to disaster and death—and worse, an invitation back to prison.

To the right of the armory was a coatrack. Hanging from it was her father's BOB, a large hiking pack with outdated aluminum bars. Beside it hung the green canvas bag Dad had brought back from Vietnam. Though her BOB was built for survival, her father's bags were stocked for a war he'd spent decades bracing for, a war he'd trained

THE OLD LADY

his daughter to fight with all the harshness of an army drill sergeant. But the training she'd received was not limited to that of the United States military. Dad had gone beyond boot camp—far beyond. He had transformed his little girl into something volatile and ferocious, blurring the lines between human, animal, and machine until all that remained was madness.

Opening her duffle bag, Tracey pulled out the little black box full of the old man's ashes and held it up before her face. Tears clouded her vision.

In his will, Dad had left the cabin to her, saying he hoped she would use it to finally do something with her life. Even in what would be his last words to her, he chose to tell her she'd been a quitter and a loser, that she'd made nothing but terrible choices. But he had no other family and, being so paranoid and distrusting, had no close friends to leave the cabin too. At the very least, he told Tracey he loved her, and encouraged her to use the cabin well, that it could be a way for her to turn her life around.

"This is it, Dad," she said to the box of ashes. "This is the end."

In exchange for giving Tracey the cabin, her father had requested she spread his ashes into the wind somewhere on the mountain.

Tracey carried the box outside, made the short walk to the compost toilet, and dumped her father down the shitter.

FOUR

MARCUS STARED AT THE DENSE forest ahead, a wall of trees and brush he hadn't anticipated. He'd sensed the trail was thinning but hadn't expected it to dead end like this. Snow and woodland debris had made the paths difficult to discern from the rest of the mountainside, but he'd been confident he could keep the group on track. Maybe a little too confident.

He peered through the icy thicket, unsure what to say to the others. Nori spoke before he could.

"Where's the trail?" she asked. Her face was pink from the cold. She sniffed a drop of moisture from her nose as her face turned sour. "Where is it, Marcus?"

He looked at the others, as if they could help him. Dylan's eyes were downcast, his head slowly shaking back and forth. Was it disappointment Marcus saw on his friend's face—disappointment in *him*? Looking at Alicia, Marcus could feel the pity emanating off the girl. He knew her empathy was genuine and well-meaning, but it felt almost patronizing. Marcus prided himself on being a man of the woods and had made many solo adventures that were much more complicated than this one. He'd had his share of failures in the wild,

THE OLD LADY

as anyone did, but he'd never lost sight of a trail before, and had never failed in front of friends like this. He'd failed in front of his instructors many times, but his friends didn't know about the trouble he'd been having with his wilderness training.

Embarrassment warmed his cheeks. "Made a wrong turn is all."

"Oh my God," Nori said in a hush.

"Just need to get my bearings."

Alicia's look of pity became one of concern. "You're not saying we're lost, are you?"

"Nah, nah," he rushed to say, whether it was true or not. "We're not lost, I just need to figure some things out."

"Oh my God," Nori said, louder this time.

Her brother frowned at her. "Would you stop that?"

"We're *lost*, Dylan!"

"Everybody just calm down," Marcus said. "We can't have deviated that far off the path."

He looked to the trails of footprints they'd left in the snow behind them, but even backtracking he couldn't make out a proper pathway. He'd been pressing on despite his growing concerns, hoping he'd find his way back onto the path, believing there was no way this could happen.

Marcus drew the map of the forest from his pocket, which was merely a pamphlet detailing the trailways that branched off the main one, which was Harding Trail. He drew his compass from his pocket and placed it flat in his palm.

"What're you doing now?" Nori asked.

"The cabin is supposed to be northeast of the pond we passed—"

"*Supposed* to be?" Dylan asked.

His incredulous tone made Marcus sigh. "It *is* northeast."

He pivoted until the compass told him he was facing the right direction. Ahead was uncharted woodland blanketed in untouched snow. No sign of a path. The terrain was cluttered and wet, with ice-caked rocks and fallen branches decorating the frozen earth.

"We cut through here," Marcus said, "and we're bound to reach the cabin soon."

"You can't be serious," Alicia said.

Dylan agreed. "No way, man. We can't hike through there. We'll just get even more lost."

Marcus glowered, trying not to take this as an insult. He was an experienced woodsman working toward becoming a forest ranger. Even if he'd failed a few written tests, that didn't mean he was any less effective in a real-life situation. Dylan wouldn't know a strike flint from a potato chip. He was a friend, but he was also soft, and that softness had been grating on Marcus' nerves as they'd gotten older. Dylan probably couldn't find his way out of a corn maze. Who was he to doubt Marcus' navigation skills?

"I'm telling you," Marcus said, "the cabin has to be just on the other side of these woods."

"The other side?" Dylan asked. "And just how far away is that? We have no way of knowing how deep these woods go, man."

"Damn it, I know what I'm—"

Alicia cut in. "Guys, c'mon. Let's just turn back the way we came. I'm sure we'll figure out where we went off trail."

Marcus shook his head. "That could take an hour. Maybe more. We cut through these woods, and I'll bet we're at the cabin in under twenty minutes. If we go northeast from here, there's no way we won't find the clearing where the cabins are."

Dylan furrowed his brow as he peered into the forest ahead. "This doesn't even *feel* like northeast, though."

"Always trust your compass," Marcus said. "Always."

"Okay," Alicia said. "Maybe you're right, but it's a big chance to take. The trail was difficult enough to hike. This will be even worse."

"We'll be fine. Just follow in my footsteps."

"Marcus, please. Let's just go back the way we came."

The tightness in his chest intensified. "Look—I don't know about you, but I'm freezing my ass off out here. I don't want to spend another hour or two backtracking in the hopes we'll find the path, only to have to march all the way back up the slope again. I want to get to the cabin and get warm, don't you?"

Nori spoke up. "I do. I'm cold and I'm tired. Let's cut across."

Alicia stared at her as if betrayed. "Nori…"

"I can't take much more of this," Nori said. "I'm sorry. I thought I could handle it, but I'm smaller than you guys. I'm freezing out here."

Dylan stood up straight, his boyishness fading with a lowering of his brow. Marcus had seen this look on his friend's face before. Despite his general softness, Dylan could be firm when it came to taking care of his little sister.

"Okay," he said. "Let's cut through the woods then."

THE OLD LADY

Alicia's jaw fell. "Dylan—"

"Look at her, Alicia," he said, pointing at his sister. "She could get frostbite out here. I want to get her warm as soon as possible."

"But if we're off the trails, we might not make it to the cabin at all. The best thing to do is go back and find Harding Trail. Now c'mon, please, let's go."

Dylan sighed and looked at his best friend. Marcus gave him an upward nod. Without words, he was asking Dylan if he was really going to let his girlfriend call the shots. Had it not been for Nori, Dylan probably would have.

"Sorry, babe," Dylan told Alicia. "But if the cabin is, like, twenty minutes from here, I say we go through the woods. Marcus knows what he's doing."

Marcus gave his friend a small nod of mutual respect.

"I'm not saying he doesn't," Alicia said. "But I think—"

"Hey," Marcus interrupted. "All this talking in circles is wasting time. Alicia, you're outvoted, alright? We're going through the woods."

Her eyebrows drew closer together. "So what then? If I don't go with you, you all are just gonna leave me here by myself? Or are you going to drag me with you, kicking and screaming?"

Marcus rolled his eyes. This was exactly what he'd expected from this white girl. People like her were just so accustomed to having things their own way. He liked Alicia well enough, but even if he hadn't, she was his best friend's girl, so he had to at least tolerate her. But that didn't mean he had to go along with whatever nonsense came out of her mouth.

"You do what you want, girl," he said. "We're taking the shortcut."

Seeing she wouldn't break through Marcus' resolve, Alicia turned to her boyfriend in a last-ditch effort to change his mind. "Babe, c'mon, this is super dangerous, and you know it."

"Hey," he said. "This trip was *your* idea, okay? I only agreed to this hike because it's what you wanted. Now can't you do something for me?"

Alicia's anger visibly faded, her eyes drooping. Marcus worried she might start to cry, but instead Alicia crossed her arms and looked away, as if she were guilty of some crime.

"Alright," she finally said. "I guess we could give it a shot."

"That's the spirit," Marcus said, wanting to encourage the group.

"This is what being in the wild is all about. Ingenuity, determination, and survival."

That last word seemed to sting Alicia. "Okay. But if we don't find anything in twenty minutes, we turn back. Deal?"

Marcus could have laughed. This would be the easiest bet he'd ever won. If the situation were different, he would have put money on it.

"Yeah, sure," he said.

Winning the argument helped rejuvenate what confidence he'd lost, and he strode into the dense, dark forest with his chin up, sure he'd get his friends to safety, that everything was going to be alright.

~

Alicia cursed under her breath as she followed Marcus deeper into the unwelcoming wilderness. It was flurrying now, and the whizzing snow created an ethereal haze. At times she could see the clusters of low, rounded mountains and scattered monadnocks in the distance, but mostly the tree coverage was too dense to see anything else. The forest was thick with dead vegetation, and the Red Spruce trees dominated the landscape, their branches bowed by snow, making them look like Christmas cards.

The group descended one slope only to march up another, the slippery granite and hidden debris creating potential hazards. Though it pained her to think it, Alicia had begun to doubt Marcus' abilities as a wilderness guide. He'd always been a wealth of information regarding the outdoors, but now she wondered just how much of it was accurate. She was not as experienced of a hiker as he was, but common sense told her trekking through these woods increased their chances of an accident. A twisted ankle wasn't much to worry about in a suburban setting where help was readily available, but out here, such an injury could create serious problems. She wondered if Marcus was truly confident about the location of the cabin or if he was simply too stubborn to admit he was wrong, and the further they journeyed, the more she feared the latter. Worse yet, she knew the further they went the harder it would be to convince anyone to turn around, if they could even find their way back.

Dylan must have sensed her unease because he squeezed her hand.

"It's all good," he whispered. "There's still plenty of daylight left. And besides, we've got a compass."

Alicia didn't reply. She'd already made her argument and lost.

THE OLD LADY

Perhaps her silence would say it better.

"You're not mad, are you?" Dylan asked.

"Just remember the deal," she said, checking her phone for the time. "Eight more minutes, then we turn back."

Dylan let go of her hand and pursed his lips. He was always even-tempered, which was one of the things she loved about him. It wasn't like him to show anger, but his frustration was obvious, and now Alicia realized the difficult position he had been put in. Dylan was the link that connected them all, being Nori's brother, Marcus' best friend, and Alicia's boyfriend. No matter whose side he chose in this argument, Dylan still lost. Alicia regretted having put that kind of pressure on him but wasn't sure what else to do. She didn't want to be the nag of the group, but she also didn't want to follow them into trouble.

"Eight minutes," she said again.

She was relieved when Dylan nodded.

"Yeah," he told her, staring straight ahead. "Eight minutes."

They traveled on until they reached level ground, and Nori pressed against her brother for warmth. Dylan put his arm around her. Alicia wished she was the one he was holding, but this wasn't the time for jealousy. That Dylan's sister was a constant barricade between them would have to be addressed some other time, when they were safe, warm, and sheltered. The strain of the hike made Alicia sweat under her layers, and she worried what trouble that dampness might cause as the sun vanished behind the clouds, further dropping the temperature. She checked her phone repeatedly, counting down every minute as they advanced across the frozen hinterland.

"Check it out!" Marcus shouted.

With less than two minutes left, he pointed ahead, and the others followed his gaze to a long, bare strip that ran through the woods. The snow upon it had been trampled by footprints and tire tracks.

"Holy shit," Dylan said. "Is that the trail?"

"Hell yeah," Marcus said with a smile. "Course it is."

"Well, it's *a* trail at least," Alicia said. "It might not be the same one. We should check the map to see if—"

"Hey, look," Nori said, pointing to the right. "You guys see that?"

Alicia squinted. With the dense tree cover and snow flurries, she might not have noticed it. The building was brown and gray, giving it the perfect camouflage against the dreary landscape. She could only see a sliver of the building, so it was impossible to tell if it was a cabin or a barn or something else entirely.

"There she is!" Marcus said with a chuckle. "See? I told you we'd find the cabin—and in less than twenty minutes too."

"How can you tell from here?" Alicia asked.

"Girl, I'm looking at it with my own two eyes. Can't you see it?"

"I see part of it. Or part of something."

"It might be one of the other rental cabins," Dylan said. "I mean, there's a couple up here, right?"

Marcus shook his head. "Man, those other cabins aren't anywhere near here. They're scattered about the mountain, miles apart."

Nori huffed. "Let's just go, already!"

Breaking away from Dylan, Nori passed the others and headed for the trail. She moved quicker now that shelter seemed within reach. The others sprinted to catch up with her, and when the group made it to the path, Alicia studied the building, but from this angle she could see even less of it. Still, whether it was the cabin was not as important to her as having found a trail. Even if they were on the wrong one, at least they weren't lost in the middle of the forest anymore. All trails eventually led to some form of civilization, and there were plenty of footprints here. Where there were human tracks, there would be other humans, and Alicia took that as a good sign.

FIVE

TRACEY THREW HER FIST INTO the Everlast bag.

Worn and wrapped in duct tape, the punching bag hung on a chain from a rafter on the back porch, just as it had when her father first taught her how to fight. She'd enjoyed hand-to-hand combat back then, because it was one of the few things that got her off the mountain.

Once they'd moved to the cabin, Dad pulled Tracey out of elementary school to "teach her more important things." Being homeschooled—if it could even be called that—left her with few chances to socialize with anyone other than her father, so she'd been eager to take kickboxing lessons, go to karate class, or do anything else that required going into town. When she'd turned twelve, Dad signed her up for a first aid course, followed by a more advanced Wilderness First Responder class when she turned sixteen. The class took a total of eighty hours before she was certified, and she'd enjoyed it because it involved socializing with new people. The only disappointing part was no one in the class was close to her age. But in her combat classes, she did meet other teenagers. Unfortunately, by then she'd been living in isolation so long that she found it difficult to relate to her peers.

She didn't get their references or understand their social cues, and they were weirded out by her unconventional way of life. That was when her social anxiety first started to take hold. Eventually, it would suffocate her.

Her teen years were long behind her now, but Tracey had retained all she'd learned. Getting in the proper stance, she bent her rear leg at the knee and shifted her center of gravity to the other. Using her core to pivot her body on her lead leg, she swung the other in a swift rear leg kick, hitting the bag at a ninety-degree angle. Her shin smacked the bag head-on, causing it to dance on the length of chain like a man choking at the end of a noose. Tracey sniffed against the cold and gave the bag a hook kick before practicing a few leads. She wasn't as limber as she'd been as a teenager, but she was still able to get her foot as high as her head and could have done even better if she weren't wearing heavy boots and snowboarding pants.

Tracey had never been on a snowboard but used the pants in cold weather for their combination of polyester and fleece, which made them warm, waterproof, and windproof. There were also plenty of pockets, and zippers at the bottoms of the legs to keep snow from collecting inside them. Most were obnoxious in color, but she'd managed to find a pair in plain gray, a shade she felt suited her best. It was every color, and yet the absence of color. Having lived most of her life without the luxury of choosing her own clothes, Tracey had no sense of fashion or desire to learn it, selecting her clothing the same way she selected anything—with only function in mind. There was a lot of flannel and wool. Her entire wardrobe—shoes and all—could fit in a single trash bag. All her worldly possessions could fit in her truck. Part of that was because she liked to be able to leave a place easily, but another part was rooted in defiance of a father who had hoarded *everything*.

The backyard was proof of that.

Behind the cabin, the tool shed and smoke shack were surrounded by old pallets stacked with plastic totes and small, wooden crates where Dad stored items he'd believed weren't valuable enough for thieves to steal but still valuable enough to hold on to. Chicken wire, twine, scrap metal, wood blocks, and bits of PVC pipe. Rusted tools, drill bits, loose gun parts, and fishing gear. Several cases of Mason jars still in their packaging. Tracey didn't have to sift through it all to know they were mostly just junk that would have to be hauled away somehow.

THE OLD LADY

She sighed in frustration. "Fuck."

Everywhere she looked, she saw another hurdle between her and getting rid of this place. Maybe she would just have to sell it *as is*. It would mean listing it at a lower price, but it would save her a lot of time, labor, and aggravation. She didn't think she could handle something as complicated as paying a crew to clear everything out, especially with the cabin being inaccessible to most vehicles.

She punched the Everlast bag again. "Bastard."

Even her father's final gift to her was just another test.

"Fucking bastard," she said, taking another swing.

She threw a couple of combinations, alternating between conventional kickboxing and what mixed martial arts moves she could still remember. Even after she'd left her father, Tracey continued to practice self-defense, knowing she'd need it to survive on the streets. Sometimes a swift kick to the head was the only thing that would make someone listen. Being able to fight had gotten her out of many dangerous situations, particularly with men.

But unfortunately, not all of them.

Watching the punching bag sway, Tracey went still and reflected on the smoldering wreckage of her life, murmuring her scattered thoughts aloud. To snap herself out of this despair, she started a mental checklist of the things she needed to do here, beginning with the deactivation of the security measures. As the list swelled, she started chewing her bottom lip, overwhelmed and anxious. She wanted another Xanax but resisted the urge, worried about running through a month's supply in one week again. Her doctor would scold her. So would her parole officer if he found out. She didn't want to risk being denied a prescription renewal of it, or her Risperidone. Tracey had tried antidepressants, benzodiazepines, mood stabilizers, and antipsychotic drugs. Some had helped more than others, but while she'd experimented with many drug combinations, she'd yet to find a chemical balance, and could only chase relief in the short term. She hated taking anything that could alter her mind, but it was far too damaged to not apply some sort of healing salve.

"Take your time," she told herself as she put both hands on the exterior wall and hung her head between them. "You've got food. You've got shelter. You've lived on much less before. Fuck it. Ain't no rush, ain't no fucking rush. One step at a time."

She focused on a single nail on one of the cedar planks. It had been hammered in crooked, creating a curve at the head. Locking eyes on it, Tracey controlled her breathing with long, slow inhalations, meditating to settle her riled blood. It only worked sometimes, but even just trying was beneficial. It reminded her that she was in control of her life now. No overbearing fathers. No corrections officers controlling her every move. No husband and daughter to disappoint or terrify.

There was only Tracey.

"That's enough horror for anyone," she said.

SIX

IT WASN'T THE CABIN.
Marcus could see that now. The building was too big, and the cleared land surrounding it was comprised of several more acres than what was allotted to the rental properties. This building was more of a ranch house, though just as rustic as any cabin he'd ever seen, with its bare wood planks and stacked log aesthetic. An American flag hung from the front porch railing, and a cracked chimney exhaled smoke that disappeared against the backdrop of the gray winter sky. The flurries had become a steady snowfall. There was another, larger building behind the main house. Its faded red paint suggested a barn, but Marcus could only see a portion of it from where they stood.

"What the hell is this?" Dylan asked.

"Somebody's house," Alicia said, "it looks like."

Hugging herself against the cold, Nori gave Marcus a pained look. "Where are we?"

Marcus struggled to answer. He looked both ways on the trail, then checked his compass again, as if it had more answers, as if it were somehow its fault instead of his own.

"You said the cabin would be here," Nori said.

"I'm sorry," he said. "I could have sworn—"

"We've been walking all day!"

Dylan touched his sister's shoulder. "It hasn't been that long."

"It's been hours." Nori shrugged his hand off her and glared at Marcus. "You promised we'd be there in twenty minutes."

Marcus opened his mouth but couldn't find the right words. He hated to admit to a mistake, especially an embarrassing one regarding his wilderness skills, but he also hated to let everyone down.

"The snow is getting heavier," Alicia said. "We need to get inside."

"I know," Marcus said. "We can't have strayed too far. We'll figure it out."

Dylan drew his phone. "Let's just call somebody."

"And tell them what?" Alicia asked. "We don't even know where we are. How can we tell them where to pick us up?" She cocked a thumb toward the ranch house. "There's smoke coming from the chimney. Someone's home. Maybe we should ask them for help."

Marcus cringed. "Alicia…"

"Look, I know this frustrates you, but—"

"No way I'm asking for help. What kind of self-reliance is that? I'm gonna be a ranger soon. How can I call myself a man of the wilderness if I ask for help on a hike this simple?"

"Everyone makes mistakes. Nobody thinks less of you for it."

"Maybe you don't, but I will. You're studying to be a journalist, right? How would you feel if someone told you to give up on a story because it got difficult?"

Alicia exhaled and looked away.

Dylan approached Marcus. "C'mon, dude. It's not a big deal."

"Shit," Marcus said, shaking his head. "What kind of man are you, anyway? No self-respecting man would ask for directions."

Dylan rolled his eyes. Marcus had to resist the urge to shove him for it.

"Would you stop?" Alicia said. "God, your views are so outdated sometimes. Enough already with the macho crap."

Before he could reply, Nori cut in again.

"You're being stupid!" she said. "I don't care what you say, I'm going up there."

Nori started toward the house, and Dylan chased after her. "Wait up!"

He reached her but she continued walking, leaving the trail and stepping onto the property. Dylan went with her but glanced back at

THE OLD LADY

the others, waving them forward. Alicia looked at Marcus. He couldn't tell if it was sympathy or disbelief she expressed with her blue eyes. They were one of her best features, which was saying something. Even when Alicia annoyed him, Marcus was affected by her physical beauty, and believed it was half the reason Dylan seemed to bend to the girl's every wish.

"Are you coming?" she asked.

Marcus swallowed hard, his pride bitter in his throat. "This is a mistake."

Alicia looked away, and this time he was sure what she was expressing. It was worse than annoyance—it was disappointment. She started toward the ranch house, sprinting to catch up with the others, and Marcus stood there watching them go, debating his next move. It would be so satisfying to keep moving and make it to their cabin before the others could, without the help of strangers. But the mistakes he'd made so far had diminished his confidence, and he didn't want to march through the woods anymore, especially with the snow coming down. He also didn't want to abandon his friends. If he did, he would only worry about them.

Marcus sighed, gripped the straps of his backpack, and followed the others onto the property. Footprints had made a trail through the fallen snow leading to the ranch house. Looking at them, Marcus was surprised by the number of different shoe sizes and styles. It seemed this was a popular place. He hadn't known about it, but there were many areas in these vast mountains he hadn't hiked before. Though he'd often journeyed off the Appalachian Trail, he didn't know this forest as well as he did others. He wondered if the house was some sort of lodge.

Now he could see the building behind it was indeed a barn. Its doors were open, and he could make out a pickup truck within its shadows. That meant there must be a drivable route nearby—certainly a dirt road. It pained him to realize just how far off course he'd taken his friends. Things could have gotten much worse.

As they reached the house, Marcus stopped when he saw the other flag in the window. It too was an American flag, but its colors had been altered so it was black, white, and navy blue. It was the Thin Blue Line flag, the "back the blue" one used to express support for the police. What made Marcus uncomfortable was knowing that where this flag waved a rebel flag was sometimes close by, sometimes even as far north as New Hampshire, which was often considered "the south of the north." The flag was primarily flown by those with far-right attitudes, people who were irritated by the notion that black lives mattered. As such, leftists often referred to the Thin Blue Line Flag as "the coward's swastika," for it was so often flown by white supremacists who weren't bold enough to admit that's what they were.

Marcus scanned his surroundings with more scrutiny now. He noticed the yellow flag on a pole near the barn. It was one of those 'Don't Tread On Me' flags with the coiled serpent. Not the most inviting signal to strangers, and an ironic partner to the Thin Blue Line Flag.

"Guys..." he said.

Alicia nodded. "Yeah. I see them too."

"Just be cool," Dylan said. "We don't have to agree with somebody's politics to accept their help."

"That's assuming they'd want to help us," Marcus said. "Only one of us is white."

"You want me to go first?" Alicia asked.

"Hell no. I ain't saying that. I'll bet you anything these people have guns and would probably love an excuse to use one on an intruder."

"You're being ridiculous," Dylan said. "Just because they're conservative doesn't mean they're alt-right maniacs."

"But it most likely means they'll be less welcoming to people of color." He looked at Alicia. "And *Jewish* girls."

"Seriously?" Dylan asked. "You decide someone is a racist just based on how they vote?"

Marcus shook his head. "I'm only going off what I see here, and it ain't a good vibe, bro." He turned to the girls. "What do you two think?"

Alicia was hesitant to answer, but Marcus sensed her apprehension. Nori, however, stuck to her goal.

"I think I'm gonna lose my toes if I stay out here any longer," she said. "Or worse."

"Guys," Dylan said. "I don't think we have any choice but to give these people the benefit of the doubt."

Marcus stared at Alicia, still waiting for an answer to his question. She shrugged as if to ask what other option they had.

"Alright," Marcus said.

He wanted to take his pocketknife out just in case but knew how bad that would look. All he could do was stay alert and be

THE OLD LADY

respectful—at least until someone didn't give him the same respect. Just because they needed help didn't mean he would tolerate being insulted by some racist cracker.

When they reached the porch, a male voice called out to them. "Hey!"

Marcus tensed. He spun toward the stranger who had appeared from the other side of the barn. The man waved at them. Dylan waved back, followed by the others. Even Marcus raised a hand in hello. The man jogged through the slush. His hands were free, but that didn't mean he wasn't carrying a concealed weapon. He was dressed in jeans and a hoodie with an indecipherable metal band logo on it. A denim jacket and striped beanie completed his cheap-looking ensemble. He had a short beard and a friendly smile. Marcus guessed him to be in his late twenties and took that as a good sign. The younger the person, the better the odds they weren't poisoned by old prejudices.

"How you guys doin'?" the man said.

Alicia spoke first. "Hey. Sorry to bother you."

He gave them a quizzical look. "You guys don't look like you're with the forest department."

The friends looked at each other, confused.

"I'm sorry," Alicia said. "But what?"

The man smiled. "Oh, there was this guy who came by. Said he was a civil servant or some shit for the forest department. Guess he's just checking on people before the storm comes."

"Oh," Alicia said. "Well, yeah, we're not with him. Didn't even know there was a storm on the way. Actually, we're a little lost."

Marcus cringed inside. The stranger nodded. He barely gave Marcus a second glance. He seemed much more interested in talking to Alicia, and his eyes alternated between her and Nori.

"Lost, huh?" he said, more statement than question. "Well, shit, I can help ya. Where you headed?"

"We rented a cabin," Alicia said, "but we went off the trail by accident. We'd appreciate it if we could—"

Before she could finish, the man extended his hand. "Jeez, where are my manners, huh? I'm Charlie."

Marcus watched carefully as Alicia shook Charlie's hand. The man's fingers were tattooed with different letters, but Marcus couldn't make them all out yet. Alicia introduced the group one by one, but Charlie kept his eyes on the girls. He didn't seem predatory, but he did seem hungry, like a man on the prowl in a singles bar. But this wasn't a nightclub. This was the middle of nowhere, and with the girls needing help, Charlie was put in a position of power.

"If we could just get warm for a bit," Alicia said, "it would make a huge difference. Nori here is very cold. We all are, really. If we could just come inside and warm up, then we could figure out how to get to the cabin, or at least off the mountain."

To Marcus' surprise, Charlie agreed without hesitation.

"Shit, yeah," Charlie said with a smile. "The more the merrier, right?"

"This is your home?" Marcus asked.

Charlie finally looked at him again but kept smiling. "Yeah. Course it is, dude."

"Sorry, it's just when you said 'the more the merrier' I thought maybe you were having a party."

"Hey, if you guys wanna party, I'm up for it." He looked at Alicia again, his smile contorting into something more mischievous. His voice lowered conspiratorially. "I got beers and weed. Hard liquor too."

"Oh," Alicia said, unable to keep eye contact with him now. "Thanks, but we're just looking to get warm and be on our way."

"Hey, one drink won't hurt, right? It'll warm you up."

Seeing Alicia's discomfort, Dylan stepped close to her and addressed Charlie. "Thanks, but we're underage."

Charlie smirked. "*Pfft*. So what?"

Dylan gestured to the Thin Blue Line flag. "Guess we just thought you'd be all about law and order."

"Nah, dude. That flag is... well, it's just a whole other thing, ya know?" He started toward the porch steps. "C'mon inside. If booze ain't your thing, I've even got some coke."

The group exchanged concerned glances with each other, but Nori followed Charlie onto the porch, her desperation outweighing whatever concerns she should have had. When Dylan went to her side, putting distance between her and the stranger, Charlie's smile faltered but he continued to encourage them toward the front door.

There was a sudden movement behind one of the window's curtains. Marcus watched as a hand parted the drapes, but the person inside remained cloaked in shadow.

"Say, Charlie," Marcus said. "I saw you got a truck in the barn there. Maybe the best thing to do is for you to just drive us back to

THE OLD LADY

our car." He didn't want to start the hike over this way, but he also didn't want any trouble, and wanted the girls to be safe. "It's just in the parking lot at the start of the Harding Trail."

Charlie gave him a dead stare. "Yeah... yeah, we got a truck."

"We?"

Alicia cut in. "That's a good idea. That way we won't be in your hair. We don't want to impose."

"You're not imposing," Charlie told her. "It'd be nice to have some new faces around, especially ones as pretty as you and your little friend here."

Alicia's polite smile wavered. "Thank you, but we'd prefer a ride, please."

Her assertiveness gave Marcus a new level of respect for her.

Charlie sighed. "Okay. But there ain't enough room for five people in the Chevy."

"We'll sit in the bed," Marcus said.

He would prefer that anyway, in case they needed to jump out for some reason.

"Tell ya what," Charlie said. "There's room for three up front and the heat works. How about you dudes sit in the truck bed, and the ladies can ride up front with me and get warm?" The group looked to each other again, but Charlie spoke before anyone else could. "Unless you're saying you don't trust me or something."

Alicia rushed in to save the situation. "No, no. We're not saying that at all."

"I hope not. I mean, you come to me for help and here I am inviting you into my house, which is what you asked for in the first place, and all of a sudden, you're turning me down. And now you're acting like you don't want to even ride in my truck with me."

"We're so sorry if we made you feel that way. It wasn't our intention. We're just cold and exhausted is all. So sorry."

Charlie pursed his lips. "Yeah. Okay. Well, come on then."

He hopped down the steps and started back to the barn. The group followed, but when Charlie wasn't looking, Marcus motioned to his friends to keep their distance from the man. Alicia slowed her pace, but there was no slowing Nori. The promise of a heated truck that would get her off this mountain, and out of the woods both figuratively and literally, was all she'd needed to hear. As she hurried with her arms crossed tight, Charlie gave her a wide smile.

"You're real cute," he said. "You know that?"

Nori didn't reply.

"You Chinese?" Charlie asked.

"Japanese," Dylan said, getting close to his little sister again.

"Oh. You from Japan too, dude?"

"We're both American. Our dad is Japanese. My mom is white, Nori's is Japanese."

"Okay, so you're her brother then, not her boyfriend." Charlie looked back at Marcus. "Wow, you four are like the high school UN. You her boyfriend?"

"She's sixteen, man," Marcus said.

Charlie chuckled. "Oops. My bad. Asian girls all look so young, ya know? It's hard to tell. Especially with all the schoolgirl stuff you see online."

"Hey!" Dylan said, his face gone hard.

Charlie laughed again. "Take it easy, dude. I'm just joking. Lighten up."

Marcus looked back, half expecting whoever had been in the house to be following them, but he saw nothing. He noticed four camouflaged ATVs parked along the side of the house. Not two, but four. He almost asked Charlie about them but decided not to. Against the same wall was a huge stack of firewood logs, a chopping block with an axe sticking out of it, and a massive, yellow machine he guessed to be some sort of mulcher.

They reached the barn. There were no animals inside, not even a horse or some chickens, but there were bales of hay and a hayloft overhead. Marcus detected a strange, chemical odor but wasn't sure if it was coming from the old truck or something else. He kept his eyes peeled, searching the stalls as they passed by them, inspecting every shadow for movement.

In one stall was a plastic pallet stacked with huge bags of fertilizer. The labels read: ammonium nitrate. There were warning signs on them saying the product was not only highly flammable, but explosive. From the look of it, there were thousands of pounds of it. The stall on the other side was stacked with metal canisters of nitromethane and DMSO, and milk crates containing what had to be close to a hundred cases of roofing nails. Something about it struck Marcus as strange. There were other items in the barn, mainly gas cans, auto parts, and farm gear, but none were as excessive as the contents of the first two stalls.

Charlie opened the truck's passenger side door. "Alright, girls.

THE OLD LADY

Your chariot awaits. Dudes, hop in back."

But now that they were here, even Nori became apprehensive. She looked to her brother, then at Marcus, as if asking for confirmation that everything would be alright.

"Don't you wanna let your truck warm up first?" Alicia asked. It was clear to Marcus that she was only stalling, but to what end?

"Nah," Charlie said. "It'll be fine. Let's go."

He put his hand on Nori's back to usher her inside. He was gentle, but Nori flinched away from him anyway. Charlie's face pinched and he pressed his fist to his mouth.

"Jesus Christ!" he said. "What's you guys' problem, huh?"

"We're sorry," Alicia said, "it's just that—"

"You keep saying you're sorry, but ya'll keep acting like dicks to me. You don't wanna get in my truck? Fine." He slammed the door shut. "Have fun walking, assholes."

"Charlie, wait—"

Alicia didn't get to finish. Another man's voice drew everyone's attention.

"What the fuck is this?" the man yelled.

Marcus turned. The man was standing in the doorway behind them. He looked to be Charlie's age, with a black goatee, flannel coat, and a trucker cap. But what drew Marcus' attention was the semi-automatic rifle the man held in both hands. It wasn't pointed at them, but he kept the barrel halfway up and his finger close to the trigger guard. Marcus didn't know much about guns, but this obviously wasn't a basic hunting rifle. This was a tactical weapon, perhaps an AR-15 or M16. Marcus swallowed hard as the man eyed the group, then stared directly at him.

"Oh," Charlie said with a nervous smile. "Hey, Wylder. Where'd you come from?"

Wylder scowled. "Who are all these people and what the fuck are they doing in the barn?"

"Take it easy. They're just hangin' out."

"What do you mean 'hanging out'?"

Alicia spoke up. "We were just leaving."

"Nobody's talking to you!" The man snapped before returning to Charlie. "Why the hell did you let them in here?"

Charlie's lower lip trembled. He looked like a child caught in a lie by his parents. "It's okay, man. They're cool." He pointed at Nori. "Check this one out. I thought you'd like her. She's single."

Despite the angry man's weapon, Marcus knew he had to take hold of the situation now. Something was going on here—something bad. Even aside from the rifle, there was a palpable sense of danger.

"Look, man," Marcus said to the gunman. "We just want to go. We won't be any trouble."

Wylder narrowed his eyes at him but said nothing.

"Whatever this is, it ain't our business." Marcus regretted saying it the moment the words left his mouth. A bead of sweat ran down the small of his back as Wylder stepped into the barn, drawing near.

"What did you just say?" Wylder asked.

"C'mon, man. All we wanted was a ride."

"I asked you a question, you black piece of shit."

Marcus breathed deep. "I just meant we didn't mean to disturb you."

"What're you doing snooping around our compound?"

"We weren't snooping."

"Bullshit. You with antifa or something?"

"What? No."

Wylder raised the barrel higher. Marcus clenched his fists at his sides.

Dylan spoke up. "Don't point that at him."

"Shut up, faggot!" Wylder said but kept the gun on Marcus.

Alicia grabbed Dylan's arm. Nori began to cry quietly, trembling from more than just the cold.

"You can't hold us here," Dylan said. "It's wrongful imprisonment."

"I told you to shut the fuck up!"

But Dylan, for all his passiveness, stood his ground. He reached into his pocket. Wylder told him to keep his hands where he could see them, and Dylan drew his phone and held it up.

"I just hit record," Dylan said. "You do anything to us, and you'll be on video."

Wylder turned his gun on Dylan. "Put it on the ground! All of you, throw your phones on the ground. Now!"

Alicia obeyed, quickly tossing her phone into the dirt. With shaking hands, Nori drew her phone from her coat pocket, and Marcus slowly moved his hand toward his.

"Just be cool, man," he said to Wylder. "I'm just reaching for my phone for you, okay? Nice and slow."

Dylan was the only one not to comply. "No way I'm dropping

THE OLD LADY

mine. This video is our insurance policy. Now let us out of here."

Wylder flushed as he barked at Dylan. "I'm gonna blow your *fucking head off* if you don't do what I tell you!"

"Dylan!" Alicia said. "Do what he says!"

"We can't do that," Dylan told her, a tremor in his voice. "This is our only defense."

Wylder screamed the order again. Instead of reaching for his phone, Marcus' hand inched toward his pocketknife while Wylder was busy ranting at Dylan. Marcus' mouth had gone dry and his hand trembled, but he knew this might be their only chance. He had to rush Wylder. It was the only thing to do when cornered by a loaded gun.

He decided not to use the knife. It would be better to have both hands free so he could try to take the rifle from Wylder. Marcus was bigger than the man was, and Wylder didn't look particularly muscular. The weapon was the only intimidating thing about him. Marcus had to try.

"You've got two seconds!" Wylder shouted at Dylan.

Charlie whispered. "Jeez, Wylder, c'mon, man…"

"Shut your mouth, Charlie! You've done enough damage." He snarled at Dylan. "One!"

Dylan kept filming, but his shaking hands couldn't hold the phone steady.

"Two!" Wylder said.

When he aimed the barrel straight at Dylan's chin, Marcus charged.

He slammed into Wylder, and they fell to the ground, Marcus trying to rip the rifle from the man's hands. The barn erupted with noise, Nori screaming and others shouting, but Marcus wasn't registering what was being said. All his focus was on obtaining the weapon. Wylder held it tight, but Marcus was more powerful. He managed to get the stock out from the crook of Wylder's arm so his hand was away from the trigger, but a shot rang out anyway.

A blunt pain filled Marcus' side, telling him it wasn't the rifle that had gone off. Though somewhat deafened by the gunshot, he could hear his friends screaming his name. Despite the intense pain spreading through his stomach and down his thigh, he kept fighting Wylder for the rifle until another shot rang out.

Marcus had just enough time to register the agony in his chest before a third shot rang out, and then there was nothing at all.

~

Alicia stopped screaming.

Seeing Marcus shot at point blank range left her too shocked to make a sound. When she'd seen Charlie draw the revolver from out of his waistband, she'd cried Marcus' name, but he'd been too busy struggling with Wylder to notice anything else. The first two shots had hit Marcus in the body, but the third one popped a hole in his head. A jet of blood spurted from the exit wound in his skull, and his head snapped back before his body hit the ground in instant death, falling on Wylder as he writhed beneath the larger man's corpse.

A sick, hollow feeling flooded Alicia's stomach. Her heart grew suddenly sluggish as dread coiled around it like barbwire. She was vaguely aware of Dylan and Nori crying. She knew she should be too, but horror had left her frozen.

"Fuck!" Charlie said, throwing up his hands. He paced nervously as Wylder struggled under Marcus' dead weight. "God fucking damnit!"

Wylder got to his feet just as Nori broke into a panicked run, screaming hysterically. Dylan called out to her but grabbed Alicia's hand before perusing his sister. Charlie grabbed Nori around the waist and lifted her. She kicked and flailed but his grip held like a bear hug.

"Everybody calm down!" Charlie said.

Dylan came at Charlie, and Wylder struck him in the face with the shoulder stock of the rifle. Alicia gasped as her boyfriend collapsed. He tried to crawl away, and Wylder jumped on him, flipping him over. Dylan fought back and managed to knee Wylder in the groin. Alicia looked about the barn for anything she could use as a weapon before telling herself it was suicide to come at a man with a pitchfork when he was holding a gun. Her whole body shook, panic cooking in her veins. But even through her tears, she saw her boyfriend looking at her.

"Run!" Dylan shouted.

Alicia did.

She bolted toward the doorway and cut a sharp left so the men in the barn wouldn't be able to see her or take aim. She heard them yelling at each other, and Charlie called her name, as if she would be stupid enough to come back. Not wanting to slow herself down by tromping through the knee-high snow, she ran on the path that wound around the back of the ranch house, and just as she darted

THE OLD LADY

into the woods beside it, she noticed two figures emerging from the house's back door.

One held a shotgun. The other had an assault rifle like Wylder's.

Alicia got low and hid behind a large tree trunk. The people who'd come out of the house must not have noticed her, for they sprinted toward the barn, responding to the sounds of chaos. When she felt they were far enough away, she broke into a run again, keeping close to the trail but staying in the woods for cover.

Her lungs ached. Her thighs burned. But she kept on running for her life.

SEVEN

WHEN TRACEY WAS NINE YEARS old, her father started telling her the horror stories of his time as a prisoner of war. As a soldier in Vietnam, and part of the frontline infantry's Order of the Viking, her father's platoon had been ambushed in early 1968, during the North Vietnamese Army's Tet Offensive military campaign, a massive armed assault on the South Vietnamese and their allies, including the United States Armed Forces.

"We were dropped in a hot LZ, outnumbered and outgunned," Dad said. "The gooks killed most of us, but me and my platoon leader, Mac, survived, though we sustained serious injuries. He'd told us not to let them flank, but there was nothing we could do to stop it. My buddy Jackson was near me when he stepped on a mine, and the blast blew me backward, singeing my flesh and breaking my elbow in the fall. Then the ambush came, and we dropped like flies. Mac had half his hand blasted away by NVA fire. Once they'd cornered us, the gooks tore our clothes off."

Tracey furrowed her brow. "They made you naked?"

"Stripped down to our skivvies. They always did that with prisoners. When Mac held up his wounded hand to show them the extent

THE OLD LADY

of his injuries, the gooks only got angry, and one of them drove a bayonet through what remained of his palm."

Tracey winced at this detail, and her father grabbed her by the chin and put his face close to hers. His eyes were like ice.

"Hey!" he said in a gravelly whisper. "You think I like talking about this? Huh? I'm telling you for your own good." He released her chin and went on. "After roughing us up and taking some pictures, the gooks had us march to one of their trucks and took us to a bamboo cage at a little internment camp deep in the jungle. No hospital or medical treatment, just a couple of blankets in a cramped cage full of insects and human feces. Mac's hand swelled to the size of a football and started to turn black. My broken arm was not put in a cast and my right side was still covered in open sores from the landmine blast." He gestured to the old scars on his face and right arm. "We both faded in and out of consciousness from the pain. It became apparent to me that Mac had gone into shock. I did what I could for him. When I shouted for the guards, they only whipped me with fan belts.

"After a day or so, I was dragged out of the cage, but Mac was left behind. Even though he was the platoon leader, I guess the NVA realized he was too fucked up to give them any answers. So instead, they took me to Hỏa Lò Prison for questioning. This was where they kept all the American pilots who'd been shot down during bombing raids. We called it the Hanoi Hilton, but that was only a sick joke, 'cause the cells in this place were only slightly better than those bamboo cages."

Tracey realized she'd heard the word "Hanoi" before—actually, she'd read it. In the compost toilet outside the cabin, the inside of the bowl had been affixed with a sticker of a woman's face inside a target, with the words "Hanoi Jane Pissing Target" below it.

"The conditions were unsanitary," her father went on. "Rats and cockroaches were fuckin' everywhere, and the food was barely edible. You think our MREs are bad? You got no idea, kid. Try living off broth and gristle." He'd stared at Tracey then, but she said nothing. "The morning after I arrived, they gave me the quiz."

Tracey had dared ask, "what quiz?"

"The gooks wanted information about American military operations. I told them I needed medical attention, and they told me I wouldn't get any until I talked. All I gave them was what was on my dog tags. They didn't like that very much, so they hurt me."

Tracey's eyes brimmed with tears. "Daddy…"

Her father's expression turned hard then, and he pointed in her face. "Don't you cry on me, understand? Don't show weakness. *Never* show weakness! That's exactly what the gooks want— what *any* enemy wants. You think I was weak when they were using rope bindings on me? Fuck no. I may have screamed in pain, but I didn't give them anything they could use—only lies, bullshit, and piddly crap." He turned his hands up to show her his scars. Tracey had seen them before, but somehow they looked worse to her in this moment. "They wrapped chains around my hands and hung me by them from rusty meat hooks. Left me like that for hours, until I felt my shoulders would pop right out of my sockets."

Tracey closed her eyes. "Daddy, please…"

"You think they listened to me when I said 'please'? Far from it, kid. No, they strapped me down in old iron stocks. The cuffs were so small they cut into my skin, turning my hands as black as poor Mac's had been. They left me to sit in my own piss and shit. Made me stand on a wooden stool for days."

Tracey began to cry then. She flinched, fearing reprisal, but her father went on instead of chastising her for displaying emotion.

"They tortured me," he said, staring into space. "They tortured *all of us*. Over 100 Americans died while in captivity in Nam, and many of those deaths were inside the walls of the Hanoi Hotel. And the goddamned U.S. government let it happen. We were supposed to be let out in '72, see? But that was contingent on our government giving four and a half billion dollars in reparations to the people of Vietnam. Our politicians agreed, but then they reneged on the deal, so the Vietcong didn't make good on their side of the agreement either. We POWS were left to fucking rot." His eyes tightened with rage. "All over fucking money. We gave everything for our country, and they repaid us with…"

Dad seemed to choke on his words then. He cleared his throat and took a deep breath to steady himself.

"I endured *years* of abuse in that hellhole," he said, "but I made it out alive. I survived the beatings and solitary confinement. Food that would make a racoon vomit. Sleeping on a cold, hard floor. Yeah, I came out with a lot of scars and my hair had turned white, but I survived. Not just because that's what a good soldier does, but because my fight to survive—my heart—was all I had." He put his hand on Tracey's shoulder. "If there's one thing I'm gonna teach you, kid, it's

THE OLD LADY

this: when your very life is put in a corner, little else matters."

~

Tracey flinched at the sound of a snowmobile pulling up outside. She instinctually went into survival mode, grabbing the shotgun from the armory in a flash. Even though she knew Dad had always kept every weapon loaded, she pumped a shell out of the chamber anyway, just to make sure, then put the shell back in. With it fully loaded and the safety off, she maneuvered in a crouch, closed the blackout drapes, and peeked through the part.

Outside, a middle-aged man sat upon the snowmobile, wind goggles and a hat with earflaps hiding most of his face. It had started snowing, and the flakes seemed to spin in every direction, further obscuring Tracey's view. The man climbed off the vehicle and stood before the edge of the property, staring at the cabin.

Just calm down, Tracey told herself.

But she was incapable of doing so, especially here. This cabin had been home base for the entirety of her training. Defending it at all costs was hard-wired into her brain, as was a deep distrust of men.

The man took a few steps forward. He appeared unarmed. As he inched closer to the pit trap, Tracey's mouth went dry. If the stranger fell in, it would create a whole new mess of problems for her. He might break a leg. It might be difficult for Tracey to get him help—if she decided he deserved help. Depending on what he was doing here, she might react differently. Part of her would want to leave him down there...or worse. She couldn't let that happen. She wasn't going to be sent back to prison, no matter what.

Though she often trembled from anxiety in her everyday life, when confronted with a real threat, a cold determination spread through her like a disease. Her every muscle tightened as her training returned in mental shockwaves. It steadied her, but also made her more dangerous. Though aware of this, she struggled with how to handle it.

Take it easy, she thought. *Easy, easy.*

But her father spoke differently. *"If a man steps on your property uninvited, you're within your right to shoot. Just tell the police you gave fair warning, but the intruder didn't comply."*

"I'm not shooting him," Tracey whispered back. "Not unless I have to."

"Hesitation is suicide."

"Opening fire will create more problems than it'll solve. You're overreacting."

"Is it really overreacting, or is it empowering yourself to never be a victim?" He paused. *"Or should I say, never be a victim again?"*

"Shut your mouth, old man," she hissed. "You don't know anything about that."

Dad hadn't known the things that happened to her after she'd left him. But this voice was not truly her father's. It was a mental tic that reflected who he'd been—partly memories and partly just an estimation of what Tracey guessed he would say in every situation. It was trauma picking at emotional scabs, the lasting impression of her father's abuse.

He barked at her again. *"I didn't leave you this cabin just so you could die in it on day one."*

Instead of snapping back at him, she went to the front door and flung it open before the man could step into a trap. Still, she kept the shotgun in both hands without pointing it at him. When he saw her, the man froze and showed her his palms in a passive gesture.

"Whoa," he said. "Easy there. I come in peace."

"Who the fuck are you?" she demanded.

He removed his hat and goggles, revealing kind—if naïve—eyes. "I'm Jeff Coleman. I work for the Department of Agriculture."

He pointed to the patches on his green jacket.

Tracey tensed. "You a forest ranger?"

"No, ma'am. I'm a civil engineer."

Hearing he wasn't law enforcement made Tracey's shoulders relax. "What exactly is a civil engineer?"

Jeff flashed a smile that made him look younger. "Well, I find solutions to land management issues. I build and maintain campgrounds, trails, and—"

"This here's private property."

"I know it's none of my business, but—"

"You're right about that. It *is* none of your business."

He took a step forward and Tracey raised the shotgun just slightly. "I wouldn't come any closer if I were you."

Jeff stopped. "Ma'am, please. I'm sorry if I've startled you. It certainly wasn't my intention. I was merely assessing damage to the trails that have obscured some paths. Now, there's always a mess in the winter, but we've had a lot of fallen trees, and with this nor'easter coming, we expect the trails to nearly disappear. I figured I'd just check on anybody who's camped out or rented a cabin to make sure

THE OLD LADY

they're safe and know what's coming. I know this is private property but, as long as I was out here, I figured I'd drop by, just in case."

"In case of what?"

He chuckled, as if in disbelief. "In case anybody needed any assistance getting off the mountain. Like I said, the trails are a mess and they're only going to get worse."

"Did you know my father?" she asked sharply.

"Your fa... oh, the man who lived here was your dad?"

"Yeah," she said, hating to admit it.

"Ah. I didn't know him very well, but yes, I knew Henry. Or at least knew about him."

"Yeah, well, then you probably know he was always prepared and didn't take kindly to people snooping around."

Jeff's smile fell. "Yes, ma'am. That was the impression he gave us."

"Well, the apple doesn't fall far from the tree."

"I understand. We'd heard he died and that someone would be coming up to the cabin to handle his things. I didn't know if anyone was here yet, but if they were, I wanted to make sure they were okay. I was just trying to help."

Tracey narrowed her eyes at him. "I don't need your help, Jeff Coleman. Now you best be on your way."

That finally shut him up. Jeff shook his head and put his hat and goggles back on. He turned back to his snowmobile, and Tracey watched him climb aboard, start it up, and drive away. She watched him until he was out of sight, then fetched the binoculars from the windowsill and scanned the woods until confident he wasn't coming back.

"Dipshit," she muttered, slamming the door behind her.

She locked every bolt.

EIGHT

"YOU MORON," WYLDER SAID. "YOU unbelievable goddamned moron."

Charlie looked at the ground. "It was a simple mistake, dude."

"No, no, no. Bringing a bunch of people we don't know into the barn isn't a simple mistake, Charlie. It's a fucking catastrophe. And now you *killed* one of them. Because of you, we've got a dead cotton picker, two chinks handcuffed in the empty stall, and this bitch running around in the woods, who may end up escaping before we can catch her."

Charlie swallowed hard. "Listen—Marcus was gonna kill you, right? He was on our property. We only did what we had to do. That's our story, right?"

Wylder pursed his lips but said nothing.

Charlie looked to Quin. At forty, he was the oldest of the group, but Quin was the silent type and had never shown interest in leading. He let Wylder dish out the lectures. Quin stroked his gray mustache and refused to make eye contact with Charlie. It wasn't the first time everyone had been angry with him for a blunder, but this was the most grievous error yet.

THE OLD LADY

Paul's dark eyes fell on Charlie, then the dead body, then back at Charlie. His birth name was Pedro, but he'd changed it to Paul after becoming a legal citizen of the United States. The Mexican was in his thirties, with a muscular frame built by constant exercise and a layered steroid regimen. He was the only non-white member of their outfit, but he'd been accepted based on his wealth of experience and proven dedication to the cause.

Paul shook his head at Charlie. Even Stan, who was only nineteen, looked at Charlie with annoyed disappointment. Once again, Charlie had allowed his appetite for young women to cloud his judgement, and he resented himself for it, but resented the girls for it even more. Part of him wanted to show Nori just how pissed he was—and knew just how he wanted to do it. But the others were less concerned about the hostages than they were about the one who'd gotten away.

Dressed in winter camouflage and combat boots, Quin carried his AR-15 close to his chest, pointed straight down the way soldiers and SWAT teams carried their assault rifles. He and Paul had been the first ones to come out of the house upon hearing the gunshots, with Stan following behind them once he'd put his boots on. Each man was armed. To Charlie, it seemed like overkill, considering they were only hunting an unarmed teenage girl, but he didn't dare object. He was in enough trouble as it was.

Wylder took control. "Stan—you and Charlie stay behind and watch the hostages."

Being left with the easiest task insulted Charlie, but he was happy to stay behind with Nori in cuffs.

"Want us to bury this guy's corpse?" Charlie asked.

Wylder took a deep breath, seeming to think it over. "Not yet. Just keep it locked in the stall here until we formulate a plan. Maybe toss some hay on it. And toss all these phones in the woodchipper." He looked to Quin and Paul. "You guys come with me. That bitch couldn't have gotten very far."

"And what are we gonna do with her?" Paul asked. "Shoot her on sight?"

Wylder furrowed his brow. "Only if you have to. Better to take her alive, I think."

"Hell yeah," Charlie said, thinking of what he could do with a fine piece of ass like that.

Wylder ignored him and addressed the group. "Let's move out. We want to follow her tracks before this snow refills them. We can gain ground on the ATVs."

Quin shook his head. "We do that, and she'll hear us coming a mile away. If we're to catch this girl—especially alive—we need to be stealthy."

Wylder nodded, taking the older man's advice. "Yeah. Yeah, okay."

As the men discussed their plan of action, Charlie lost focus and began fantasizing about what sort of panties Nori might be wearing. It wouldn't be so bad if he just peeked, right? He and Stan got along well, and with Stan being the new guy, Charlie outranked him in an unspoken rule. *At least I outrank somebody,* he thought. Charlie doubted Stan would object to having a little fun with the girl while the others were away. He didn't want to rape her exactly, and had never done something like that before, but he wasn't opposed to seeing what she looked like naked, and flirted with the idea of feeling her up, at the very least. He'd already killed a man today. Might as well go whole hog and make the best of a bad situation.

The realization that he'd murdered someone kept returning to him in powerful waves. He'd never shot someone before, let alone killed them. What surprised him most about it was his complete lack of feeling. Except for fear of punishment, the killing hadn't upset him, only surprised him. It was surreal but hardly devastating. Considering what the group had planned, being numb to murder was a benefit. It made their mission easier.

Marcus' race hadn't been a deciding factor for Charlie when he'd pulled the trigger, but Wylder seemed to think killing a black man was easier to get away with than killing a white female or even the Asians. Charlie figured he could claim self-defense, but that didn't matter. This wasn't going to be reported. The group had made a sacred vow, and their code of silence was unwavering. Even Stan, who seemed the most rattled by what had happened, made no objections to what was going on, and showed no signs of dissent. Aside from Wylder, everyone seemed clear-headed, their hard eyes brewing with determination. Charlie knew them well enough to know that while the men were angry about what he'd done, they were also excited to put their skills to the test with the challenge of hunting human prey. Despite the unfortunate circumstances, Charlie believed this would actually be good for the group.

"The keys," Wylder said to Charlie, holding out his hand.

"You're taking the truck?"

THE OLD LADY

"No, you idiot," Wylder said, "but obviously you can't be trusted with them."

Charlie reddened. "Hey now…"

"You're offering rides to anyone who comes by. Now give 'em to me."

Charlie started to object, but Quin interrupted him. "Just give Wylder the damned keys."

Annoyed, Charlie dug them from his pocket. When he handed the keyring to Wylder, Paul handed Charlie a smaller set of keys. Dylan and Nori had been handcuffed by Paul, with Nori gagged with a bandana and Dylan's mouth stuffed with an oily rag. But Charlie worried if the siblings stayed out here, they might spit out the gags and scream for help. The girl was also still shivering from the cold.

As Wylder, Paul, and Quin left for the woods, Charlie turned to Stan and smiled. "Well, I guess we should take care of our guests. Let's get them to the house and put them in the root cellar."

Stan ran his hand over his shaved head. "Right."

Charlie studied him. "You okay, man?"

The young man gulped. "It's… it's just a lot, you know?"

"I hear ya. But don't worry too much. It'll all work out. Remember—we're the patriots, the real heroes."

Stan didn't seem convinced, but he nodded anyway.

"C'mon," Charlie said, starting toward the stall with his pistol in hand. "You take the boy. The girl's all mine."

~

Hearing a snowmobile, Alicia got low, then lay flat on her stomach. Peering through the bare trees, she watched the rider zip by. Goggles and a hat covered his face. She wasn't sure if it was one of the men from the compound, but he wasn't wearing the same clothes as them. He was dressed in dark green.

A ranger?

Knowing she was being pursued, she was hesitant to take any chances. Even if she did, the man had moved quickly, and was now too far away to flag down, and wouldn't hear her yelling over the noise of the snowmobile. But the men chasing her might hear her, and then they might find her.

Alicia wasn't sure where they were. Maybe she'd lost them, but she also felt lost herself. It seemed like she'd been running for hours, but without her phone she couldn't check the time. The weather had darkened the sky, casting the woods in heavy shadow. It would make her harder to locate, but also made it harder for her to see. When she'd first heard the men's voices on the trail, she'd left it completely and darted deeper into the woods, escaping before they could spot her. Now her poor sense of direction was failing her, as she knew it would in the wilderness, and she had no tools to guide her. Marcus was the one with the compass and map.

Marcus...

Alicia fought the urge to cry, but when she closed her eyes, all she could see was her friend's head snapping back as a bullet went straight through it.

Had they killed Dylan and Nori too?

The thought made her guts twist. How was it fair that she'd gotten away while they hadn't? How could she have left her boyfriend and his little sister behind?

It was your only chance, she told herself. But the guilt weighed heavy on her mind anyway.

If they found her, would they kill her too?

Alicia slowly pushed off the ground. She'd escaped for now, but she had other pressing problems. She wanted to find her way back to the lot they'd parked in, even though the car belonged to Marcus, and he'd had the keys. But she had to get off this mountain and had to do it before dark. She needed to find help—*fast*.

Moving through the forest, Alicia watched her steps closely out of fear she would snap too many branches and give away her position. Though she'd seen ATVs on the compound, she didn't hear any, and assumed the men were still pursuing her on foot so they could sneak up on her. This part of the woods was also too treacherous for even ATVs to journey off the trails. She wondered if the men had hounds that could follow her scent. Charlie and Wylder seemed like the kind of guys who would have hunting dogs, but so far, she'd heard no barking.

Perhaps she'd really lost them. She hadn't seen or heard anything for what seemed like a long time until that snowmobile had passed. Though she still wasn't sure if it was one of her pursuers or not, she was already regretting not trying to flag the man down, even though she knew it would have been futile. He might have been her only hope. Now he was gone.

Tears rolled down Alicia's cheeks, and she quickly dried them with the back of her gloves to keep the breeze from freezing her wet face. Her nose was numb, and her lower lip trembled uncontrollably. If she

THE OLD LADY

stayed lost out here, the men wouldn't have to kill her, because the mountain would do it for them.

You can't die, she thought. *You must get help for Dylan and Nori.*

Reaching the crest of another hill, she looked around the mountainside in every direction, trying to get her bearings. All she could see was snow-covered wilderness and the hulking blue shadows of more unforgiving mountains in the distance.

Alicia had no idea where she was going, but she had to press on. She'd never been a quitter, and despite the terror that kept her heart racing, she had more motivation than she'd ever had before. Putting herself to the test was the reason she'd wanted to come up here in the first place. She'd gotten way more than she'd bargained for but wouldn't let that be a deterrent. Giving up on herself meant giving up on her friends, and she simply couldn't accept that as a viable option.

Keep moving, she told herself.

Alicia scurried down the slope, sinking deeper into the forest.

NINE

TRACEY WAS COMING OUT OF the tool shed when it all began.

After tallying the inventory, she exited with her notepad in hand and slipped the military tactical pen into her pants pocket. It was forged of tungsten steel and could be used to break glass in an emergency. The notepad was scribbled with her chicken-scratch handwriting, nearly indecipherable to anyone but her. Once she'd been envious of how artful other women's penmanship was. Now she couldn't imagine caring about something like that.

As she walked back to the cabin, a sudden movement caught her eye, and she gazed downhill to the treeline at the end of the property. Someone was coming. It wasn't Jeff the Civil Engineer. This shape was much smaller. Tracey guessed the stranger to be female. It made her less nervous, but she still watched the figure closely as Tracey came around to the front of the cabin.

Spotting Tracey, the stranger raised both hands, waving frantically. Tracey didn't wave back, only watched. Her hunting knife was strapped to her belt. She doubted she would need more than that, but she stayed near the front door in case she needed to duck inside for

THE OLD LADY

a gun.

"Help!" the stranger cried out, her voice confirming her as female. When she made it to the path, she ran faster toward the cabin. "Please, help me!"

Tracey scanned the woods. This could be a set-up. The girl might not be alone. She could only be bait.

"Help me, please," she cried.

If she were acting, it was a great performance. Perhaps the girl had hurt herself while hiking or had gotten lost. Neither of these situations would make her Tracey's responsibility, but curiosity pulled her in. If this really was some sort of trap, she wanted to know as soon as possible, so she watched the girl closely.

Tracey gasped when she recognized her.

Olivia?

But that couldn't be right. Her daughter didn't know where she was and hadn't known for years. Tracey had never even told Olivia or her ex-husband the location of the cabin. As far as Tracey knew, Olivia didn't know about the cabin at all. Tracey had wanted to spare her daughter those horror stories.

So how was it Olivia was running toward her now?

Tracey stepped forward, her stomach fluttering. She maneuvered around the hidden pitfall and watched the girl closely, still not acknowledging her as she cried for help.

An illusion? Tracey wondered. Had her tortured mind projected this? Were her antipsychotic medications causing hallucinations? She'd tried many narcotics in her life, including copious amounts of acid and psychedelic mushrooms, but she'd never had a hallucination as realistic as this. It couldn't be a figment, couldn't be a dream.

Tracey started toward her. As the girl drew closer, her pink cheeks and watery eyes only underlined the fear in her face. Tracey blinked rapidly as the teenager's appearance blurred, and when her vision cleared, Tracey realized this wasn't Olivia at all. Noting the girl's outfit, she recognized her as one of the kids she'd seen hiking up the mountain when she'd first arrived.

"Please," the girl said, panting from exhaustion. "Please... these men are after me... my friends..."

Tracey put her hands on her hips, a body language move that made people pay closer attention. She also preferred her hand to be close to her weapon.

"Please," the girl said between heavy breaths. "They've got my friends… they killed one…"

Tracey's shoulders tightened. "*Killed?*"

The girl nodded. "Shot him in the head."

"Why?"

"I… I dunno… it was all so crazy."

Tracey squinted. "Who are you? Why'd you come here?"

She gave her name and Tracey gasped.

"Your name is *Olivia?*" Tracey asked.

The girl shook her head. "No. I said my name's Alicia."

Tracey only stared at her.

"Please," Alicia said. "I lost them for a while, but I'm pretty sure I heard their voices a few minutes ago. I need to get help. Can you get me to the police?"

The mention of law enforcement made Tracey's chest feel tight. She instinctually scanned the woods surrounding them, but the snow was falling heavier, obscuring everything, and she saw no one. Her eyes returned to the terrified girl.

"How old are you, anyway?" Tracey asked.

The girl seemed confused by the question. "Eighteen."

Again, Tracey stared at her in silence.

"Do you have a phone?" the girl asked.

"No."

The girl gave her an incredulous look. "You don't have a *phone?*"

"I said no, and I meant it."

Alicia continued panting, fear making her eyes dart. "Please… help me."

"There's not much I can do for you, kid. Ain't got no phone or snowmobile or anything like that. And I ain't gonna trek all the way back down the mountain. Not in this weather."

The girl looked at her in disbelief, fresh tears filling her eyes. "You don't understand. These guys murdered my friend and took my other friends hostage. One of them is only sixteen—just a girl. Now those men are after me. Can you at least let me in your cabin?"

Despite the girl's panic, Tracey had her doubts about Alicia's story, particularly because it was so thin. She needed to know more if she was even going to consider taking the girl inside.

Tracey was about to tell Alicia this when the men appeared behind the treeline. She spotted them but Alicia hadn't yet. Tracey watched their shadows closely as they emerged from the woods, and when she saw their rifles, she put her hand on Alicia's back and gave her a little

THE OLD LADY

nudge.

"Move," Tracey said.

Alicia obeyed, but she also looked behind her. When she saw the men, her mouth opened to scream, and Tracey pressed her palm over the girl's mouth to mute her. She threw her arm around Alicia and walked her toward the cabin, steering clear of the traps.

One of the men called out. "Hey!"

Tracey ignored him as she and Alicia made it to the porch, Tracey advising her to skip a step. She'd left the door unlocked when she'd gone to the tool shed, so they made it inside quickly. Tracey pushed all the bolts and deadlocks into place, then rushed to the armory, her thoughts racing. After quickly making sure they were loaded, she shoved the Glock into her waistband at the small of her back and grabbed the .22 rifle. Alicia whimpered something but Tracey ignored her. She considered giving the girl the .38 revolver but didn't trust her enough yet. From the look of Alicia, Tracey doubted the teenager would even know how to handle a pistol. Darting to the window, she snatched the binoculars and parted the curtains just enough to peer through the gap.

The men were jogging up the pathway leading to the cabin. She only saw three of them but knew there may be others coming around the rear of the building. She slid the window up a crack and leveled the business end of the rifle with the sill so she could fire easily without the men seeing the firearm sticking out. Her father's voice echoed through her head, shouting instructions like a drill sergeant, but as the men approached, his voice was cut off when one of the men shouted out.

"Hello in there!" he said in a pleasant tone.

Tracey didn't reply. She only aligned the rifle's sights with his skull, even though the men weren't aiming their assault rifles at the cabin. Her every muscle flexed, sweat pouring down her head despite the cold. An ill fear was spreading through her like a virus. She resented it and resented the men for instilling it in her. This anger gave her fuel.

"We need to talk to the girl," the man said.

He looked to be in his twenties, with a black goatee, flannel coat, and a trucker cap on his head. Maybe five foot-ten, one hundred and fifty pounds.

"Please," Alicia whispered. "Don't tell him I'm here."

Tracey kept her eyes on the men but hissed back at her. "Shut the fuck up and stay down."

Alicia whimpered as she got down on the floor.

"*I said shut up*," Tracey said in a whisper-shout. "Not a sound, and not one fucking word."

Alicia nodded and sucked in her lips, tears streaking her young face. She looked so much like Olivia then. Tracey had seen her daughter frightened many times, and more often than not, Tracey had been the cause of that fear because she didn't behave like a normal mother or even a human being.

"We just wanna talk," the man outside said. "C'mon, Alicia. Let's clear up this misunderstanding. What do you say?"

Alicia didn't speak, but Tracey did.

"This is private property!" she shouted. "If I were you, I'd step the fuck back."

The young man smirked and shared a glance with his older buddies—a gray-haired man with a mustache and a bulky Mexican with a leathery scowl.

"We've got no beef with you, ma'am," the young man said. "We just need to sort things out with Alicia."

"No."

The man shook his head. "Look, lady. That girl in there stole from us. You're harboring a thief; did you know that?"

Tracey didn't believe him. His body language assured he was lying.

The man went on. "You need to open the door. My friends and I are very serious about this matter, and we intend to resolve it, right now."

"If that's all you wanted, you would've called the cops."

"We were hoping we could handle this without having to get Alicia arrested. We're doing her a favor here. Trying to be understanding."

"Understand this," Tracey said. "I don't call cops. I handle things myself. Catch my drift?"

He gave a small laugh. "You know, if you're trying to threaten us—"

"There's no *trying* about. I *am* threatening you, dipshit. All of you. I want to make that very clear."

"And just who am I talking to?" he asked, smirking.

Tracey stared down the barrel. "Pain."

The young man's smile faded. He looked to his friends and the gray-haired man moved past him, approaching the cabin.

THE OLD LADY

"Enough of this," the grayed man said to the young one. "She's just some lady. What is she going to do?"

His assault rifle was still held to his chest in a downward position, but his finger was close enough to the trigger guard to make Tracey's skin pimple. She resented his infantilizing, sexist sentiment—the tired male opinion that a woman couldn't take of herself during a conflict—but more deeply resented the way he'd said it. It was too similar to what another man had said before assaulting her.

"Don't come any closer!" she ordered.

But the grayed man kept coming, slowly making his way up the path. Tracey grimaced. She had given these trespassers fair warning. If he wanted to keep walking, then she would let him.

The grayed man started to say something, but his words became a shout as the ground beneath him gave way. The pitfall opened, sending him down into the hole with a thud. All went still for a second, and then scream rose out of the pit like a desperate cry from Hell.

Adrenaline burned through Tracey, and she controlled her breathing to steady herself.

Her father echoed through her mind. *"You know what to do."*

Though everything was happening fast, somehow it seemed as if the universe had come to a halt. Tracey's thoughts were quick but clear, predicting what the other men would do next, and debating how she would respond. She didn't want to go back to prison over someone else's problem, but it was too late to back out of this situation. Alicia's problem was now Tracey's problem, and the men outside would have to be dealt with swiftly and efficiently.

Her father's words returned to her. *"Worry about the six that will kill you, not the twelve that will put you away."*

When the grayed man fell into the pit, the young man took a panicked step backward. The Mexican raised his rifle and looked all around, as if the pitfall had been caused by some exterior force. He spun back, facing the cabin with the stock of his tactical weapon pressed to his shoulder and the barrel leveled at the window. Tracey wasn't going to wait to find out if he intended to fire it. Before he could shoot off a round, she got a lock on him and pulled the trigger of her .22 rifle. Gunpowder burned. The Mexican's body gyrated as the bullet entered his chest, and because he didn't fall immediately, Tracey fired two more shots, tagging him twice in the belly. That dropped him. His gun went into the snow, and he fell backwards, screaming in agony just like his friend in the pit.

Tracey lunged away from the window just before the young man opened fire with his AR-15. The windowpane exploded. Alicia screamed and covered her head with both hands, curling into a ball. Broken glass showered the cabin floor. Canned vegetables on the shelf popped, and pieces of wood flew like shrapnel when the walls were struck by bullets. The man's rapid firing told Tracey his rifle was equipped with a bump stock, allowing him to spray bullets quicker. But he only shot in a quick, short-lived burst, then ceased fire.

Though the gunshots had shocked her eardrums, she could still hear the anguished screams of the men outside. Two were down but not dead yet. The gut shots she'd given the Mexican might not kill him, but it would likely hurt worse than any pain he'd ever experienced before. And the man in the pit wasn't just crying out because he was trapped. His screams told of serious injury.

Using the strap, Tracey slung the rifle over her back and crawled on her elbows to Alicia to whisper in her ear. "Stay down. Don't move. Don't follow me. Don't try to run."

Alicia whimpered, still holding her head in both hands. Tracey wasn't sure if the girl was calm enough to comprehend. She could only hope Alicia was smart enough to take her advice.

Shuffling to the rear corner of the cabin, Tracey shoved away the fake fern that concealed the breakaway plank at the bottom of the wall. Removing the plank, she was relieved to see her father had maintained the tunnel. It looked a lot smaller and tighter to her now that she was a fully grown adult, but she was lean enough to fit through the cramped space. It was like an air vent, only forged of cold dirt and wooden buttresses.

Tracey crawled the way her father had taught her, using her elbows and knees to propel her body forward. She took deep breaths through her nose and focused straight ahead, utilizing meditative techniques to keep her nerves from snapping. Her chest shuddered as if filled with thunder and she cursed her own heart, demanding it to slow down. As she made it to the exit, she gently pushed the trapdoor open. It exited to the rear of the cabin. Tracey got to her knees and slung the rifle off her back. She'd fired three rounds. That meant she had seven left in the magazine. She rose to her feet but moved in a hunched over stride, sticking close to the wall of the cabin as she gingerly approached the front yard.

When she reached the end of the wall, Tracey pressed her back

THE OLD LADY

against it, holding the rifle close to her. She listened. One of the wounded men was screaming in horror. The other was crying for help.

"Wylder!" he cried. "Wylder, help me!"

Slowly, Tracey peeked around the side of the cabin.

The young one called Wylder held his AR-15 high, still pointed at the blown-out window. His expression was not one of rage or determination—it was chalk-white terror. Even from afar, she could see he was shaking. This was both good and bad for her. The good part was he obviously wasn't trained in combat and had been totally unprepared for this. The bad part was his fear would make him reckless and impulsive. In this state, he would not hesitate to shoot at anything that moved. If Tracey called out to Wylder and told him to drop his weapon, it would only give away her position, and his rifle was far more powerful than her own.

She was closer to Wylder now than she'd been inside the cabin, and getting a better look at his face, Tracey gritted her teeth. He reminded her of someone she'd long wanted to forget, another man with a black goatee who'd committed acts of evil upon her. When she blinked, Wylder *became* that man, just as Alicia had become Olivia, and Tracey shook her head hard to shake the image loose. Blinking, she saw Wylder for who he was again, but the traumatic memory left a lingering hatred. What had happened to her was forever imprinted on her soul; what was happening now seemed destined to become another painful memory, but just how painful depended on what she did next. That was enough to spring her into action.

With the rifle raised in both hands, Tracey came around the corner firing. Years of practice returned to her—all the target shooting, plinking, and small game hunting she'd done in her youth. Before Wylder even noticed her, she'd clipped him. He yelped and spun, dropping his rifle so he could clutch his wound, and her next shots barely missed him as he retreated toward the path in a panicked run. Tracey got a lock on him and aimed at the center of his back. Killing him would be easy.

No, she told herself. *So far this has been self-defense but shooting a man in the back is an express ticket back to prison.*

She kept Wylder in her sights as he raced toward the treeline, clutching his bleeding arm. Part of her hoped he would draw a pistol from his coat and spin around, just so she'd have a good excuse to separate his brains from his head. But he only kept running away. As he got closer to the woods, he struggled in the snowbank and tripped over his own feet. Tracey couldn't help but smile. For all his strutting machismo, Wylder was a piss-poor soldier. Someone like him didn't even deserve to own an AR-15. Not only would his foolishness endanger others, but he was also likely to blow his own dick off. Wylder groaned as he got up and continued toward the woods. He was limping now.

The voice of Tracey's father rose from the shadows of her mind. *"Don't let him get away!"*

"Damnit, old man," she said aloud. "I'm not going back in the slammer over this shit."

"You let him escape and you'll live to regret it—but you sure won't live very long."

"Nobody asked your opinion."

"I raised you better than this," he snarled. Even after decades of estrangement, Tracey remembered his gravelly voice perfectly, every inflection and word choice. *"You know damned well that asshole is not going to let it end like this."*

"He's scared shitless and I've disarmed him. He's not coming back."

"Maybe not alone."

It was a valid point, but even if Wylder had other goons, Tracey wasn't planning on waiting for a war to come to her. Finishing every battle wasn't what survival was about. She didn't care how heavily the snow was falling or how obscured the trail may have become. Once she gathered Alicia, she was getting off this mountain. She could figure out her next steps once they were speeding away in her truck. If the girl gave her any argument, Tracey would leave her here.

But first she had to check on the other men. Though they'd stopped screaming, she still heard their suffering grunts. Her eyes narrowed as she watched Wylder vanish into the forest. Though her head told her she'd made the right decision, her gut disagreed. Just because Wylder was a poor soldier didn't mean he wouldn't try to save his friends, and she doubted he was the type of man who would let go of a grudge. The young punk would want retribution—not just for his wounded arm, but for his wounded pride. Tracey had to move fast.

First, she went to the Mexican. The man in the pit wasn't going anywhere, and even if he was still capable of firing his weapon, he wouldn't be able to get the right angle for a shot unless she peered down from the edge of the hole. The Mexican had been shot three

THE OLD LADY

times and was on his back in the bloody snow, but his assault rifle was within his reach. Tracey kept her aim on him as she hurried over.

His torso was bleeding profusely. He held his hands over his stomach wounds and stared straight up at the sky, moaning and coughing blood. Tracey was close enough now that the man could see her, but he didn't acknowledge her presence. He didn't ask for help or beg for his life, didn't curse her or try to fight. When Tracey used her boot to push the Mexican's assault rifle out of his reach, he didn't make a grab for it. He was too focused on holding in his guts.

Tracey pointed her rifle at him. "Who are you?"

He only sneered at her, so Tracey pressed the barrel against his knee and held it there. The Mexican's eyes widened.

"Tell me who you are," she said, "or you can say goodbye to your right kneecap, followed by your left."

The man grunted. "Paul…"

"I don't give a fuck about your name. I meant *who are you guys*? What do you want with the girl?"

He closed his eyes tight as a trickle of blood sluiced through his clenched teeth.

"Did one of you kill her friend?" Tracey asked. "Did you take two hostages?"

Paul shook his head, but she couldn't be sure if he was answering her or just writhing from the pain.

"Where'd you guys come from, anyway?" she asked.

This land had always been practically deserted, with only a few cabins on the mountain. But having not been here for so long, it was possible other buildings had been constructed which she knew nothing about. The thought was a little unsettling. Tracey preferred to have a clear mental map of the mountainside, the way she'd had as a child. But she wasn't a child anymore. She was a middle-aged woman, and a confused one at that, just unhinged enough to make life a constant struggle.

"I asked you a question," Tracey told Paul when he didn't respond.

The man murmured with his eyes still closed. Tracey leaned in slightly to try to hear him better, and with the sound of the snow crunching beneath her, Paul suddenly came alive and reached for the barrel of her rifle. Despite his injuries, he was a big man, and *strong*. But the barrel of the .22 was still hot. It burned his hands and Tracey snatched the rifle away, and without thinking about it, she turned it over and hammered the butt of the stock down on Paul's face. His nose crunched, sounding like bubble wrap popping, and his mashed nostrils gushed blood into his mouth.

"Answer my questions," Tracey said. "If you don't, I'll keep hurting you until you beg for death."

The pleasure Tracey took in beating him almost surprised her. She'd thought prison and therapy had tamed her tendency for wrath. That had been the goal of those in charge. But Tracey had always harbored a propensity for taking violent situations to another level. The prison shrink had diagnosed her with intermittent explosive disorder, a condition that caused people to overact to situations with an unreasonable amount of anger. Medication helped, but only to a point, and when truly pressed by aggressors, Tracey's corroded heart grew blacker, her blood hotter.

The fear of going back to prison was starting to dissipate. Though it remained in the back of her mind, a vehement bloodlust was beginning to stew.

Paul's eyes rolled and his arms fell to the ground with his palms facing up, exposing his belly wounds. The rounds had grouped close together, creating a hole that looked in on his punctured intestines. His groans of agony diminished into wet, clicking noises in his throat, and his whole body shuddered as if electrocuted.

"Looks like you don't need to beg for death," Tracey said with a sigh. "Time's up."

Paul fell slack. Tracey stared at his lifeless body, her anger cooling as a pitch-black dread coursed into her veins. She tried to gulp but her throat had gone dry.

She'd killed him.

It was in self-defense, but with her police record, she'd be extremely lucky to be charged with just involuntary manslaughter. Investigators and prosecutors would grill her relentlessly, digging up her past to question her present. They would insist Tracey was still a powder keg of uncontrollable rage, incapable of shutting off her violent impulses.

"Now you've done it," she told herself.

She suddenly felt weighted, and her shoulders curled forward. Her eyes began to water but she stopped them, having been trained how to hold back tears. The problem was, her swallowed sadness blossomed into fury so easily, an emotion she often couldn't control.

Staring down at Paul, she kicked him in the ribs to make sure he

THE OLD LADY

was dead. He didn't flinch or make a sound. She stomped on his neck, pressing down firmly and holding there to see if he choked. Getting no reaction, Tracey picked up the man's assault rifle by the stock so not to smudge his fingerprints on the trigger and carried it to the front porch. Putting it down, she approached the pitfall. There was no longer any screaming or even moaning. The hole was as silent as a grave, and perhaps it had become one to the man within it.

Bringing her .22 to her shoulder, Tracey aimed the barrel downward as she inched toward the edge. If she called out to the man in the pit, he might wait for her to appear over the edge like a Whac-A-Mole and blow her head apart with his assault rifle. But if she approached quietly and appeared suddenly, the man likely wouldn't be able to react before she leveled the end of her rifle with his heart. Tracey chose the latter, but her head swirled with various, tortured thoughts, visions of extreme violence striking her like an earthquake. When she reached the edge, she paused to brace herself, then let the rifle lead the way, pointing it into the hole first to see if the man opened fire. When he didn't, she inched close enough to look down into the pit.

What she saw chilled her.

The grayed man was on his back in the frozen dirt. He'd gone pale and his lips were turning blue, but he was breathing rapidly and three of his limbs were shaking. The only one that wasn't was his left leg. The man's femur had snapped in the fall, and the broken bone had ripped out of his thigh and through his slacks. Blood was everywhere, and there was a spatter of vomit beside his head. Though Tracey stared down at him, he never looked at her. His wide, dilated eyes looked straight up, staring into the ashen sky.

He's in shock, Tracey thought. And judging by the condition of his leg, his pain must have been excruciating, but it wasn't his biggest problem. *If that leg fills with blood, he could die.*

"*Fuck him*," her father's voice said. "*Let him die.*"

"It's not that simple," she replied.

Even when she spoke, the man below didn't look at her. But Tracey stared at him as she pondered what to do next.

Maybe she didn't have to do anything at all. He'd either go into toxic shock and die, or if he'd severed his femoral artery, he would bleed to death. It would be the fall that killed him, not Tracey. She certainly wasn't going to lower ropes or a ladder and try to get him out, especially with his rifle so close by.

"*Bury him,*" her father whispered through her head.

"He ain't dead yet."

"*You got a problem with burying the living?*"

"Of course, I do."

But they both knew that wasn't true. Tracey felt no remorse for anyone who tried to hurt her. Her only reservations against acts of further cruelty stemmed not from sympathy, but from a fear of persecution in a courtroom.

"*You've already killed one man,*" her father said. "*What's one more?*"

Tracey bit her bottom lip, refusing to reply to her own mind. But now another thought was forming.

If she dragged Paul to the pit and tossed him on top of the man below, she could bury them both and conceal the murders altogether. All she'd have to do was collect the empty shell casings, tarp the window, and clean up inside. It wasn't like Wylder was going to call the police. He and his pals had been chasing a teenage girl with rifles. They had ignored the *No Trespassing* signs and Tracey's clear warnings to leave. They had started this—she'd only finished it. But the police might never find out about this if Tracey didn't report it. Problem was, Alicia would, especially if she'd been truthful about Wylder taking her friends hostage and killing one of them. So, unless Tracey was ready to kill the girl too, the plan was too faulty to move forward with. She was also certain Wylder would soon return—perhaps with more gun-toting buddies. Time spent filling the hole would be better used getting off the mountain before things got worse.

The grayed man released loud, rapid breaths. When a grunt escaped him, the hairs on Tracey's nape and arms stood up. She knew that grunt. She'd heard it before from a man who had once crawled on top of her. The sound she heard now had the same tone and duration—a perfect echo of the grunts that had been made in her ear years ago.

"You son of a bitch," she snarled at the man below.

She didn't know him, but she knew his kind.

The reason the intruders had been chasing after Alicia suddenly became clear, and a vicious heat spread through Tracey as the revelation struck her. Her pulse quickened, making her feel twitchy, edgy. Aggressive flashbacks pounded her skull.

This spell was harsher than her usual anxiety attacks. In the support group she'd been forced to attend in prison, the counselor had treated Tracey for post-traumatic stress disorder, telling her these

THE OLD LADY

sudden spells of horror were the aftershocks of the brutal ordeal that was her life. Tracey had learned just how easily she could be triggered. Most of the time she could control her reactions but now, engaging in a violent altercation for the first time since the event that had put her in prison for years, the spell was so intense as to seem unbreakable. Her heart shuddered and her vision blurred, the world around her becoming a vibrating dome of her own dread. And within that dome, a screaming, red Hell of rage burst to life, setting her soul ablaze.

"Never again," she snarled at the man in the pit.

Tracey stepped back from the rim and slung her rifle over her shoulder before turning back. She passed by the cabin, marching through the snow and slush with grim determination until she reached the tool shed. Finding what she needed, she removed the rifle and put the pack of dual canisters on her back. A hose running from the tanks was attached to the tool she carried with both hands as she made her way back to the pit.

As she passed the cabin, she heard a small voice. She wasn't sure if it was real or imagined until she turned to see Alicia standing on the porch. The girl was trembling, tears and snot wetting her face.

"What... what's going on?" Alicia asked.

Tracey gave her a stern look. "Get back inside. Now."

When Alicia saw the tool Tracey held, she furrowed her brow. She looked away but didn't move, only scanned the horizon with nervous eyes.

"Get inside!" Tracey said louder. "That's an order!"

Alicia gave her a worried look but retreated into the cabin and closed the door behind her. Tracey returned to the pit and stepped to the edge, no longer cautious. The fury within her outweighed any concern for own safety. Even the fear of returning to prison for a life sentence couldn't deter her in this clenched moment. Impulse reigned. Anger silenced every other thought.

Her eyes narrowed as she pointed the tool at the man below. "You were going to rape her. And then, you were going to rape me."

The man only gasped for air.

"Pretty young thing like her... you boys must've planned on a grand old time, huh? Tell me I'm wrong. Tell me I'm wrong, you fucking rapist!"

But the man told her nothing. He wouldn't even focus on her. Instead, his eyelids fluttered, and his jaw fell slack, but still he breathed, still had the audacity to live.

The tears Tracey had been holding back returned to her, and this time, she let them go. Her cheeks grew wet, lips quivering before they curled in hatred. She flicked the ignition switch, and the tool made a soft hiss.

She and her father had only ever used it to remove snow and ice.

Now the flamethrower would serve a more noble purpose.

Pressing the trigger, Tracey held the barrel up into the air as the nozzle sprayed fire, taunting the crippled man below. It may have just been a result of going into shock, but his eyes widened, giving Tracey hope the bastard understood what was going to happen to him.

"You don't deserve the peaceful death of bleeding out," she snarled. "Men like you only have one thing coming, and I'm here to give it to you." She aimed the nozzle into the hole. "Tell my Dad I said hello."

Tracey released a jet of flame into the pit. As the man began to cook, he let out one final cry. Keeping the trigger pressed, Tracey moved the nozzle from side to side, filling the entire hole with fire. The man's body shook as he was burned alive. His flesh blackened and cracked, his face melting to reveal the raw tissue beneath. The foul odor of singed flesh struck Tracey, but she ignored it. All that mattered now was retribution. It was the only thing that would release the spell's hold on her, the only action that would soothe the old demons within. As she continued shooting flames, the orange glow reflected off the darkness of her unblinking eyes, and she didn't stop until she realized the only screams left were her own.

TEN

ALICIA WATCHED IT ALL FROM the window.

The woman who'd saved her was setting the pit on fire. Having stayed on the floor during the shootout, Alicia didn't know what was in the hole, but she could guess. There was only one reason the woman would be burning whatever lay inside, and it was a macabre thought for Alicia to stomach.

Why go fetch a flamethrower? she thought. *Why wouldn't she just shoot him? And if he was trapped down there, why would she have to kill him at all?*

Alicia didn't like the implications of that, but also hadn't seen everything that transpired. She'd been curled into a ball, praying for her life, and her prayers had been answered in the form of this heavily armed old lady. Alicia was grateful, and yet afraid of her at the same time. She couldn't help but eye the escape hatch on the floor where the woman had crawled out of the cabin. If Alicia stayed, the woman could help her get to safety, but judging by her actions, staying with her might not be safe.

She set a man on fire.

While the woman had initially acted in self-defense, burning someone to death was a dark step to take. That she had successfully defeated three armed men was impressive, but also damning. What had she been into before Alicia had come here? What kind of life had she lived to make her such an effective shooter? Looking at the well-stocked shelves surrounding her, Alicia ascertained that the woman was not just a hoarder, but some sort of prepper. The supplies and survival gear were too plentiful to be just for a simple emergency. This cabin wasn't stocked for a harsh winter or weather disaster—it was stocked for doomsday.

All the people Alicia had encountered on this mountain were dangerous, with each one being weirder than the last. First, she'd met Charlie, who'd turned out to be far worse than the basic creep she'd perceived him to be. Then there had been Wylder, a man who carried an assault rifle around like it was a normal thing to do, and then the other men who'd come out of the house to hunt her down like a deer. Now, Alicia had come across a one-woman army. It would have been reassuring if the old lady wasn't so strange. Alicia had heard her yelling at the men when the gunfire died down. She'd also heard the woman yelling at herself, as if having a conversation with someone who wasn't there. She'd threatened one man with blowing his kneecaps off. The other she'd accused of being a rapist, for some reason. Alicia hadn't mentioned any sexual assault, so why did she jump to the conclusion that the men were out to rape them both?

Because she's nuts, Alicia told herself.

Outside, the woman walked to the other man, the one she'd shot down. Putting the gun of the flamethrower into its holding latch on the pack, she grabbed the dead man's ankles and dragged him toward the burning pit, then got on her knees and rolled his body into the smoking hole. She then doubled down with the flamethrower, filling the pit with jets of fresh flames to devour the bodies below.

Alicia cringed. The direness of her entire situation fell upon her in a crushing swoop, and it frightened her to not know if things had gotten better or worse.

The front door swung open, causing Alicia to flinch. The woman stood in the doorway, silhouetted against a backdrop of muted daylight. When she stepped into the cabin, she removed the flamethrower pack and placed it under the coatrack. She went back outside, then returned with the .22 rifle and what looked to Alicia like a machine gun—one of the men's weapons that was more appropriate for military use than civilian. Another rifle lay on the porch, and the woman kicked it into the cabin too.

THE OLD LADY

Shutting the door behind her, the woman placed the firearms on the floor and exhaled deeply. She drew a pack of cigarettes from her pocket and lit one with a Zippo. Her bloodshot eyes landed on Alicia, giving her chills as she realized the woman had been crying too. Alicia couldn't blame her. As the woman stepped closer, Alicia took one step back and put her hands halfway up.

"At ease," the woman said.

Alicia put her hands down but swallowed hard. "You saved my life. Thank you."

The woman gave her a small nod, puffing smoke.

"What... what happened?" Alicia asked.

The woman glowered. "What the hell do you think?"

"You..." Alicia couldn't bring herself to finish.

The woman finished for her. "I killed them. All but one."

Alicia's eyes went wide. "One got away?"

"They called him Wylder."

"What? Where'd he go?"

"Back into the woods. I tagged him in the upper arm with at least one round, and he twisted his ankle pretty bad before he made it to the treeline." She pointed at the assault rifles on the floor. "The dumb shit dropped his weapon too."

Alicia shivered. "He's gonna go back to the compound."

"What compound?"

"The one they're keeping my friends at."

"How many men are there?"

"I don't know. At least one. This weird guy named Charlie."

The woman's hard face went even harder. "*Charlie?*"

"That's what he said his name was."

"Fuckin' Charlie." The woman shook her head with a sour laugh. "*Charlie*. How do you like that, Dad?"

Alicia furrowed her brow. "What?"

The woman seemed to return from some deep cavern in her own head. "Never mind. This compound—you think you could find your way back to it?"

Alicia crossed her arms and dropped her gaze. "I can't go back there."

"Your friends' lives may depend on it. Who knows what Wylder and Charlie have planned for them. You say they killed one already, and they tried to kill you too. They could be doing anything to those kids."

A shudder went through Alicia when she imagined her boyfriend and young Nori being abused by these violent strangers. She still didn't know what they really wanted or why they were so angry with her and her friends.

"Can't we just get to the nearest police station or find a phone?" she asked.

The woman shook her head. "It'll take too long, especially with this snow coming down hard. It'll be hours before we can get help, and then more hours before the police can get to the compound. In that time, your friends could be raped and tortured, maybe even killed."

Alice winced. "But what can we do if we go there?"

"We make this a rescue mission. Get your friends out of there by any means necessary."

Stunned, Alicia took a deep breath. "Are you, like, black ops or something? I mean, who are you?"

The woman didn't answer at first. Her eyes roamed the shelves as if evaluating the inventory. Finally, she replied.

"I'm Tracey."

It was all she offered, and while Alicia wanted more, she was too intimidated to press her. She remained silent, unsure what to say.

"Look, kid," Tracey said. "My first thought was to get us the fuck off this mountain. I didn't ask to be dragged into your fiasco. But things have changed. Two men are dead. They had it coming, but the cops won't see it that way."

"Why not?"

"They just won't. Not with me." Tracey's face twisted with consternation. "But the bigger issue at hand is this—I fucked up by letting Wylder escape. No one had been killed yet, and I wanted to avoid that, if I could. But now two of his buddies have been murdered, so I know he's going back to that compound with vengeance in his heart, and if he can't take it out on us, he's gonna take it out on your friends—especially that sixteen-year-old girl."

The weight of this hit Alicia like a sledgehammer to the gut.

"Trust me," Tracey said, "you don't want to know what men like that will do to a little girl. It's an evil you can't even imagine."

Tears welled in Alicia's eyes.

"What are your friends' names?" Tracey asked.

"Nori and Dylan."

"Well, Nori and Dylan's only chance is for us to go after them,"

THE OLD LADY

Tracey said. "Otherwise, they will be raped and killed. Unless you can live with that, I suggest you suck it up and come with me."

Tracey reached behind her back, and Alicia flinched when the woman drew a pistol. She'd forgotten Tracey had even put it there. Tracey held it by the barrel, the handle pointed at Alicia.

"Take it," Tracey said.

Alicia hesitated.

"I said take it!"

Alicia slowly took the pistol in her hand.

"You ever use a firearm?" Tracey asked.

Alicia shook her head.

"Well, this here's a Glock. There's no safety on it, no tricks to learn. Just point it at what you want to die, bend your knees, and squeeze the trigger. Don't yank it too hard and fast. Squeeze with a steady amount of pressure. And make sure you hold it with both hands. None of that movie cowboy bullshit, and none of that sideways shit the street gangs do. Understand?"

Alicia nodded.

"If you understand, say so."

"I understand," she whispered.

"*I can't hear you!*"

Alicia straightened up and raised her voice. "Yes! I understand."

"Good. Now listen up. I can see you don't know shit about fighting—that's why you shouldn't use one of these assault rifles; they'll be too much for you. And we don't have time for me to teach you about combat. You just stay behind me and do exactly what I say. Understood?"

"Yes." Alicia looked at the gun in her hands, then back at Tracey. "How do you know so much about this stuff? Were you a marine or something?"

Tracey held her gaze. "Something like that."

"A cop?"

Tracey gave a small laugh. "Far from it, kid."

"Look... I'm very grateful to you for saving my life. If you're worried about the police, I promise I'll tell them how brave and protective you were. I won't say anything but good things, I swear."

"You're wasting time. We need to get moving."

Anxiousness made Alicia tingle. "I don't think I can do this."

"You have to."

"I've just never been in a situation like this."

"Life is full of bad situations, kid, because the world is a terrible place. Right now, fear is a luxury you can't afford. If you don't fight back, the bastards will only hurt you worse—you and everyone you love."

"But why are *you* doing this?" Alicia had to ask. "I know I asked for your help, but *this*? This is a whole other level. Why are you risking—"

"My reasons are my own."

Tracey picked up a large backpack and slid her arms through the straps, then pointed at another backpack and told Alicia to put it on. When she did, the weight of it wasn't too bad, but the weight of what she was doing was as heavy as a whale.

"C'mon," Tracey said. "There's some things we need to get from the toolshed."

ELEVEN

EVERY STEP WAS AGONY.

Wylder wasn't sure if he'd broken his foot or merely sprained it, but it didn't matter right now. The important thing was getting back to the compound, but to move he had to lean on trees, barely letting his injured foot touch the ground. This alone was enough to put him at a turtle's pace but making matters worse was the bullet in his arm. It was his right arm, so his dominate hand was numb. The pain was strong but dull, feeling like the bullet had hit bone. He'd touched it gently, trying to feel how deep the bullet was, but even grazing the wound with his fingertips sent hot blades of pain through him.

But things could be worse. He could have been taken down like Paul and Quin. The way they'd screamed his name as he'd run away haunted Wylder, his memory an echo chamber that tortured him, telling him he'd been a coward. He wondered if his fellow soldiers were still alive. Based on the behavior of the woman who'd shot at them, Wylder worried she may have used lethal force. Quin had fallen into a pit, and who knew what that crazy bitch had put down there—spikes, hot coals, a goddamned alligator? She'd also blown several holes through Paul without hesitation.

Who the hell is this psycho cunt?

Having tracked Alicia, he and the others figured they could get to her even if they had to go through some female hermit living in the woods. Like Quin had said, this was just some old lady, so what harm could she have done to three men so heavily armed?

Apparently, it was a lot of goddamn harm.

What the fuck are going to do now? Wylder asked himself.

Thinking of Charlie's huge mistake made him seethe. If Wylder had his way, Charlie would be expelled from the group, but it wasn't his call. He also didn't have final say about what would be done with the hostages. He knew he'd made the right decision chasing after Alicia, but that had ended in disaster. Not only was Wylder returning without her, but also coming back without two senior team members.

And then there was the problem of the woman, which Wylder now suspected would be the biggest problem of all.

He grunted as he trekked through the mounting snow. He wished he had a phone or radio to contact Charlie and Stan, but such devices were banned. The trail back was more difficult to discern than it had been when he'd left the compound earlier, and snowflakes were whizzing in every direction, the cruel winter wind creating a cyclone. Finding a large branch, Wylder painstakingly bent over and picked it up to use as a hiking stick. His progress was pathetic, but it was the best he could do.

What if the woman comes after you? he thought. But he doubted she would be that invested in this to try. It was Alicia's problem, not hers. Why would she further endanger herself for some teenager she didn't even know?

They'll get the police. You can bet your ass on that. And if the girl can find her way back to the compound, we're all fucked.

Something had to be done about this, and fast.

Wylder struggled on. "Damn you, Charlie."

~

The cellar was dimly lit and smelled of dust and dried rat feces, but it was warmer than outside, and Charlie had given Nori a dog bed to sit on. He'd even brought down the old CD boombox so they could listen to music. Before Stan went back upstairs, they had put Dylan on the other side of the cellar, facing the wall with his hands tied to a pole behind his back and the gag in his mouth secured with duct tape. Nori was kept with her hands cuffed in front of her, but that was the extent of her confines. He'd even taken her gag out, so they could

THE OLD LADY

talk. Charlie hoped she would appreciate all he'd done for her. He also hoped she would show that appreciation, but when he put his hand on her thigh, Nori flinched and scooted away.

"Take it easy," he said.

The young girl's chocolate eyes watered, her face pinched in fear.

"Everything's gonna be alright," he told her. "That whole thing with the black guy was just an accident, okay? I only meant to stop him from killing my friend. This whole thing is, like, one big misunderstanding."

Nori hung her head, and when her hair hid her face Charlie tried to brush it behind her ear and noticed it was scarred and had a hearing aid attached. Nori yelped, causing her tied-up brother to grunt in protest even though he couldn't see what was going on. Charlie sighed. This was getting annoying.

"For Christ's sake," he told Nori. "Will you chill out? I told you, I'm not a bad guy. And in this place, I'm the best friend you're gonna have. So, unless you don't want me to help you get out of this, I'd start being nicer to me if I was you."

Nori whimpered. "P-please… please d-d-don't hurt me. Please d-d-don't hurt muh-my brother."

Her stutter was almost cute. Charlie glanced back at Dylan, then smiled at Nori. "Like I said, I can help you, but if you keep being cold to me—keep being rude when I'm treating you good—I'll have no reason to treat you like a friend."

He let that sink in. Nori didn't say anything, but this time when Charlie placed his palm on her thigh, she didn't resist him. He ran his hand up and down her leg, petting her like a pussycat as a pop country song played in the background.

God, she looks good, Charlie thought. Even wet with tears and her face scrunched by fear, she was as tender as could be. Charlie hadn't been laid in eight months, and even then, he'd had to pay for it. And he'd never fucked an Asian. Now he was cuddling close to a ripe, Japanese teen he suspected was a virgin. He would have cut off his left pinky to have a girl like this, and now here she was, at his mercy, ready to bend to his will. The power he held over her only increased the eroticism, but he didn't want to abuse it if he didn't have to. It was better for her to want it, perhaps even beg for it.

He reached up slowly and ran the back of one finger up and down her cheek, feeling the warmth of her tears as they wet his skin. Just below the knuckles on both his hands, each of Charlie's fingers bore a letter, together spelling out "Born Free." Reaching for her chin, he gently turned her head up, so she was facing him.

"Look at me," he whispered.

Nori looked at him but struggled to maintain eye contact.

"I'm the best chance you've got," he told her. "I may not look like much, but I'm a nice person. That should count for something, right? Women should appreciate a nice guy."

Nori sniffed, seemingly unable to respond.

"I've just been lonely," Charlie said. "We all get lonely sometimes, right? Even a pretty girl like you must get lonely now and then. This cellar could easily be the loneliest place on earth for you. I'm the only thing keeping that from happening. Do you get what I'm saying?"

Still Nori wouldn't answer. But she also didn't do anything when he ran his hand up and down her back and pulled her in for a hug. She trembled in his arms, and Charlie shushed her, telling her everything was alright. His sniffed the top of her head. The girl smelled of youth, like the flesh of a baby. She didn't flinch until he kissed her good ear, but he soothed her again, so she settled down.

"Just a little kiss," he said, inching his lips closer to hers. "Just to tell me you understand, to show me you want to be my friend too."

TWELVE

TRACEY HAD ONLY BEEN HOMELESS for three weeks when she had her first violent encounter. Being only eighteen-years old, she knew better than to get close to strangers, especially men, and tried to stay hidden as she wandered from town to town. She didn't hitchhike, talk to other homeless people, or put herself in any other situations that had the potential for danger. Mostly, she kept to herself, relying on her training to get by.

She slept in the woods, using the tent kept in her BOB, and did so fully clothed, including keeping her boots on, just in case she had to flee or fight in a hurry. She rationed the small amount of food she'd brought along in the bag. Being springtime, Tracey was able to forage, sustaining herself by boiling ground nuts (which were like small potatoes) in her portable camp stove, and boiling a lichen known as rock tripe. The fungus was bland, but safe to eat. She made tea out of Hemlock needles and ate salads of dandelion, which hadn't gone bitter yet because it was May. It was too early in the season for any Chicken of the Woods mushrooms, but when she was lucky, Tracey found wild blueberries, and sometimes dared to steal fruits and vegetables from suburban gardens.

She also hunted successfully without using the .38 snub-nosed revolver she'd stolen from her father's armory. The gun was only for protection. Using it to catch game was not only unnecessary, but it would also waste ammunition and draw the attention of anyone in earshot. Instead, she made traps for squirrels and cottontails by day, and by night stalked frogs for their leg meat, confusing them with the beam of her flashlight so she could pick them up. Sometimes she let other predators do the work for her. She watched for owls and other large birds because they were good providers. Often a hawk would kill a hare or partridge, but their bounty would be too heavy for them to fly off with, leaving Tracey to reap the spoils. Other times when one was feeding on fresh prey, it was easy enough to scare them off and secure a hassle-free supper. When she found owls perched in the shadows, Tracey would strike them down with large rocks. Though they were smaller up close than they appeared when high above, owls provided excellent sustenance. When near a water source, she would refill her canteen and purify it with a few drops of bleach, and did some fishing with a collapsible pole she kept in her BOB. Occasionally, she was lucky enough to catch a beaver and slit its throat with her hunting knife before it could defend itself.

Due to stress more than her varied diet, Tracey often suffered stomach upsets and loose stools. She used the medicines of the earth whenever she could but went through her stash of paregoric tablets faster than she'd anticipated. Whenever she ran out of something like this, she went into town to shoplift supplies. Store employees gave her the side-eye whenever this dirty teenage girl entered their establishment with her BOB on her back, so she tied the hiking pack high up in a tree for safekeeping before leaving the woods. Mostly she stole isobutane cans for her stove, hygiene products, bags of Ramen noodles, candy bars, and toilet paper rolls from public bathrooms. But now in need of medicine, Tracey went to the nearest drugstore, wearing her coat despite the warm, sunny day. Watching for staff, she pocketed stomach medicines, a bottle of aspirin, and a box of Reese's Pieces. As she made her way to the exit, sweat boiled in her armpits, but she kept a slow, steady gait. When the sensor opened the sliding doors, a man called out to her.

"Excuse me, young lady," he said. "Hey there, miss."

Tracey acted like she didn't hear him and moved into the foyer, approaching the second set of motion activated doors.

"Hey, you!" the man called out. "Stop."

THE OLD LADY

Tracey ignored him, but as she reached the doors a hand fell on her shoulder.

Being grabbed—especially from behind—caused Tracey's pulse to race. She became acutely sensitive to every sound and sight, the world tightening around her head like a vice. Acting on impulse, she gripped the hand on her shoulder, then used the other to grab the man's forearm. Though he was bigger than her, he was slow to react, and Tracey knew how to use someone's body weight against them. Pivoting, she spun the fat man forward, his eyes going wide with shock as a teenager propelled him with extreme force. The doors started to open, but the man slammed into one of them before it could, causing the doors to stop on the tracks. Stepping across him in a forty-five-degree angle, Tracey rose on the balls of her base foot, pivoted, and roundhouse kicked the man in the head. He fell hard into one of the doors, causing the glass to crack in spiderwebs, and before he could regain his senses, Tracey kicked him square in the chest, sending him not just into the door, but through it. The center bar broke and he fell through the shattered glass. His head smacked the pavement, sounding like a coconut being opened, and little pinpoints of blood from the glass shards appeared through his shirt. His nametag lay crooked, the words "Mike Patch, Assistant Manager" hanging from his breast.

Tracey ran.

People walking down the sidewalk stared as she charged past them, getting out of her way when she got too close. It was for the best, because she would have hurt them if they'd tried to stop her. No one pursued, and she made it back into the woods before police could arrive on the scene. But she knew it all must have been on camera, which meant she would have to get as far from this town as possible, as quickly as she could.

For over a week, she stuck to the woods, using her compass to stay on track as she journeyed south. To make herself look different from the girl on the security cameras, she cut her hair short and used the bleach to dye her hair, leaving enough left over to purify her water until she could shoplift another bottle small enough to carry.

She didn't leave the forest until she'd made it across state lines into Massachusetts.

Being alone for so long gave her too much time to think about what had happened with the drugstore manager, and she ran through different scenarios in her head, wondering what had happened after she'd left. The sound of his skull colliding with concrete recycled in her mind, jabbing at her when she was at her most vulnerable. Though she felt no sympathy for him, she worried that if he had died, the police manhunt would be far more intensive than it would be for a simple shoplifter, even one who'd assaulted somebody.

He touched me first, she thought. Any unwanted touching was assault—she knew that from the self-defense books her father had made her study—so really, she'd only been protecting herself. She was a teenage girl, and the manager was a grown man who had physically accosted her. The courts might side with her, but it was a chance Tracey wasn't willing to take, especially as a drifter.

As much as she disliked busy places, Tracey figured it might be best to go to a city so she could disappear amongst the crowd for a while. She could also check newspapers for any information about the incident at the drugstore, giving her a better idea of what she would be up against.

She followed her compass southeast, heading toward Boston.

THIRTEEN

AFTER LOADING UP ON THE toolshed's supplies, Tracey led the wide-eyed girl toward the trail Alicia had come in on. Along with the Ruger .22 rifle slung over her back, the pump action 12-gauge in her hands, and her large hunting knife, Tracey had attached a variety of instruments to her BOB and hung a splitting maul on the small loop. She wasn't interested in the men's AR-15s. They were too big and bulky, and often malfunctioned, failing to feed, eject, and extract rounds. A jam wasn't a big deal at the gun range, but in an actual shootout, it was the difference between life and death. Whenever possible, Tracey preferred old fashioned weaponry over high-tech.

Wanting Alicia to have more than a pistol, she'd clipped a stun gun and pocketknife to the girl's waistband. Tracey also had Alicia wear her balaclava, so she would appear more intimidating to their enemies. The teen was nervous, and understandably so, but Tracey needed her to show the way to the compound, and she could also use a second set of eyes for lookout. She didn't expect a teenager to go on offense in a battle but hoped Alicia wouldn't hesitate to defend them both. The only other option was to leave her behind at the cabin, but that was a terrible idea for a variety of reasons.

The cabin.

Just being back there was traumatic enough, digging up the graves of demons she'd long wished would stay buried. But Tracey had learned, time and again, that demons don't die, only lay in wait. Her father's voice was such a demon—perhaps, the leader of them all.

"*You have to be thorough,*" he warned. "*When there are ants in your kitchen, you can't just crush the ones you see. You have to hunt down the whole lot and wipe every trace of them from your home. You must kill every fucking last one.*"

The snow swarmed as they proceeded down the path. Tracey watched the wooded sidelines for other foot soldiers, but sensed Wylder was on his own now, at least out here. In his crippled state, they could gain on him, and if he chose to hide, they would get to the compound before he did, possibly giving Tracey the element of surprise over those who held the kids captive. Alicia said there was at least one man at the compound, but Tracey expected more.

In a way, she even hoped for more.

She was in attack mode. She was not thinking straight and knew it—her intermittent explosive disorder had steered her into trouble before—but there was no choice now. Fleeing was unacceptable when there were enemies to destroy. And she did have to destroy them. If she didn't, they would only come after her. And she didn't want to alert the police because she'd already killed two men and aimed to kill at least two more. There was no turning back from this, and there would be no compromises. Tracey knew that from experience. When this hunger came upon her, only blood would satiate it.

The trail widened as they moved along, giving Tracey a sense of unease. She'd taken away Wylder's AR-15, but he might have another firearm stashed on him, and could be waiting for them in the trees like a sniper. Guiding Alicia into the woods for cover, Tracey kept them close to the pathway to stay on track and noticed drops of blood in the snow—a red breadcrumb trail to Wylder. He was sticking to the path itself. It left him wide open for attack but, being hurt, he probably had no choice.

Tracey pressed the stock of the 12-gauge to her shoulder.

Alicia flinched. "What? What is it?"

"He's close."

Alicia frantically looked in every direction.

"Calm down," Tracey told her. "We've got the upper hand here."

Alicia's hushed voice was garbled by emotion. "I don't think I can

THE OLD LADY

take this."

"Hey. We've been over this already. You *must* do this."

"It's just... I'm just so scared."

Tracey locked eyes with the girl. "Let me tell you something, kid. Everything you want out of life awaits you on the other side of fear."

Alicia bit her bottom lip.

"Once a woman starts to run, she never stops," Tracey said. "You said you're eighteen now—an adult by law, old enough to go to war and die. Alicia... it's time for you to stop running."

Tracey didn't wait for the girl to reply. Time was wasting. Though she had never met Nori and Dylan, Tracey worried for them—especially Nori. Having been abused as a child herself, Tracey couldn't bear the idea of leaving the hostage girl behind, not even for the time it would take to get help. In that time, Nori could experience things that would scar her for life. Tracey couldn't let Nori end up like she was. No one should have to suffer that greatly.

The trail of Wylder's blood disappeared and reappeared, but when Tracey looked ahead, she couldn't see him. The dimmed daylight and falling snow limited her vision even when she used her binoculars. They continued hiking, and Alicia didn't protest.

Tracey believed in what she'd said to her. How many men Alicia's age had been drafted into wars they didn't even understand? How many boys under the age of twenty-six had won the Vietnam lottery? The conflict's Extract Data File contained records of over fifty-thousand U.S. military fatalities. How many of those corpses had been too young to even buy a beer yet? And how many of the young men who'd survived the war returned home in the same permanently damaged mental state her father had?

Tracey didn't envy Alicia's initiation into violence, but she also wouldn't accept a coward. Not when they were heading into battle.

~

Wylder gasped when he saw them.

He'd looked back after hearing voices, and though the view was obscured, he made out the shadowy forms of the two women. Unfortunately, he'd been right to think they would come after him.

Heart palpitating, he got behind a thick maple and slid to the ground. He drew his pocketknife—his only weapon. Thinking of the tapestry of artillery back at the house, he cursed himself for not bringing other guns, but he'd had no reason to believe three men with assault rifles would need more to capture an unarmed teenager. He'd not known there would be some psycho out there too.

Staying low, he watched from behind the tree as the figures journeyed through the woods on the other side of the trail. If he'd chosen that side, he might not have had a chance, but if he could avoid being seen here, he increased his odds of surviving this. He believed the woman coming for him would kill him if he were caught. His fear of her was absolute, the sort of fear he never would have thought a female could instill in him. Wylder would have been ashamed if others were around, but being alone out here, he didn't challenge himself with stubborn male bravado. Instead, he flattened in the snow, wedging himself deep for camouflage, and prayed the crazy old lady wouldn't find him.

Please, God. Please save me.

Even once they'd passed, Wylder didn't move. He watched them proceed toward the compound until they were out of sight, but even then, he stayed put. Without a gun in his hands, his courage disappeared. He was wounded, he was afraid, and he'd failed. Now, if he moved, he was sure he would be executed.

Wylder lay there and cried.

FOURTEEN

THE COMPOUND APPEARED DESERTED, BUT appearances could be deceiving. Crouched behind the treeline at the edge of the property, Tracey scanned the area with her binoculars.

A ranch house. An old barn with a pickup truck inside. ATVs on the side of the house, and a huge pile of firewood, along with an axe chopping block and a curiously large industrial woodchipper. Was it possible this was some sort of logging camp?

The truck drew her interest. It told her there must be a dirt road somewhere nearby. The windows of the house were too dark to see anything. She waited and listened but heard nothing.

"We go around back," Tracey told Alicia, pointing to a dip in the land behind the ranch house. "First the house, then the barn. Follow me and watch our backs."

Alicia held her Glock with both hands, her index finger grazing the trigger guard. She was shaking but Tracey chose not to mention it. When she moved, the girl walked behind her, staying close. They descended onto the property and sprinted toward the side of the house in a crouch, trying to avoid the windows even though the curtains were drawn. Tracey spotted two security cameras perched on the rooftop beside floodlights. Shooting them out would be too noisy, and if someone were watching the monitors right now, they would know Tracey and Alicia were here anyway.

They had to move fast.

Leading Alicia to the back of the house, Tracey stuck close to the walls as they moved in. She hoped the girl was right when she'd said only one of the men had stayed behind. As they approached the back door, Tracey heard voices, but ascertained it was just a television set. That was good. It might drown out the sound of them breaking in, and if the man was distracted and sitting down, he'd be slower to react to this home invasion.

They had to be careful not to kill a hostage by accident. That Tracey didn't know where the kids were being held was the only thing that kept her from shooting through the door before making her grand entrance. But when she reached for the handle, she realized there was no need to bust inside.

The backdoor was unlocked.

Tracey turned to Alicia and put one finger to her lips before turning back to the door. She cracked it open slowly, put the barrel of the shotgun through the gap, and peered inside. She couldn't see much—just an empty kitchen—but the sound of the television told her where her target might be. When Tracey dared to look around the door, she saw the entryway into the living room. A couch was positioned with its back to the kitchen, and the back of a man's head was visible. He appeared to be alone, but in case he wasn't, she had to do this quietly.

She stepped inside.

When Tracey gently put her shotgun on the counter, Alicia gave her a shocked look from behind the balaclava. Tracey put up one hand to tell her to stay back, pointed at Alicia's pistol, and then pointed at the man, silently telling Alicia it was up to her to shoot the man if something went wrong.

Tracey drew her hunting knife from its sheath.

At fourteen inches long, it was more like a small machete, with one side a razor-sharp blade and the other a serrated saw. Tracey slowed her breaths again, hushing herself as she crept behind the bald man on the sofa. A game show yammered on the TV. Looking from side to side as she exited the kitchen, Tracey was assured they were alone in this part of the house, but the hallway to the bedrooms was to her right and could be hiding any number of people. She looked back at Alicia, pointed at her own eyes, and then pointed right, hoping

THE OLD LADY

the girl would understand. Alicia nodded, aiming her pistol in that direction, her arms as unsteady as an earthquake.

Returning her attention to the man on the couch, Tracey could see, even from behind, that he was young. Maybe just a little older than Alicia. But if he were one of Alicia's friends, she would have recognized him and said so. Tracey crept up behind the young man, grabbed him by the forehead and snapped his neck back, and pressed the smooth edge of the knife to his throat. Startled, the young man made a small grunt, and she whispered in his ear.

"Make a sound and I'll dig out your Adam's apple," she told him.

The young man shut his mouth and gulped, his rapid breaths flaring his nostrils. He was boyishly handsome, his stubble blonde and patchy, his blue eyes stunning in their paleness.

"Put your hands out in front of you," Tracey whispered.

He complied. Tracey looked around the couch and coffee table but saw no weapons within reach. Now that she had him, she briefly took in the inside of the house. It was rustic and masculine in appearance, with dark brown furniture and minimal decoration. No plants or artwork. No personality.

"Is this Charlie?" Tracey asked Alicia.

Alicia shook her head.

Tracey tensed. If this wasn't Charlie, that meant there was at least one other man to worry about. She pressed the blade deeper into the handsome boy's neck, opening the surface of his skin. He whimpered, sounding even younger than he looked.

"Who are you?" she asked.

"Stan... please, don't—"

"Who else is here?"

Stan hesitated to answer, assuring her there were others.

"Where's Charlie?" she demanded.

"Please, I—"

Tracey slowly dragged the blade across Stan's throat, slicing into his neck without opening his jugular. It was a flesh wound, but he didn't know that. When he made to scream, Tracey moved her hand from his forehead to cover his mouth. She pressed her lips to his ear.

"That was just a warning, pussy," she said. "Next time, I won't be as gentle. Now, if you lie to me, I'll bash your teeth down your throat with the handle of this knife until you choke to death on your own molars. And if you try to scream, I'll have torn your trachea out before anyone can help you. Nod if you understand."

Stan nodded and she slowly removed her hand from his mouth, but kept the knife pressed to his Adam's apple.

"Charlie…" Stan said. "Charlie's down in the cellar."

"Where are the hostages?"

"Down there with him."

"Anyone else?"

Sweat rolled down Stan's forehead. "No. I swear. Nobody else is here. Please…"

"So, you just left that little girl down in a cellar with this guy?"

Stan didn't seem to know how to reply. "Please…"

Tracey turned to Alicia. "Keep your eyes on the hall and don't look back until I say so."

Alicia turned her head. She kept her gun on the hall, but that wasn't the real reason Tracey had asked her to look away. The familiar, mean heat was swelling in Tracey's chest now. That the man was barely out of his boyhood didn't matter. He'd made his own choices, and they'd landed him in the position he was now in.

Gazing down into his beautiful eyes, Tracey thought of all she'd missed out on in her youth—all the cute boys and school dances, the prom she never went to and the college she never attended. There'd been no dates to the movies or trips with friends to see a concert. No school football games or loitering around a local diner. There'd only been pain—pain and the mercy of the void when life was kind enough to let her go dead inside.

Looking at Stan, Tracey's eyes went cold and dark, a stare as empty as she felt within.

She removed the knife from Stan's throat, giving him a moment of relief before she hacked into his neck. His throat opened in a gush of gore, thick blood cascading down his chest like syrup. He tried to scream but it came out as a wet gurgle. Gritting her teeth, Tracey swung and swung, chopping into Stan's neck like a tree, pulverizing the meat and chipping at bone. Stan writhed, swatting at her, and Tracey leaned over the couch and sunk most of the fourteen-inch blade into his stomach. His body caved inward as his guts were punctured, and when Tracey drew the knife out, the saw edge of the blade hooked a piece of intestines. A nugget of the pale tube popped out of Stan's belly in a grotesque peekaboo. When he bent forward, trying to put his guts back in, Tracey stabbed him in the side, aiming for his kidneys.

Alicia let out a small cry of horror. The foolish girl had made the

THE OLD LADY

mistake of looking.

Tracey didn't look back at her. The fuse had been lit, and the flame in Tracey's chest had become a roaring fire, threatening to annihilate everything in her path.

"*There is no good sportsmanship in war,*" her father echoed through her mind. "*Every move is acceptable, no matter how sneaky or brutal. There can be no mercy, no forgiveness, and no second chances. Destroy your enemies before they destroy you.*"

Tracey stabbed Stan in the back, and as he was about to fall forward, she grabbed him by the forehead again and chopped his neck until he stopped twitching. When he finally expired, she had nearly decapitated him.

The couch was a sea of red. Tracey pushed the corpse onto its side so it wouldn't make noise by crashing through the coffee table. Her extremities tingled, her heart palpitating with adrenaline. The rush of endorphins brought a smile to her face as she wiped her blade on the back of the couch. When she looked at Alicia, the girl was practically convulsing. When Tracey moved closer, Alicia scurried back.

"Don't be scared of me," Tracey said.

Alicia wept but did so with her mouth shut, maintaining silence as best she could. Tracey was proud of her. When Alicia finally spoke, her voice was a stuttering whisper.

"Y-y-you killed h-him…"

"It had to be done," Tracey said.

Alicia looked about in a panic, her legs bent as if she were preparing to run. Tracey raised one hand to touch the girl's shoulder but withdrew when she realized it was covered in blood.

"Easy now," Tracey told her. "It's almost over. I think he was telling the truth. There's only one of these bastards left. Our boy Charlie."

"You… you killed him," Alicia said again, her face twisted by horror.

"Would you rather I left him alive to *kill us* like they killed your friend? Christ, Alicia, this scumbag would have raped, beaten, and sodomized you, over and over and over again. You must know that."

"But—"

Tracey shushed the girl, turning to the door on the other side of the kitchen.

The cellar.

Picking up her shotgun, Tracey stepped to the door. She steadied her aim at it, just in case someone below had heard them, but as she got closer, she noticed music playing behind the door.

"Stay in the doorway, facing out," Tracey told Alicia. "If anyone comes—anyone other than me or your friends—shoot them and come down the stairs. Otherwise, stay right here."

But Alicia was a mess. She was shaking so hard now that Tracey worried about her holding the pistol. But she couldn't risk disarming the girl. She was the only backup Tracey had. While she understood Alicia's terror, part of Tracey wanted to discipline her for it, to yell in this little girl's weepy face the way Tracey's old man had. She resisted the urge, rationalizing that it would only make things worse, but it irked her that Alicia was so afraid of her, considering all Tracey was doing for her and her friends. She couldn't understand why Alicia was behaving this way. Perhaps Tracey had been brutal, but Stan's death required silence, so she'd used the knife. She'd only kept stabbing him until she was sure he was dead. As she'd done it, Tracey had felt like she was burning inside, and her urge to cause grievous bodily harm became irresistible. Her mind shook with traumatic memories, but with every hack and slash of Stan's body, relief had flooded her veins like morphine, and the jarring static of her mind cooled. Butchering him left her calm and collected. His murder was a validation—proof Tracey wasn't going to tolerate abuse ever again.

Shotgun in her fist, Tracey opened the door.

FIFTEEN

WHEN THE DOOR AT THE top of the stairs opened, Charlie flinched, expecting Wylder to have returned with the others. Stan had promised not to bother Charlie while he was down here, so it almost certainly wasn't him. Charlie sighed. He and Nori were still sitting on the dog bed, and he'd only just gotten her shirt undone. He hadn't even gotten to the bra yet (not that there was much for it to cover, though). Before he could really enjoy himself, he was being interrupted. Another pleasure denied. It was so typical of his luck with women.

As the figure descended the staircase, Charlie realized it was someone he didn't know, and a female at that. She was older, with a hard face and dark eyes like a mad bull. She carried a shotgun, a backpack, and a rifle slung over one shoulder. Though he'd never met her, Charlie figured the woman must be a new member of the team.

"Hey," he said, pulling his hand away from Nori's chest. "Are you a friend of my—"

Just as he noticed the blood on her, the woman suddenly rushed him. Before Charlie could react, the butt of the shotgun struck his face like a sledgehammer. Pain cut into him as his cheekbone was broken, and as he fell to the side, Nori scooted away from him, screaming. Stars swam across his vision, dizzying him as he tasted blood.

"Fucking rapist," the woman snarled.

Charlie spat red. "Wha? Naw, naw, I wasn't gonna—"

He was kicked in the ribs and fell on his side, gasping for the air he'd been robbed of. The woman towered over Charlie, a menacing silhouette against the single bare bulb in the ceiling.

She looked at Nori. "Get upstairs."

The girl hesitated, frozen by fear.

"Go now!" the woman demanded.

Holding her shirt closed, Nori ran to the staircase, taking the steps two at a time. When Charlie looked up, he saw someone in a black mask at the top of the staircase.

"Nori, it's me," the masked figure said. "It's Alicia."

Charlie lowered his brow. "What the—"

He was silenced by another kick to the side. The power of the blow told him the old woman was wearing steel-toed boots.

"You were gonna rape and torture that poor girl," the woman said. "You and your buddies. You were just gonna line up and fuck her and beat her until she wouldn't resist anymore."

Charlie shook his head. "Nah… I was just talking to her… just wanted to be her friend."

The woman seemed like she was about to stomp him, so Charlie raised both hands as if he were surrounded by police, hoping she would accept his surrender.

"Please," he said. "I swear I wasn't gonna—"

Charlie's right hand came apart before he even heard the shotgun go off. He screamed in agony as his palm was shredded by the blast, and three of his severed fingers smacked against the wall behind him and fell to the floor. He convulsed uncontrollably as everything seemed to go into slow motion. Grabbing his wrist, the sight of his mutilation threatened to make him vomit. He was aware of the woman saying something, but the blast of the shotgun had been amplified by the small, concrete room, leaving Charlie unable to make out her words. He only heard muffled threats and Dylan crying out from behind his gag. Charlie shut his eyes tight against the pain, but they snapped open again when he felt the barrel of the shotgun press against his crotch.

"Where are the keys?" the woman shouted.

THE OLD LADY

Charlie shuddered. "W-w-wha... what?"

"The keys to the handcuffs." She nodded toward Dylan, whose hands remained cuffed behind the back of the pole. "Where are they?"

Under duress, Charlie's memory failed him. "Um... I, uh..."

She pressed the mean end of the shotgun harder against his testicles, making them ache, and Charlie felt the heat of the recently fired barrel through his jeans.

"Tell me where they are," the woman said, "or you lose your dick and balls. Probably your asshole too, given the spread of this here shotgun. Mossberg doesn't fuck around when they make one of these. Give me the keys right now or I'll make every part of you hurt so bad you'll beg me for death, and yet I still won't let you go that easily. I'll drag it out like a fucking crucifixion."

Charlie grew cold, from fear as well as blood loss.

"Upstairs," he said, unsure if it was true. "Keys are upstairs."

"Get up," the woman said, pushing him with the sole of her boot.

Charlie rose slowly, still dazed, and clutched his wounded hand against his chest, trying to stop the bleeding. His sweater bloomed red like an opening carnation. The woman got behind him and pressed the barrel to the small of his back, nudging him toward the staircase. As he walked, he felt the bulge of keys in his pocket. They had to be for the handcuffs because Wylder had taken the keys to the pickup truck from him, a symbolic punishment after Charlie had offered strangers a ride.

"Wait," he said, stopping at the foot of the stairs. "I forgot. They're in my pocket."

"Give 'em to me."

Charlie would have complied, but the keys were in his right pocket, and he no longer hand a functioning right hand. He tried to get his left hand into the pocket but struggled. His head was spinning, and the fierce pain of his wound had spread up his arm. He tried to dig the keys out from the bottom of his pocket but couldn't get a grip.

"I... I can't..." he said. "My hand..."

"Fuck your hand."

"I can't get them."

The woman grunted. To Charlie's surprise, she put the shotgun down and leaned it against the wall.

"Don't fucking move," she warned him. "I promise you'll regret it."

She shoved her hand into his pocket, digging for the keys. Charlie knew he didn't have much time. To get to the shotgun, he'd have to get past the woman first, and with only one hand, she would probably defeat him if it came to blows. But as much as he wanted to believe the old lady would let him live if he complied, he doubted someone this ruthless would show such mercy. This moment was his only chance.

With the woman's hand buried in his pocket, Charlie caught her arm in the crook of his and spun. Catching her off guard, he managed to slam her into the banister. The woman took the blow to the chest and fell to her knees, but Charlie knew she wouldn't stay down long. Ignoring his pain and blurred vision, he raced up the short flight of stairs before his attacker could collect herself.

As he reached the door, Nori and Alicia backed away from him. Nori screamed hysterically. Alicia cried and raised a pistol, her whole body shaking as she took aim. Charlie kept running, not even noticing the bloody living room as he sprinted to the back door. He worried he would be shot in the back as he fled the house, but Alicia didn't fire. Launching himself outside, Charlie was struck by a gust of snow-filled wind. He'd not had time to put on a coat, and the chill cut into him like thousands of stinging bees. Several inches of fresh snow had accumulated, and he struggled to run in it as the wind chill threatened to freeze the blood on his face. He heard the woman shouting but was too delirious to understand her. He wasn't even sure if she were yelling at him or the girls. Staggering along, he went to the side of the house where the ATVs were, hoping to escape, but just as he reached one of them a shot rang out. The back of his knee burst, his thigh and buttocks burning with the sprayed pellets of the fired round.

Charlie fell to his knees, and the one that had been shot gave way beneath him. Something in his leg shifted and snapped, and with only one hand to break his fall, he collapsed into an icy pool of slush. He groaned before crying out for help, hoping Wylder or Quin or *anyone* might hear him before it was too late. He wanted his friends. He wanted his teammates. And more than anything else, he wanted his dad. If his mother were still alive, he might have called her name.

"Somebody help me!" he wept.

The falling snow absorbed the sound, and when he tried to scream a boot pressed down on his neck. One side of his face was pressed into the slush, and he looked up at the woman with one eye. Her face was a pink mask of concentrated rage.

THE OLD LADY

"I warned you," she said.

Charlie closed his eyes tight, bracing himself for a shotgun shell through the skull. Instead, he heard something drop, and when he opened his eye, Charlie saw the woman had tossed the shotgun, but he couldn't see where to. It didn't matter. He was in no shape to make a grab for it. The woman drew something from a leather loop on her backpack. At first, Charlie thought it was a hammer. But when she turned it sideways, he realized it was a one-handed splitting maul, and he whimpered just before it was swung down into the back of his blown-out knee.

~

The bastard twitched, bleeding at her feet, just where he belonged. With many good swings, Tracey managed to sever his leg at the knee. Charlie was shaking, face down in the frozen mud, bleeding out but still alive, still *conscious*. His words became a garbled mess, blood and mucus choking him as Tracey rolled him on his back and dug the keys out of his pocket. She checked the ring for a key to the truck, but there were only two small keys for the handcuffs. She also searched him for a phone, but he didn't have one on him.

Seeing the chopping block nearby, Tracey bared her teeth in a combination of smile and snarl. She could drag Charlie to the block, set up his head like a log, a cleave it down the middle with the axe sticking out of the wood. Her mind buzzed with visions of violence, both stunning and energizing her, calling her to action.

Memories of her father teaching her to be impervious to pain flooded Tracey's consciousness until she could almost feel the tip of his hot knife going under her fingernail. Flashbacks of horror pounded her from within—a drugstore manager thrown through glass; a man's rough hands tearing her panties off; fists hitting her, driving the back of her skull into concrete; her father chasing her as she fled into the woods; a gang of prison inmates jumping her. She recalled drunken, blackout nights and endless days of suffering. And when she looked down at the bloody mess of Charlie, she saw in him every brutality she'd ever been subjected to.

Suddenly a beheading wasn't good enough.

Sticking her splitting maul into the chopping block, Tracey grabbed Charlie's wrists. The wounded arm was slick with blood, but with her fingerless gloves she got a grip near his elbow and managed to drag him to the industrial woodchipper beside the mountain of timber. The machine was four times the size of woodchippers designed for home use. The men must have been doing some serious logging to require one this huge.

The control panel was self-explanatory, the key still in the lock. Tracey got the motor going, and stared into the large, square opening where the blades churned, looking like rows of metallic shark teeth. Keeping it running, she stepped around the shivering Charlie, retrieved his severed leg, and waved it in front of his face.

"You know," she said over the roar of the motor. "It being in the snow like this, your leg might have been kept cold enough to be reattached."

Blood from the leg dribbled onto its previous owner's face. Tracey stepped to the woodchipper and shoved the leg into the opening. The machine pulled the limb in, tearing the boot from the foot, peeling the flesh from Charlie's leg, and pulverizing the bones. Bits of tissue sprayed back at Tracey, splashing across her face. She didn't back away from it. The warmth of the gore was comforting on her cold cheeks—a baptism by blood.

Then she returned to Charlie.

He had lost a considerable amount of blood, leaving him a delirious mess. *Probably in shock*, she thought. She wasn't even sure if he knew what was happening when she lifted him in a fireman's carry and brought him to the opening of the woodchipper's shaft.

It was going to be a tight fit.

Though he only had one, she put him in feetfirst. When the blades hit him, Charlie's eyes went wide, awakened by fresh pain. He screeched and struggled, and Tracey pushed on his shoulders, blood spraying her in a hot shower as she drove him deeper into the shaft, staring face to face with Charlie until he was completely devoured by fangs of stainless steel.

SIXTEEN

WHEN TRACEY RAN PAST THEM in the kitchen, Alicia held Nori against her as they retreated from the crazed woman. She'd expected Tracey to scold her for not shooting Charlie as he'd fled, but she was too focused on catching him, on *killing* him. It was something Alicia had been unable to do. Once Tracey was outside, Alicia was compelled to flee into the woods before the old lady returned. Having seen her slaughter Stan like a strung-up deer, Alicia was even more terrified of Tracey than before, and having glimpsed the mangled corpse, Nori had thrown up. Her hands were cuffed in front of her, but they could worry about that later. The important thing was she could run. There was only one hurdle keeping them from escaping.

"Dylan?" Alicia asked.

Though she was a sobbing, stuttering mess, Nori managed to tell her Dylan was alone in the cellar, gagged and cuffed to a pole. Alicia helped Nori button up her shirt, not asking why it was undone, knowing but not wanting to know.

"Where are the keys to the cuffs?" Alicia asked.

"I th-think Ch-Ch-Charlie has 'em."

Alicia cursed. She looked at the Glock but doubted it would be safe to try to shoot the handcuffs off the others. The metal link connecting them was too small, and it would risk injuring Dylan by accident. But she had to try something.

"C'mon," she said, taking Nori's arm as she headed downstairs.

The cellar floor was slick with blood. Alicia cringed seeing tattooed fingers in a red puddle. As they reached Dylan, he moaned behind his gag, and when Alicia removed the balaclava, his eyes went wide with surprise. Tears ran over the duct tape on his mouth, and Alicia tore it off so he could spit out the gag. He took in deep breaths. Alicia rolled up her mask to her forehead, kissed his cheek, and hugged him.

"Are you okay?" she asked.

"My nose is stuffed up from crying," he said, panting. "It was getting so I couldn't breathe." His eyes fell on his sister. "Did that son of a bitch hurt you?"

Nori sniffed and stammered. "N-n-no... I'm o-k-ka-kay."

"What the hell is going on?" he said, nearly weeping.

"I'll explain later," Alicia said. "Right now we've got to get you out of these cuffs."

She couldn't see any way to break them, so she tucked her pistol into her waistband and grabbed the pipe with both hands, shaking it. It wobbled slightly, connected to the ceiling and the floor. It was about twenty inches around. When she knocked on it, there was an echo. Could she shoot at the top, away from Dylan, and break the pipe? Or did things like that only work in the movies? She wasn't even sure what the pipe was for. It could be water, or it could be gas. If she busted a water pipe but couldn't bend or break it enough to get Dylan free, the cellar could flood and drown him. She didn't even want to think about what might happen if it were gas.

Alicia looked about the cellar. It was mostly bare, with a few water-damaged cardboard boxes against one wall and two dusty, window unit air conditioners sprinkled with mouse feces. There was small workbench and a few power tools, all of which looked too large to be of any use. Going to the boxes, she peeled back the flaps on one, finding outdated electronics—a stack of blank CDs, a digital camera, random wires, and video cassettes. She threw it aside and opened the next box, uncovering a miscellaneous junk pile, and dug through it until finding a screwdriver.

Rushing to Dylan, Alicia wedged the screwdriver between the link of the cuffs and the pipe.

THE OLD LADY

"This will hurt your wrists," she told him, "but I've got to try."

Her boyfriend nodded. "Okay."

Using the screwdriver as a crowbar, she pried the cuffs away from the pole. As she applied pressure, Dylan grunted, his hands changing color.

"You're h-h-hur-huurting him!" Nori said.

"Well, we have to do something," Alicia said.

She pressed harder, putting her weight onto the handle, but the link didn't give.

Finally, Dylan cried out in pain. "Stop! Stop!"

Alicia eased off. The cuffs fell back in place, revealing pink rings they'd left on Dylan's wrists. Unless she could think of something better, she had to either reconsider busting the pipe or try to shoot the handcuffs, so they'd separate. If she pressed the barrel to the link before firing, it might do the trick. It also might blow shrapnel in her face or burn and mutilate Dylan's wrists. The bullet could even ricochet and kill one of them.

Alicia shouted in frustration just before she heard a loud motor come to life.

Nori jumped, grabbing Alicia. "Wh-what's that?"

The three of them went still, listening with dread. Under the roar of the machine was a human scream that wouldn't end.

"Jesus," Dylan whimpered.

Nori squealed, hysterical.

We have to get out of here, Alicia thought.

Not knowing what else to do, she returned to the boxes, hoping to find a paperclip or bobby pin she could try to jimmy the handcuffs' lock with. Among the other screwdrivers, she found a tiny one like those used to repair eyeglasses. Working it in the lock, she wiggled and twisted it, having no idea what she was doing. Hearing the outside motor turn off increased her sense of urgency, adrenaline making her hands tremble as she worked.

"Just go!" Dylan said. "You and Nori get out of here and find help."

"No!" his sister said.

Alicia wanted to agree with her, but the situation being what it was, she couldn't help but consider Dylan's suggestion.

"Maybe he's right," she told Nori.

Grief scrunched the girl's face. "*No!* W-w-we're not lea-leaving my buh-buh-brother here!"

104

"Go now!" Dylan insisted.

Alicia was awed by her boyfriend's bravery. Even locked in this hellish dungeon, surrounded by blood and screams, he was more concerned about the two of them than himself. Dylan was afraid, but he was strong, and she loved him even more because of it.

You can't let him die here, Alicia thought.

If Charlie had killed Tracey, he could return any second. But somehow Alicia doubted he could defeat the madwoman. At this point, would it be any safer for them if Tracey came back instead of Charlie? She seemed to be in an uncontrollable spiral of rage, particularly against men. With no more enemies to slaughter, would Tracey find a new victim in Dylan?

Hearing a door open upstairs, Alicia feared they were about to find out.

The trio listened to the footsteps above them, no one making a sound. Alicia drew her pistol and aimed at the foot of the stairs. From their position, they couldn't see the top of the staircase, and whoever might be up there wouldn't see them until they came all the way down. Alicia told herself she'd shoot first and ask questions later, but she doubted that was true. She'd hesitated to shoot Charlie, even though he would have deserved it. That she'd failed to act bothered her. But the person coming now could be a police officer or forest ranger responding to all the gunshots. What if whoever was up there had come to rescue them?

Something jangled at the top of the stairs, sounding like tags on a dog.

"I've got the keys," Tracey said. "I'm coming down. Don't shoot."

Each step she took sounded like an old coffin opening, the wooden steps bowing beneath her weight. Alicia held the Glock out in front of her even though she wasn't sure what she intended to do with it. Perhaps it all depended on what Tracey chose to do. She watched the woman come down, her legs appearing first, then the barrel of the shotgun, which pointed straight down as she carried it with one hand.

When Tracey rounded the corner at the bottom of the staircase, Alicia at first thought she'd applied war paint. The woman's face was entirely red, her body splattered with blood, flesh, and bone shards. Her eyes were like lost planets, cold and black in their vacuuming voids. She looked not just like she'd stepped out of the ninth circle of Hell, but that she owned the place and ruled it with an iron fist.

THE OLD LADY

"Lower your weapon," Tracey said. "It's just me."

Alicia swallowed hard, hesitating, but ultimately did as Tracey said. Even with the woman in her sights, she was far too afraid of Tracey to challenge her.

"Catch," Tracey said, throwing something.

Alicia flinched as the keys fell at her feet.

SEVENTEEN

AS ALICIA UNDID THE BOY'S handcuffs and the kids gathered themselves, Tracey returned to the kitchen. There was no landline phone, but even if there had been, would she have called the police? She doubted it. But she wouldn't mind having a cellular phone on her, just in case. Entering the living room, she searched Stan's body, but just like Charlie, the young man had no phone on him. Tracey found that odd. These days it seemed everyone always had a phone on them, as if it was an extra appendage.

Returning to the kitchen, she washed up in the sink. It was filled with dirty dishes. Stan and Charlie had eaten their last meals without knowing it. Patting herself dry with paper towels, she tossed the used wad on the floor and sniffed. The stench of human offal in the next room had permeated the kitchen now, stinking up the house as if it were an abattoir.

Putting both hands on the counter, Tracey breathed deep. Her head was pounding, as it often did in stressful situations. The doctors attributed her migraines to what they called a "traumatic brain injury," a fancy term for her skull having been repeatedly slammed against the concrete of a back alley.

THE OLD LADY

These headaches always made her remember.

The bar had been closing up, and she'd taken the guy who'd bought her drinks into the alley to fool around. She was in her twenties then and excessively promiscuous, using sex the same way she used drugs and alcohol—tonics to ease the pain of being alive and save her from her own mind. The city of Boston offered her a lot of opportunities for a good time. Though she'd been there for many years by now, she'd continued to hop from section to section, often living on the outskirts. For work, she took lousy jobs with small businesses that paid under the table, including janitor, convenience store clerk, and gas station attendant. But most of the time she waitressed and bused tables at greasy spoons, slinging pancakes and burgers, and sneaking home the leftover portions customers left behind. She rented small rooms during the coldest and hottest months, and in the milder seasons she went on to smaller towns like Bedford and Wayland where there were plenty of woods to camp in. Eventually, she saved enough money to buy a used car that ran just well enough to not be a total lemon, and she lived out of it most of the time. The rest of her cash went to booze and dope, but men often supplied her with these for free.

Only nothing in life was ever truly free.

On that night in the alley, she'd leaned on the wall with her skirt hitched up, letting the stranger screw her from behind. They stood the whole time, not wanting to get down in the rank filth of the alley floor. Drunk and stoned, Tracey had been too numb to have an orgasm, but just having him inside her was a great, if momentary, release from the dismal hellscape she lived in every day. When the man finished, Tracey had stumbled as she stood up straight again, feeling the remnants of their lovemaking running down her leg. She tried to kiss him, but he turned his head away in disgust. Tracey glowered then. She'd seen that look of disdain before. It was the same look of revulsion some men wore the very moment after they'd climaxed, the sort of face that told Tracey how little they really thought of her. She was always a queen before they'd stuck it in her, but after that, she was just a dirty whore to these pigs, and she sickened them as much as they sickened themselves for being with her.

Tracey had grown immune to their disrespect, and in all honesty, she used them just as much as they used her. She didn't like them either and often felt just as disgusted with herself as the men seemed to be. They simply fulfilled a need, however temporary, by filling a hole in her both literally and figuratively. Not all men had treated her poorly after she'd had sex with them. Many had tried to build some sort of relationship with her, as if she could ever be wife material. But in those cases, Tracey had been even more eager to dispose of them. Getting close to anyone was too terrifying. She hadn't truly loved a man since her father, and seeing how that had worked out, she had resigned herself to being single forever.

So, this night behind the dumpster hadn't been too bad, despite her lover pushing her away before he'd even zipped up his fly. It only turned bad when his friends came out the side door and saw Tracey stumbling with her skirt hiked up around her waist and her panties taut above her knees. These young men hadn't been as good-looking as her lover, and she'd had no interest in them, but that hadn't stopped them from taking an interest in her. Inebriated and uninhibited, their hands grabbed at her, squeezing and groping as she'd batted them away, trying to readjust her clothes. Her lover, being buddies with the other two, had only laughed and done nothing to stop them—so Tracey had to stop them herself, her way.

The mean heat had boiled inside her. She'd heard her father's voice then, telling her she'd been careless and sloppy, putting herself in a situation she should've known better than to ever get into. And the worst part was, he was right.

When one of the men put his arm around her neck in what he seemed to think was a playful headlock, Tracey bit him so hard he screamed. He'd tried to withdraw but she held on like an attack dog, bruising his muscle tissue and busting capillaries. His friends tried to pull her off, but she'd shook her head back and forth, tearing flesh from the arm. Her captor finally released her then, screaming and bleeding, calling her a cunt. She'd tried to back away, wanting only to get to her car and leave, but the men weren't teasing her anymore—they were pissed.

The man who had fucked her threw the first punch.

Still woozy from excessive drinking, Tracey had tried to fight but her equilibrium was off, so she hadn't been able to spin a kick without losing her balance. She'd landed a few good punches before the men managed to get her on the ground, but from then on, every time she'd fought her skull had been hammered harder into the concrete of the alley floor.

After that, things had taken a turn for the worse that night… but not for Tracey.

THE OLD LADY

Alicia's voice suddenly brought Tracey out of the black pit of that memory and back into the present.

As the kids came up the stairs, Alicia was assuring her friends things would be okay. The well-meaning lie brought a bitter smile to Tracey's face. Though the kids had survived, they did not yet know the struggle that would come with surviving the memory of this day. Violence and physical pain were merely nuisances compared to the eternal horror of a broken mind's recollection.

Drawing the first aid kit from her BOB, Tracey popped three aspirin, chewing them so they'd take effect faster. The bitter taste pulled her further back to reality.

When the kids entered the kitchen, the boy gagged at the bloody display in the living room.

"Don't look," Tracey said, addressing them all. "Some things you can never unsee."

The kids averted their gaze and huddled close together. With their hands free, Nori and her brother embraced each other, then brought Alicia in for a group hug.

"Save the love fest for later," Tracey said, zipping up her BOB. "We need to move."

"Okay," Alicia said. "But what about Charlie?"

"He's no longer a concern."

Alicia gulped. "What about a phone? There must be a—"

"There isn't. I looked."

Alicia furrowed her brow. "Not one phone?"

"I checked the bodies and looked around a little. Nothing. Couldn't even find keys for the truck."

"They took our phones. They must have them somewhere."

"We don't have time to search the whole house for one, okay? It's more important that we get out of here—fast."

Alicia appeared to despair, sighing at the floor, but she didn't argue. The others didn't argue either. They seemed to agree with Tracey, wanting to flee this horrible place more than anything else.

"You okay there, Nori?" Tracey asked the young teen.

The girl nodded. "Yuh-yuh-yes."

"You don't sound like it."

"I h-ha-have a stu-stut—"

"A stutter?"

The girl nodded.

"It used to be really bad," the boy explained. "It took a lot of speech classes for her to get rid of it. But after all that's happened here, I guess the stress must have—"

Tracey cut him off. "I don't need the whole story."

She looked back at the petite girl. Tracey had seen her when she'd first entered the cellar, the girl's shirt undone, Charlie feeling her up. Hopefully that was as far as things had gone. Turning to the boy, Tracey asked his name, having forgotten it. When he told her, she asked Dylan if he was alright, and he nodded just like his sister. They were young enough that they still looked very similar, with soft features and tender skin, Dylan's face sporting a little acne along his jawline where the first facial hairs had appeared. As with Alicia, Tracey felt like she was looking at babies instead of teens, and in each of them, she saw glimpses of the child she'd abandoned.

Well, she wouldn't abandon these three.

Tracey promised herself that.

"What did you do with the handcuffs?" Tracey asked.

To her surprise, Alicia drew them from her coat. "I wasn't sure what to do with them, but…"

"Good. Better to take them in case we need them."

"But Charlie didn't have the keys to the truck?"

"I told you—I searched both the bodies but didn't find any car keys, so we're going on foot. Now let's get the hell out of here."

Dylan hesitated. "Wait… what about Marcus?"

Tracey narrowed her eyes. "Who's Marcus?"

"Our other friend," Alicia explained. "The one who was shot."

"You mean the one they *murdered*?"

Dylan and Alicia nodded. Nori blinked tears from her eyes.

"He's dead," Tracey said. "So what about him?"

"Well, like, we can't just leave his body in the barn," Dylan said. "His family will want to bury him properly."

"Fuck what his family wants. If we don't move quickly, we'll be going to our graves too. There are no rescue choppers coming to haul away the dead, and we're not carrying a corpse all the way down the goddamned mountain."

Alicia gave her boyfriend a sympathetic look. "People will understand."

"Fuck people," Tracey grumbled, her head aching as she started toward the backdoor.

Her father agreed. "*Fuck the world.*"

She repeated his sentence out loud without even realizing it.

THE OLD LADY

The kids followed behind her, whispering, asking Alicia who this strange woman was. Alicia whispered back, but her words were muffled by the wind, and Tracey didn't hear them. It wouldn't have mattered to her much anyway. How the teenagers felt about her (or any of this) wouldn't change a thing.

Having reloaded from the side saddle after killing Charlie, Tracey held the shotgun with both hands, scanning their surroundings for any sign of Wylder, the one who'd escaped after the shootout at her father's cabin. The bastard was still out there somewhere and would have to be dealt with.

"*Burn the house down,*" Dad told her as they left the ranch house.

"There's no time," she mumbled.

"*You're leaving too much to chance. You don't really think this is over, do you?*"

Tracey swallowed hard. "No."

She still wasn't sure what these men were. Rapists and child molesters, for sure, but what were they doing on this compound deep in the White Mountains? Were they some sort of Nazis or a cult? Were they anti-Asian bigots who'd kidnapped Nori and Dylan because of their race? The men certainly had enough weapons to be a militia. Was that all they were? A group of weekend warrior gun nuts with delusions of starting a second Civil War?

A rumbling sound in the distance turned Tracey's head. She wasn't sure if it was real or imagined until she looked back at the kids and saw them searching for the source of the noise too. The rumble continued, a low roar like a mechanical tiger.

And it was coming closer.

Tracey stared at her daughter and her friends.

"Olivia…" she said. "*Run!*"

The four of them darted into the bare branches of the forest, snow pelting them from every direction as they disappeared into the coming storm.

PART TWO
HOME OF THE BRAVE

EIGHTEEN

THE TRUCK RUMBLED UP THE hill, the massive tires kicking up snow on the muddy dirt road. Lance shifted gears and adjusted the yellow lens glasses on his nose. Though a redhead, Lance kept his head shaved bald, but wore a goatee that ran down past his neck. Beside him in the passenger seat, his wife Regina held an AK47 across her lap. The semi-automatic rifle was a cobalt blue, reflecting the glow of the dashboard clock, looking like city lights at twilight. Her green eyes complimented her hair, which she'd dyed a dark russet, and her thin lips were sealed tight in silent contemplation.

The large truck's roof covered the entire vehicle, making it a sort of giant van, and came with a spacious backseat between the front seats and the huge, empty space at the rear, which was fifteen feet long and nearly eight feet in both width and height.

Sitting behind the heavyset driver, Ed Bartlett ran his hand over his gray mustache and down over his chin. His hard, leathery face was ghost-like in the dimly lit truck, concentration deepening his wrinkles. Watching the windshield wipers push the falling snow away, he frowned at the rotten luck. The night before, the weather forecast had predicted light flurries for today, but by morning that was upped to

THE OLD LADY

one-to-three inches of snow accumulation. Looking at the road ahead, he estimated they'd already surpassed that amount, and the storm was only getting worse.

As he cursed under his breath, his cousin Julie glanced at him. She was in the backseat beside him, her dark eyes drilling into him until he was forced to say something.

"What?" he asked.

Julie gave him a small smile that didn't reach her eyes. "It's gonna be fine, Bart."

Everyone called Ed Bartlett that, shortening his last name into a nickname that had stuck since high school. Now in his late fifties, he'd accepted it, and didn't even mind when he'd found out the other members of the team had started referring to him as "Black Bart." Being white as Wonder Bread, the name had confused him at first, until he'd found out it had been derived from a nineteenth century outlaw who robbed banks and left behind poetic messages. Now he could see how appropriate his new moniker was.

"If this storm buries the roads," Bart said, "we might be stuck until it melts."

"Nah," Julie said. "We've got the plow we can put on the pickup."

Bart smirked. "That old hunk of junk can barely haul a bale of hay, let alone shove that rusted plow with any real force. But it'll have to do."

"Well," she said, gesturing to the interior, "this truck we're in now seems big enough not to let a little snow hold it back."

Exhaling, Bart looked away from her. "Guess we'll see. Once everything's in the back, the added weight could help it handle the ice and snow better, but not if the truck's buried up to the goddamned grill."

From the front seat, Lance glanced at Bart in the rearview mirror. "You don't think we'll have to postpone, do you?"

"I said we'll see. Our best bet will be to try to get ahead of the snow. We should plow these roads ahead of time, in preparation for tomorrow, and keep up with it overnight if it keeps coming down."

Bart didn't like rescheduling things. He hated any form of delay. But if he was going to do something, he was going to do it right.

"We can't afford to get stuck in a snowbank in this thing," Bart said of the new truck. "Especially not once the back is fully loaded."

The others were silent in agreement. They were good soldiers—most of them, anyway. Sometimes Bart sensed an individual's displeasure in the way he was running things, but he was not met with disobedience, let alone mutiny. He was the leader now. The majority of the team respected that. Only Regina gave him any trouble, and unfortunately, her husband wasn't any good at keeping her in line. That alone made Lance a liability, but his overall dedication to the cause sustained his value.

Julie was dedicated too, but she had ulterior motives. That she didn't try to hide them gave her Bart's forgiveness, but if she hadn't been his younger cousin, he doubted he would have kept her on. She was an effective soldier when she wanted to be, but also unstable, allowing her bizarre appetites to rule her life in a flagrant lack of self-control. But it was those same dark desires that had led her to a lucrative business, one that kept the team financed for more important things.

Bart watched his cousin tuck a lock of her brown hair behind an ear riveted with seven earrings. Now in her mid-forties, Julie's once pretty face had hardened, leaving her an attractive but intimidating presence. Her penchant for black clothing only intensified an inner darkness that seemed to encircle her at all times, and her refusal to wear makeup only added to her cold, pale stoicism.

They made it to the crest of the hill, and when Lance turned down the private dirt road, the truck was wider than the path, and its sides cracked branches from the dead trees as they headed toward home base. Bart shifted in his seat, readjusting his shoulder holster and the Glock 22 it cradled. The pistol was the same type of gun he'd carried for a quarter century, but not the same one he'd been given all those years ago. That one had been taken from Bart, along with so many other things that had once been so important to him. Now he had other things that were important, things that could make up for everything he'd been robbed of.

Arriving at the compound, Lance parked in front of the barn and the team exited the truck. Lance huffed as he stepped down from the driver's side, his extra weight slowing him. Regina waited for him, holding the stock of her rifle and resting it on one shoulder, like a marine without the stiff posture. Bart and Julie walked ahead of them, and as the team drew closer to the ranch house, Bart saw the ATVs were all there. Usually on a snowy day, the men spent their downtime riding around on the four-wheelers, particularly the younger guys. But perhaps, with the news of a coming storm, they'd been smart enough to stay indoors rather than get lost on the mountain, which was easier

THE OLD LADY

to do than most people realized.

As they drew closer, Bart spotted red snow.

The ground below the woodchipper was stained a sickly burgundy, with brown chunks and pulpy tendrils of yellow.

"The fuck is that?" Julie said.

Bart's face hardened as he drew his pistol from his coat. He put up one hand, signaling to the group to stop walking and be cautious of their surroundings. They all fell hushed, looking to the surrounding woods, but their eyes kept returning to the discolored snow under the woodchipper's exit chute.

"Jesus," Regina whispered, readying her rifle with both hands.

"Shit," Lance said. "Bart, is that what I think it is?"

Bart didn't answer. He was too focused on scanning the perimeter, looking for any signs of danger. He saw footprints going from the rear of the house into the dense woodland that ran alongside the nearest trail. Seeing as the falling snow hadn't concealed the footprints yet, Bart knew they were fresh.

With an annoyed sigh, Julie looked at Bart and nodded toward the crimson mess. "What the hell did those idiots put in there? A goddamn doe? A sack full of rabbits?"

"C'mon, now," Regina said. "I can't imagine any of them killing an animal like that. It's too cruel and pointless."

"Well then, what is it?"

Regina didn't have an answer for that.

Lanced grumbled. "Dang it, I told them boys not to fuck around with my chipper. It's a serious piece of machinery, not a toy."

The compound had once been a small logging camp where Lance had worked, which was how the team had come into its possession. He continued to make his living as a lumberjack and woodworker, and because the chipper was more difficult to move down the mountain than it was worth, he'd purchased it from the company for his own use.

Bart drew closer to the redness, and with each step he was more certain it was gore, and when the stink hit the group, they knew it for certain. Bart had gutted enough deer to recognize the overwhelming stench of organs and entrails. Lance and Regina backed away, putting their hands over their noses as they gagged. Julie lifted the collar of her shirt over half her face like a mask. Only Bart stepped closer.

The pool of blood was large enough to have been a doe or a small bear, but there wasn't any fur, only little bunches of hair. Amongst the pulverized tissue and offal were bone fragments the woodchipper had reduced to splinters. Squatting at the edge of the mess, Bart saw bits of shredded clothing and boot leather, and a chill went through him when he spotted most of a severed human ear.

He stood quickly and gave the command. "Guns."

Regina already had hers ready for war. Lance drew his .44 Magnum from his hip holster. Julie, having always disliked the added bulk of carrying a gun, drew her small .22 pistol from its hiding place in her right boot.

Regina grimaced as she stared at the bloody chunks. "Is that… Jesus, is that a *human being*?"

"You two," Bart said to her and Lance. "Go around front. Julie and I will enter through the back. Be on your toes."

"Oh my God," Lance said, staring at the carnage. "That really is a person, ain't it? Shit, you think it's one of our boys?"

Regina moaned at the thought and Bart couldn't blame her. But they had to be strong right now. They could grieve once they were sure they were safe.

"It could be anybody," he said, desperately hoping it wasn't one of their own.

"The guys wouldn't do this, though, would they?" Lance asked. "Even if for some reason they did, they wouldn't leave this kind of mess out in the open."

Julie glowered. "Someone has infiltrated our camp. Infiltrated with a vengeance."

"But who?" Lance asked. "Who even knows we're—"

Bart silenced them all. "Shut up and move!"

The group separated, approaching the ranch house as Bart had commanded. As Regina and Lance vanished around the bend, Julie spoke more freely with Bart now that they were alone.

"The fucking *woodchipper*?" she said. "That's not some simple strike against our cause. That's personal."

"C'mon," he said, leading them toward the backdoor.

"Who do you think—"

"Just shut up. I don't know who it is, but I aim to find out."

It pained him to realize she'd been asking about the identity of whoever had attacked the base, not the identity of the person who'd come out the nasty end of the woodchipper. Julie had always been cold, but could she really be this indifferent to the casualty? Bart's throat had gone tight. His finger gently touched the trigger of his

THE OLD LADY

Glock, already itching for payback, no matter which man had been lost, if it had been one of his men at all.

Or one of his boys.

Bart's jaw clenched as he tried to deny the possibility. Reaching the backdoor, he noticed it hadn't been closed all the way. In this kind of cold weather, it was the sort of mistake that would have been easily noticed by those inside. He looked at the footprints going from the door to the treeline. Some were too small to belong to any of his team members. *Children?* He and Julie pressed their backs to the wall surrounding the doorframe, and when Bart counted down from three, he and his cousin burst into the kitchen. The same pungent odor of evisceration permeated the inside of the house. Bart noticed drops of blood on the tile floor, and a wadded-up paper towel that had been stained red. The door to the cellar was wide open, country music rising from the depths.

Bart wanted to check it out, but as he moved around the table, he saw the horror of the living room just as Lance and Regina came through the front door. Seeing the body in full, they both cried out. Bart came around the couch in slow, cautious steps, and Julie tailed behind him like an emotionless phantom.

The mutilated corpse lay on its side, throat slit, midsection punctured in several places. Realizing it was only Stan brought Bart some relief. Losing a soldier to a method of death this brutal was upsetting, but better him than…

"God in Heaven," Regina said, shutting her eyes against the horror.

Lance went out to the front porch and puked over the railing before returning to the living room.

"Get it together," Bart said in a low tone. "Whoever did this may still be here." He pointed Lance and Regina in the direction of the hall. "Check the rooms. We're going down to the cellar."

The couple did as they were told, however reluctantly, and Bart returned to the kitchen with Julie close behind, heading to the staircase.

Julie started to say something. "Bart, I think—"

He spun back to her sharply. "Shut your fucking mouth, Julie. Do you understand? Not one more fucking word."

Her dark eyes showed no feeling, her face a pallid, lifeless mask. She said nothing and followed Bart down into the cellar, where they found more blood. It wasn't as gruesome of a sight as the other two had been, but a there was a significant red splatter on the wall, still wet. Bart noticed what looked like several small sausages spattered with blood.

Fingers, he realized.

When he saw their tattoos, he swallowed a scream.

NINETEEN

WYLDER FINALLY MADE IT HOME.

Trying to avoid the woman and Alicia, he'd avoided the trail and cut around to the rear of the property. Seeing the big truck parked in front of the barn, he sighed with relief. The rest of the team had returned. Bart would know what to do. Wylder hated having to deliver the news about Paul and Quin to his commander, but their deaths weren't his fault. He wasn't the one who had set all of this in motion. It wasn't him who had let strangers onto the property, and he hadn't shot that black boy in the head. Wylder didn't want to snitch, but he wasn't going to take the fall for Charlie. Bart deserved to know the truth, no matter how ugly.

Still holding his arm to pressurize the bullet wound, Wylder limped along, thanking God when he heard the voices of his leader and fellow teammates.

"Nobody in the barn," Regina was saying.

"And all the equipment is still there," Bart replied.

When Wylder came around the side of the building, four guns were turned in his direction, and he rushed to get his hands up despite the pain in his arm.

"Don't shoot!" he said. "It's just me."

Bart, Julie, Lance, and Regina lowered their weapons, staring at him in silence.

Wylder limped closer. "Man, am I glad to see you guys. Bart, we've got real trouble."

Bart looked him up and down, his eyes landing on the blood running down Wylder's sleeve. The commander's face was a granite wall, making the hairs on Wylder's neck stand up.

"What the hell happened here?" Bart demanded. "Who did this?"

Wylder glanced at the barn. "I guess you saw the body."

Bart's eyes narrowed. "Yeah. I saw the body."

"Okay," Wylder said, taking a deep breath. "This whole thing is not my fault. I hate to say it, but it's all Charlie's fault."

Bart's eyes darkened. "*Charlie's* fault?"

Wylder had anticipated a bad reaction to this fact, but Bart's expression still chilled him, causing him to talk faster. "I'm sorry to tell you, sir, but this whole disaster never would've happened if Charlie hadn't acted so stupidly. I mean, he acted like a total idiot, and now we're—"

A punch to the face cut him short. Bart's fist slammed into the side of Wylder's head in a mean right hook, stunning and confusing him. Before he could ask why he'd been struck, Bart hit him again, his left fist pounding Wylder's ribs. Wylder cowered back, holding his hands up with his palms facing out.

"Boss, I—"

Bart socked him in the jaw and Wylder heard something click inside his skull. His vision filled with stars, and he stumbled on his sprained ankle, but as he was falling Bart grabbed his wrist, so Wylder only dropped to his knees. Bart yanked on his wounded arm.

"Wait!" Wylder begged. "I've been shot and—"

His next words became a scream as Bart found the bullet wound and dug his thumb into it, widening the hole as he wiggled inside Wylder's mangled flesh. The pain was all-encompassing, drowning out any other thought so it was all Wylder was aware of. He cried out, begging Bart to stop, terrified that he may be begging for his life without knowing why.

"I should shoot you again," Bart growled in his face. "I should blow your nutsack off and feed you your own balls!"

"Boss, I'm sorry, I—"

"*Sorry?* My son is dead and you're calling him an idiot, and you're

THE OLD LADY

sorry? You have the gall to tell me his murder is his own fault, and you're fucking *sorry?*"

Wylder's stomach went hollow. "*Murdered? Charlie?*"

Bart grabbed him by the collar, pulling him close so they were face to face. "Listen up, asswipe. You better explain yourself real fast. Tell me what the fuck happened here, or I swear to Christ I'll make sure you spend the rest of a very short life screaming."

Wylder glanced at the others. Regina's eyes were brimming with tears, and all the color had left Lance's face. Julie watched on with her arms crossed, impossible to read, if the woman ever had emotions at all.

"Look at me!" Bart demanded.

Wylder gulped and did as he was told. "Boss, please... I didn't know Charlie was..."

"Then what *body* were you thinking of?"

"The black guy."

"*Black guy?* What black guy?"

"In the barn. We put his body in a stall and threw a tarp over him... put some haybales around him too, to conceal him. We were gonna bury him but wanted to wait to see what you wanted us to do."

Bart furrowed his brow and glanced back at the barn. He nodded at Lance and the large man entered the building to investigate.

"I would've called and told you right away," Wylder said, "but with your cellphone thing..."

Bart glared at him. Wylder realized this wasn't the right time to bring up the commander's rule against anyone having a cellphone because they could be easily tracked.

"Oh, man," Wylder said, gasping. "I mean... shit, is Charlie really dead?"

Bart pursed his lips and returned his gaze to Wylder. He reached into his coat pocket, withdrew a folded dishtowel, and unfolded it to reveal two and a half human fingers. The tattoos made the identity of their owner unquestionable.

"Ah, fuck," Wylder said. "I didn't know, boss. Honest."

Bart took a deep breath, his wide chest rising and falling. "Stan's dead too. Somebody cut him up like swine. We brought his corpse out of the house to get the smell out, but the ground is too hard to even bury the poor kid. There's also a mound of human remains on the side of the house. Somebody was shoved down the woodchipper." His eyelids tightened. "The woodchipper, Wylder. The *fucking woodchipper!*"

"Oh, no…" he whispered, more to himself than to Bart. "That old lady…"

"Old lady? Is that what you just said?"

Wylder's heart picked up speed. "I… I just…"

"For fuck's sake, tell me what happened!"

"I don't know… I just got back."

"Back from where? And where the hell are Quin and Paul?"

Wylder swallowed hard. Paul had screamed for his help as he'd run away. Wylder told himself he'd done the only thing he could, that he wasn't a coward or deserter. But feelings of self-disgust persisted. Though he feared being beaten again, Wylder knew he had to give Bart and the team the whole story but could omit how he'd left Paul and Quin to die. Maybe the commander would show him mercy if he realized Wylder had done all he could to prevent this mess.

"Boss," he began. "I'm pretty sure Quin and Paul are dead too, sir."

The rage in Bart's eyes faded to something hollow, his weathered face going slack and pale. He looked like a man lost at sea, a lonesome traveler with no place to call home. Wylder could understand why. Though not a parent himself, he knew the bond of father and son—not from personal experience but from TV and the movies. Despite their differences, Bart loved Charlie, even though his son was known for his blunders, this one being the most detrimental of all. He deserved answers. He deserved the truth, no matter how bitter it would be to swallow.

Wylder started at the beginning, telling his commander everything.

TWENTY

AS A JOURNALISM MAJOR, ALICIA read the news every morning and recapped at the end of the night, scanning articles on her phone as she lay in bed. She was familiar with the cruel nature of humanity, and the decline of civility in modern society. Every day there was a new story about a mass shooting, a mother strangling her children to death, or police officers murdering unarmed people. These tragedies seemed to duplicate at alarming speed, be they homeland cruelties or wartime atrocities in foreign countries. But despite the regularity of such terrible events, Alicia had never thought such horrors would invade her personal life.

Now she realized just how naïve she'd been—just another American youth who'd thought violence and tragedy was reserved for other people, ones she didn't know. She'd never experienced such things firsthand before. The suffering of others had always been viewed through the filter of media. Now it had been thrown into her lap, kicking and screaming. The raw horror of this day caused her to view the ones she'd read about with wider eyes. Murder was much more upsetting in person than it was in text, and nothing like what she'd seen in movies. In real life, seeing someone killed—whether they were your friend or someone who'd attacked you personally—left a burn mark on your soul, like cattle branded with hot iron. Though it was still fresh, Alicia knew this feeling of abject horror would never truly leave her, only diminish over time, bit by bit. Dread and disgust were now integral parts of what made Alicia who she would no longer have any choice but to be. She was tainted by it, stained by blood and tears, and feared she would carry the burden of these violent memories the rest of her life.

But at least Dylan and Nori were okay. Marcus was gone, but she'd managed to rescue the rest of her friends, much to her own amazement. Alicia had never been a coward, but there were limits to what she could handle, and she'd far surpassed them today. For that, she was proud of herself. They were all safe.

Or were they?

Wylder was still out there. And what about the noise they'd heard before leaving the compound? It had sounded like a dump truck. What if the men who'd attacked them had called in other friends?

The other element of danger was Tracey. The woman had rescued them all, and Alicia was grateful to her, but every moment she spent with Tracey only increased Alicia's fear of her. Tracey seemed as if she'd been born to kill, that the acts of extreme violence which left Alicia so rattled were nothing to the woman. She didn't seem to enjoy murdering people as a sadist would, but she did not hesitate to kill, and even seemed to make it her default in dangerous situations. It caused Alicia to wonder if Tracey had previous experience in taking lives, a notion that haunted her as they returned to the trail.

Alicia thought of her mother. Right now she was probably working from home on her dual monitors in the den. Alicia wished she was with her, safe and warm. She thought of her father, who had moved to North Carolina after her parents' divorce. They spoke and texted regularly, and she visited him in the summer, but it was hardly the same. Alicia longed to have his arms around her now more than ever. That her parents weighed so heavily on her mind seemed like a grim prophecy. Was she mentally preparing herself to never see them again? Underneath her relief of having escaped the compound, had a foundation of doubt been built, leaving a bitter sense of impending defeat?

She couldn't allow that. If they were ever going to get off this mountain, and if she wanted to see her parents again, she would have to stay positive. Feelings of hopelessness only led to true

THE OLD LADY

hopelessness. She'd struggled with sadness enough to know that. Before finding Dylan, she'd been convinced romantic love was a lie, her heart having been bruised by too many boys. That sourness had only made it harder for her to accept love when it came around again. How many potential boyfriends had she turned away based solely on her negative attitude? Dylan had only managed to pierce that armor by chipping away at it slowly, being a friend to her first before showing her it was okay to love again, that she shouldn't be afraid of being happy.

Optimism didn't have to be foolish. Positivity didn't have to be a weakness. Holding on to them in times like this was the greatest strength someone could have, and the smartest thing they could do to get them out alive.

Alicia held Dylan's hand as they followed Tracey up the trailway, going back the way she and Alicia had come. Her boyfriend squeezed her hand and kissed her cheek.

"Thank you," he whispered. "Thank you so, so much."

She kissed him back.

Everything's going to be alright, she told herself. *You've made it this far. Now you just need to get down the mountain.*

But that was a trek of multiple miles down a rocky slope covered in ice and snow. They'd known to expect a little snow accumulation after seeing the weather forecast but hadn't expected it to come down as hard as it was now. They also hadn't wanted to give up the non-refundable money they'd spent booking the cabin. If she'd only known how much was at stake.

Another grim thought struck her.

Marcus had driven them here. He'd died with the car keys in his pocket. Even if they made it down the mountain, they would still need Tracey. She would have to drive them into town for help. So no matter how reluctant Alicia was to stay with the killer, there was no other choice. Tracey was her only protection, a golem in female form. Alicia would just have to trust that Tracey's violence wouldn't extend to her and the others. There was no reason it should, but Tracey seemed immune to the behavior atypical to normal human beings. Alicia had never known anyone could be so driven by a single emotion, but Tracey was the embodiment of rage. Something had happened to her long ago that she'd never recovered from. Perhaps she couldn't. Perhaps she no longer wanted to. Tracey had found her own solutions to life's hardships, ones dipped in gun powder and blood. It pained

Alicia to be grateful for the woman's wrath, to have benefitted from such unbridled brutality, but she could not object to the one thing that had saved the lives of her and her friends.

Today she'd learned that sometimes, the only answer was destruction.

Sometimes, murder was for the greater good.

They marched in silence, listening for anyone in pursuit or any sign of Wylder. Alicia hoped he'd bled to death and felt no remorse for her feelings. After what she'd been through today, her liberal views against capital punishment had evaporated. Not all human life was precious anymore. Some of it was repulsive and could be exterminated justifiably, like cockroaches and mice hiding in the walls. She understood that now, and it welcomed the Glock 19 in her hands. Dylan had looked down at it but said nothing. He'd never liked guns and had always been afraid of them. Alicia wondered how he felt about them now.

Snow buzzed around them, creating an ivory hive. It blew in tornadic bursts, the force of the wind shaking the remaining dead leaves from the trees. The hemlocks bowed as boulders vanished under blankets of white. It was enough to make her feel blind. The world around them was slowly disappearing, taking the trail with it.

Tracey stopped and checked her compass.

"Are we still headed the right way?" Alicia asked.

"Yeah. But we'll have to backtrack to my cabin before we can turn around."

Alicia swallowed. She didn't want to go back to that dreadful place.

"That's where this trail leads first," Tracey explained. "Then it branches off, with one path leading back to the Harding Trail you're looking for, the same one you all came up on."

"There's no faster way down?"

"Not from right here. Or if there is, I don't know of it. And if we go off trail it'll be ten times harder." She stared at the teens. "I won't lie. This isn't going to be easy. But it'll be a lot easier if you just do what I say."

Alicia looked to her friends. Dylan took a deep breath, resigning himself to the difficult task ahead. Nori was huddled into herself again, shivering in the cold. Noticing this, Tracey slung her backpack off and started rooting through one of the zippered pouches.

"You three really don't know how to handle winter in the woods,

THE OLD LADY

do you?" she asked, only it wasn't a question. "All three of you are in jeans. Denim is about the worst fabric you can wear in the wild. It isn't insulating enough, and when it gets wet it takes forever to dry. You can literally freeze your ass off in snow like this." She dug out a small, plastic bag with something silver inside it, and handed it to Nori. "That's an emergency blanket. Wear it like a coat until we get to the cabin. There's some better snow clothes back there that may be loose on you but will be worth it."

Nori unfolded the blanket and wore it like a shawl. The material looked like tinfoil, and Alicia was glad there was no sun to make it shine. It would have made them too easy to spot if Wylder was hunting them.

"Th-thank yu-yu-you," Nori told Tracey.

"Don't thank me yet, kid. This ain't over."

Tracey moved on and the teens followed, but Nori suddenly stopped and grabbed her brother's arm.

"What?" Dylan asked.

"C-Can wu-wu-we say a p-prayer?"

"Nori, I think—"

Tracey answered before he could. "We don't have time for that horseshit."

"Oh," Dylan said, giving her a curious look. "You don't believe in God?"

"How could I?" She sneered. "How could *you*, given what's happened? There is no God, kid, but fuck him anyway. We don't have time for superstition."

Nori recoiled a little, clearly uncomfortable with the blasphemy.

"You must believe in something," Dylan told Tracey. "If you don't believe in God, then what do you believe in?"

Tracey's face was a blank. "I believe in death."

Silence dropped upon the group, leaving only the thrum of the cold wind.

Finally, Nori spoke. "Le-let's just guh-guh-go."

"We'll say one while we walk," Dylan told her. "Okay?"

"Well, fucking do it quietly," Tracey said. "God may not be watching, but I have a feeling someone else is."

130

TWENTY-ONE

WATCHING IT A SECOND TIME, Bart played the security footage in slow motion. Wylder's story had been a wild one, but it seemed he was telling the truth. Though the footage was in black and white, the outdoor cameras had captured clear images of two women—one older and the other very young. The latter had been wearing a balaclava, but her long blonde hair and the shape of her body gave away her gender. They entered through the back door, and then left with two skinny kids with black hair. There were no cameras inside the house, so he couldn't see what had happened to Stan. That was probably for the best, seeing how he'd been practically eviscerated, and his head was barely attached to his body anymore. It would have made for unpleasant viewing and wouldn't have gotten Bart any closer to identifying the old lady. Wylder had told him she was some kind of soldier. There was a little more footage of her, but it was the hardest for Bart to stomach.

The westbound camera had caught the leadup to his son's death.

Bart watched as his only child was chased by the woman, holding his mangled hand as he stumbled through the snow. Bart flinched when she blew out Charlie's leg. His son fell, and Bart looked away

THE OLD LADY

as the woman hacked at him with what looked like a small axe. The video was silent, but when Bart looked back, he could see his boy was screaming as the bitch stomped his face into the slush. Then she dragged him off camera, toward the woodchipper.

He was still alive, Bart thought with a bitter grimace. *She put my Charlie in there while he was still alive.*

Bart looked at Wylder, who was sitting behind him, nursing his wounds. Regina had managed to patch and stitch the bullet wound in his arm where a bullet had gone through the triceps clean without hitting bone. Wylder's sprained ankle was up on a table with a bag of frozen peas under it, and he held an ice pack to his jaw. When Bart's eyes met Wylder's, the younger man looked away in shame.

"And you don't have any idea who she is or why she's doing this?" Bart asked again.

Wylder shook his head. "No."

Bart addressed the group. "Who is this crazy cunt?"

But no one knew any more than he did. The team huddled around their leader, awaiting the command they must have anticipated.

"She must be with somebody, right?" Lance asked, still holding the bucket of cleaning supplies he'd been using on the messes.

Julie crossed her arms. "Like who?"

"I dunno," Lance said. "Maybe she's a bounty hunter or something."

"Ain't no bounty on us."

"You know what I mean."

"Do I?" Julie stepped closer to him. "This bitch put my family—a boy I consider a nephew—in your woodchipper, Lance. You really think she's on the side of the law?"

The big ginger didn't have a response to that.

Regina spoke for her husband instead. "Could be a mercenary."

"But sent by who?" Julie asked. "No one knows about us or what we're doing here."

"We'd like to think so, but maybe we're wrong. Maybe someone's on to us but didn't want to call the FBI. Maybe they have their own personal vendetta against our cause."

Bart spun in his chair. "The only people we know she's with now are those kids who showed up here asking for directions."

"You buy that story?" Lance asked. "I mean, what if they were in on it?"

"Don't be ridiculous," Julie said. "A bunch of teenagers teaming up with a mercenary to take us down? That's retarded."

Regina huffed. "You know I don't like that word."

Bart groaned. He couldn't listen to Regina's sob story about her mentally challenged brother again, especially not now.

"I'll say whatever I want," Julie told Regina, her face a blank.

"Cut the shit," Bart told them. "You two hens can peck each other's eyes out later. Right now, we've got to move. Every second, this bitch and her brats are getting further away."

"You think that's it?" Lance asked. "You think she's their mom?"

Wylder spoke up, still holding the ice pack to his swollen jaw. "She can't be everyone's mom. The old lady's white. Two of the teenagers are Chinese and the dead one's a black."

"Could be adopted though."

Bart turned to them sharply. "I don't give a damn who these people are to each other. It's fucking irrelevant. Now strap up and meet me outside." He looked to Wylder. "You're gonna take us to that bitch's cabin."

"I can hardly walk," Wylder whined. "I mean, I barely made it back here."

Bart stepped into him, making Wylder squirm. "You know I consider you responsible for all this, don't you? You want to a be an officer in our troop, but as soon as I leave you in charge, we lose four men."

"It wasn't my—"

"Shut your mouth, son. Grab yourself a hiking stick because you're absolutely coming with us. I don't give a damn if your foot turns black and falls off. You owe it to Charlie. You owe it to all of us."

Wylder didn't argue it further.

The group separated, heading for their well-stocked armories. For this situation, Bart wanted to bring out the big guns—literally. Julie followed him as Bart opened the closet and grabbed his bag of emergency reserves with the secret stash of special weaponry.

"The hunt is on," Julie said.

Bart ignored her and kept preparing.

"This is gonna be our main focus now?" she asked.

"They killed my boy, Julie. *She* killed my boy."

"Wanting revenge is only natural, but—"

"My son and your nephew."

"But what if this hunt goes on into the morning? We have a

THE OLD LADY

mission to think about."

Bart bared his teeth. "Charlie is *dead*, Julie! And he died horribly. All other missions take a backseat to a father's vengeance."

"I understand, Bart. Really, I do. But we cannot alter the plan this late in the game."

Bart hefted his bag over his shoulder. A cold emptiness was spreading through him, a blackness so thick and unrelenting it removed every thought that didn't involve violent retribution. All his missions were an act of revenge, but this was the most personal grudge of all. Hell had sprung a leak.

"Things don't always go according to plan, Julie," he said. "You must learn to adapt when everything turns to shit in your hands. I won't be able to focus on the mission until I've got that cunt's head on a stick. Distraction causes mistakes, and mistakes cause failure. We've worked too hard on this plan to allow anyone to fuck it up—even me."

Julie looked about the room, avoiding Bart's eyes. "Okay then. Give me something bigger than my lousy .22."

"You know it. But just one thing."

She smirked but there was no humor in it. "Let me guess. The rest of us can take her down, but no one kills her but you?"

Bart nodded. "After what I'm going to do to her, death will seem like a favor."

~

Julie knew Bart wouldn't want to use the ATVs, but it still annoyed her when he said so. They could gain ground on the escapees so easily and be back here in plenty of time to go over the plan again before tomorrow morning. But Bart insisted the sound of the four-wheelers would only alert their prey to their presence. Time was not an issue to Bart right now, which was very out of character for her cousin. He'd always been meticulous and calculated. But the gruesome murder of his only child had obliterated his good sense. And while Julie couldn't blame him for his fury, it was still a disappointing thing to witness.

The remaining members of their team trekked uphill through the snow and ice and gray misery, doing their best to discern the tracks left by the woman and the kids. Bart seemed confident their prey would retreat to the old lady's cabin, where Wylder insisted Paul and Quin had likely died by her hand too. But if Julie were them, she'd be hauling ass down this mountain as quickly as possible. The old lady didn't know just how dangerous and determined Ed Bartlett could be, but if she didn't get out of these woods soon, she was going to find out, and would regret it the rest of her short life.

Thinking of the teenagers she'd seen on the video, Julie hoped they could capture them alive too, or at least the females. Girls that age could bring in a hefty paycheck from her employers in the consortium. Luckily, Bart had agreed to trying to kidnap them again rather than kill them on sight. Though he morally disapproved of Julie's involvement in sex trafficking, the missions he planned weren't cheap. Supplies, weapons, trucks, and even this secluded compound had mostly been paid for through criminal enterprises, with the bulk of their finances coming from Julie's wealthy clientele.

As a woman, it was easier for her to gain the trust of young ladies in desperate situations. She found them in bus stations and shelters, loitering on street corners and sleeping in Pittsburg alleys. They worked odd jobs off the books and lied about their ages to perform in strip clubs, some already turning tricks. Julie was a shaper of these sophomoric minds, conditioning underage runaways and feeding their drug habits, painting their downward spirals into pursuits of feminist freedom to convince the girls they were living their lives the way they wanted to and nothing else mattered. Once they'd been properly transformed, Julie brought these young women to one of the boarding houses where they were either handled by the outfit's pimps or sold at auction to silent partner millionaires.

Julie's own carnal desires had led her to this lurid profession. A ravenous bisexual, she'd gone on lust vacations in countries with legalized prostitution, indulging her cravings in Berlin, Amsterdam, and Tijuana. Back in her home country, the only legal prostitution was in Nevada, and the cost of a half hour with a hooker was astronomical. It wasn't until her trip to Thailand that she began seeing the potential of trafficking and considered starting her own business in the oldest profession. After renting out a townhouse, Julie ran her own illegal brothel on the east coast, one where she was the only madam. The girls were considered independent contractors who gave Julie a cut for the use of her rooms, but most of them were permanent residents who paid the madam in cash and sexual favors they performed on her and her best clients.

When the police finally raided the brothel, it was Bart who'd helped Julie with her case, so she served a short sentence with time served, and was out on probation within two years. Julie had gotten

THE OLD LADY

lucky with the timing of the raid, with none of the current girls being under eighteen, which would have made her offense much more serious, resulting in a much longer prison sentence.

Once she'd been released, she contacted one of the most powerful men she'd protected by keeping her mouth shut and refusing to enter a plea deal. Her new position with the high-level criminal consortium was secured, and she'd been grooming girls for them ever since.

There would be no grooming for the two teen girls who'd escaped here. They would be sold into slavery and pumped full of so much heroin that they wouldn't even know what was happening for the first few weeks. Then, once they were properly addicted, they would suck and fuck as much as they were told to. Otherwise, they would face the agony of withdrawals, as well as beatings with sacks full of oranges, to lessen the bruising, which was a turnoff for paying customers.

The blonde would bring in a minimum of four figures.

The underage Asian could sell at auction for over five, especially if she were a virgin.

TWENTY-TWO

LEADING THE KIDS IN A silent expedition, Tracey reflected on all the people she'd murdered. She'd had some time to cool, the fire in her belly that came with intermittent explosive disorder now simmering to a single wick. Her antipsychotic pills were in her bag, but she needed to be alert, so she dismissed the idea of taking one. The fits of rage she suffered would come in handy if it turned out they weren't alone in these woods.

Still, her acts of violence haunted her. It was not guilt or remorse that riddled Tracey, but an amazement at her own bad luck. Somehow, she'd found herself in situations like this time and again—dangerous encounters that forced her to fight with everything she had, using all the training her father had given her, harsh classes she'd once been so sure would be useless in everyday life. It pained her to accept that her old man had been right about anything, but it was especially hard when he'd been right about something that had been traumatizing to learn.

Marching back to the cabin now, she recalled one of the lessons her father had made her go through again and again until it was forever cemented in her mind.

THE OLD LADY

"A man tries to grab you," Dad would say. "How do you react?"

Tracey always replied with the answer she'd been taught. "I kill him."

"Correct. Any unwanted touching is assault, and you have a right to protect yourself. But if you initiate combat with someone—especially someone bigger and stronger than you—you must be prepared to take it to the most extreme level as quickly as possible, to ensure your own safety. Any hesitation to hurt others could result in them hurting you or worse."

Tracey would sit in the wooden chair, head bowed, waiting for the next question.

"A stranger approaches you in a dark alley where no one else is around," Dad would say. "What do you do?"

"Kill him."

"A man breaks into our home in the middle of the night."

"Kill him."

"A woman breaks into our home in the middle of the night."

"Kill her."

"You've just beaten some rapist in a fight, so he couldn't assault you. Now you've got a gun on him and he's begging for his life."

"Kill him."

"A group of people chase you through the woods, Tracey. What do you do?"

"Kill them all."

"And how?"

"By using all the survival techniques and combat skills you've taught me."

Back then, Tracey had thought such recitals were feed for her father's vanity. Now she realized he'd been driving home an important point. He'd been preparing her for situations people thought were unlikely to happen but did happen. Tracey had learned the hard way just how right the old man had been. The world was cruel and heartless. People were capable of great evil. And not all human life had value. Most of it was better off wiped from the earth.

As she continued through the snow, her father's voice returned to her, quoting himself.

"A group of people chase you through the woods, Tracey. What do you do?"

But they both knew the answer. The question was whether she was being pursued or not.

As they continued along the trail, Tracey scanned the woods for

Wylder. She kept her eyes peeled and used the binoculars whenever she thought she spotted something. But the snowstorm had made it easy for Wylder to cover his tracks. If she'd been on her own, Tracey would have hunted him down first and foremost, to eliminate the threat instead of waiting for it to come to her, but with the kids in tow, getting to safety was a higher priority.

She also believed Wylder wasn't alone.

The men who'd attacked the cabin, and the other men at the ranch house, were part of something bigger. She'd sensed that even before hearing the truck approach the compound. It only stood to reason that it was filled with more members of their cult or militia or whatever the hell it was. Tracey couldn't be sure what they were into. All she was sure of was the men she'd killed today were only a fraction of a much larger threat.

Knowing how dangerous groups were, Tracey had grown to hate them in every form. Organizations, associations, teams, clubs, political parties, gangs, police squads, armies—all of them made her recoil. Groups led to group thinking, and nothing was more volatile and insipid than that. To allow yourself to be told what your opinion should be, and be threatened with exile if you should disagree, was the submission of a fool. Individuals could potentially be liked and perhaps even relied on, but the groups they belonged to were never to be trusted under any circumstances.

Even having the three kids with her left Tracey a little uneasy. They were close friends, with two even being family. Tracey was the outsider. She was the crazy old lady and knew it. Surely the kids knew it too. If any of them were pushed into a corner, how quick might they be to betray her? Could they be trusted not to talk under torture? Somehow Tracey doubted they had been taught how to endure pain the way she had, or that they'd learned the futility of bargaining with people who intended to hurt you either way.

"Never talk," her father had always said. "Never be a snitch. Don't tell your enemies anything. Don't tell the police, the ATF, the FBI, or any form of law enforcement anything, even if you only *saw* what they're talking about and had nothing to do with it. Even if the President of the United States asks you a question, you tell him to fuck right off."

Having not taken these words to heart, she'd later learned at her own expense that her father was right. Now Tracey considered these words gospel.

THE OLD LADY

"Trust no one," Dad whispered in her head.

Tracey muttered. "Tell me something I don't know."

She spotted the smoke before the cabin. The pitfall was still smoldering, and the stench of burnt flesh crept upon the air. The kids coughed and groaned but kept following her, no doubt being quietly reassured by Alicia. As they finally reached the cabin, Tracey guided them to avoid the tripwires. The trail of blood left behind when she'd dragged Paul to the pit had been aptly concealed by the snow, and when she peered over the edge of it, she saw the charred bodies were heavily coated in snow too.

"We're not staying here long, right?" Alicia asked as they came to the front step.

"As long as it takes to get ready."

"Ready for what?"

Tracey opened the door, and the kids followed her inside, Dylan and Nori marveling at the strange surroundings.

"Olivia..." Tracey began.

"It's *Alicia*."

Tracey blinked her daughter's image off Alicia's face. "Alicia, I thought we agreed you'd all do as I say."

"Yeah, but, I mean, Wylder is still out there. He might come back here looking for us. He might bring others with him."

"Well, you're not stupid, I'll give you that." Tracey put down the shotgun and slung off her BOB and rifle. "We're going to take a quick break here and get warm. Then we need to stock up on supplies and gear before we head back out."

"What supplies? We're just going down the mountain trail."

"That's not as simple as it was earlier today. There's the blizzard to contend with, not to mention Wylder and any reserves he may have called in."

Nori looked up at her with harrowing eyes. "You mean there's m-more of them?"

"We don't know, but it's better to expect the unexpected. Anything could happen out in this storm. We need the proper tools to survive if we get in a jam. I can't carry everything, so you all will have to haul some stuff too." Tracey dragged her father's BOB across the floor and put it at Alicia's feet. "Take it."

Dylan reached for it instead. "I can carry it for her."

Tracey narrowed her eyes. "I said it's Alicia's."

Dylan looked to his girlfriend as if for permission. She picked up the bag instead.

"I know it slows you down a little," Tracey said, "but it's very important that you hang on to it, understand?"

Alicia nodded. "I will."

Tracey drew a small rod from her pocket and handed it to Alicia. "That's a ferrocerium rod," Tracey said. "It's small, but contains a paracord, whistle, steel flint, and most importantly, a compass. Even if you lose everything else, keep this in your pocket, okay?"

Alicia nodded again and stuffed the rod in the front pocket of her jeans. "Okay. I will."

Tracey held the girl's gaze, underlining her point, and then turned to Nori.

"You," Tracey said, pointing at her. "There are snow pants and a heavy coat in the trunk over there. I don't want you getting the umbles. Just put them over your clothes so they'll fit better, and roll up the cuffs of the pants so you don't trip over them. I have safety pins you can use to secure them."

Following direction, Nori went to the trunk. Tracey stepped to her father's armory and retrieved the .380 Automatic Colt Pistol. She extended it to Dylan, and the boy's eyes went wide. He backed away with his hands up.

"Whoa, whoa," he said. "I don't do guns."

Tracey stared at him in disbelief, anger sending tingles through her extremities. "You don't have a choice, kid."

Alicia tried. "Dylan—"

"I'm just not comfortable with guns," he said. "I've always been against them."

"Look, sonny boy," Tracey said. "It's guns that saved your girlfriend's life when she came here, and a gun is what blew the hand off the man who would have otherwise raped your sister."

"I know, but guns just cause more prob—"

"Take the fucking gun." She held it out, but Dylan didn't make a move for it. "Take the gun, you pussy!"

"Calm down," Alicia told her.

"I'll calm down once I know your boyfriend has *our* backs the way we've had his."

Alicia turned to Dylan. "Sorry, babe, but she's right. You can go back to your stance on guns once we're home safe."

Dylan looked from his girlfriend to the pistol and back. Though he finally relented and took the gun, Tracey no longer saw the use in

THE OLD LADY

it. The boy wouldn't know how to handle a firearm and would certainly be hesitant to shoot people with it. She could see in his eyes that he'd never been in a fight, that he'd coasted through life with few hiccups until this fateful day. Dylan was soft, and that made him dead weight in dire situations. He was just another child for her to look after. But better to know that now than to learn it when bullets started flying.

"Is there, like, a safety?" he asked, holding the .380 like it was a spent condom.

"There's an integrated trigger safety," she told him. "But it's off. I suggest you keep it like that. That way, all you have to do is point and shoot. I don't want you fumbling when the shit hits the fan."

Dylan was about to say something, but Tracey's hard stare shut him up. She returned to the armory and transferred select items to her BOB. Then she took an empty tote bag from the kitchen area and started filling it with supplies for Dylan to carry.

"A purse would suit him better," her father said.

Tracey stifled a sardonic laugh. She trusted Alicia with her father's BOB more than she would Dylan, because the girl had shown her bravery and exhibited an intelligence Tracey had yet to see from the boy. Though she may not have been trained for this, Alicia was a survivor. Even without Tracey's guidance, she would make better use of the contents of the bag than her boyfriend would.

Nori finished dressing, and Tracey gave her the safety pins to secure the baggy clothes. She also handed the girl a stun gun. Nori reached for it gingerly but didn't object to weapons the way her brother did. Tracey showed her how to use it, and the teens all jumped at the loud spark. A smile curled the corners of Nori's mouth. Seeing it, Tracey snatched the machete from the tool board and handed it to the girl too.

"Clip the stun gun to your waistband," Tracey said, "and carry the machete. It has a longer reach. If it fails you, you'll have the stunner as backup."

Nori stared at the long, black blade. Tracey selected it because it was lightweight and effective. The only other pistol was the .38 snub nose, and judging by Nori's tiny hands, there was no way the girl could handle it. Tracey doubted Nori could handle any kind of firearm at all, but at least she wasn't showing the aversion to weapons her brother had. Still, putting a pistol in the shaky hands of a petite teenage girl was basically placing an order for a fatal accident.

"Alright," Tracey said to the group. "You guys warm up while I make a quick run to the toolshed. If someone other than me comes to cabin, what are you going to do?"

Dylan's eyes went wide.

Alicia took a deep breath.

Nori gripped the handle of the machete. "Kill them?"

TWENTY-THREE

BART HAD HOPED TO MAKE things right with Charlie.

He knew he hadn't been the best husband to Sandy, and with her gone, becoming a better father was the only way he could have compensated for his poor behavior as a husband. Nearly two years after a miscarriage that had threatened to tear their marriage apart, Bart and Sandy had been blessed with an unexpected pregnancy. Though born slightly premature, Charlie grew up healthy, with no physical ailments beyond what was considered normal. His only abnormalities seemed to be emotional, but they didn't manifest until he was a teen. He'd been the opposite of his father—awkward around girls; submissive around other boys; quick to give up on important tasks and slow to catch on to obvious things. Social cues had always eluded Charlie. Even once he'd entered his twenties, he didn't care for sports and had no strong opinions on politics. His obsession with video games, careless drug habits, and addiction to internet porn had only further deracinated him from the real world.

Bart had bailed his son out of trouble time and again, and yet he'd felt it was Sandy who'd really enabled the boy. Bart was always busy with work, pulling long hours, and regularly brought the stress of the job home with him. Because Sandy only had a part-time job filing for an accounting firm, Bart had considered it his wife's responsibility to raise their only child right. It was one of many perceived injustices that had caused him to lash out at Sandy as frequently as he had—mostly verbally, but sometimes physically, though he limited the violence to smacking her across the face, shaking her, and pushing her against walls. In retrospect, Bart realized it was his profession that had turned him into a domestic monster, not anything his wife had done. But this revelation came too late.

Sandy died of breast cancer while Bart was still a rage-fueled animal in a cage that was rattled daily. He hadn't yet learned to focus that anger into productivity instead of unleashing it on the person closest to him. Bart's final promise to his wife was that he'd always take care of their child, their miracle boy. And now, some crazy bitch had taken away his right to make good on that promise, his one chance at redemption for a marriage he had poisoned. While she was alive, he'd taken Sandy for granted. Now that she was gone, he'd disappointed her memory. And though he knew he should be more focused on mourning his son right now, he kept returning to this remorse over his wife as he marched on through the cold and unforgiving wilderness of the White Mountains.

The weight of the Heckler & Koch G36 felt good in his hands. He longed to make the cold assault rifle warm at the expense of those who had wronged him. A bullet for each of the woman's knees and elbows would still leave him with twenty-six rounds in the magazine to play with. Bart fantasized about shoving the hot barrel of the rifle down the woman's throat and blasting her guts apart from the inside, then reimagined doing the same thing through her colon.

Beside him, his cousin carried an identical Heckler & Koch. Julie had opted to wear a ski mask against the snow, and its concealing red and black design only intensified her stoicism. The others were also heavily armed, with Regina wearing a belt of extra magazines for her AK47. Though they had enough instruments of death to take on a small SWAT team, the goal was to take their enemies alive. Bart needed to know just who these people were and how much they knew about his team's operation. But more than that, he had to make his son's killer suffer—not just for Charlie or for himself, but for Sandy.

The wind whistled as it hurled snow flurries into the team's faces. Lining the trail, the dead trees towered and sulked, their branches

THE OLD LADY

raking the ashen sky like black streaks of lightning. Bart's grimace deepened as drops of sweat began to freeze in his mustache.

How many times had he been a part of an armed squad like this, doing raids or responding to calls about violent offenders? Despite all his experience, this was his first time as part of a manhunt since he'd left the force, and it made him anxious. There was more riding on this, and not just because it was personal. When he'd been a police officer, he'd always had the law to back him up, no matter how ugly things got in the aftermath. As a civilian, he had no such armor. If this was handled wrong, the consequences could be severe, even if the team was initially successful. These actions, much like all the major decisions he'd made in recent years, were felonies. He couldn't afford to muck this up any more than he could afford to let the woman and kids escape. He had to be meticulous. They all did.

It was too easy for a cop to be a target these days, even if they were an ex-cop. U.S. law enforcement agencies had increasingly been attacked from all sides of the political spectrum. In 2021 alone, forty-three percent of domestic terrorist plots had targeted law enforcement, government, and even the military. Regardless of the perpetrator's ideology, cops were the new punching bag. Bart had both lived it and researched it. The far-left selected law enforcement in nearly half of their attacks, and the far-right, for all their "back the blue" rhetoric, selected law enforcement in thirty-seven percent of their terrorist attacks. The capitol riot was a perfect example of that.

Because of all this, Bart looked upon both sides of the political spectrum with equal vehemence. He did not share his disgust for conservatives with his fellow teammates however, for he knew most of them subscribed to conventional militia mentalities. His associates had their own platforms—close the border, end welfare, stop gun control—but Bart considered these minor issues. Only Julie knew Bart's true motivations, for only she truly understood them. That's why he trusted her with information he never offered to the others.

Bart saw the American Dream as being assassinated by its own leaders, and his goal was to fight a system that had failed people like him.

These days, most terrorist attacks occurred at demonstrations. Bart felt that was all for show—a rage-fueled celebration of team rivalry, just like the bad blood between the Boston Red Sox and the New York Yankees. He was smart enough to know the better route was to strike off-camera, ducking the spotlight to generate as much damage and instill as much fear as possible. But the shrill hippie protestors and redneck MAGA trolls of this country were too dim-witted and self-righteous to understand that, which was to be expected from a generation who believed their Twitter accounts amounted to activism.

Bart's generation had grown up believing the cops were the good guys. Somewhere along the way, that public opinion had been reversed. And where once the country had united to destroy Nazis, communists, and Salafi-jihadists, now American citizens were too dedicated to destroying one another to unite against anything.

A house divided against itself cannot stand.

Lincoln had said that. Bart agreed with the sixteenth president but was no longer interested in mending America's frayed and rotted union. Rather than work to put out this blustering garbage fire, he would supply it with oceans of gasoline.

First things first, Bart thought.

Upon the crest of the next hill, a dark cabin loomed.

TWENTY-FOUR

ALICIA TRIED HER BEST TO explain it all to Dylan and Nori, but she didn't quite understand it herself. Everything that had happened seemed like a bizarre fever dream, from Marcus' murder to this moment of loading up supplies in this prepper shack.

How was she supposed to explain the crazy woman to her friends? How could she tell Dylan and Nori she'd been running for help and thought she'd found a female recluse, but had actually awakened a terrifying golem?

When she was a child, Alicia's grandfather had told her stories from Jewish mythology. Most were warm fables meant as guides for God's chosen people while others served as poignant lessons. But one that had always sparked her imagination was that of The Golem.

The classic tale told of Rabbi Judah Loew of Prague and the golem he created to defend those in the Jewish community against antisemitic attacks. The creature was a statue made of clay, dust, and earth—inanimate materials that magically came to life when in complete human form. The golem was a giant that proved to be an effective defender of the Jews, but eventually it became a relentlessly violent, fearsome beast, much like Frankenstein's monster, and the rabbi was forced to destroy it.

As Alicia had grown older, she came to understand the story as a composite of the same fears and anxieties that underlined other mystical tales about demons, ghosts, boogeymen, and dybbuks. But in the case of the dreadful golem, there was the additional message of the danger of calling upon violent forces beyond one's understanding.

By involving Tracey in her crisis, had Alicia unleashed such a beast?

"We need to get out of here," she told her friends. "That guy who escaped knows where this cabin is."

"You said he was badly hurt," Dylan said.

"Yeah, but he might have more friends, right? You all heard that truck."

"We don't know if the truck was heading to the compound though. It could've been going anywhere. With this weather, it was probably a plow."

"I doubt there'd be a plow this high on the mountain."

He exhaled. "C'mon, babe. We don't even know for sure that it was a truck. It could have been snowmobiles or something."

Alicia looked to Nori, as if the girl could better explain things to her brother, but Nori was walking by the shelves with wide eyes, taking in the staggering inventory of survival gear.

"I'm more concerned about this woman we're with," Dylan said, lowering his voice. "I don't feel safe around her. She's unstable."

"Hey, I'm not exactly comfortable with Tracey either, but she's saved all our lives, and without her help we might never make it off this mountain."

"But she's a murderer, Alicia. And a brutal one."

Alicia sighed. "I know, I know. As soon as we can get away from her, we will. But right now, she's our best shot of putting an end to this whole nightmare."

"Even though she's part of the nightmare? I'll never forget that body in the living room. Never."

"We've all seen things today we never should have had to. But there's nothing anyone could do about it. Tracey did what she felt she had to do to rescue us."

"But the way she did it was so barbaric. I think she's a psycho. I mean, she must be to do things like that."

Alicia nodded. She didn't *think* Tracey was psychotic; she *knew* it.

"My grandpa always told me beggars can't be choosers," Alicia

THE OLD LADY

said. "We'll just have to be careful around Tracey. Really, really careful."

~

That night in the alley, with three young men encircling her as she lay on the filthy concrete, Tracey managed to knee the crotch of the heavyset man who'd been beating her head in. It happened just as he was fumbling with her panties and threatening her with sodomy. The man's friend—not Carl, the one she'd had sex with, but the other man—had distracted the potential rapist, telling him to lay off Tracey before he did any serious damage. She'd taken advantage of this distraction by nailing her attacker in the nuts, and when he leaned forward groaning, she punched him in the throat, and he began choking on the air trapped in his passages.

Shoving him off, Tracey kicked Carl in the knee, making him buckle, and as she rose to her feet the third man who'd passively tried to defend her backed away with his hands up, telling her to just take it easy even though her eyes were filling with her own blood. Her scalp had been split by the heavyset man who'd repeatedly bashed her skull into the concrete, leaving her dizzy and panicked. Carl started to rise, calling her a whore, but before he could stand up straight, Tracey leaned back and snapped a turning kick into his stomach.

Carl groaned as the front of his pants bloomed with piss. As he leaned over, Tracey grabbed him by the hair with both fists and hammered his face with a series of knee butts until his nose exploded with blood. The sound of it snapping echoed loudly through the alleyway. She kneed him again, splitting the bottom lip she'd sucked on earlier that night. The third man continued to stay back, but Tracey went at him anyway, preferring to go on the offense rather than give him any opportunity to strike her. He kept his hands up to block her blows, but when he threw a punch to defend himself, Tracey managed to grab his arm, twist it, and slammed her elbow down upon the back of his. The man's elbow bent in the wrong direction, and he screamed like a baby as she went at his eyes with her thumbs, digging her press-on nails in as deep as she could, expelling ocular fluid that ran red with blood. Then she slammed the back of his head against the dumpster before letting him fall blindly in the filth and trash and blood and drops of his buddy's semen.

Tracey grabbed her purse from the ground and ran.

She heard the men collecting themselves as she exited the alleyway. Panting, she bolted into the small parking lot behind the tavern where she'd left her car. Though there were several other vehicles, no other people were in sight. Her hands shook and she struggled to get her keys from her bag. As she climbed inside the car, she spotted a shadow coming from behind her, and heard the shouts of the men. She couldn't process what they were saying. It didn't matter anyway.

Starting the car, Tracey put it in reverse, and when she checked her mirror, she saw two of the men getting behind her car to block her in. The one she'd blinded wasn't present. The heavyset one who'd tried to get her panties off stood behind her car, pounding the trunk just as he'd pounded her skull. The one she'd had sex with hobbled toward the driver's side door.

Tracey pressed the accelerator and the brake simultaneously, revving the engine, and then released the brake, sending the car rocketing backward. The rear bumper slammed into the heavyset man, sending him back a few feet and causing him to stumble against another parked car. As he tried to right himself, Tracey kept the gas pedal to the floor, sandwiching the man between her car and the parked one. He cried out as his legs were crushed. Tracey didn't let up. The tires spun in the loose gravel, the four thousand pounds of her automobile pulverizing the heavyset man's shins as his cries were drowned out by the lion's roar of the engine.

Carl pounded on her door. He didn't seem angry anymore. Instead, he looked pale with fright. "Stop! Stop! You're killing him!"

As Carl tried to bust out her window with his fist, Tracey heard her father's voice.

"A man tries to grab you. How do you react?"

Keeping the accelerator down, she reached for the compartment under the arm rest, and withdrew the .38 pistol she'd been carrying since fleeing her father's cabin.

She didn't even bother rolling down the window.

It exploded, creating a shower of safety glass as the bullet whizzed over the head of the young man she'd eagerly had sex with half an hour ago. He flinched and stumbled, catching himself with his hands, and ran away. Tracey raised the pistol, aiming at the fleeing man, but despite her father's demands to kill Carl, she was too nervous to shoot someone in the back.

Lowering her revolver, Tracey cut the wheel, her nerves telling her to escape while she still could, but her training kicked in, forcing her to put the car in park while keeping the engine running. She stepped out, still holding the revolver, and looked around the parking lot for

THE OLD LADY

any other people or security cameras. Seeing nothing but empty darkness, she went to the man she'd crushed. Crippled and pinned, he cried out as she approached.

"Please...," he whimpered. "I wasn't really gonna do anything to you, I swear."

Tracey didn't reply. She raised the pistol, putting the barrel four inches away from the space between his eyes.

"*Finish it*," her father whispered.

Instinct told her to do the same, but Tracey struggled with the idea of murdering the heavyset man. Not because she would feel guilty about it, but because being a wanted killer would make her life even more miserable than it already was.

The man continued to plead for his life. "I'm so sorry... I was just trying to scare you. Honest."

"*You know what you have to do,*" her father whispered.

"Fuck you," she said, both to her father and the man she'd crippled.

Tracey headed back to her open car door, then remembered there was still one man left. Was he still writhing on the alley floor clutching his punctured eyeballs, or had he gone for help?

"*Finish it*," her father said again.

Steadying her breathing, Tracey looked toward the alley, but the sound of a distant siren froze her in place. She couldn't tell if it was a police car or an ambulance.

"Shit," she hissed through clenched teeth.

Panic returned, hindering Tracey's lungs. Her limbs shook so hard she feared she was going to lose hold of the gun. She looked all around, still seeing nothing, but the sound of the siren was getting louder, closer.

Tracey hopped into her car, and as she pulled away the heavyset man's body finally collapsed, the bloody ruin of his legs giving out from under him.

The exit path was tight. When the loose gravel of the lot became pavement, she struck potholes without decreasing her speed. Tracey gasped as the car shook about like a rollercoaster cart.

"*Slow down*," her father's voice advised. "*Too many people get caught committing a misdemeanor while fleeing a felony.*"

Tracey decelerated but maintained the speed limit. Fleeing the scene, she was several blocks away before another car passed her in the opposite direction. When its headlights flashed her, Tracey clenched the steering wheel, sure the car was going to cut her off so another could box her in from behind. But it wasn't a policeman. The civilian had only flashed her because Tracey had forgotten to turn her headlights on.

She spent the next few days camping out in the woods, hiding from all she'd done and yet waiting for law enforcement to capture her. But they never came. Tracey checked the news at the library, but while the assault on the three college students was reported on, they were the only witnesses to the event. They'd concocted a story that painted Tracey as the villain, omitting their assault on her which had preceded her violence against them. Even the one who'd told the others to back off her gave an unfair version of the events of that night, because he and his friends had been attacking a woman, and the truth would only incriminate them.

As a result of Tracey's attack on the man's eyeballs, he'd only regained his vision in one eye. Carl had gotten away with only minor injuries. The heavyset man she'd pinned between two cars had been paralyzed. Doctors remained uncertain if he would ever regain the use of his legs.

Luckily, none of them had thought to get her license plate. She wasn't worried about them knowing her name, because she never used her real one while picking up men in bars and wasn't a regular anywhere. She liked to keep her anonymity and felt freer when she could lose herself in a fantasy persona, and so Carl, and everyone else in the bar that night, had only known her as Jasmine. She'd worn heavy makeup for the role, and the police composite sketch looked nothing like Tracey did in her everyday life.

But still she worried. The fear ate her from the inside as she slept under the stars with one eye open. She started to believe letting the men live was a mistake. Without their testimony, the police would have even less to go on. But on the other hand, they would probably pursue the perpetrator of a triple homicide with more vigor.

After a week of hiding in the woods of Bedford, Tracey returned to the car she'd hid in the rear parking lot of a long-abandoned convenience store. The driver's window was gone, and the rear bumper was cracked, but she'd cleaned the blood off with Amor All wipes. She could get these repaired, but not anytime soon, and not in this town.

Starting the car, Tracey pulled away, leaving behind the meager life she'd made in Massachusetts.

THE OLD LADY

And for her first major acts of violence, she was never caught.

TWENTY-FIVE

HAVING LOADED UP ON SUPPLIES, Tracey returned from the shed to gather her brood. Craving something to calm her nerves, she drew a cigarette and lit it with her Zippo. When she stepped inside the cabin, the three kids looked at her with drained faces. Distributing the gear so they all shared the burden of carrying what they might need to survive, Tracey replaced the spent rounds in her pump action shotgun and checked her .22 rifle before slinging it over her shoulder.

"Everybody good to go?" she asked the kids.

Alicia nodded. "As ready as we'll ever be."

"Do we really need all this stuff?" Dylan asked.

"Two is one and one is none," Tracey told him.

"What?"

"Never mind. Just do as I say and carry it. Let's move out."

Hefting their bags, the group started toward the front door. Tracey sensed the palpable fear emanating from the teenagers and couldn't help but wonder how much of it was caused by her. She dismissed the thought. There was no time to pacify these three. Sometimes survival got ugly. Sometimes you had to paralyze people or slit their throats or blow their hands off. And in the worst of

THE OLD LADY

situations, you had to kill. The kids should be grateful to have someone willing to go to such extremes. Left on their own, Dylan would likely be dead, and the girls would be getting gang raped right now. Both fates were far more horrible than what they'd already been through.

Tracey grabbed the doorhandle, then stopped and looked back at the kids.

"One question," she said, puffing smoke. "Do any of you have any idea what those guys were up to?"

They all looked to each other, seeming lost.

"Did they say anything to you while you were there?" Tracey asked. "Did you hear or see anything that might explain who they are?"

Silence.

"Did you see anything out of the ordinary?" Tracey asked.

Finally, Alicia spoke up. "There was something that seemed weird to me. In the barn, there were huge stacks of fertilizer—and I mean, *huge*. Like, thousands of pounds worth."

"That's right," Dylan said. "The stalls were stacked with bags of it. And there were a lot of cans marked DMSO, and some other thing called nitro meth or something."

Tracey's face hardened. "Nitromethane?"

"Yeah, that's it."

"And nails," Alicia said. "Hundreds of boxes."

Dylan nodded. "It's like they were building something in there. Something big."

Tracey rubbed the bridge of her nose as she processed this frightening information. Everything the kids were saying made perfect, horrible sense. These men were even worse than she'd suspected.

"Think it means anything?" Dylan asked.

"Not sure yet," Tracey lied, unable to tell them the truth. It would only feed their fear and rightly so. "If you remember anything else, let me know."

Nori stepped up, holding her machete at her side like a jungle warrior. Seeing the Asian girl like this made Tracey's mouth dry. Though a Japanese American, Nori now looked like a junior member of the North Vietnamese Army, whom Tracey had been taught to hate and distrust, and had grown up fearing because of the prejudice her father had brought back from the war. Tracey was aware of the reason behind her apprehension, and told herself she was being ridiculous, but a murmur of paranoia remained.

"Charlie," Nori said.

Charlie, Tracey thought. *Victor. Charlie. VC.*

"Those little motherfuckers in black pajamas," her father's voice whispered. *"The gooks; the dinks; the zipperheads."*

"Charlie said something to me," Nori said.

Tracey remembered now. This was the name of the little bastard she'd shoved down the woodchipper. Her father's racist grumbles retreated to the back of her mind, and Nori continued. Tracey was glad to see the girl's stutter had faded since they'd escaped the compound.

"He was trying to get me to like him, I guess," Nori said. "I was s-scared… and he said I shouldn't be afraid of him 'cause he and his friends were the good guys. Said he was a freedom fighter."

Her suspicions confirmed, Tracey nodded. "What else did he say?"

"Mostly he just tried to get me to warm up to him. Kept telling me how p-pretty I was. But then he started telling me about his life when he was my age, to like, try to relate to me. Told me bands he liked and stuff. But then he mentioned being a little kid and watching a raid on live TV with his dad. Something called Waco."

Tracey tensed, her hands gripping the shotgun harder. "And what did he say about Waco?"

"Charlie was re-really intense about it. He said Waco wasn't a movie or TV show, that it was real and made a lasting im-impression on him. I think he was trying to say this Waco thing inspired him, but I wasn't sure what he was even talking about." Nori shrugged. "I mean, what's Waco?"

Tracey looked to Alicia and Dylan, wondering if they also hadn't learned about the law enforcement siege on the Branch Davidians in 1993. The young couple seemed equally lost. While Tracey remembered the standoff vividly, she was much older than these kids, who hadn't even been alive during the 9/11 terrorist attacks, let alone the Waco Massacre that had occurred three decades ago.

"Waco's a place in Texas," Tracey said. "And Texas is full of assholes like Charlie."

Dylan furrowed his brow. "You think it's, like, a gun control thing?"

"*What?*"

"The gun laws in Texas are some of the loosest in the country. These guys who captured us were armed to the teeth. So maybe that's

THE OLD LADY

what Charlie was trying to say? That Texas inspires him and his friends? Like, in their minds they're freedom fighters for going against gun control."

Tracey was surprised by Dylan's logical fallacy, but this wasn't the time for a history lesson on cults, American tragedies, and government overreach. She'd gathered noteworthy information from the teenagers but explaining things to them would be time consuming, and time was in short supply.

"Never mind that now," Tracey told Dylan before addressing the group. "I guess if there's sense to make of all this, we'll know it once it's over. But only if we make it down alive." She opened the front door a crack, and a vicious wind entered the cabin like a glacial breath. "Stay close to me. Keep an eye on each other. And most importantly, keep an eye on yourselves."

~

"I know this place," Bart said as his squad approached the cabin.

"You do?" Wylder asked.

"You sure this is it?"

"Positive." Wylder pointed to a black hole in the earth. "That's where Quin fell."

"And Paul?"

Wylder looked about nervously. "I dunno."

Raising the Heckler & Koch to shoulder level, Bart clenched his jaw and proceeded toward the cabin with his team close behind him. The mounting snow was daunting, and Wylder struggled even with the hiking stick. Bart was wearing ice cleats over his combat boots, but they were hardly the same as snowshoes. His feet were swallowed with every step.

Julie walked beside him. "How do you know this place?"

Bart only shushed her.

The rustic cabin was a gray square among the hills of white, like a mausoleum of rotted wood in an abandoned cemetery. The thought was fitting, considering what Bart knew about the place. The reclusive man who had lived here was dead. The flagpole was still standing, with the Gadsden flag fluttering in the storm wind, and the *no trespassing* signs also remained. Had the cabin already sold to a new owner—this madwoman? Bart figured a maniac like her was more likely to be a squatter than a landowner.

He was about to tell his squad to fan out, but as he raised his hand to give the order, Bart noticed a trail of footprints going across the property toward the Harding Trail that led downhill. There were several sets of prints in different sizes, all still fresh enough to see the treads of the boots. They were just like the ones left back at the compound.

"They've been here," he said. "But now they're gone."

Julie followed the footprints with her eyes. "They're trying to get off the mountain."

"Oh, fuck," Wylder said. "We've gotta catch up with them before that happens."

"Yeah, no shit."

As Bart approached the pit, a vile, burnt meat stink struck him, carried on the remaining wisps of black smoke rising out of the hole. He was so focused on this that he failed to see the tripwire until he'd hit it. The braided fishing line pulled taught, and Bart flinched, expecting a small detonation or spring trap to fill him with spikes. But nothing happened. He looked up at the cabin, realizing he'd set off an alarm, nothing more.

Quin and Paul hadn't been as lucky.

When Bart reached the pit, he saw the charred remains of his soldiers beneath the fallen snow. He bit his fist. The death of Quin was particularly hard to take, for their friendship went back decades. Even with what Wylder had told him, Bart struggled to understand what had happened here. Had the pit been filled with landmines? Had the woman doused the men in gasoline and tossed down grenades or Molotov cocktails? Just what kind of artillery was she packing? And just how dangerous was she? That she'd taken out this many men with such cruelty indicated she was not to be underestimated.

"Bart," Julie said. "We can mourn them later. Right now, we need to avenge them. All of them. Especially Charlie."

The image of his son's leg being blown off returned to Bart's mind. He wished he hadn't watched the video. It would replay in his mind the rest of his life on a horrible marathon. It would intrude upon better memories of his son, like Bart teaching Charlie how to ride a bike or the time the whole family had gone to Disney World. Now when Bart thought of his only child, the first thing that would come to his mind would be that Charlie had been eaten alive by a woodchipper. He'd died screaming in agony, and somehow, Bart felt it was his fault, though he wasn't sure exactly how or why.

If he'd only run things differently. If he'd not allowed Charlie to be part of the team and kept him away from the compound, his son

THE OLD LADY

would be alive. And if Bart hadn't set the rule about no cellphones being allowed on base for security reasons, the men could have contacted him before this whole situation had gotten way out of hand. Even old flip phones without GPS signals had been banned because it was too easy for the lines to be unsecure, and Bart had banished landlines because they could be tapped. He believed in thorough precautions, but perhaps these rules had been a detriment to the safety of his crew and only son.

Looking upon the cabin, Bart debated breaking inside, even though the footprints made it obvious the woman and teenagers had fled. He almost raised the assault rifle to shoot at the place, just to vent some of his rage, but decided against it. He didn't want to give their position away to anyone in earshot, and also worried about the contents of the cabin. There could be explosives inside that would be set off by gunfire. And there were bound to be more boobytraps.

He turned to Wylder. "Go look in the window."

Wylder gazed at him stupidly, his mouth open. "But... you said they were gone."

"Well, I want to be sure. Now go look."

"Boss, I—"

Bart invaded Wylder's person space. When he spoke, spittle flew from his mouth onto Wylder's cheek. "Maybe you forgot you're the one who got us into this mess, but I haven't! Now look inside, damn it, or you're going in the pit with poor Paul and Quin!"

Wylder gulped and looked at the others. Regina wore an expression of sympathy, and her husband couldn't look Wylder's way at all. Julie had raised her mask and now smiled at him, but her eyes were dark and dead. Because he needed one hand free to support himself on the hiking stick, Wylder was unable to handle heavy artillery, and only carried a Glock 45—a small, lightweight version of the pistol. Bart had told him it was more than enough for a real man to be able to handle himself.

Drawing the Glock from his clip-on holster, Wylder limped toward the cabin. Bart could almost feel the young man's sweat. The last time Wylder was here, he had been shot and his teammates were killed. Coming back only to be forced to peek in the window was bound to fill him with terror, and that's exactly what Bart wanted. The little prick deserved to be punished, and if by some chance the woman was inside and blew Wylder's head off, Bart would only have lost what he now considered his most expendable soldier.

"Boss, I'm worried there's gonna be another trap," Wylder said as he approached the porch.

"We're about to find out," Bart said.

Regina whispered to him. "Bart, c'mon…"

Bart didn't even look at her. He only watched Wylder as the young man gingerly stepped upon the first of the stairs. Nothing happened, and Wylder put his foot on the second stair. A loud noise boomed. In a panic, Wylder fell backward and landed on his ass in the snow. Bart and the rest of the team flinched and backed away, but soon relaxed when they realized it was just an airhorn. Bart sighed in aggravation. Wylder had set off an alarm, one that could be heard a mile away. This gave away their position, telling the woman and kids exactly where the team was.

Infuriated, Bart grabbed a rock at the edge of the pit, walked toward the cabin, and hurled it at the intact window with all his might. The glass cracked into spiderwebs but didn't burst.

Security window film, Bart thought. This made the glass harder to penetrate and kept the shards in place when they broke, unless they were struck by a barrage of bullets, which he guessed the other window had been.

Too pissed to care about playing it safe anymore, Bart raised his G36 assault rifle and fired four shots at the intact window. Wylder yelped and scurried away like a crab. The window exploded and the ratty curtains fluttered halfway outside.

There was no returning fire.

The airhorn continued to wail but Bart couldn't see the source of it. Grabbing Wylder by the collar, he hoisted him up and shoved the young man back toward the porch.

Bart said nothing. He didn't need to.

Wylder was shaking as he returned to the steps, moving on his tiptoes with his gun raised in one fist and the hiking stick in the other. He moved slowly, a slug in human form.

"Today, Wylder," Bart snapped. "You're wasting valuable time."

If someone was here, they would have shot at us by now, Bart thought.

Pale and wild-eyed, Wylder jumped in front of the window, glass crunching beneath his boots, and fired twice into the opening before looking inside. He brushed the curtains aside with the barrel of the Glock and peered through the broken window.

"All clear," he said. "Just a bunch of canned goods and shit."

Looking up, Wylder pointed his pistol at the roof's overhang and

THE OLD LADY

fired. The airhorn went silent as it broke into pieces.

Bart shook his head.

"You okay, boss?" Lance asked.

The leader turned back slowly and looked upon his crew with hard eyes.

"No," Bart said. "No, I'm not. But I know what will make me feel better."

Leaving the property, Bart followed the trail of footprints, leading his vengeful army into the cold embrace of the woods below.

TWENTY-SIX

TRACEY REPEATEDLY WENT THROUGH THE mental checklist of the supplies in their bags. Though the trip down Harding Trail normally wouldn't require such extensive gear, the dire situation they were in could add hours to the journey. They might have to hide from their pursuers, go far off the trail, or be forced to settle somewhere overnight. One of them could get injured or they might get split up. Anything could happen, and in Tracey's experience, if something could go wrong, it did.

First, there was sustenance and hydration. The group had two water bladders, some high calorie protein bars, and water purification tablets. For light, there were LED flashlights and a few twelve-hour glow sticks. She opted not to bother with flares, as they would be too intense and give away their position to the enemy. For comfort in the cold, there were body warmer patches, blankets, and the tube tent in her BOB. She allowed Alicia to keep the balaclava, but the girl was wearing her winter cap now, the mask tucked in her pocket. There was a wide variety of tools—Tracey's compass, a long rope, a compact entrenchment shovel and pick combo, a first aid kit, card multi-tools, and her Zippo. She'd also made sure Alicia had the ferrocerium

THE OLD LADY

rod she'd picked out just for her, with the glow-in-the-dark compass. Tracey had also modified this rod with a special feature, which she kept secret for now.

For weaponry, Tracey had her Mossberg Maverick shotgun, the Ruger 10/22 rifle, and her massive hunting knife. Tucked in her BOB was the loaded .38 snub nose, some of the metal shivs used for spring traps, and three of the small devices her father had kept in the shed. These special devices were the same kind Tracey and her dad used to make together, so she was very familiar with how they operated.

Alicia had the Glock 19, a stun gun, and a pocketknife, with some extra goodies in her backpack, and her conscientious objector boyfriend had the .380 Automatic Colt Pistol. Nori had her machete and the stun gun tucked into her waistband. Tracey kept second guessing whether she should give Nori the .38 revolver too but stuck with her opinion that it would be too much for the child.

The group was well-stocked. The only thing they lacked was a source of communication to the outside world. Tracey had never owned a cellular phone and the kids had been stripped of theirs by the men at the compound. The only tool available that connected them to the outside world was her father's hand crank radio, which was only good to receive weather updates and could not send out transmissions.

Despite the plentiful supplies, Tracey felt unprepared. She kept thinking back to all the gear and goods in the cabin, wondering if she should have packed more. But it was better to travel as light as possible, so not to further slow them down in the snow. The BOBs and bags were packed tight but contained nothing heavy. Even the entrenchment tool was small, collapsible, and lightweight.

The foursome trekked downhill. They tried to stick to the trail, but as Jeff the Civil Engineer had predicted, the path had been blurred by heavy snow and downed trees. Busted branches and thin, frozen streams stemming from a nearby pond made the path especially treacherous and indiscernible. Tracey relied on the miniature compass she kept stashed in the hollowed-out chamber of her hunting knife's handle, along with a few other essentials. And whenever the path became clear again, they would tromp back to it and continue on until they reached another impasse.

The blare of an airhorn froze them in their tracks.

"Shit," Dylan said. "What is that?"

Tracey spoke calmly. "Relax. It's just an alarm."

"What does it mean?" Alicia asked.

"It means someone is on the front porch of my cabin."

Nori gasped. Dylan cursed, a frightened whisper.

"What do we do?" Alicia asked Tracey.

"We haven't heard any vehicles yet," she said, "but that doesn't mean they aren't on some."

"*They?*"

"I seriously doubt Wylder would have come back alone."

"Oh my God…"

"If they're trying to be stealthy, they'll be on foot. That'll buy us some time. And if Wylder is with them, he'll still be struggling with that busted leg and the hole I put in his arm."

Tracey took a deep breath.

"*You should have killed him when you had the chance*," her father's voice grumbled in her brainpan. "*I told you you'd regret it.*"

Trying to ignore him, Tracey bit the inside of her cheek. Sometimes physical pain could drown out psychological. But it wasn't enough to silence the old man today.

"*You let an enemy get away*," Dad said. "*He's still alive. You call that playing to win?*"

Tracey hissed under her breath. "Shut the fuck up."

Alicia heard her and gave Tracey a puzzled look. "What?"

"Nothing. Let's just keep moving. We'll go off trail and follow the compass. Stay hidden in the woods."

Tracey didn't wait for the kids to say anything else. She held out her compass, heading southwest through the thicket, boots crushing the dead vegetation that rose through the snow in defiant wisps. Moving cautiously down the slanted hillside, she braced herself on trees and got low to hold on to jagged boulders, keeping her balance as she descended. She turned her head to check on the kids. They were still following her. Alicia looked up at Tracey, her soft eyes fraught with worry, seeming to beg Tracey for answers she just didn't have and promises of safety she couldn't guarantee.

The sound of gunfire startled them. Tracey squatted and waved at the kids to get low to the ground. The girls whimpered. The boy whispered "oh fuck" repeatedly until Tracey shushed him. Shotgun clenched in her fists, Tracey listened, scanning the forest for any sign of movement, but after the shots were fired, there was only the sound of the airhorn still howling. Still she kept the kids frozen in place, squatting in the slush and ice, gripping weapons they barely knew how

THE OLD LADY

to use.

Another shot rang out and the airhorn went silent.

"They're coming," Tracey's father told her. *"They're coming and you're not ready."*

She nearly snapped back at him but couldn't find the words because her father was right. There was more to getting away than just running, and on this terrain, they couldn't run at all, only baby step down the vertical hinterland. Hanging her head, she struggled with feelings of defeat, of impending death. Tracey breathed deep to resituate her state of mind, but her father continued to criticize.

"You never do anything right," he said, *"and then you wonder why you always get into jams like this."*

Tracey gritted her teeth against him.

"Goddamnit, girl. You know what to do! I taught you better than this."

Glowering, Tracey slowly rose to her feet. "Alright."

The teenagers looked up at her. But she hadn't been talking to them. Tracey did another scan of the woods, devising a plan of action. She spotted a small, trickling stream, half-frozen with clumps of ice. It ran down the mountain, and she followed it with her eyes until it became too hard to discern. Drawing her binoculars, she found the stream again in the distance, and spotted a clearing and a flat, white surface. She double-checked her compass, making sure this destination wouldn't take them too far off track. It was southbound. If they could make it there and cut back west, they would eventually cross over to the trail again.

"Look here," she told the kids, pointing to the trickle between the rocks. "This stream leads to a pond, maybe a hundred yards away. I want you three to head down there."

Nori furrowed her brow. "Without you?"

"I need to set up a few things. You three stay hidden in the woods and follow the stream. Alicia, use your compass to stay on track. When you reach the pond, wait for me there, but don't wait too long. You may hear a commotion. If I'm gone more than thirty minutes or if you hear someone other than me getting closer, take off and head southwest."

"A pond?" Alicia asked, looking confused. "On a mountain?"

"It's not that uncommon. It's really a depression in the rock big enough to have become a pond."

"Tracey…" Alicia said but found no words to follow.

"I'll be fine. Just go on before they get any closer, and let me do what I have to do."

"*What you were born to do,*" her dad said.

Alicia nodded but her body language revealed her reluctance. She drew the ferrocerium rod from her pocket, keeping its compass upright in her hand. She flinched when Tracey took her wrist.

"Whatever you do," Tracey said. "Do *not* lose this rod. Understand me?"

Alicia nodded again. "Yeah. Okay."

Tracey released the girl and titled her head toward the pond in the distance. "Get going."

As the teens came together, Nori looked back at Tracey with haunted eyes.

"Thank you," the young girl said.

Tracey didn't reply. She didn't know how. And so she just watched the kids as they followed the trickling stream, her daughter leading them with the compass. A dull ache went through Tracey as she realized she was leaving Olivia all over again, still refusing to say a proper goodbye. When she remembered the girl was not her daughter, it hardly lessened Tracey's grief. The sick feeling of being unloved flooded her senses, a cruel reminder that she would always be alone. If she were to die today, would anyone even mourn her? Her ex-husband Gavin and their daughter must have moved on by now. Tracey certainly hoped so, for that had been her goal all along. She'd wanted her family to be safe from harm and knew that, despite her being in prison at the time, the greatest threat to Gavin and Olivia would always be her. At the expense of her own heart, Tracey had pushed them away until they could no longer reach her. It was the hardest gift she'd ever had to give. Even fighting for these kids' lives was easy by comparison.

"Focus," she told herself.

Tracey started back the way they'd come, hiking uphill until she reached a section that was clearly part of Harding Trail. Sling her BOB off, she fished out the entrenchment shovel and one of the devices she'd taken from her father's shed.

Just holding one of them again made the tiny hairs on her body rise in salute.

"*Atta girl,*" her father said as she started digging.

~

Wylder was slowing them down.

Now that he'd led them to the cabin, his usefulness was spent, so

THE OLD LADY

Bart told him to wait there in case the woman returned, though he did not expect her to. Wylder seemed relieved, which irked Bart, but he let the minion stay behind anyway. Julie, Regina, and Lance joined him as he headed downhill, following the footprints to Harding Trail.

Lance held his .44 Magnum in both hands, pointing it at the ground, but Bart knew the big man would be ready to raise it if he heard so much as a snapping twig. Julie carried her assault rifle pressed to her chest, like a soldier at ease. But Regina kept her AK47 high to her shoulder with her finger on the trigger guard, her auburn hair pulled back in a bun tight enough to forge a diamond from coal.

Observing the woman, Bart was reminded of how she'd rejected him. A few weeks ago, while Lance was out buying more fertilizer with Quin and Wylder, and Paul was at his day job and Charlie had gone to see the latest Marvel movie, Bart had finally been alone in the ranch house with Regina and decided to make the play he'd been fantasizing about.

Bart was the troop leader now and had been struggling to get Regina to respect that. The woman wasn't nearly as obsequious as the others. She always seemed to be questioning his orders and got pissy when he refused to budge. At first, he'd taken this insolence as a sign she was outraged that he'd been next in line for commander, that she was jealous, as if a woman could ever lead them. But based on the subtle signals he'd observed from her—the sideways glances; the way she puffed her chest out when challenging him; how she sometimes pulled him aside to talk to him privately about the mission—he'd begun to think she was as physically attracted to him as he was to her. Despite all her behavioral problems, Regina was fit and had the sort of long legs that made Bart foam. And a large part of his desire was based in wanting to dominate her sexually, to show her and her body who was boss. He'd even come to convince himself that it was exactly what Regina needed—an older man who could take control of her the way her husband never could.

But Bart had been wrong.

On the day they were alone, Bart had advanced on Regina in the kitchen, coming up behind her as she washed dishes. He put his hands between her arms and body and scooped her ample breasts in his hands. Regina gasped and twisted around. Believing she was into it, Bart reached down and cupped her crotch, rubbing the tight jeans and claiming that pussy as his own. It was one of his many fantasies about being the leader of this outfit. He often daydreamed about bringing on more people, especially women, so he could turn this team into a family of sorts, with him filling the role of cult leader, giving him full access to every female member.

Regina knocked that fantasy out of Bart's head by slapping him across the face. She didn't slap like a huffy woman either. Regina smashed her hand against his cheek with the force of a man. The whole left side of his head panged with sharp tingles, his jaw rocking from the impact. Bart bent sideways, and when he righted himself and looked at Regina, she whacked him again, making his left ear ring.

"Don't ever touch me, you son of a bitch!" she said.

Seeing Regina's scowl, all the domination Bart had lusted after dissipated.

"I'm sorry," he said. "I read you wrong."

"I'm a married woman, Bart. And even if I wasn't, groping me like that wouldn't be the right move to make."

It wasn't like Bart to apologize, but he did so again. "I'm sorry, Regina. Really, I am." He needed to make this right for the sake of the mission, so he dug up an excuse. "I've been lonely a long time, having lost my wife. Somehow, I got it in my mind that you… that you wanted me too."

Regina looked upon him as one did a pathetic creature. "You need a girlfriend, Bart, but I ain't it. I *love* my husband. I am bound to him, just like I'm bound to our cause. You should respect both of these things too."

"I do."

"Oh, really? Funny way to show respect for Lance by grabbing his wife's tits and shoving your hand into—"

"For Christ's sake, Regina, I said I was sorry. I fucked up. I admit it. It was a stupid mistake, and I won't make it again."

Regina narrowed her eyes. "You swear it to me?"

He nodded. "On my wife's grave."

Regina looked away, sucking in her bottom lip. She made Bart wait for her next words, digging in the wound.

"I ought to tell Lance," she said.

"Regina—"

"But I ain't gonna." She looked Bart in the eyes again. "He's a proud man, and he respects you… for some reason. If he knew what happened here it would crush him, and he'd want out. It would blow the whole mission. My husband and I have worked too hard on this to bow out now."

THE OLD LADY

Bart exhaled with relief. "You're making the right decision."

"Yeah, we'll see."

"So, we're going to pretend this never happened?"

"Yeah, but it *did* happen, and you'd best not forget it. You pull anything like that with me again and I'll—"

"I know. Trust me, it won't happen again."

Regina eyed him, then shook her head as if she were fed up with a misbehaving child. "From now on, think with your big head, not your little one. All that's important is that we achieve what we've come together to do. You'd be best to keep that in mind."

Bart offered a smile. "Yes, ma'am. You are right at that."

Regina didn't smile back, but she was true to her word and kept her silence.

Looking at her now as they marched through the snow, the desire to slam her to the ground and fuck her hard returned to Bart, as it often did. It was not just sexual arousal, but also a craving to pay her back for her harsh words. But when Regina realized he was looking at her, Bart turned away. He hated to admit she was right, but he did need to focus on the mission. But first, he had to dominate the one woman who'd pissed him off more than Regina ever could.

The Old Lady.

That's what Wylder referred to her as, but judging by all she'd done, Bart expected the woman to be over thirty but under sixty. If Wylder saw her as old, she was probably around fifty, which was still several years younger than Bart was. These days, sixty was the new forty—or at least, that's what people in their sixties said. Bart, on the other hand, was dreading the fast-approaching milestone.

Lance hopped over a decayed log, and his momentum hurried him down the slope until it leveled out again. Bart wondered what Regina saw in the tubby redhead. At thirty-five, Lance was twenty-three years younger than Bart, but was in worse physical shape. Even now he was breathing heavy from the hike, even though it was all downhill. At his age, Bart's knees and hips ached from this freezing journey, but he still moved with more grace than the ginger.

Bart still respected Lance, despite his failed effort to cuckhold him. The lumberjack was a loyal, sycophantic soldier who worked harder than anyone else on the team, but his ever-expanding waist size had become a concern. Once this was over, Bart would have to start a dialogue with him about a weight loss plan. It would behoove everyone if the fat man stripped away a few layers of flab.

Bart stepped over the log and the women followed. As they reached the level area of the trail, Lance kept walking but looked back at them to speak.

"I think if we—"

Lance's words were cut short as he was blown up.

The detonation came from the ground below his right foot, a hot burst of flame, sparks, and smoke. The big man screamed as his leg was mutilated by the blast, dropping him into the snow. Regina screamed. Julie got down, her rifle raised as she frantically looked in every direction.

"Jesus," Bart said.

He scanned the dense thicket with the butt of his assault rifle pressed against his shoulder, gazing down the barrel, hoping for any sign of a life he could snub out.

Crying her husband's name, Regina went to the fallen soldier.

Lance rolled onto his back, revealing the damage in full. The front of his calf was exposed, his pants shredded, a black burn running from his ankle to his hip. His boot was ripped apart, exposing the toes he'd lost in the blast. The stink of roasted human flesh rose from his body in a grotesque perfume, combining with the odors of sulfur and gunpowder. Lance was covered in shrapnel—not just pieces of the device that had gone off, but shrapnel that must have been deliberately inserted into the homemade landmine. He was now like a bloody pincushion, his flesh pocked with ball bearings, nails, darts, and the other jagged pieces of metal that had been shoved into his body by the force of the explosion. If not for the man's size, Bart and the women would have been hit with the projectiles too, but Lance's large frame was just enough to shield the others.

Lance moaned. When he blinked his eyes open, Bart saw a razor blade had gone into the lumberjack's right eyebrow, the wound dribbling blood into his eye. His face was pierced with several more blade shards, with long cuts torn into his cheeks. Part of his earlobe was missing. His coat had protected him from the minor pieces, but much of the heavy shrapnel had torn right through his clothes, and his torso wept red.

"Oh my God," Regina said as she squatted over her punctured husband. "Oh my God, oh my God, oh my God."

Bart didn't have the heart to tell her to shut up.

He looked at Julie. "Cover us."

Julie continued to stare down the barrel of her Heckler & Koch,

THE OLD LADY

watching the woods for movement. Bart squatted beside Regina, placed his rifle in the snow, and examined Lance closer. His right leg looked like loose, burnt hamburger meat, but it hadn't been severed and Bart couldn't see bone. Hunks of twisted metal decorated the limb like a Christmas tree, screws and nails wedged into his singed thigh.

"Can you move?" Bart asked.

Lance groaned and shivered, not answering, perhaps unable to. Shock could be setting in.

"We need to get you up and back to the compound," Bart said.

Regina held her husband's blood-spattered hand. "We're gonna need a stretcher."

Julie spoke up. "We don't have a stretcher. Not even back at the house."

"Well then we can build one!"

"We need to address these wounds fast," Bart said. "Anyone have first aid supplies?"

But he knew no one did, and the women confirmed this.

"Lance?" he said. "Can you hear me?"

Lance moaned. "Bart…" He fluttered his eyelids. "I can't see!"

"Relax, there's just some blood in your eye. Can you move?"

Lance raised his good arm and cleared the blood from his eye socket, winking at the ashen sky above. Bart tucked his hands under the big man's back, and together they got him to sit up. Lance winced and the cuts on his face dribbled. When he looked down at the multiple piercings in his body, he murmured in fright.

"It's okay, honey," Regina said. "Everything's gonna be alright."

Bart doubted it. He removed his coat, then his sweater, and then put his coat back on. Using his pocketknife, he tore strips of cloth from the sweater to use as gauze. He nursed the leg first, it being the most decimated. Making a tourniquet to stop the access blood flow, he tightened it by turning the pocketknife's handle in the cloth before tying the knot. Bart and Regina removed some of the loose pieces of shrapnel from Lance's wounds but were hesitant to yank out the parts imbedded deep. Fears of blood poisoning and accidentally breaking off smaller pieces inside of Lance caused Bart to sweat as he did his best to stop the bleeding. He opened Lance's coat and shirt, and then tried to wrap the sleeve torn from his sweater around the wound below Lance's belly button, but the lumberjack's waist was too big. Regina removed her coat and sweater too. Bart chopped the sweater up, and they tied all the sleeves together to form a belt that pressurized the hole in Lance's lower belly. Just as the man's size had shielded Bart and the others, his blubber had absorbed much of the shrapnel, sparing his organs.

They got the lumberjack to his feet, Bart and Regina bracing him on both sides. Lance cringed when he tried to put weight on his bad leg. He wobbled, blinking rapidly as he tried to maintain consciousness.

"Christ, Bart," Regina said. "He can't walk like this. What're we gonna do?"

Bart considered their options. It didn't take long because he didn't have time to weigh them all. The woman was still out there and could be watching them right now, waiting for the right moment to open fire. More likely, she and the kids could be using this time to gain ground and make their escape.

"Lance," Bart said. "Lance, look at me."

The big man turned his head toward Bart. "Yeah, boss?"

"I know you're in pain, but I need you to suck it up so you and Regina can get up that hill." He pointed back the way they'd come. "You go up there and get back to where we left Wylder at the cabin. He can help you guys the rest of the way back to home base."

"*Wylder?*" Regina asked, incredulous. "But he can barely walk either. How is he—"

Lance interrupted his wife. "I can do it."

"Honey—"

"We gotta do it."

"No! Bart and Julie should help us get up there and return to base."

Lance objected before Bart could. "We can't do that. That old bitch and her kids are still runnin' 'round out there. We let 'em get away, and we're all as good as dead, and so's the mission. Bart and Julie gotta go after her."

Regina's face wrinkled. "But, honey, you're—"

"I know," Lance grunted, easing some of his weight onto his mangled foot, keeping what remained of his sweater-wrapped toes pointed up. "I'm a big ol' mess. But I couldn't live with myself if that bunch got away and ruined everything. I'd rather limp back to base than have everybody carry me. Better I suffer than put the whole outfit at risk."

Lance took a bold step forward. His face went tight with pain, and

THE OLD LADY

he screamed as he fell back. Bart got behind him just in time for he and Regina to keep the big man from hitting the ground. Lance closed his eyes, and then they snapped back open as if he'd been jolted by an electric shock.

"He can't do this," Regina said through tears.

Bart ran his hand over his mustache. "Okay, new plan. Regina, you go up and fetch Wylder, and bring him back down here to help you with Lance. There may not be a stretcher in the cabin, but there must be a sled or a big piece of plywood, some ropes or *something* you can use to haul Lance uphill."

"You go," she said. "I'm staying right here with my husband."

"You don't understand, Regina. No one is staying here with Lance. You go get Wylder. Julie and I must keep after these people we've been hunting."

Her face twisted in anger. "You son of a bitch…"

"Listen to me. Hell, listen to your husband! Those kids get to the police, and we're finished."

"I am not letting him out of my sight!"

"If we don't stop them from getting to the cops, you and Lance will spend the rest of your lives in separate prisons. Then you'll *never* see him again."

He let that sink in. Tears cascaded down Regina's pained face as she turned pink. Bart took hold of Lance and slowly lowered him to the ground, propping him up against a tree trunk. When Regina took his hand in hers, the lumberjack gave her a small smile.

"It's okay, honeybee," he said. "Just do like the boss says."

Regina stopped weeping just long enough to stare up at Bart with eyes like knives. It made him wonder if she regretted not telling her husband what his leader had done to her. Bart had experienced regret about keeping his son in the outfit, which ultimately led to his death. It only made sense that Regina might be having similar regrets, wishing she'd told Lance the truth so they would have left the compound for good. If they had, her husband wouldn't be a human corkboard right now.

Regina kissed a clean spot on her husband's forehead. "I'll be right back, darlin'. I swear it."

"I'll be here," he said with a chuckle that was clearly more for her benefit than anything else.

As Regina got to her feet, she clutched her rifle with white-knuckled fists and glared at Bart and his cousin. It was a look that carried more loathing than words ever could. She sprung forward and bounded up the slope with a speed Bart wouldn't have thought the woman was capable of.

Bart looked down at Lance. His .44 Magnum had fallen in the snow, so Bart picked it up and put it in Lance's good hand. It was his left—not his dominate hand—but the right was too heavily peppered with shards of scrap metal.

"They're going to get you back safe," Bart said, though he wasn't so sure.

Lance leaned his head against the tree and closed his right eye as blood flowed into it again. His remaining eye stared into Bart as if he were digging for the man's soul.

"You just make sure my Regina is okay," Lance said. "I can't take the idea of her rottin' in prison. So you blow a hole in that old lady's head as big as a half dollar, boss."

Bart nodded at his fallen soldier. "Rest assured, I won't stop until she's dead or I am."

Standing up, Bart readied his weapon, nodded at Julie, and the two of them proceeded down the trail, watching every footfall to avoid any other landmine pipe bombs.

~

Flat on her stomach with binoculars to her eyes, Tracey watched the show from the treeline. When the obese man drew closer to the circular bomb she'd covered with snow and dirt, she held her breath, hoping the device wasn't too old to function properly. But when the man stepped down onto the trigger button, the match heads inside the device were pushed forward, striking the coarse flint, and igniting the smokeless powder and potassium nitrate. The weighted plate erupted in a geyser of merciless metal bits, dropping the victim but unfortunately not killing him upon impact. It was possible her father had coated the darts and razors with a toxic compound, but she couldn't be sure, and therefore couldn't be sure if the man would die from his injuries. But watching him try to stand, Tracey smiled, knowing that if he survived this, he'd still spend the rest of his life limping in pain.

"Suck on that, you fat fuck."

Through her binoculars, she'd watched the group of four come down the trail. If not for their heavy artillery, she wouldn't have been sure they were the ones that were after her and the children. But they had assault rifles, including one that looked like an AK47, which had

THE OLD LADY

been the Viet Cong's weapon of choice during the war. Obviously, hunters wouldn't need that kind of firepower, and wouldn't be out in this shitty weather anyway. Wylder was not among this group, but he'd been similarly dressed and armed. Tracey was certain this crew was her new enemy. Two men and, surprisingly, two women. Judging by his mannerisms, the gray-haired man seemed to be in charge.

Having traded out the shotgun for her .22 rifle, Tracey propped herself on her elbows and steadied her aim, but she was far away, and the tree coverage was thick. If she opened fire, she would give away her position, and would be easily outmatched by the heavily-armed squad.

Tending to the fat man would take the group some time, which Tracey could better spend catching up to the kids. They must have made it to the pond by now.

Crawling downhill until she was sure she was out of sight, Tracey ignored the aches in her bones, her age nagging her. Rising to her feet, she darted through the woodland in a crouch, trying to stay as small a target as possible as she fled from those stalking her. Following the thin stream, she traversed clusters of loose rock and crashed through bramble that tugged at her clothes. She pressed on until the white sheet of the frozen pond appeared. She spotted Alicia and Nori staring out at it with their backs to her, but before Tracey could sigh with relief, her nerves went taut as she saw Dylan walking across the ice.

TWENTY-SEVEN

"I SAY WE BAIL OUT," Dylan said.

Tracey was still up the hill, but they'd just heard an explosion. Alicia's heartbeat accelerated, making her sweat despite the cold.

"We shouldn't leave Tracey behind," Nori said.

Dylan glowered at his little sister. "Don't you understand? The woman is insane. She's dangerous. We're better off getting away from her. We have the compass and all these supplies, right? We stand a better chance of getting out of this now, especially if we keep moving."

Conflicted, Alicia looked to the woods behind them and the land ahead surrounding the pond. The surface of the water was a complete sheet of ice.

"Which way is southwest?" Dylan asked.

Alicia checked the compass on the ferrocerium rod. Leaning over her shoulder, Dylan watched the dial spin beneath the bubble. Southwest lay dead ahead, directly across the pond.

Her boyfriend peered across the ice, biting his lower lip. "I say we cut across the pond, rather than go around it."

Alicia tensed. "Oh, I don't know about that."

THE OLD LADY

"The fastest route is always a straight line. Think of the time we'll save."

"But the ice might break."

Dylan scoffed. "Nah, just look at it. The water is frozen solid. And, like, people skate on this kind of thing all the time." He looked to his sister. "Dad goes ice fishing. It's the same thing."

"We should wait for Tracey," Nori said.

Dylan shook his head at his sister.

"It'd be a lot safer to just go around the pond," Alicia said.

"It'll also take twice as long to get where we need to go," Dylan said. "I want us out of here as soon as possible."

"Even if we get back to the car, we don't even have the keys. We'll need to hitch a ride with Tracey. I really don't think we have any choice but to wait for her."

Dylan sighed. It made Alicia uneasy because she knew how impatient he could be, and how impulsive. Sometimes Dylan didn't think things through before he acted, especially in stressful situations, and this was the most anxiety-inducing experience of their young lives.

"If we cut across quickly," he said, "and get to the parking lot, there's a sign there, remember? With a big map showing where all the trails go? We can use that to find the nearest ranger's station, where we can get help, and get a ride with someone less dangerous."

Alicia hadn't thought of that. The plan was promising but flawed.

"Any trail to the ranger station will be just as wrecked as Harding Trail," she said. "And we don't know just how far away one might be. All of that will keep us in the woods longer, giving the people hunting us more of a chance to track us down."

Her boyfriend stared across the pond. "I'll go then."

"What?"

"I'll go on my own. I can get help and—"

"We can't split up! Are you crazy?"

Nori tugged her brother's sleeve. "Dylan, no..."

"We need to do *something*," he insisted. "Let me just test out the ice, okay? See if we can cut across it. I'll bet we can."

The girls tried to reason with him, but Dylan stepped onto the ice anyway, still carrying the bag Tracey had given him, the Colt pistol tucked into his waistband. He stepped cautiously, careful not to slip, his arms extended for balance. Alicia watched for any hairline fractures, but the ice held beneath his weight. Unlike Dylan's ice fishing father, they had no drill to test the ice's durability, and none of them knew enough about frozen ponds to test it any other way than how Dylan was now. Alicia didn't ice skate or play hockey, so she wasn't sure how many inches thick ice needed to be to support the average person. The ice appeared white, but she wasn't sure if that was good or bad. That her boyfriend was taking gentle steps did little to ease her worry, but he continued several feet further without any trouble.

Suddenly, Alicia's attention was drawn away by a rustle in the brush behind her. She raised her pistol in shaky hands, then lowered it when she saw the top of Tracey's grayed head within the dead shrubbery. The woman was moving quickly.

"Dylan!" Tracey yelled for him without raising her voice too high, trying to remain stealthy, which told Alicia the hunters were nearby. "Dylan, get off the ice!"

Either the wind on the pond was loud enough to drown her out, or Dylan simply ignored her. He took another step, putting him a good six yards from the shore. He took a step further, advancing to nineteen feet away. Tracey called his name louder, but it was too late.

There was an intense snapping sound just before Dylan disappeared.

Falling through the ice, he went all the way under, his head dunking beneath the dark surface. Alicia jumped. Nori shrieked. As Dylan returned to the surface, gasping for air and flailing his arms, Tracey cursed and flung off her backpack, unzipped one of the pouches, and dug out a rope.

"Help!" Dylan shouted from the freezing pit.

Tracey tied the end of the rope into a loop.

"Dumb son of bitch," she muttered. "I knew he'd fuck things up."

Alicia wasn't sure if Tracey was talking to her and Nori or just herself.

She wasn't sure of anything anymore.

~

Wrapping the other end of the rope around the nearest tree, Tracey came to the edge of the pond and swung the other end of the rope—the one with the loop—over her head like a rodeo cowboy.

She shouted at the flailing boy as she hurled the rope across the water. "Grab on!"

Fortunately, the rope was long enough to reach Dylan while still being secured to the tree with a knot of two half hitches. At the edge of the ice, Tracey managed the middle of the rope with both hands. The girls stood on either side of her, watching Dylan with wild eyes.

THE OLD LADY

The boy reached for the rope and missed, breaking away more ice. Watching him writhe in panic made Tracey wince. It was as if the kid were deliberately doing everything wrong. It almost made her want to let him drown and turn into a popsicle, but that would only upset the girls and make them harder to manage. She also supposed being an inexperienced fool at seventeen wasn't enough to earn Dylan a premature death, so she called out to him again, telling him to grab hold of the loop, which she'd designed to be a handle. He made a few desperate lunges for it before finally snatching the rope.

Tracey started pulling. Realizing what she was doing, Alicia and Nori joined her like a tug-of-war team.

"Hang on tight!" Alicia called out to her boyfriend, a little too loud for Tracey's comfort.

The boy came closer, chunks of ice breaking away from his path, but he hit a stiff section that stopped him in place.

"Pull yourself onto it!" Tracey said. "Roll out!"

The boy grabbed the rope tight and heaved but wasn't strong enough to get out of the water.

"Break the ice!" Tracey said.

Dylan tucked the rope under his arm, still holding the loop, and bashed the frozen surface with his fist. He yelped when the ice resisted.

"The gun!" Alicia yelled out to him. "Use the butt of the gun!"

Dylan reached down, drawing the Colt from his waistband, and began using it like a hammer. He successfully broke through a segment, but as he tried to shatter the next sheet, his arms slipped on the surface, and he dropped the gun so he could grab the rope with both hands. The pistol sunk into the murky water and was gone.

"Pull harder," Tracey told the girls. "On three."

They counted down and drew their shoulders back, using all their upper body strength and bending their knees, and Dylan came out onto the ice, up past his waist, then planted a knee and drew himself out, rolling onto his side.

He was less than ten feet away now.

Tracey pulled, hand over hand, and the girls copied her technique until Dylan was back upon the shore.

He was already blue. Before the girls could dote on him, Tracey put her hands on the boy's right leg and shoulder.

"I'm gonna roll you," she said. "Don't fight it."

She pushed his body, rolling him in the fluffy snow.

"*What're you doing?*" Nori asked. "He's already freezing!"

"I'm blotting him. The snow will absorb the water on his jacket."

The coat was somewhat waterproof, but unfortunately, Dylan's jeans wouldn't benefit from anything but drying. But at least the boy was breathing. While out there, he'd seemed to remain conscious, but Tracey knew how intensely cold water could put a drowning victim in a bizarre state of suspended animation, reducing the need for oxygen and halting respiration. The body forced blood to the organs that needed it most, preventing brain damage for up to forty minutes. They'd gotten him out quickly. Their biggest concern now was hypothermia.

After blotting him with snow, Tracey went for the boy's boots.

"Alicia," she said, "untie his other one."

They got his boots off, and Tracey stamped them into the fluffy snow to blot them. She removed his socks, then undid his belt and zipper. As she started stripping his lower body, underwear and all, Dylan resisted.

"Don't fight it," she told him again.

"Are you sure he should take his clothes off?" Nori asked, looking away so not to see her brother's privates.

"We need to get him dry—fast. His clothes are soaked through. In this weather they'll freeze solid, and so will he." She looked at Nori, who was still wearing the extra layer of clothes Tracey had given her. "Take that layer off."

Nori removed the snow pants and top. Tracey and Alicia stripped Dylan nude as he shivered to the point of convulsion, his lips already the color of blueberries.

"Tracey," Alicia said in a whimper. "What do we—"

"Take off your clothes," Tracey told her.

The girl blinked in confusion. "What?"

"We can't build a fire. The smoke will give away our position. We must get him warm."

"But what does—"

"You're his girlfriend, aren't you?"

Alicia furrowed her brow. "Yeah."

Tracey turned to Nori. "Get the heat patches out of my backpack. They're in the uppermost pouch." Nori went for it and Tracey returned her attention to Alicia. "I'm gonna wrap him in blankets with the heat patches. You're gonna get naked and lay in there with him, and I'll pack you two in like a burrito. Put his feet between your legs

THE OLD LADY

and his hands in your armpits."

Alicia flushed; from embarrassment or from the cold, Tracey couldn't be sure.

"Hurry," Tracey said before the girl could think of anything to say.

As Alicia disrobed down to her bra and panties, Nori returned with the heat patches and Tracey applied them to the shivering boy's torso and told Nori to fetch one of the blankets from her BOB, then opened Alicia's backpack for another. The second was the emergency blanket with the silvery, waterproof exterior and thick fabric on the inside. She placed the regular blanket inside of it for an additional layer, then lifted Dylan and placed him on the center of the pile.

When she was ready, Alicia laid on top of him, stomach to stomach, and hissed when her warm body touched her boyfriend's cold flesh. Tracey maneuvered the blankets around the kids, Alicia stuffed Dylan's hands and feet as instructed, and Tracey and Nori tucked them in, cocooning them. Through the blankets, Tracey rubbed her hands up and down the boy's back to create friction, and Nori did the same to his legs. Alicia whispered to her boyfriend that he was going to be okay. Dylan shook like puppy left out in the rain, but they'd tended to him quickly, so Tracey figured Alicia just might be telling him the truth. They might just be able to keep him from getting the umbles—grumbling, mumbling, stumbling, and fumbling—and other effects of hypothermia. That he was shivering was a good sign. It meant his heat regulation systems were still functioning.

But they couldn't stay here like this very long. They had to keep moving. Tracey removed her boots and waterproof socks. The boy's boots wouldn't have time to dry, and even wrung out his socks were now useless, but she could give him her socks to keep his feet relatively dry in his damp boots.

Tracey would just go without socks.

It was the best she could offer, and the sacrifices she continued to make for these kids surprised her.

I knew he'd fuck everything up, she thought again.

That's why she'd given the important things to Alicia.

By losing his bag to the pond—as well as the .380 Colt pistol—Dylan had robbed the group of glow sticks, snacks, and other supplies, but not the essentials. And not the ferrocerium rod, which Tracey saw Alicia had secured to her wrist by the cloth tie at the end of the tool.

That's my girl, Tracey thought.

TWENTY-EIGHT

SNOOPING THROUGH THE CABIN, WYLDER marveled at the extensive supplies. It was as if he were standing inside an aboveground bomb shelter, a shack designed for the aftermath of the apocalypse. With the woman gone, he would have to come back here when he was healed up, and swipe some of this gear. The team could use this kind of backstock at the compound.

It was almost a shame he and the woman had gotten off on the wrong foot. She might have made for an excellent recruit, with her survival skills, weapons expertise, and tendencies toward the prepper lifestyle. Wylder wondered how long she'd been living here. Did she sustain herself in this doomsday adobe, living off the land in isolation like some female Ted Kaczynski? Did she share some of the Unabomber's views?

It didn't matter now. After what she'd done to his fellow team members, the old lady was marked for death. And those teenagers were similarly sentenced. Wylder knew Bart well enough to predict the man's wrath, which would be callous and merciless in avenging his son. Wylder would be glad to see it happen too. For all Charlie's blunders, Wylder had considered him a friend as well as a

THE OLD LADY

teammate—much more so than Paul, who'd been a foreigner, and Quin, the fuddy-duddy. Being close to the same age, Wylder had bonded more with Charlie, and he lamented his failure to protect his buddy. If he'd taken out the old lady during their gunfight, Charlie would be alive, and would probably be nailing that little Chinese girl right now. Wylder and Charlie had often joked about wanting to be rapists for hire. They'd also commiserated over how hard it was to get girls these days.

"Why do you think mass shootings are an epidemic?" Wylder had once asked his friend. "Women aren't women anymore, and men are mad as hell, and we're not gonna take it any longer."

"Yeah," Charlie had agreed. "This used to be our country."

"Want to get rid of incels? Want to drastically reduce the amount of mass shootings in this country? Then either teach girls to not be such selfish, stuck-up bitches or legalize prostitution."

"Wow, man," Charlie said with a smile. "That's fuckin' brilliant. You know, I've used an escort here and there, but they're so damned expensive. Plus, they're risky. If it were legal, it'd be cheaper, and I wouldn't have to worry about getting arrested and embarrassing my old man."

"And better still, we wouldn't have to put up with women's bullshit. For less than it would cost to take them on a bunch of dates only to *maybe* get laid, we just pay a set fee and get the pussy we need and deserve."

Wylder still believed that, amongst other opinions people claimed were misogynistic, and he vowed that once the teen girls were captured, he would fuck them both in Charlie's honor, and do it with a cruelty preternatural even to rapists. Payback would be kinky.

The sound of footsteps on the front porch gave him a start. He snatched his Glock and pointed it toward the hole where the front window used to be.

"Wylder? You in there?"

He recognized Regina's voice and lowered his pistol.

"C'mon in," he said.

Regina entered alone, her face puffy and wet from crying.

"Jesus, you okay?" Wylder asked. "Where is everybody?"

Regina sniffed. "It's Lance."

Then she told him all that had happened, and what they had to do.

"Holy shit," Wylder said. "This bitch has *landmines*?"

"Some sort of homemade pipe bomb, yeah. It was full of nails and darts and stuff." She looked about the cabin with bloodshot eyes. "There must be something here we can use as a sled for Lance. Something we can put him on and drag him back home."

The thought of pulling the fat man back up the mountain made Wylder cringe. He was in enough pain already.

Regina noticed his hesitation. "Unless you think you can get him in a fireman's carry."

"I doubt it. I mean, how much does he weigh?"

"Over three-hundred. But in the shape he's in, it'd probably be too painful for him to be carried that way anyhow." She wiped her eyes with her sleeve. "Fucking Bart. How many more of us have to get wounded or die before our fearless leader ends this?"

Wylder wanted to reiterate that they had to catch the woman, but given his injuries and the rising death toll, he found it hard to argue with Regina.

"I just can't believe one old lady has caused this much damage," he admitted.

"Yeah, well, she's gonna pay for everything she's done to us. Mark my words. Bart and Julie better find her quick." She tightened her eyelids. "If that bitch gets away and my Lance dies, I will hold Bart responsible, and I swear I'll kill the prick myself."

Regina's mutinous attitude shocked Wylder, but given that her husband had been *exploded*, she was bound to be upset with the way things had been handled. Maybe she was right. Maybe Bart didn't know everything. Maybe he wasn't going to lead them to victory in this manhunt. And if he couldn't succeed in this, was he really the best person to lead them on their big mission, the one they'd been working on for months?

"I saw some pallets out back," Regina said, starting toward the door. "Let's see what we can do with one. Maybe find some rope or something."

Wylder followed. "Yeah, okay."

"And let's do it fast. My poor husband is down there all alone... what kind of wife am I?"

But Wylder still wanted to find a way to get Lance to the base without having to give himself a hernia in the process. "Maybe we should go back and get the ATVs and—"

Regina's stare silenced him.

THE OLD LADY

Tracey allowed Alicia to warm Dylan for only twenty minutes—enough to save him from hypothermia, but not as long as would be best for the boy. There was no time. Not only were they being hunted, but sunset came early this time of year, and it was only getting colder.

Alicia redressed and Dylan wore the layer Nori had taken off, along with Tracey's socks and his boots. Taking the balaclava from her pocket, Alicia put it over her boyfriend's head. He wanted to keep the blankets around him like a shawl, but Tracey refused to let him. They would just get caught on twigs and branches, and generally slow him down if they suddenly had to run. Once they'd packed everything up again, Tracey led them around the pond and into the southbound woodland. The snowfall had lightened to flurries and sleet, but off the trails, the accumulated snow reached the middle of her shins. She tromped on, telling the kids to step in her footprints. They marched in silence—miserable, broken, and distraught, sniffling back tears. Tracey knew the kids were developing fresh trauma that would never fully leave them, but she also knew from experience that if they could survive this horrible ordeal, they could survive its memory.

The grayness of the afternoon deepened. Tracey was about to check her compass again when she finally spotted Harding Trail. It was snowed over here, but clear of any serious debris.

"Everyone get low," she whispered.

The kids crouched behind her. Tracey drew her binoculars and scanned the area, wondering if the squad tracking them had continued on the trail or if they'd worked together to get the fat man she'd nuked back to safety. Some of them may have split up in search of her. Tracey and the kids had taken a shortcut through the woods, but given the break they'd taken to warm Dylan, their hunters could be further down the trail than they were. Getting back on it was a gamble. Then again, everything was.

Seeing nothing, Tracey moved ahead, getting closer to the break in the trees so she could see better. She looked through the binoculars again, up and down the trail, observing as if she were trying to cross a busy highway on foot. She held her breath and listened, stretching her ears against the muting effect of the snow.

Nothing.

But the hunters could be hiding, waiting for her to make an appearance so they could fill her with lead. She wished she'd had a vest of Kevlar or some sort of armor. Even shoulder pads and a football helmet would be better than nothing. There was probably something buried in her father's toolshed, but there hadn't been time for her to dig through the massive clutter.

Tracey grabbed a rock the size of a softball, reared back, and heaved it onto the trail, hoping to spook anyone hiding nearby into shooting at it. Instead, the stone instantly sunk in the snow without so much as a whisper.

"Shitballs," she said.

Because her attackers might be in the distance, she switched out her shotgun for her rifle, and peered down the barrel in every direction as she inched toward the edge of the trail. The kids remained where they'd been, huddled together, shivering.

"This is your chance to leave them behind," her father said from the cobwebs of her mind. *"They're only slowing you down and putting your life at risk."*

I can't do that, she thought back at him.

"Yes, you can. They're not your responsibility, Tracey."

I've made it my responsibility, she thought.

"This whole mess is their fault," Dad replied. *"And saving them won't save your relationship with Olivia. You know that, don't you?"*

But Tracey wasn't sure what she knew anymore. Every day, the line between reality and delusion grew fainter and fainter.

A mechanical roar rose in the distance. Tracey turned toward the sound and raised her rifle. The noise grew louder, whatever it was coming closer. She soon recognized it as a motor. Not a large one like an automobile, but a smaller one like a dirt bike or…

An ATV.

There'd been several of them back at the cabin. Had the hunters gone back for them, or was their squad bigger in number than she'd thought?

The machine continued to growl as it drew nearer. Tracey bent her knees and put her finger against the trigger of the .22 rifle. She didn't blink. Her breathing slowed. There was no sense in letting one of these bastards move in on her. She had to go on the offense.

The engine revved, pushed to bring the vehicle uphill, and as the black shape of the ATV and its rider appeared, Tracey took aim, letting the hunter get a little closer to guarantee a direct hit.

The shadowy rider came into the sight at the end of her rifle.

Tracey fired.

The vehicle kept moving but the rider jolted backward, falling off the ATV and into the snow with a thud. Tracey didn't hear any

THE OLD LADY

screams. The vehicle swerved off trail and came to a stop in a tangle of branches along the edge. It was then that she saw it was not an ATV, but a snowmobile.

Tracey gasped.

Sprinting down the trail, she approached the fallen rider, her angst increasing when she saw the man was dressed in a green jacket now spattered red.

No, no, no...

Though a hole had been blown through the top of his nose, Tracey recognized her victim as Jeff, the civil engineer who'd visited her about the storm. He wasn't breathing or groaning or coughing up blood. Tracey's shot had landed true, sending a round through his face, killing him instantly.

"Now you've done it," she said to herself. "You stupid, crazy bitch."

She was definitely going back to prison now. Killing the kidnappers could be excused but taking out an innocent man—one who had only been out helping others—was an express train back into the joint. And this time, the book would be thrown at her much harder, because she'd failed to learn her lesson and stay out of trouble. Looking down at the dead man's shattered face, Tracey realized she might deserve it, that prison was where she belonged no matter how much she hated it. She'd become withdrawn and deracinated in recent years, and kept to herself as much as possible, but obviously the self-imposed ostracization hadn't been enough.

But she couldn't face a life of confinement again.

"I'm not going back to prison," she muttered to the corpse.

Tracey had been only thirty the first time she'd gone away. It hadn't been her first offense, the drug was an ounce of cocaine, she'd had her father's pistol without a permit, and she'd been staying in a public housing unit, all of which added to the severity of her charges. Tracey was sentenced to eighty months, but with good behavior got out after six years. Every day she'd been inside she'd cursed herself for the party lifestyle that had made her sloppy, and lamented that she hadn't done more to fight off the police when they'd raided the housing unit, which was a known drug den. She might have gotten away if she'd crippled them, but she also might have earned herself a bullet between the eyes, just like poor Jeff here. Back then, she'd valued her life and safety above all else. Now, she valued her freedom more.

"I'd rather die than go back," she told Jeff's body.

Looking both ways again, making sure the hunters hadn't come, Tracey slung her rifle over her shoulder, freeing her hands. There wasn't time to bury Jeff—she knew that despite her urge to break out the entrenchment tool—but she had to at least make him harder to spot by dragging his carcass into the woods and covering him with snow. But as she was about to take his heels, she saw movement in the corner of her eye, and when she spun around, the kids were standing at the edge of the trail, watching her. Alicia's jaw was slack, and Nori was covering her mouth with both hands. Dylan, still recovering from his ice fall, only stared at her with dead eyes, his face a blank behind the balaclava.

"Oh my God," Alicia said. She pointed at the dead man's jacket patches. "Oh my God, is… is that a ranger?"

Tracey was breathing heavily now. "No. He's a civil engineer."

"You know him?"

"Not really."

"Why did you—"

"I thought he was one of *them*. I thought someone had come back on one of those ATVs we saw back at the compound."

Alicia's face twisted. It was not only grief Tracey saw in her now, but unbridled fear. Not just of the situation they were in, but of Tracey. The girl pressed into her boyfriend, and Dylan put his arms around both girls, as if to protect them.

"It was an accident," Tracey said. "Okay?"

But she knew it wasn't okay. These kids were right to fear her. Despite all she'd done to rescue them, she was nearly as dangerous as the hunters, and probably less sane. Every screw that held a person together had rusted to ash within Tracey. She was a berserk ape, a monster with delusions of heroism.

Dad had told her to leave these kids behind to save herself. But what Tracey realized now was that it was they who should be leaving her behind.

She nodded toward the snowmobile. "See that? That's your ticket out of here."

The kids looked at it but didn't speak or move. Tracey crouched beside the man she'd killed and started digging through his pockets. The kids remained still, the girls burying their soft whimpers into Dylan's chest. Finding what she'd been hoping for, Tracey stood up and showed them Jeff's phone.

"Here you go," she said, starting toward them. "It's locked, but

THE OLD LADY

you can still call 911. You just need to get somewhere with a decent signal. Have any of you driven a snowmobile before?"

Silence and shaking heads.

"Well, it's pretty easy," Tracey said. "If you've ever been on a four-wheeler, it operates almost the same way. Handles control the throttle and brakes, just like on a bike. It's all about keeping your balance, really. Think one of you can handle it?"

Tracey was surprised the girls looked at Dylan. They still hadn't realized he was useless.

"Alicia," Tracey said. "Come here."

Dylan spoke up. "Just let us go. Please."

Tracey's eyebrows drew closer together. "What?"

"Please... just let us go on... without you."

The insult stung, considering all she'd done for these kids, but Tracey swallowed the hurt. There wasn't time for feelings. They'd always proved to be a nuisance anyway.

"Look at this thing," she said, pointing at the snowmobile. "It's just barely big enough for your three skinny asses. So yeah, I'm *not* going with you—okay? Listen to me. Alicia, you drive. Dylan's still too frozen."

"I can do—"

"I said you're too frozen, Dylan. Now shut up and listen, like I told you. Alicia drives, and you two hold on tight. There'll hardly be any cellular service this high up in the middle of nowhere, but once you get back to the car park, you might be able to get enough of a signal to get through to 911. But honestly, you're probably better off just gunning it as far down the mountain roads as you can rather than wait for the cops to arrive in this shit weather. The roads won't have been plowed, so the snowmobile will work. And once you get to a road that has been plowed, you'll know you're close to civilization, and then you can place the call, but don't just sit around and wait for rescue, because these people will still be after you. Get to a public place, like the nearest gas station. They're one of the few businesses that'll still be open in this storm."

She paused there, letting the kids look at each other, waiting for approval as if any of them were the leader. Clearly, Tracey was the only leader they had.

Nori admitted it. "We won't make it without you."

Dylan shushed his sister. "Nori, don't..."

"You have to," Tracey told them. "I can't fit on the snowmobile with you, and it's your best chance to get away. You'll have to leave the bags behind. Just take your weapons and what few small things you might need, like Alicia's ferrocerium rod."

Alicia fingered the rod at her wrist. "But what about you?"

"I'll be fine. I'm gonna set up some more traps and slow those pricks down. Then I'll get to my truck and go." She didn't mention her concern it would be snowed in. "If I see you along the way, I'll pick you up, but I'm confident you'll be long gone by then." She locked eyes with Alicia, with Olivia. "I always tried to do what was best for you, kid. You may not see it that way now, but remember I said that."

TWENTY-NINE

AFTER REGINA LEFT, JULIE AND Bart told Lance to stay quiet and wait for help, and then they entered the woods. They were scouting for the woman, thinking she must be close by if she'd planted the bomb that took down one of their men. Seeing Lance get blown up had made Julie even more nervous about her own safety, but there was something about watching someone else suffer that had always titillated her. Lance had been burned, shredded, and pierced—all methods of torture she'd used as a dominatrix. It was difficult for her to see a man in pain and not get at least a little turned on, especially when his injuries were so extensive. Still, her arousal surprised her, given the precarious nature of their situation.

Trenching through the snow, she and her cousin noted no footprints. The coppice was thick with tangling bushes and fallen tree limbs, but Bart knew the terrain well.

"There's a short trail near here," he said. "It leads down the rock wall into a copse, then winds back onto Harding Trail. If we hurry, we could cut the bitch off at the pass."

"You don't think she left the kids, do you?" Julie asked.

"I doubt she would've for long, but if I were her, I'd have let them get a head start instead of making them wait around while I planted landmines… and whatever other booby-traps we've been lucky enough to avoid, at least so far."

Julie's shoulders tensed at the thought. "So, what do we do?"

"She planted one bomb on Harding Trail already. There's bound to be more buried nearby. Best for us to stick to the woods and take the shortcut, and just hope she doesn't know about it."

Facing the dense, white grove, Bart started toward the slab of black rock leading down to the craggy footpath.

The low rumble of a motor hummed in the distance.

"Must be one of the rental cabins' generators," Bart said. "Trees have fallen all over. Hope we don't lose power at the compound too."

Julie followed him, her shoulders hunching as the wind picked up. The forecast predicted temperatures to fall into the teens by nightfall, with the storm bringing a windchill well below zero. The thought of staying out here past sunset filled her with unease. Catching the intruders was imperative, but the storm could soon become just as deadly as the woman they were chasing.

"Bart," she said as they scurried downhill. "If we don't find them soon, we may have to come up with a new plan. Otherwise we'll turn into icicles out here."

Bart stopped, turned his face to the sky, and closed his eyes, letting the flurries melt upon his flesh. He did this sometimes—a sort of stoic meditation that cleared his mind, allowing for the construction of new proposals.

Julie stopped behind him. "I'm just saying, we—"

"I know what you're saying," he said without looking at her. "But we've also been over this already, and I'm sick of discussing it. I don't care if it rains frogs, we're not leaving these woods without either hostages or corpses. It's the only way, Julie, and you know it."

Before she could reply, Bart continued along the path, leaning on the rock wall with one hand as he scurried down the slope.

All Julie could do was follow.

The downward momentum allowed them to move quickly, and they landed in the basin, cut through the forest again, and returned to Harding Trail, having gained considerable ground. Just to the south was a loose gravel parking lot—they couldn't see it from here, but Julie knew it was nearby—and to the north was the trail they'd bypassed.

They examined the trail from the cover of the woods. Seeing what

THE OLD LADY

appeared to be the faint remainder of snowmobile tracks, Julie turned to her cousin.

"What the hell?" she said. "They can't have a vehicle, right?"

"No. They were definitely on foot. And even a two-seater couldn't carry all four of them. This must've been someone else."

"Maybe that's what we heard, not a generator. Jeez, what idiot would be out in this if they didn't have to be?"

"The world is full of idiots."

"Could be a cop or a ranger or something."

"Could be anyone. But more than likely it's just somebody else with a cabin up here."

"If they cross paths with the woman and her kids…"

Bart grimaced. "Yeah. But if she notices someone coming, she'll probably think it's us and hide."

Julie believed he was right. "How long ago do you think they made these tracks?"

"Hard to tell with the snow coming down like this. But I'm happy there's something I *don't* see."

Julie looked at the path. "No footprints."

"Exactly. We're ahead of them. Even if they've stuck to the woods, they'll eventually have to come back to the trail to reach the parking lot, and we know that's the only place they could be going."

"Should we keep going then, to sabotage their cars?"

"Nah. They're probably buried in snow by now anyway. Even if the plows come through, they won't clear the lot, and if they do, that'll just create bigger mounds of snow that'll trap the cars in."

"So what then? We just wait?"

Bart was about to say something, but the crack of a rifle interrupted him. The sound was too far away to make them hit the ground, but they raised their Heckler & Kochs.

"Something tells me our snowmobiler was in the wrong place at the wrong time," Bart said.

"You don't really think she'd kill somebody just to steal their snowmobile, do you?"

"Maybe, maybe not. But somebody shot at something, and I doubt it was quail." He looked back at the rocky slope they had just descended. "If we take a spot somewhere up there—not too high, but enough to give us a sniper's position—then we'll have the advantage when they come this way, on foot or on a snowmobile, it doesn't matter."

194

As they turned back to find a spot, Julie confirmed with Bart once more. "Still trying to take them alive, right?"

Bart nodded. "Don't worry. If it's at all possible, you'll get your little girls. And I'll get the bitch who killed my son. We need to know just who she is and what's she's really up to."

"And what about the boy?"

Bart stepped onto the black cluster of rock, not giving an answer.

Julie knew what that meant.

~

Alicia was both relieved and troubled by Tracey's sudden exit. Despite what her boyfriend thought, she wasn't sure if they were better off without the woman. Though absolutely unhinged and lethally dangerous, the golem had been their noble protector. Without Tracey, they had to take care of themselves, something she had little confidence they were up for.

She also wasn't comfortable with the lack of a proper goodbye. Tracey had told her to remember she'd always tried to do what was right for Alicia, and then darted back into the forest like a fox. After all they'd been through together, this departure seemed anticlimactic and impersonal, leaving a sour aftertaste. Though she feared Tracey, she was also grateful to her and always would be. She felt as if she owed something to the woman, a debt she could never possibly repay. The least she could have done was hug her goodbye. But she hadn't wanted to and doubted Tracey would like to be embraced by anyone. A golem was not open to such tenderness. They were beings made of stone with one singular purpose—destruction.

She and her friends threw their bags as far into the woods as they could, and as they loaded up on the snowmobile, Alicia tried the civil engineer's phone. Just as Tracey had predicted, they were in a dead zone. No bars, no signal. But what Alicia knew and Tracey didn't was that even without a signal a smartphone could place a successful emergency call, provided there was a cellphone tower within range. The bars only signified they weren't near a tower belonging to this phone's service provider. If they could reach any brand of tower, an emergency call might get through. Unfortunately, with the phone being locked, she couldn't access the settings to use a signal booster or close all the tabs and apps that might impede the phone's functions.

She swiped and placed the call.

At first, she heard nothing as the phone desperately tried to find a signal.

THE OLD LADY

"Hey," Dylan said. "Let's get out of here first and call for help later."

He'd put himself in the driver's seat despite Tracey's insistence Alicia drive. Alicia held up one finger, asking him to give her a few more seconds.

C'mon. Pickup, pickup.

She was about to give up when she heard a faint ringing. The hairs on the back of her neck sprung up, and when she heard a muffled voice, tears filled Alicia's eyes.

"911. What is your emergency?" a woman asked.

"*Oh my God.* Hello?"

Dylan and Nori watched her with hopeful eyes.

"Yes. This is 911. What is your emergency?"

"Oh, thank God." She didn't know where to begin, so she went with the shortest version of events. "My friends and I. We were attacked. Our friend Marcus was shot. They killed him. These people at this compound—they shot him."

Dylan was telling her to say something specific, but Alicia ignored him, trying to better hear the faint voice of the operator.

"Are you in a safe place now?" the woman asked.

"We got away but they're coming after us."

"Where are you?"

"In the woods. Up in the White Mountains. On Harding Trail."

"Okay. What's your name?"

"Alicia."

"Alright, Alicia. I'm going to help you, so just stay calm for me, okay? I'm trying to pinpoint your location but can't seem to find you."

"I'm on somebody's else's phone. I used the emergency call feature."

"Does the phone show that it has a signal?"

"No."

"Okay. Without a signal, your phone can't deliver your location to our call center."

Alicia made a small, pained noise.

"Don't worry," the operator said. "I will dispatch officers, but I need you to give me as much information as you can. Harding Trail winds all through the White Mountains, and they cover nearly a quarter of the state. It goes on for miles. Do you know which of the mountains you are on?"

Alicia's chest tightened. She looked to her friends. "Which

mountain are we on?"

"White, right?" Dylan said.

"That's the name of the whole range."

"I think this one is called Black Mountain," Nori said. "I think that's what Marcus said."

Alicia returned to the call. "We're not sure. On the way in, I saw a sign saying we were in Jackson, but we may have gone past the town. We came up this winding road and parked in a gravel lot with a big sign that says 'Harding Trail' and a map of the trails." Hearing herself, Alicia winced. She wasn't being helpful at all. There must be several lots like the one they'd parked in, all scattered across the mountains, miles apart. Tears choked her. "I… I just don't know."

The operator said something, but her voice was fractured by static.

Dylan called to her again. "Alicia, let's *go*. We can call again once we're safe."

"We have to keep moving," Alicia said into the receiver. "We… we, um, found a snowmobile." She hesitated to tell the operator what had happened to the civil engineer. "We're going to try and get down the mountain on it and find a gas station or something."

The garbled voice returned. "I have… officers… the snow may delay their…"

Alicia shut her eyes as the call dropped. Rather than try again, she stuffed the phone into her back pocket and climbed onto the snowmobile behind Nori, who had her arms around her brother's waist. Alicia grabbed on to Nori. Without the extra layer of clothing, the poor girl was shivering in the cold again. Her cheeks were pink and chapped. Sandwiching her would at least provide her with some body heat. It was a tight fit getting them all on the two-seater, but Nori's petiteness made it possible.

Dylan cranked the throttle and the snowmobile heaved forward, then stopped, then moved again as he adjusted to the handlebars' functions. He managed to get the vehicle turned around and told the girls to hang on tight as he hit the throttle again. The powdery snow splashed away from the rolling tracks, making small waves of white as they were propelled down Harding Trail. The acceleration flooded Alicia with a sudden sense of relief. Now they were putting distance between themselves and the horrors of the day at a much faster rate, and with every corner they turned, she could feel the parking lot getting closer.

Soon they would reach the road they'd come in on. Soon they

THE OLD LADY

would return to civilization, to safety, to the normal world. Thinking of her family again, Alicia was warmed by her memories of them and the growing feeling that she would see them again after all. Even her annoying sister was going to get a bear hug. She thought of the homework that had been daunting her and the stress of her classes, all of which she would be happy to tackle now. All the things that had bothered her before coming to this dreadful mountain now seemed like spilt milk. Even the parts of her normal life that had once gotten her down were welcome, for today's experiences in true pain and suffering had awakened her to just how easy her life had been all along.

On this mountain, there were no hopes and dreams for the future, no academic goals or career prospects or thoughts of having children one day. There was only the blood-pumping instinct to survive. This place had made her primitive. It had damaged her sanity, crippled her emotions, and scarred her for life, just as it had all of them. But it had not taken their lives. Poor Marcus had been murdered, but Alicia had survived, her boyfriend had survived, and Nori had survived. Despite everything else, there was something to be grateful for, the thing that mattered most.

Dylan dodged fallen branches, slowing to skirt around debris and then picking up speed again when the path was clear. The wind whipping past them was bitter and Alicia could feel the skin on her face starting to chap. She tucked her head into Dylan's back, looking over his shoulder at the white world racing by.

Let her skin crack and bleed. That was nothing to her now.

They were going home.

She was thinking this just as the first bullets struck the snowmobile.

Everything happened at once. The gunfire was rapid—the pops of assault rifles. Nori screamed. Frantic, Alicia looked all about but couldn't see where the attack was coming from. Holes appeared in the front end of the snowmobile, bits of plastic and metal bursting as the engine was struck. Blood sprayed across Alicia's face, coating it, and Dylan groaned in pain, his shoulder gushing, and his grip on the throttle faltered. He lost control of the vehicle, and it careened toward a dark mass half-buried under snow. As they struck the fallen tree, Dylan was propelled forward, his chest slamming into the handlebars. Nori lost her grip on her brother and Alicia lost her grip on Nori, and the girls tumbled over the side, crashing into the tangled brush at the edge of the trail.

Alicia fell hard on her butt, and she felt the phone in her back pocket shatter as she hit a frozen rock cluster. But it was the least of her worries. Her boyfriend was draped over the snowmobile's handlebars like a rag doll, blood cascading down his back. His quivering limbs were the only sign of life. She called his name, but doing so drew more fire from the hidden assassins.

Nori was shrieking. Alicia blinked her boyfriend's blood from her eyes and saw the girl on her back in the snow, clutching her knee. Alicia wasn't sure if Nori had been shot or hurt herself in the fall. She started toward her, but the snowy ground around them popped as more bullets rained down. Two muzzles flashed from the rocky slope on the other side of the trail, revealing there was more than one shooter. When Alicia saw a large man scampering down from the crags, she had no choice but to start running.

She called for Dylan and Nori but could not wait for them to follow her. She didn't know if they were even able to run. And if Alicia tried to return fire with her Glock, she would be killed. She wasn't a skilled enough shooter, and a pistol was no match for dual assault rifles.

All she could do was run.

Run and cry.

PART THREE
COME HOME TO ROOST

THIRTY

TRACEY HEARD THE GUNSHOTS JUST as she finished setting another trap.

"No…" she whispered.

She picked up her shotgun and ran downhill as quickly as she could in packed inches of snow.

"Alicia…"

The rapid gunshots continued, filling her head with horrible visions of the kids being massacred. She followed the snowmobile tracks, her chest tightening as if she were wrapped in rachet ties. There were several more shots, followed by a girl screaming.

Negative emotions pummeled Tracey—fear, emptiness, grief, anger. The internal heat that came to her in times like this flooded her veins, her complex disorder pushing her anger into outright rage. Thinking of the hunters, her finger itched against the shotgun's trigger guard.

If you hurt her, I swear to God, I'll make you die slowly.

Though she wanted all three of the kids to be safe, it was Alicia she was the most concerned about. The girl had become like her surrogate daughter, and Tracey the protective mama bear. In her mind,

THE OLD LADY

Alicia's face once again merged with that of her real daughter, the child Tracey had left behind now an amalgamation with the one she shouldn't have allowed to leave her. And as Tracey charged downhill, her heart ached with the distant memories of the family she'd once had, and the chance for a normal life she'd squandered.

The gunfire ceased, and the silence left in its wake was even more unsettling. It meant there was nothing left to shoot at, that the battle was over.

It meant death.

"Olivia," Tracey whispered into the wind. "Olivia…"

~

Tracey was thirty-six and fresh out of prison when she'd met Gavin MacKinnon. One of the terms of her parole was she had to attend group counseling for drugs addicts, even though she'd had no choice but to go clean during her time in the slammer. She was warned being free would tempt her to start using again, and while Tracey would never admit it, the parole board had been right to anticipate that. The temptation was there, despite the pride she felt for having kicked her habits. And so she went to the drug addicts' equivalent of Alcoholics Anonymous twice a week, but never "shared" the way the others did. Tracey felt her demons were no one else's business and saw only weakness in those who needed to share with others. Though she knew she was mentally disturbed, she still preferred to be self-reliant, even regarding therapy.

Gavin was a couple of years older than she was. He had thinning hair and a beard that couldn't decide if it wanted to be black or silver. Having spent some time in jail but never gone to prison, Gavin came to the meetings of his own volition, determined to never go back to his days of smoking weed all day and shooting heroin every other night. He was weening off prescription methadone, which Tracey saw as just another version of the same problem, but the meetings were always heavy on coffee and cigarettes, two other addictions that everyone seemed okay with, oblivious to the irony. Tracey steered clear of coffee because caffeine made her manic, but she chain-smoked Marlboros, and one afternoon Gavin had joined her outside and bummed a cigarette off her.

Normally, Tracey tried to avoid getting to know anyone, but after six years in prison, she craved a man with a terrible thirst. Gavin had humble good looks—no movie star but no goober either. Kicking heroin and eating right had given him an appealing muscle-to-fat ratio. And so Tracey made small talk with him, doing her best to impersonate a normal woman by stifling her constant urge to flee from others. After that, they paired up during every smoke break, until he finally asked her out.

"How about dinner tonight?" Gavin asked.

"How about dinner at your place?" Tracey suggested.

He smiled, bashful and surprised. "Sounds good. But I'll warn you now, I'm not much of a cook."

"Doesn't matter."

"I suppose we could order out or—"

Tracey shut him up with a kiss, her body tingling at the connection of her lips with a man's. They slept together that night, and Gavin proved to be a generous lover and a good lay, so she decided to keep seeing him. At first, it was merely physical, but then she grew to like him for other reasons. Gavin was thoughtful and caring, things that initially made her suspicious, but she soon grew to understand this was just true to his nature. There was something about him that she'd rarely experienced with someone else, a feeling of peacefulness and belonging, of togetherness. Before she knew it, she was in her first real relationship. Her feelings for Gavin bloomed, which scared her, but her enjoyment became a sort of addiction of its own. Instead of drugs, she was self-medicating with a man's affection. Instead of floundering through life and wallowing in the charred wreckage of her past, she was now rebuilding from the rubble, and she and Gavin as a couple became her true support group.

Having been through his own version of Hell, Gavin was more patient with Tracey's mood swings and general brokenness than any of the men she'd been involved with before. Slowly, he chipped away at her wall until, finally, she let him in, and while her fear of love remained, the therapeutic joy of being loved was impossible to reject. Though she would never confess to it, Tracey didn't just want Gavin, she needed him. Love, for all its volatility, was allowing her to heal.

They moved in together, giving Tracey a proper home after nearly two decades of drifting between rented rooms, shelters, campsites, and prison cells. Gavin worked retail and Tracey went back to waitressing. They lived modestly but happily. He was more capable of happiness than she was, but Tracey gradually learned to welcome love and laughter. She still had many bad moments, and often woke up at night not knowing where she was, but Gavin was understanding, never seeming to lose patience with his damaged girlfriend, and

THE OLD LADY

within a year's time, she was pregnant with his child.

They married in a courthouse. Tracey didn't want a big ceremony because she had no one to invite. Only Gavin mattered—Gavin and the baby he'd put into her. Their country of three. By now, her husband had weaned off methadone and they were both living clean. Though they rented, Tracey had a house to call her own, and better yet, it was a real *home*. It was such a positive situation that she grew increasingly worried things would collapse. In her experience, nothing good ever lasted. Imagining every possible scenario for disaster was a habit she'd developed based on her father's teachings, and the practice had never bothered her... until now. The thought of losing her family filled her with the most horrible sense of unease she'd ever known, which was saying something. She wasn't sure how to handle it, so she struggled with it in silence, never sharing these feelings out of fear they would drive Gavin away.

Olivia MacKinnon came into the world, and Tracey fell into a deep post-partum depression. It put extra strain on her husband, but as always, he proved resilient, patient, and caring. His kindness was so absolute that Tracey began to resent how levelheaded and supportive he was when she was in a constant state of disrepair. She not only struggled to be helpful with the baby—she struggled to even care about it. She knew it was wrong for her to feel this way, but it was beyond her ability to change. Controlling her feelings had always been a weakness. In the past it had made her a bad friend, worse employee, and even worse girlfriend. But being a bad mother was unnatural, and she knew it. It made her hate herself.

"Some people just aren't cut out to be parents," she eventually confessed to Gavin.

"You just need time, honey," Gavin said with his typical insufferable sweetness. "Post-partum depression happens to a lot of women, but in most cases, they overcome."

"I was already damaged before the baby. Maybe I'm too fucked up to be anybody's mommy."

Months went by, and her depression and anxiety only deepened. She was in her late thirties, trapped in a house with an infant that never stopped crying, and in a constant state of dread and self-disgust. While pregnant, she'd feared losing her family. Now she feared being suffocated by it. More than that, she feared failing Gavin and Olivia. She knew it was unavoidable. It was happening already.

Still, Tracey hung on. Gradually, she started taking care of the baby, but it only added to her resentment toward it. Its needs were infinite, its dependency absolute. She began to wonder why she'd agreed to having it in the first place. She'd had a wonderful life with Gavin, and just as she'd predicted, something had come along and ruined it.

A year went by, then two. Olivia became a toddler, and Tracey started teaching the girl. That's when things became truly tumultuous in her marriage. Without meaning to be, Tracey was a stern mother, casting a shadow of her father's tough parenting. Though to a lesser extent than what she'd gone through as a child, she taught her daughter with a harsh tongue and a firm grip, making Olivia cry on a regular basis. This too was beyond Tracey's control. She easily got angry with her little girl and tended to yell and slam doors. And for the first time in their relationship, Gavin couldn't show her emotional support. He had a child to care for now, and much to Tracey's chagrin, Olivia meant more to him than she did. Her husband became critical of her and more protective of their daughter, until Tracey started to feel like the monster of the house. Unfortunately, it was a designation she couldn't dispute.

That's when Tracey started drinking again. She did so in secret, stashing airplane bottles throughout the house and larger bottles in the toilet tank and other compartments that were rarely checked. She would tell Gavin she needed some personal time and would go out for a walk, only to end up at the nearest bar. And as with all secrets, the truth was finally revealed. One night, Tracey came home drunk, and after that, Gavin got on her about quitting. Though his intentions were good, giving up booze only led Tracey back to drugs. First it was weed, then pills, and then she was back on cocaine, the same drug that had sent her to prison a decade ago. As a former drug addict, Gavin couldn't be around someone who was using, but more than that, he didn't want his daughter to be afflicted by the nastiness her mother's bad habits brought out in her.

He begged Tracey to go into rehab.

Instead, she left.

One night, she packed up some supplies and fashioned a BOB, and snuck out while her family was asleep. She quit her job without notice and hit the road again. Gavin was right. She was being abusive to their daughter, their marriage, and herself, but she couldn't see a way to stop it. In Tracey's mind, leaving them was best for everyone, despite the initial pain it would cause. That pain was brutal on her,

THE OLD LADY

and every day she chased a high to ease it. She drank and smoked and did whatever non-needle drugs she could get her hands on, returning at forty to the dangerous, bar-hopping, party life she'd led in her twenties. And just like when she'd been a young woman, it didn't take long for her to get into serious trouble.

~

The man stood over Dylan, who was on his back in the snow. His female companion was twisting Nori's arm behind her back to get the girl to stop struggling. Tracey didn't see Alicia anywhere and hoped she'd gotten away. The snowmobile was wrapped around a fallen tree. The man held an assault rifle, and the woman had a duplicate one strapped to her body.

Tracey had drawn her rifle too. From the cover of the brush, she could pick the man off, but shooting at the woman would be too risky with Nori held so close to her. And if she shot the man, would the woman kill Nori in a swift act of vengeance?

"Shit..." Tracey whispered to herself.

Should she sniper or sneak attack?

"*It's too late for them now,*" her father echoed through her brain.

"Bullshit," Tracey whispered back. "No soldier left behind."

"*That's bumper sticker talk. You need to think practically, in real life terms. Not trying to save these kids may hurt your pride, but what's more important—honor or self-preservation?*"

"The lives of children are more important, but I wouldn't expect you to understand that."

"*Right,*" Dad said in a flippant tone. "*I was so bad to you. My training is what has kept you alive this far, but I was the worst father ever for putting you through it.*"

"You tortured me."

"*I toughened you up. There's a difference.*"

"I was just a little girl."

"*And I did what I had to do to make sure you'd be strong enough to grow into a woman. A real woman. One who doesn't take shit from nobody. One who can survive anything. You know how to survive this, but you're letting your emotions get in the way. If you don't change course, your feelings are gonna get you killed.*"

"I don't consider this life a treasure."

Her mental remnants of her father started to say something, but Tracey's mind shut him off like a switch as she watched the man drag Dylan to his feet and tear off his balaclava. Even from this distance,

Tracey could see the boy was seriously hurt. He could barely stand up and blood was cascading down his sweater.

The man drew a knife.

Tracey raised the rifle and stood, finger on the trigger, but the hunters were holding the children in front of them, facing Tracey even though they didn't know she was there. The kids were human shields. Tracey had to wait and hold her stance until the hunters changed positions.

But then the man shouted out. "Tracey!"

That he knew her name chilled her. One of the kids must have confessed it to him.

"Tracey!" he called again. "I know you're out there somewhere!" He pressed the tip of the knife against Dylan's throat. "I have two of your kids! But what I really want is you! Their lives mean nothing to me, Tracey! *Nothing*! So the choice is yours!"

He waited for a reply she didn't give. The woman dropped Nori to her knees and aimed her assault rifle at the back of the girl's head. The hunters scanned their surroundings, but Tracey was well concealed in the snowy thicket on the edge of the trail, some thirty yards away.

"Tracey, do you hear me?" the man called out. "I know you must have heard the gunshots and come running to save these brats. If you are listening, this is your last chance to rescue them! Come on out with your hands in the air! If you don't, I will slit the boy's throat and stab him in the belly until his guts fall out."

Tracey heard a whimper but wasn't sure if it came from Dylan or his sister.

"The girl will die too!" the hunter said. "But first she will pay for things *you* did. She will be raped and tortured, just for the hell of it!"

Tracey's ribcage seemed to compress, a lump rising in her throat.

"You can prevent all of this!" the man said. "But you have to act now."

Gritting her teeth, Tracey stared down the barrel of the .22, holding it so tight it trembled. She figured she had an eighty percent chance of success if she tried for headshots, but one of the kids would almost certainly die. She could call the man's bluff, but doubted he was lying about hurting the kids, and she was certain the consequences would be dire if she tested him.

Tracey put the rifle down and set it beside her shotgun, which she'd placed upon a stone slab. Her mind offered dozens of

THE OLD LADY

objections to what she was doing, including her father's critical voice, but she put her hands in the air anyway and slowly stepped toward the trail.

"I'm coming out!" she shouted.

The female hunter raised her assault rifle while the man continued to hold Dylan at the edge of a knife. As Tracey stepped out from behind cover, snapshots of her life flickered across the strained hemispheres of her brain. There was a good chance this was the end, and Tracey found she wasn't exactly upset about it. For a long time, she'd been tired of being alive, surviving on instinct without having any worthy reason to go on. Every day was a war within her own skull, self-hatred a nightly lullaby. Suicide ideation had become a hobby. Now, Tracey had an honorable reason to die. If it meant saving these kids, she could sacrifice herself. The only problem was, she didn't trust these hunters at their word. She knew she wasn't buying Dylan and Nori their freedom. She was only buying them time. It was the best she could offer.

Tracey emerged from the woods and stood in the center of the trail. She stared at the hunters, saying nothing.

"Hands on your head," the woman with the rifle said.

Tracey obeyed. The hunters looked at one another. Tracey exhaled with relief when the man let go of Dylan, but he shoved the boy to his knees beside his sister. The woman kept them at gunpoint while the man traded his knife out for the pistol in his hip holster and started toward Tracey, holding the gun with both hands, aiming at her heart.

"Let them go," she said.

"Shut the fuck up," the man barked. "That knife you got sheathed—take it out slowly and drop it on the ground."

Tracey tensed. She needed the knife, more for what was inside the handle than anything else.

"Now!" the man demanded.

She undid the latch, slid the blade out, and dropped it. The man eyed it but quickly brought his attention back to her.

"Your gun," he said. "Where is it?"

Tracey used her head to point. "On a rock over there. Two. A rifle and shotgun."

"No hidden pieces? No ankle holster or something tucked in your waistband?"

"No."

He narrowed his eyes. "So what's in the backpack?"

"Tools. Supplies."

"A bug-out bag?"

She nodded.

"Any more of those homemade landmines in there?" he asked.

"No."

"You sure? No pipe bombs or dynamite or anything?"

"No."

Drawing closer, he stared into Tracey's eyes. She stared back, unflinching.

"Alright," he said. "Now the bag. Lower it, don't drop it."

She slid the bag off her shoulders and gently placed it in the snow.

"Any other weapons of any kind?" he asked.

"No. That's it."

"You make one move, and my assistant there is gonna turn your little friends into pudding. Understand?"

"Yes."

He watched her closely as he picked up her knife, drew her bag to him, and opened it. "Anything in here that can stick me? Needles or razors or anything?"

"No."

"If you're lying—"

"Then the kids are dead."

The man squatted and dug around inside the BOB, checking out the contents. Satisfied it was clean, he stuffed her hunting knife into it and zipped it up, then stood. He asked her the same questions before frisking her and turning her pockets inside out, discovering the keys to her truck. He jingled them before Tracey's face as if she were a baby.

"Looks like you missed your ride," he said. "My men found car keys on the dead boy back at the barn and told me these little shits all came here together."

Tracey said nothing.

Bart took a deep breath as he put his Glock into its holster again.

"Okay then," he said.

His fist flew.

Tracey's jaw shifted as the man struck her. The blow spun her to one side, and the man hit her with a left hook, spinning her back the other way. Her hands left her head as she tried to regain her balance, but she didn't try to fight back, knowing it would only make things

THE OLD LADY

worse. She put her arms up only to block his attack and curled forward as he hammered down on her with his fists, rabbit-punching her and pounding her back. Her vision filled with stars and blood dribbled from the corner of her mouth. When she finally dropped to her knees and put out her hands to keep from falling, the big man kicked her in the side of the head.

Her body wanted to give out, as did her consciousness, but Tracey allowed neither. She stayed on her hands and knees in the snow, trying not to tense up as she braced for more of the man's violence. Instead of another blow, he grabbed her by the hair, snapping her head back, and spit in her face.

"You cunt," he said. "You goddamned, psycho cunt."

Tracey remained stoic.

"You fucking bitch," he snarled in her face. "Fucking animal! Do you even know what you did?"

She didn't respond.

"I saw you on video. I saw what you did to my boy." He spat at her again, hitting her in the eye. "You crippled my son, and when he was helpless, you shoved him into a fucking woodchipper!"

He drew his Glock and pressed the barrel into her belly. Tracey closed her eyes and tried to steady her breathing, but it kept coming out of her nostrils like the snorts of a bull.

"Any father would want vengeance," the man said. "But few would take the matter into their own hands. They'd be worried about the consequences of committing murder. But me? Hell, killing is nothing new. It's as easy as tying my shoes. I could kill you right now, but that would be too kind." Pulling her hair tighter, pistol jabbed under her ribs, the man guided Tracey back to her feet. "Now move."

The hunter walked her to his assistant and the children. Both kids had their heads down and their eyes closed, but hearing the footsteps, Nori looked up and her teary eyes locked with Tracey's. At least she didn't appear to be seriously injured. The female hunter gently pushed the back of Nori's head with the Heckler & Koch, and the girl turned her face to the ground again.

"On your knees," the man ordered Tracey.

She lowered to the ground again, still trying to catch her breath and recover from the beating. The man got in front of her, and when Tracey looked up, she couldn't keep the hatred from curling her mouth.

"Don't give me that look," he said, staring down at her. "I'm not gonna make you suck my dick or anything. It'd be a pleasure to degrade you, but I'd never stick my cock in any part of a nasty, shriveled skank like you."

Tracey hung her head like the other hostages. A splinter would hurt her more than this man's words. She merely lowered her head as a show of obedience, hoping to keep the man calm.

The female hunter said, "C'mon, Bart. We need to hurry this up."

Bart, Tracey thought. That the woman used his name was a bad sign. It meant they didn't care if she and the kids knew their identities, which meant they didn't plan to ever let them go alive.

"We need to get back to Lance and the others," the woman said. "And get out of this snowstorm before I freeze my tits off."

Tracey watched Bart from the corner of her eye. He gave his companion a sour look, but then seemed to agree. "Yeah. Okay. But first…"

Bart raised his pistol and fired.

Gunpowder burned as the crack of the Glock shocked Tracey's eardrums. She flinched, expecting the next thing she felt to be a hot lead entering her forehead. Instead she felt a warm spray.

Nori screamed.

Dylan did not.

THIRTY-ONE

THE BOY'S BODY FELL BEFORE Tracey, giving her a clear view of his bloodied face and the bullet hole in his forehead. Dylan's blood wept into the snow, turning it the color of strawberries. His sister wailed and the female hunter shouted at her, but Nori was unable to control herself.

The old rage bubbled within Tracey. She itched to lunge at their attackers and beat them to death with her bare hands. Bart seemed to sense this, and he pressed the still-hot barrel of the gun under her chin, singeing her flesh.

"An eye for an eye, bitch," he snarled. "You kill my boy, I kill yours."

Tracey spoke through clenched teeth. "He isn't my son."

"*Wasn't.*"

"Look at him. He's Japanese. Do I look Japanese to you, you dumb son of a bitch?"

"Better watch your mouth when you're talking to me, sweetheart. This zipperhead might not be your kin, but he was as close to an Old Testament revenge as I could get, at least to start off. Besides, I only shot him. I didn't shove him down a woodchipper because I'm not an utter maniac like you. Maybe now, you know just what you're dealing with."

"I only know I'm dealing with a child-killer and a liar. You said you'd let them go."

"And I told my late wife I'd always keep our child safe from harm. So I may be a liar, but you're the one who first made a liar out of me." Bart looked at his assistant. "Keep your gun on them while I drag this corpse into the woods there."

"Jesus," she said. "We're just gonna leave him out here for anyone to find?"

"Just for now. I'll cover him with snow, and we can come back for the body later."

Tracey listened to the sound of a teenage corpse being hauled through slush and briar, a horrible duet with the cries of his grieving sister. When she glanced up, the trail of blood was thick and speckled with bits of brain matter. She only hoped Nori had the good sense to keep her eyes closed.

A dark spell of uncertainty came over Tracey. If it were only her with a gun to her head, she would rush it, knowing it would be her only hope of getting out of this; but with Nori there, she needed a better plan than that. With Dylan slain, Tracey was now certain they wouldn't be shown mercy, and surely wouldn't be let go. Better to take a bullet than wait and see what nightmare of misery Bart and his bitch had in store. If she couldn't overpower the hunters, this form of suicide was the best option for both of them, but perhaps if she just held out, a better opportunity to strike would present itself. She just had to be patient… but that had never been one of her virtues.

She wondered where Alicia had gone. There was only one way to find out, but Tracey didn't have access to that now. Seeing no other bodies, she ascertained the girl had gotten away. Imagining Alicia stumbling through the snow with bullet wounds made Tracey ache inside, so she tried to picture the girl escaping and getting to town. Maybe Alicia had been able to place the 911 call. Hopefully, her daughter still had a chance.

Gathering Tracey's weapons, Bart brought them back to the trail and shoved the pump-action shotgun into Tracey's BOB and zipped it up with the barrel sticking out of the top. He slung the bag over his shoulder and passed Tracey's Ruger 10/22 Rifle to his assistant.

"We really need all this shit?" she asked.

"Now we have weapons with her prints all over them," he said.

THE OLD LADY

"May come in handy. If not, it's always good to have extra firepower for the crew."

"Typical hoarder."

The woman slung the rifle over her shoulder while Bart kept his gun pointed at Tracey's head. The woman gripped her Heckler & Koch again, and Bart holstered his Glock, trading it out for his assault rifle, so the hunters matched like a pair of SWAT team stooges.

"On your feet," Bart told his captives.

They stood, and he raised the rifle at them. Nori shut her eyes tight and whimpered. Tracey just stared at Bart because he wasn't going to kill them yet. If he were going to do that, he wouldn't have gone through all this trouble.

"Now then," he said to Nori. "The blonde—Alicia, right?" She nodded, and he looked at Tracey. "Where do you think she might be going?"

"Is she hurt?" Tracey asked.

"Don't know or care. But she took off like she wasn't. Darted into the woods there, but that land's nothing but dense forest and rock walls that are impossible to climb without the right tools. I'd have thought she'd be going to the parking lot ahead, but she must've gotten discombobulated 'cause the bimbo ran in the wrong direction. Any idea where she might be going? Maybe back to the cabin?"

Tracey was silent.

"Yeah," Bart said. "That's what I thought. Poor little bitch just ran into the woods blind. She has no plan at all, does she? Just a dumb kid like her friends." He grinned. "*You* were their leader, Tracey, and just look where your leadership got them."

~

Bart debated what job he should give Julie. He could send her to look for Alicia, so he could march the hostages back to home base, or he could let her escort them so he could chase after the escapee. He was confident he'd be better at either task, but Julie was a strong soldier and did not hesitate to do what needed to be done, no matter what. If Tracey pulled anything, Julie could handle her. The problem was, Julie had a cruel streak that outdid Bart's, and he didn't want Tracey killed until he had a chance to question her about who she was and what she might know about their operation. But they also had to find Alicia. Her freedom was a dangerous loose end that needed to be tied, and Bart was a better tracker than his cousin.

"Take these two back to base," he told Julie. "If Tracey pulls anything, kill the girl first."

He knew Julie wouldn't want to damage the teenage merchandise, but it was merely an empty threat meant to keep Tracey in line, so Julie agreed.

"Hands behind your backs," Bart told their captives.

They complied, and Bart drew the Zip Ties from his coat pocket and tightly cuffed the hostages. As he did so, he noticed the hearing aid in Nori's ear.

"Well look at that," he said with a smirk.

Bart plucked it from the girl's head, causing her to flinch, then hurled the device into the woods. He told Julie to walk the captives uphill to catch up with the others, who had probably returned for Lance by now. Then Bart entered the woods Alicia had fled into. There were some footprints but no drops of blood. She hadn't been hit, but she may have been bruised in the crash or broken an arm.

Would she have a gun on her? It was possible Tracey had given her one, but Alicia hadn't fired back during the ambush, so perhaps she only had hand combat weapons. If she did have a firearm, he doubted it was as powerful as his Heckler & Koch, but either way, as an experienced lawman in his fifties, he would be a better shot than any teenage girl.

Ex-lawman, he reminded himself.

His country hadn't appreciated his service. When he'd needed it most, even the support of his department and superiors had thinned to a trickle. Bart's history of successful arrests and convictions had gradually been overshadowed by multiple filed complaints—conduct unbecoming of a police officer; abuse of process; attentiveness to duty; and violating the Law Enforcement Officer's Code of Ethics. Slowly, a sordid permanent record had developed that kept him from moving up. Feeling betrayed and out of options, Bart started taking bribes and stealing from criminals. He swiped money, drugs, and other goods instead of turning them in as evidence. He was never caught red-handed, but eventually the mounting complaints against him—including some made by other officers—threatened his position, so he'd quit bitterly before a full investigation could commence.

Those who had wronged him would pay.

Everyone was going to pay.

Bart followed the footprints, but they were rapidly fading as the snow came down, filling the holes, and the divots in the land and denseness of the brush made the tracks harder to discern. They led

THE OLD LADY

down to a rocky stream, then disappeared.

"Son of a bitch," Bart grumbled.

The snow was getting heavier, the wind meaner. His body ached from the cold. Julie was right. It was getting worse out here. If he stayed outside much longer, he might suffer frostbite or hypothermia. Once it got dark, he could very well freeze to death.

But the same went for Alicia. With no vehicle, she would be trapped on the mountain for hours before she could get off it, especially if she were wandering around in the forest instead of using the trails, which were also rapidly vanishing. Wylder had told Bart they'd confiscated all the kids' phones, but he'd found a broken one at the snowmobile crash. He guessed it belonged to Tracey. It didn't matter. The girl would be without a phone either way. The problem was, she may have called the police already. Getting a clear signal was nearly impossible this high up in the wilderness, but there remained a chance. In this weather, rescue would be slow getting here, but who knew just how long ago Alicia may have called?

As a former cop, Bart knew how to talk to police, and there was always a comradery between members of law enforcement. But it still wouldn't look good if he were found stalking the woods in a snowstorm with such heavy artillery. However, if the police came to Harding Trail and found nothing but fallen trees and mounted snow that would hinder their search, they might attribute the call to a prank and turn back, or at least would have a difficult time getting uphill. They also wouldn't know where to look for the compound, which was isolated and far off Harding Trail. Even if they somehow found it, they couldn't just barge into every property on the mountain based off a single 911 call. They would need to have reasonable grounds.

Bart thought about it all as he followed the stream. Eventually it led to a cluster of boulders, trickling through the cracks and down a steep slope of igneous rock. Huge icicles dangled from the overhang like white swords.

The Sword of Damocles, Bart thought. *Right above your head.*

He'd lost the girl.

No matter how he seethed, the trail had gone cold. He had no idea where she'd gone and no easy way to locate her in this increasingly hostile weather. Bart backtracked, looking for any footprints he may have missed, but if the girl had left any, the storm had already covered them up. The snow was hammering down now and whipping in all directions, making it difficult to see, and the eastern sky had grown darker, threatening the coming of night.

If you can't handle it out here, Bart thought, *then that little girl doesn't stand a chance.*

Presently, searching for Alicia was futile. Bart didn't have to kill himself trying to kill her. A stormy night on the mountain would take care of the execution for him. His crew could return later and search for her frozen corpse. Right now, he needed to get warm, and get answers.

~

She was going to die out here.

This realization had struck Alicia several times throughout this ordeal but receded whenever she'd escaped. Now, it seemed a certainty.

She was alone deep in the woods, stranded in the freezing wind and gathering darkness. She had no supplies, only the Glock 19, the stun gun/flashlight combo, and the ferrocerium rod she wore like a bracelet. It had a compass, flint, and whistle. These were the extent of her survival tools now that she'd jettisoned the backpack.

Alicia was cold and tired and hungry. More than anything else, she was afraid.

Guilt weighed down on her like a hex. She'd left her friends behind to save her own ass. She'd had no other choice but was ashamed of it anyway. The gunshots and screams would echo in her memory as long as she lived.

At least that wouldn't be much longer.

She was confident she'd lost the hunters, but she remained stalked by death. If she didn't get to shelter, the below-freezing winds would send her right into the reaper's arms.

Alicia kept moving, clearing her tears so they wouldn't turn to ice on her already irritated skin. Thoughts of Dylan and Nori battered her, making her efforts seem even more hopeless and futile. She wondered where Tracey was. Surely all the gunshots had drawn her attention. Regardless of how scary the woman was, Alicia wished for her company right now. She was tempted to blow the whistle, but it would attract the people hunting her too.

Traveling on, she tried to keep going southwest, but the woods were thick and cluttered and treacherous, and she often had to deviate from the instruction of her compass. Even if she managed to make it to the parking lot or another place she recognized, getting into town on foot before dark would be impossible. Without help or a vehicle, she would die long before she made it to any gas station.

THE OLD LADY

Again she wondered if the 911 operator had been able to send the police to the right location, or if police were dispatched at all. Were they on their way now? If they did manage to get here, they would be looking for her on Harding Trail, not deep in the woods. But the hunters were back there, and Alicia didn't want to step into another ambush. This Catch 22 put her at a terrible impasse. Even if she weren't so exhausted and distraught, she would still have difficulty figuring out where to go from here.

Alicia wanted to find a cave or even a hollow log, something to hide in and shield her from the blizzard. But she had to resist this urge. She had to keep moving, keep the blood pumping. If she rested, she might fall asleep and never wake up. The cold would simply devour her.

And so, she marched on, for what else was there to do?

THIRTY-TWO

BART CAUGHT UP WITH JULIE and the captives where Lance had been waiting. Regina and Wylder had returned from the cabin with a wooden pallet they'd affixed with chains and had helped Lance onto it. As Bart arrived, Julie was forcing Nori and Tracey to the front of the pallet so they could help drag it with their arms still cuffed behind their backs. Nori had hurt her leg falling off the snowmobile, but it was a minor scrape, and while Bart had knocked Tracey around, she was still mobile and strong.

Regina radiated rage as she stared at Tracey. Bart could understand why. For nearly killing her husband, she would want to break the woman's bones just as strongly as Bart did. Lance might still die too. He was a bloody mess, shifting in and out of consciousness. If not for Regina's sense of urgency regarding taking care of her husband, she probably would be stomping Tracey's head in the ground right now, but presently, rescuing Lance took priority.

Though Wylder groaned about it, Bart made him help Regina and the hostages drag the pallet uphill, hauling big Lance home. Julie and Bart kept their guns in hand, in case the captives tried to run, or Tracey decided to fight, but assisted the others when they came to a

THE OLD LADY

difficult part of the trail.

At one point, Tracey stopped walking, and Bart told her to move.

"You don't want that," she said. "We keep going this way, and we're going to set off another trap."

Bart tensed. "How many did you plant?"

"Enough. Let me steer this ship or we all explode."

"Why the hell should I trust you?"

"You don't have a choice. Either we move several feet to the left, or we're all gonna look like the fat fuck here."

Regina started to curse the woman, and Bart raised a hand to silence her. "Alright," he said reluctantly. "Everyone move to the left."

"Wait," Julie said. "Shouldn't we locate these landmines and take them back with us?"

"Later."

Regina huffed. "Some kid could find them and blow themselves to bits."

"*I said* we'll find them *later*." Bart said, growing frustrated. "You want to dig around for landmines, or do you want to get Lance home?"

This shut Regina's mouth. The rest of the way up, Tracey advised the steps they took. She didn't say how many traps she'd set or pinpoint their locations but made them alter their route. By the time they reached the top of the hill, it was twilight time. Bart and Julie turned on the flashlights attached to their rifles, and they used the less-traveled pathways as night fell in full, marching like spent warriors through the unrelenting snow. It made Bart feel like a man on an exhibition, some traveler of old trying to climb Mount Everest or walk across Antarctica.

When he felt they were close enough, Bart suggested Julie run ahead and fetch one of the ATVs so they could hook the chains to it and drag Lance easier. Each of the vehicles were 500cc and could haul at least eight-hundred pounds. But after a short discussion with the others, it was clear an ATV couldn't make it through snow this deep without a plow attached, and the only one they had was for the pickup truck, which could never fit down this thin path. So they continued on foot, huffing and grunting, the team taking turns hauling but never giving Tracey and Nori a break, even as the young girl stumbled and wept.

Finally, they arrived at the compound. They helped Lance into the house and Regina tended to his wounds in their bedroom, bandaging and stitching him while feeding him Tramadol for the pain. Bart and Julie marched their prisoners down into the cellar, with Wylder tagging along, carrying down folding chairs as instructed. The house was warm, but the cellar was frigid, so Bart flicked on the electric heater they kept down there. Bart put Tracey's BOB on the floor. Seeing the blood on the concrete, he wondered how much of it had belonged to his late son.

"She needs to get warm," Tracey said, gesturing toward Nori with her head.

"No shit," Bart said. "We all do."

"Look at her!"

Bart did. The girl seemed confused and drowsy. She shivered so hard it almost looked like she was strapped in an electric chair, and her exposed skin was blue and ashen.

"She's frostbitten," Tracey said, "and suffering from hypothermia."

Wylder smirked. "Sucks to be her."

Tracey ignored him and kept her eyes on Bart. "She's too small to take this. If you don't tend to her, she'll be dead soon."

"Maybe that's what I want," Bart said.

"If you did, you would've killed her already."

Bart turned to Wylder. "Bring that space heater closer to the girl. And go make some chicken soup."

Wylder pouted but brought the electric heater close to Nori. He unfolded the three chairs. Nori was sat in one, Tracey in another. Bart used Zip Ties to secure Tracey's feet to the legs of the chair, then took his seat in front of the hostages as Wylder went back upstairs to the kitchen, still limping with his sprained ankle.

"You're right," Bart told Tracey. "I do want this girl alive. Or at least, my cousin here does." He nodded toward Julie, then smiled at Tracey. "You wanna know why?"

Tracey's face was a granite wall, expressing only contempt.

"She's a human trafficker," Bart explained. "I know I threatened to rape the girl, but frankly, I'm not a rapist and have no interest in that. And she's a little young for my tastes anyway. However, my cousin brings in a lot of money putting young women into prostitution, money we need to invest in our enterprises."

"You mean terrorism," Tracey said.

Bart squinted at the woman. "What makes you say that?"

"As your fat ass friend can tell you, I know a thing or two about

THE OLD LADY

bombs. You've got a barn full of ammonium nitrate and fertilizer, and when you came home earlier, you were in a huge truck. So obviously you're planning to be the next Tim McVeigh. You gonna blow up a daycare too, you fucking child killer?"

Bart resisted the urge to slap her. "And just how do you know all this?"

"You're a militia. It's what you yahoos do."

"You don't know all this for another reason?"

She gave him a curious look. "What? You think I'm some kind of spy?"

"Are you?"

"Wow. You really are stupid."

Now he did slap her. Tracey turned her head and spat, but her stoic expression remained unchanged. She had one of those thousand-yard stares. It made Bart wonder just what it would take to get her to cry out in pain. He aimed to find out.

"These kids were just hiking," Bart said. "I want to know what *you're* doing up here."

"Picking huckleberries."

"That's real cute. What're you doing in Henry Thompson's old cabin?"

Bart saw something flicker in the woman's eyes. He was on to something.

"Did you buy it after he died?" Bart asked.

Tracey didn't reply.

"Who are you?" Bart asked.

Again, Tracey said nothing.

Bart reached for the woman's bag, unzipped it, and drew out Tracey's large hunting knife, slapping the blade in his hand. "You know, we may want to keep Nori alive, but I just might want you to talk more than I want to sell her to rich pedophiles. Besides, I don't think they'd mind too much if she had some scars, as long as they weren't on the face and all her important holes still worked." He waited for Tracey to curse at him, but the woman only stared. Keeping his eyes on her, he gestured at Nori with the knife. "Tell me what I want to know, Tracey. From this point on, if you stonewall me or hand me bullshit or piss me off any further, I'm gonna start using this knife on the little dragon princess here."

Tracey breathed deep. "I didn't buy the cabin. I inherited it."

"*Inherited?*" Bart asked. "You're telling me you're some distant relative of Henry's? Some long-lost niece or cousin or something?"

"No. He was my father."

Bart furrowed his brow. "Henry didn't have any children."

"Yes, he did. One daughter. We were estranged is all. When he died, he left the cabin to me. I came here to fix it up and clean it out so I could sell it."

"Shit." Bart sat back and shook his head. "So that's why he didn't leave it to the cause."

Tracey narrowed her eyes at him. "What're you talking about?"

Bart was going to enjoy this. He leaned toward her again, smiling wide. "Your old man was part of our crew. In fact, he was our leader."

~

Every inch of Tracey ached. Her extremities were numb from the cold and her joints were tight with pain from hauling the fat man uphill on a pallet. But she could handle all of this. What she couldn't handle was this new information.

"Your father was the head of this outfit," Bart repeated. "I was his right-hand man and took over when he died. You call us terrorists? Well, your daddy was one too."

The news made Tracey burn inside. She didn't care enough about her old man to be disappointed in him; she was merely outraged by his limitless evil, and furious at how he could continue to hurt her from beyond the grave.

"I shouldn't be surprised," she said. "He was an asshole too."

"He was a freedom fighter. A good man."

"He was psychotic."

Bart snickered. "In that case, the apple doesn't fall far from the tree." He shook his head and smiled. "Henry had a daughter. How 'bout that? Now I understand how you know so much about explosives. See, I'm a certified explosives breacher, so I have experience with det cord, shock tube, and blasting caps. But your old man had that military training and he'd dedicated years of his life to being an expert in bombs, guns, traps, and everything else that could annihilate enemy forces. I was his right-hand man, so he allowed me to go to his cabin on occasion but wouldn't let anyone else on the team know about the place. He swore me to secrecy on that."

"What exactly was he hoping to accomplish by teaming up with a bunch of rednecks?"

"He had a very clear vision. We continue to do his work."

"Oh, please," Tracey said. "You're probably just Proud Boys or

THE OLD LADY

some other far-right loons."

This seemed to irk Bart. His mustache arched in a scowl.

"Proud Boys was started by a British Canadian," Bart said. "That's not American enough for me. And they're also focused on the wrong things. Tea Party, MAGA—it's all the same weak, unorganized, ineffective shit. The January 6th attack on the capitol proved that. Bunch of clowns in antlers making a mess and accomplishing nothing. And who did they hurt? *Cops*. Not leaders or politicians—just cops. This from people who claim to back the blue. It's all so stupid it makes my head hurt." He huffed, slapping the blade against his palm again. "Then you've got the leftist protestors on the other end, who are really just anarchists using protest marches as an excuse to riot, to steal and destroy property and assault police and anyone who doesn't agree with their sanctimonious, radical ideas."

"You're doing a lot of crying on behalf of pigs," Tracey said, hoping to pull more information out of him. "Makes me think you're in law enforcement. Or at least *were* in law enforcement. What happened? You get kicked off the force for beating a black seven-year-old to death?"

Bart slapped her again. She tasted blood but smiled anyway as she examined her surroundings—the workbench; the pole Dylan had been tied to; a washer and dryer in the back.

"In my day," she said, "all the rednecks living in the woods hated cops. Now they wave 'Back the Blue' flags from their porches, just like you. But still the dumb hicks like to call themselves outlaws. Pathetic morons. Fucking Nazi assholes."

"You think we're white supremacists?" Bart belted out a laugh. "Maybe that's what some people would make us out to be. The left calls the right racists, and the right calls the left pedophiles, and they're both right, but it goes both ways, and both parties have lost their fuckin' minds. This outfit though? We are not Nazis, skinheads, or Klansmen. We don't blame ethnics for all our country's problems. It goes much, much deeper than that. You don't know a *damn thing* about this outfit."

"How can you say that when I'm the daughter of your exalted leader?"

"Okay, bitch. You want to talk about this? We can do that." Bart leaned forward in his chair. "Your father loathed the U.S. government for forcing him to go to a war he wasn't even allowed to win. He resented the poor treatment he received as a veteran, so he wanted to take out government buildings. You call it domestic terrorism—we call it activism. *Real* activism. Not whining on social media and not organizing some pointless march. Real activism gets things done. You want change? You've got to strike fear into the owners of this country." He leaned closer to Tracey, his foul breath making her wince. "It's all tied together. Just like the domino effect of Ruby Ridge, The Branch Davidians, and McVeigh in Oklahoma City. How does my team's bombings differ from the American government bombing hospitals in Afghanistan, Serbia, or Iraq? With these strikes, we are operating with clinical detachment."

"Do you use clinical detachment when you sell children into sex slavery?" she asked.

"Casualties of war."

"This isn't a war."

"It's as good a name as any. People are driven to extremes over election results and Covid restrictions. Their media pushes them into a frenzy over trivial shit to distract them from the bigger picture. I say fuck all these knee-jerk reactions to social and political issues. I'm not going to be some homeland soldier for one of the two parties that have equally ruined my country. I am *not* leading a terrorist organization. And we're *not* a militia. Modern militias waste their time defending corporate businesses from looters like a bunch of fools. We're defending *ourselves*, and we're going to make our own stand. Your father felt the same way."

Tracey spat a bit of blood from her mouth onto the floor. "I already told you—my father was a psycho son of a bitch. Any ideology he could've had would only be crazy, stupid, and cruel. Now he's dead and the world's a better place without him. Just like it will be better off when I kill you."

Bart's lips thinned, his eyes blazing with resentment. "And just what ideology do you subscribe to that makes you feel so superior?"

"Nothing. If *any* group of people share a belief, you can bet your ass I'm against it."

The only sound then was footsteps as Wylder came down the stairs with a comforter and a large mug full of soup. He draped the blanket over Nori and held up a spoonful of noodles in front of her. She only stared at it.

"It ain't poisoned," Wylder told her.

Tracey turned to the girl. "Go ahead. You need to get warm. If these assholes want to poison us, they'll find a way to do it anyway."

THE OLD LADY

Nori slurped, the steam from the mug rising about her chapped face. Tracey worried the soup might contain drugs to knock the girl out, but perhaps that would be best for her, a reprieve from the grief, horror, and pain she'd suffered all day. And if she were to be raped, better for her to not experience it. As Wylder continued to feed Nori, he looked the girl up and down in a way Tracey didn't like.

"So who're you blowing up next?" Tracey asked Bart.

Bart shook his head. "You just mind your own business. I'm asking the questions here."

"Yeah, well, I've already told you everything."

"Not everything," he said, his voice deepening. "You haven't told me why you thought it was necessary to kill my son the way you did."

"Your son was a kidnapper and a rapist. That's why."

Bart glowered, anger tightening his eyes. "My son was not a rapist."

"He was at least an attempted rapist."

"Charlie was a mixed-up kid, I'll give you that. But he was a good boy. There's not a whole lot left in this world for me to love, but I loved him. And you took him away from me."

"With pleasure."

The comment earned her a devastating backhand. Her nostrils burned, one releasing a trickle of blood. Bart stared at her, long and hard, but said nothing. It seemed the leader was all out of questions and lectures. Silence hung in the room, broken only by the static hum of the space heater.

Finally, Bart spoke. "I've asked you where the other girl is. You say you don't know, but I need to be sure you're as worthless to me as you seem. And we *really* want to find that little bitch."

"She's probably got a SWAT team coming up the mountain as we speak."

Tracey was bluffing and knew it, but it was worth a try.

"Yeah, maybe," Bart said, aloof. "Or maybe she's got a bullet in her and has already bled to death. Or maybe she's as frozen as a fudgesicle. Either way, I will find her. But I'd rather do it quickly, so we're gonna find out just how much you two know." He sneered. "Or maybe I just want you to hurt for what you did to my boy."

His female assistant stepped forward, her pale face like a death mask.

"This is where Julie comes in," Bart said. "I've never been one for torture, myself. Don't have the stomach for it. But Julie? Well, she's got what you'd call a kink. Get my drift?"

He passed Tracey's knife to Julie, and she held it up so the blade covered one side of her face.

"Julie's going to interrogate you now, Tracey," Bart said, rising from his chair. "And little Nori here is going upstairs so Wylder can rape her."

Nori gasped and Tracey struggled against the Zip Tie cuffing her. Bart pushed her back in her chair so hard that it tipped over backwards. She hit the hard floor, the air leaving her lungs. When she opened her eyes, Wylder was hauling a kicking and screaming Nori up the stairs, a sinister grin on his face, his eyes on Tracey, mocking her. Bart put his foot on Tracey's chest so she couldn't get up.

"Maybe with a dick in her ass that little girl will talk," Bart said.

"Bastard!" Tracey shouted. "She's just a girl. She doesn't know anything. Alicia ran off! We don't know where she is any better than you do."

It wasn't entirely true, but Bart didn't know that. Neither did Nori.

"I guess we'll find out," Bart said.

"You wanna torture someone, make it me," Tracey said. "Leave the girl alone. You're a father, you should know—"

"I'm not a father anymore, remember?" he said, soft and low. "I'm gonna go upstairs where it's warm and have a coffee. I'll let you and Julie have some girl time."

Julie twirled the knife and smiled down at Tracey. "Maybe we'll start by doing our nails, huh?"

"If she talks," Bart told Julie, "get on it first thing. Finding the girl is more important than your little games, alright?"

"Sure thing, boss."

Bart gave Tracey one more loathsome glance. "Everything you experience from this point on is for Charlie. But don't worry. Julie will make you wish you were dead, but she won't kill you. That pleasure will be all mine."

Then he proceeded up the staircase, leaving Tracey alone with the dead-eyed woman holding a knife the size of her shin.

THIRTY-THREE

"THIS'LL BE A LOT EASIER on you if you just do what I say," Wylder told the shivering girl on his bed.

Nori refused to look at him. She sobbed quietly, the events of the day having broken the teenager. She'd fought him on their way up the stairs, but now it seemed what little energy she'd had left was spent.

"Not only did I serve you soup," Wylder said, "but I brought down a blanket for you, without anyone asking me to. Now, I'm no simp like Charlie was, but I'm trying to go easy on you, considering all you've been through. So maybe you oughta—"

A knock at the door interrupted him. Wylder poked his head out, seeing Bart.

"Yeah, boss?" Wylder asked.

"You doing what I asked?"

"Just about to, yeah."

Bart lowered his voice so only Wylder would hear. "Alright. Just don't hurt her too badly."

Wylder deflated. He'd been looking forward to hurting Nori, considering all she'd put him through. His plan was to soothe the girl, to lick her wounds, warming her to him so it would be even more painful when he finally resulted to violence. But Bart had other ideas, and he was the boss.

"You don't train a dog by kicking it," Bart told him. "Remember, Julie needs these girls to be shaped and molded. Forcing them won't do. You need to coax her, to make her submit."

"Yes, sir."

"You have the keys to the truck, right?"

"Yeah."

"Hand 'em over."

Wylder did.

Bart exhaled with exhaustion, looking his age. "I'm gonna take the plow out and get a head start on clearing the road for tomorrow. You've kept the gas cans in the barn full, haven't you? And not used it all up riding around on those damn four wheelers?"

"No, sir. Six of the five-gallon cans are full."

"Good. When I get back, we'll start loading everything into the other truck."

"Okay."

Bart took a deep breath. "I want you done here before I get back. You foresee any issues with that?"

Wylder couldn't resist. "Just one. The problem with fucking a Chinese girl is that half an hour later you wanna do it again."

He'd hoped to get a chuckle out of Bart, or at least a smile. Wylder had been trying to get back on his leader's good side all day. But Bart offered nothing.

"Be dressed and ready when I get back," Bart said, then closed the door and left.

Wylder whispered to himself. "Miserable old prick." He returned his attention to Nori. "Stand up, sweetheart."

The girl did, and when Wylder drew his pocketknife, she flinched.

"Relax," he said.

Wylder slid the knife between her hands and cut the Zip Ties. He gently turned her around and removed her coat. Nori didn't resist or make a sound. Wylder took that as a good sign. Maybe the girl had enough sense to not make things worse for herself than they had to be. As he removed the coat, he found something small and hard tucked under her sweater, hiding beneath her waistband. He drew it out.

Seeing what it was, Wylder shook his head. "They get on me for

THE OLD LADY

every little thing, but they miss a *taser* while searching you? Did they not bothering patting you down at all, or what?"

The question was rhetorical. Wylder put the stun gun on the dresser, a smug smile on his face. He was eager to tell Bart and Julie what he'd found just to rub it in their faces, but it could wait.

"Nice and warm in here, huh?" he asked Nori.

She didn't respond in any way.

Wylder turned her around to face him. Her cheeks were cracked and raw, her eyes blank from trauma. But Charlie had been right about her. She was a pretty girl. Wylder had done some things to women they hadn't appreciated, but he'd never done something like this. He was going to enjoy it, and wherever Charlie was now, Wylder hoped he'd enjoy it too.

"You ever get fucked before?" he asked, gliding his finger under her chin.

Nori trembled. "P-p-please…"

It was all she was able to get out.

"You're a virgin, aren't you?" he asked, only it wasn't a question.

She shut her eyes, forcing out tears, but she nodded.

"Well," he said gently, "if you don't resist, it will only hurt for a little while. First, we're gonna get you out of these clothes. You play nice and I'll play nice. You try to hurt me, and I promise you'll regret it the rest of your life. Understand?"

She hung her head, whimpering, and Wylder lifted her chin she so faced him.

"I need you to tell me you understand," he said.

He wiped a tear from her cheek and ran his thumb along her lips.

"Y-ye-yes," the girl stuttered. "I un-un-under—"

Wylder slid his thumb into her warm little mouth.

~

With the tool plugged in, Julie raised Tracey off the floor and sat her upright again. Her wrists remained bound behind her back with her ankles strapped to the chair legs. Julie undid the woman's coat, humming as she did so. Then she started unbuttoning Tracey's heavy flannel. She expected Tracey to say all the things women always said at times like this, to ask how Julie could do this to another woman, to beg and plead and try to bargain. But Tracey was a blank, as if made of stone. That was fine with Julie. With the right tools, even the toughest stone could be broken.

She undid the woman's belt and started yanking her snow pants.

Tracey didn't help her any, but Julie managed to get them down around her calves. Being tied to the chair, Tracey's legs were forced open just enough. Julie picked up Tracey's huge hunting knife again, smiling at her prisoner as she flicked the tip of the blade.

"Nice and sharp," Julie said.

She carefully ran the flat side of the blade up Tracey's leg, not cutting the woman as she inched closer to her panties. Tracey didn't even flinch when Julie slipped the blade between her flesh and underwear. A few tugs and the panties gave, leaving Tracey exposed.

"I've never seen a bush like that outside of '70s porn," Julie said. She pushed pubic hair up and found what she was looking for. "Ah, there's your button. Something tells me it's been a long time since anyone's flicked it for you."

Julie grabbed a fistful of pubic hair, held it taught, and sliced through it with the knife. She wasn't gentle about it, but it still failed to get a rise out of Tracey. The woman didn't even whimper, let alone cry and beg. She just sat there like a propped-up corpse. She seemed lost in thought, as if she were concentrating on something outside of her present dilemma.

"You know," Julie said, her face level with Tracey's, "the Arabs—Muslims, of course—have a practice called 'Tahor' or 'Sunna'. Much simpler words than what we call it in America, which is a Clitoridectomy. Know what that is?"

Nothing.

"People tend to think men do it to their wives to keep them from cheating, but it's often done to young women by older women, as a sort of rite of passage." She gently glided the flat of the blade over Tracey's privates, not cutting her yet. "For example, in Ethiopia, girls are cut at just nine days old. In half the countries that practice female genital mutilation, most girls have it done before they even reach their fifth birthday. In the Central African Republic, Chad, Egypt, Somalia—the wide majority of girls are cut to mark their passage into adulthood, a coming-of-age ritual that—"

"Jesus, you prattle on worse than your cousin," Tracey said.

Julie turned the blade and pressed the sharp edge against Tracey's clitoris. The women locked eyes in a death stare. Julie pressed a little harder, the blade just breaking the surface. Tracey held her gaze, unflinching.

Julie smiled and cut Tracey's clitoris in half.

As she stood up straight, Julie's smile faded. Tracey hadn't

THE OLD LADY

screamed. She wasn't writhing against her ties. Even though her genitals were bleeding, the woman continued to stare at Julie with silent loathing.

Furious, Julie went at the woman again, putting a long gash in Tracey's leg. It was only surface level, but the blood began to flow, exciting Julie. She put the knife under Tracey's t-shirt and sawed it open. Tracey wore no bra. Julie grabbed one of the woman's breasts and gently sliced open her nipple.

Not a grunt. Not a hiss. Not a curse.

Nothing.

Julie stepped back and her brow furrowed in confusion. Tracey stared right at Julie, not even bothering to check her wounds.

"So," Julie said, "you're a hard ass, huh? I thought you might be." She ran her finger over the old scar on Tracey's neck. "Fortunately, I'm creative."

Placing the knife on the workbench, Julie picked up the tool she'd prepared. It was ready now. She gripped the handle but kept it plugged in. The little red button was lit, assuring her it was on. The coils at the end of the device seemed almost as eager as she was as she held it up before Tracey's face.

"Ever use a magnetic induction heater?" Julie asked.

The death-stare continued.

"It's a flameless heating tool used in auto repair," Julie explained. "Almost looks like a curling iron, doesn't it? Mostly, it's used to take out stubborn bolts. But you see, I've learned it is equally good for taking out stubborn bitches."

Feeling the heat coming off the device, Julie tingled with anticipation. She stepped closer to Tracey and squatted so she was between the woman's legs.

"It's hot now," Julie said, "but it's still warming up. It's going to get very, *very* hot. But by the time it reaches its max temperature, it will have already been inside you for several minutes."

Finally, Julie saw a twitch in Tracey's eyelids.

~

To teach her to ignore pain, Tracey's father had put her through torture exercises.

"You get captured," he said, "and our enemies will want information out of you. They may want to know where our cabin is, or want to know about me or any number of things. And some of them won't hesitate to ask you these questions at the edge of a knife, get me?"

In her pre-teens, Tracey had been tied to a chair and given a belt to bite down on as her father pushed pins beneath her fingernails. He held her bare foot over the flame of his Zippo until the sole blistered and turned black. One day, he decided to break the pinkie on her left hand, then set it again with a splint. He starved her and deprived her of water, all the while telling her he was doing this for her own good, that he was doing it out of love, and that even though she might not understand it right now, she would one day.

And slowly, Tracey did learn how to ignore pain. Her father made her stand on a stool for hours on end, recreating the nightmarish treatment he'd received as a POW, and Tracey had no choice but to take it all until she began to harden, inside and out. Eventually, she realized the trick to it was to never show her father that the things he did hurt or upset her. She found a way to leave her body and flee into the fractured passages of her own mind, escaping into an almost meditative trance while remaining completely aware of what was happening around her. First, she didn't scream or struggle. Then she learned how to control her reflexes and keep herself from jumping, wincing, and clenching her teeth.

That's when her father stopped putting her through it all. He was satisfied that his daughter was impervious to torture, or at least the sort of torture he was comfortable subjecting her to. With Dad, there were never any sexual molestations or beatings brought on by anger. The child abuse Tracey endured at his hand was much different from everything she would later hear about in group therapy discussions, over and over again. And while he'd inflicted minor injuries on her body, they were able to heal. The same could not be said for the mental and emotional scars that resulted from those long days and nights when she was locked inside that cabin and strapped to a chair, much like she was now.

Julie came closer with the magnetic induction heater. While the sadistic smirk on the bitch's face was infuriating, it wasn't what made Tracey ball her fists behind her back. They'd been balled the entire time as she pulled the end piece of the Zip Tie with her thumb and index finger, tightening the loop while simultaneously pushing her hands away from each other. Her wrists were chaffing and raw, but it was just another physical pain she could easily ignore. She kept creating tension on the tie by pulling her wrists in opposite directions, and just as she felt the radiating heat of the tool's coils inch closer to her

THE OLD LADY

genitals, Tracey snapped the Zip Ties, freeing her hands.

Though her feet were still tied to the chair, Tracey lunged at her tormentor. Frazzled by the sudden movement, Julie's eyes went wide, and Tracey grabbed her skull with both hands and shoved her thumbs into the sockets. The hot tool fell from Julie's hands, and she grabbed Tracey's wrists and shook her head violently to free her eyes from the assault. Tracey punched Julie in the face, instantly splitting her lip, and then grabbed her skull again and started bashing it against the concrete floor. Julie fought back, clawing at Tracey, trying to wiggle out from under her, but even with her legs tied to the chair, Tracey overpowered the woman, and kept bashing Julie's skull into the pavement until she saw a burst of blood.

Julie's eyelids fluttered as she went slack. Her legs twitched instead of kicked, arms falling at her sides. But Tracey continued to slam her skull against the concrete. Finally, she heard something crack, then dropped the woman's head. Julie mumbled, but was in no condition to flee, fight, or even scream for help.

Tracey snatched her hunting knife from the workbench and cut her feet free. She pulled up her pants, sheathed the knife, and glanced at the induction heater on the floor. The old, familiar fury caused her heart to beat rapidly, and now that she was free, she began to feel the pain Julie had caused her body. Growling, Tracey undid Julie's pants and underwear, thinking of grabbing the handle of the induction heater with one hand, pushing open Julie's buttocks with the other, and sodomizing her with the coil, shoving it in deep so it would cook the woman's colon from the inside. But when Tracey rolled Julie onto her stomach, it exposed the cracked skull. Blood spread from the fracture. Tracey positioned Julie with her face in the puddle and straddled her.

Then she grabbed the heating tool.

Tracey jammed it into the woman's head wound, pushing through the fractured bits of skull to burn the brain. Julie's eyes shot open, her face twisted in a grimace of agony unlike anything Tracey had ever seen, and just as Julie took in a breath to scream, Tracey put her hand over the woman's mouth and drove the tool in deeper.

THIRTY-FOUR

REGINA FOLLOWED BART OUT TO the barn, continuing to plead with him as he finished putting gas in the pickup. He placed the plow mounting bar before the pickup's front bumper.

"Please," she said. "If we don't get him to a doctor, he's gonna die."

"You stitched and bandaged him up, didn't you?"

"Of course, but I'm not a doctor. He needs professional treatment."

"Regina—"

"Please, Bart. With the plow, we can get down the mountain and get Lance to a hospital."

Bart shook his head and sighed. "And then what? Huh? How do we explain that he stepped on a homemade landmine?"

"I know," she said, looking away as if shamed. "I'm aware of the risks but he's my husband. Without a doctor, he ain't gonna make it."

"Doctors call the police when they get someone who has been shot. What do you think they're going to do with explosive wounds, huh? They'll open a whole investigation, that's what. Then we're all fucked, and the mission is fucked too."

THE OLD LADY

"Damn it, I don't care about the mission!"

Bart snapped his head toward her, the anger that had accumulated throughout the day becoming a single beam of hatred focused on the woman standing before him.

"You don't *care*?" he asked.

Regina hesitated. Bart relished the fear in her eyes, but she stood her ground.

"I know we worked long and hard on this," she said, "but nothing is as important to me as my husband's life. Surely you understand that."

Bart punched the side of the truck, startling Regina.

"Here's what I understand," he said, pointing at her face. "You're willing to risk everything on the off-chance Lance might not recover from his injuries. You want to throw away everything your husband and the rest of us worked so hard on the past few months, and put us all in jail, just because you're afraid."

Tears filled Regina's eyes, but her face remained wrinkled in irritation, and her objections persisted.

"Goddamn, Bart. When are you gonna wake up and realize we've already lost? We were all supposed to be safe—that was the promise, wasn't it? We'd all be far away by the time the bomb went off and only government officials would be taken out in the blast, right? Well, newsflash, dipshit—four members of this team are dead, and now we might just lose a fifth. I *never* would've asked you to focus on the mission if there'd been a chance to save Charlie, so don't you *dare* tell me to sacrifice my Lance."

Bart seethed. "Don't you ever talk about my son again."

"Then at least listen to this. We are *fucked*. Got that? Four deaths—six with the dead kids—two hostages, that Alicia girl on the loose, *and* this blizzard, and you still can't accept that there's no way we can pull the mission off anymore."

Bart grabbed Regina by her coat and pulled her into him. "Now you listen to me, you condescending bitch!" He held her tight as she tried to twist free. "*I'm* still the leader of this outfit and *I* make the calls. You've been testing me since day one and have only gotten pushier since I grabbed your titties. You just can't let that go, can you?"

Regina started to say something, so Bart shook her.

"Shut the fuck up!" he said. "I am the team leader, and I decide when a mission is on and when it is off—and this mission has never been more on."

He released her and the momentum caused Regina to stumble backward and fall. Now the fear in her eyes was at the level Bart needed it to be. He didn't help her up, only watched as she struggled to pull herself out of the snow. Her face contorted between rage and grief, but she didn't talk back to him now.

"Have I gotten through that thick skull of yours?" he asked. "Are you finally going to listen to your commanding officer?"

Regina paled. "Sure, Bart. Whatever you say."

"Good," he said, flipping the locking pins of the plow. "Now get in the damn truck. I need these roads clear for tomorrow, and you're coming with me so I can keep my eye on you."

~

Tracey slid her shotgun out of her BOB, put it by the front door, and continued to creep through the empty living room. The house was eerily calm and silent, a stark contrast to the rest of the day she'd had. Her body ached from injuries, but she was able to walk and secure the butt of the shotgun to her shoulder.

The kitchen was as empty as the living room, so she stepped into the hallway with gentle, silent footfalls. She heard a man's muffled voice and followed it to one of the bedrooms. The other rooms were silent. She didn't even hear a TV or radio going. As she reached the door, she realized it was Wylder she heard on the other side of it.

"That's a good girl," he was saying.

Tracey looked at the doorknob. There was no keyhole, no lock. She turned it slowly, and when she felt the bolt slide out of the latch, she inched the door open.

Wylder was standing with his back to the door with Nori on her knees in front of him. His jeans were undone, and he was staring down at the girl. Tracey couldn't see exactly what he was making Nori do, but she didn't have to see it to know.

"Watch your teeth," he told Nori, unaware of Tracey's presence.

Tracey would have blasted his head right off his shoulders if she weren't trying to keep quiet. Instead, she came at him with the butt of the shotgun. Sensing someone was there, Wylder spun his head just in time for the shoulder stock to bust his mouth. Wylder grunted and stumbled, and Nori rose quickly to get away from him, darting toward the dresser. Two teeth fell from Wylder's lips.

Watch your teeth, Tracey thought.

She put one leg in front of Wylder and jabbed the butt of the gun

THE OLD LADY

into his back, tripping him. He fell against the bed before dropping to the floor, facing her, and Tracey shoved the business end of the shotgun under his chin.

"Not a word," she told him. "Don't scream. Don't move."

Wylder blinked in disbelief. "You…"

She pressed the shotgun into his bottom jaw. "I *said* not a word."

Gulping, Wylder sealed his bloody lips and closed his eyes. Before Tracey could give any further instruction or ask him where the others were, Nori ran toward them and shoved something against his ribs.

The crackle of the stun gun seemed as loud as fireworks in the silent house, but Tracey didn't stop the girl as she zapped her assaulter. She closed the door and watched it with her shotgun at the ready. Nori continued to stun Wylder. He convulsed on the floor, whimpering through clenched teeth. The girl was crying and snarling at the same time. A terrible fury had taken her somewhere dark and merciless. Tracey knew that place well, so she let Nori have her just revenge, and when Tracey looked back, Nori was sending electric currents through Wylder's exposed genitalia. He was frozen by the volts running through him and could do nothing to resist as his scrotum began to turn black.

Tracey drew her hunting knife and came over to them. Wylder was now splayed out on the floor with Nori crouching over him, her face tight with hatred, her eyes like black caverns, hollowed by the waking nightmare she'd endured.

"Enough," Tracey said.

Nori reluctantly pulled back with the stun gun.

Tracey held up her knife. "Let me finish this so we can get out of here."

"No," Nori said. She reached out with an open hand. "H-he's muh-muh-mine."

The girl had the same look she'd had when Tracey had given her the machete back at the cabin. It seemed like years ago now, but Nori had that same grim determination, and though she'd been forced to abandon the machete, the knife she was asking for was nearly as big, and a girl as petite as Nori would need both hands to use it.

Having been where Nori was right now—distraught and ashamed and stripped of her humanity—Tracey wanted to give the girl the knife and let her vent as brutally as she desired, but she also knew the permanent stain murder put upon one's soul.

"You don't want this, kid," she told her. "I know you think you do, but—"

"Guh-give it to m-muh-me."

Their eyes locked, and Tracey realized the Hell of all the girl had been through had already stained her soul, even painted it in full. Her life had been derailed and the wreckage would be smoking for a long time. Who was Tracey to deny Nori the same vengeance she'd taken against her attacker? Who was she to try to save somebody who had already been broken?

"Alright," Tracey said, extending the knife, handle first. "But make it quick."

Nori took the knife in both hands, wielding it like a sword, and as the hunger for murder flamed through the teen, Tracey saw a reflection of another sad, shattered girl, one she'd not seen since she'd first left the cabin all those decades ago. In Nori, Tracey saw herself, and what she saw sickened her.

But it was too late.

Nori had already raised the knife over her head, and now the blade was coming down at Wylder as he struggled to compose himself after being worked over with the stun gun. The knife entered the side of Wylder's neck, squirting a jet of blood from his punctured jugular. Nori tried to pull the knife out to stab him again, but it was stuck inside him, so she put her foot against his shoulder for leverage and yanked the blade free, causing more blood to burst from the rapist's neck. He grabbed at the wound in a futile effort to pressurize it, and gargled what may have been pleas for mercy as Nori came down with the knife once more, sinking the blade halfway into Wylder's belly.

Weeping, Nori scurried away from the man as if suddenly terrified of him again, leaving the blade in his stomach. Wylder was in no condition to do anything with it though. He was bleeding out rapidly. Though he was presently alive, Nori had killed him. But she didn't need to know that. Despite her reservations, Tracey pulled the knife from Wylder's belly, grabbed his hair, snapped his neck back, and slit his throat. It wasn't necessary, but Tracey felt it might lessen any guilt Nori may experience when this was all over.

Tracey wiped the blade on the bedsheets and sheathed the knife. "Let's go."

Drying her eyes, Nori put on her coat. Tracey was picking up her shotgun when she heard a truck rumble outside. Going to the window, she peeked through the gap in the curtains, watching the pickup as it plowed snow off the path.

THE OLD LADY

So that's where they are, she thought.

It made sense that they would want to get a head start on the snow now, especially if they planned to execute their terrorist attack soon. She wondered how much time this would buy her and Nori. She also wondered how many members of the team had gone off in the plow truck. Bart and that other woman perhaps, but certainly not the fat fuck, if he were even still alive.

Tracey intended to find out.

She told Nori to stay close and the girl clutched her stun gun as Tracey led the way with her shotgun. It was then she noticed the drops of blood leading to the second door on the right. The door was open a crack, but the room was dark. Tracey told Nori to stay back, then took a deep breath and kicked the door open, ready to spray hot lead. But when she saw the only person in the room, she realized she didn't have to.

The light from the hall fell across the fat man's slack face. His eyes were open, but they responded to nothing. His tongue hung out of his mouth and his big belly was still instead of rising and falling with breaths.

She'd been wondering how long it would take for him to die.

Her father had always dipped the nails, darts, and other shrapnel in cyanide and rolled the bits in rat poison before inserting them into the bombs, so if the blast didn't kill his enemies, the poison would.

The sound of the pickup truck grew fainter as it drove away.

If the fat man's wife were still here, she would have been by his side. She had to be in the truck. She and Bart were the only ones left now, and Tracey didn't think Bart would let an important task be done without him, so she ascertained they both had gone out to plow.

But how far would they go? How long would they be gone?

"C'mon," she told Nori. "Let's grab my BOB and get the fuck out of here."

At the front door, she dug into the bag for extra shells, making sure the shotgun was fully loaded. Then she dug out the pouch of first aid supplies and dropped her pants. Seeing the blood running down the insides of her legs, Nori looked away as Tracey applied an alcohol wipe and gauze pad to her cut vagina before pulling her pants up. She searched through the bag, hoping Bart had put her keys in it, but they were nowhere to be found. They were probably still in his pocket with the keys to the bigger truck. The only transportation Tracey and Nori could steal were the ATVS, but they would be useless in snow this deep.

She slung the bag over her shoulders, but as they were about to leave, Tracey noticed the gun rack on the other side of the living room, and there was the weapon the fat man's wife had been carrying earlier. The cobalt AK47 seemed to call on her like a spotlight.

"Okay," she said, turning to Nori. She handed the girl the shotgun, telling her how to pump a fresh shell into the chamber after firing. She pointed out the safety and told her to keep it off. "You don't have to be a good shot with this because it creates a spray. Just keep your finger off the trigger until it's time to shoot, and make sure I'm nowhere in the line of fire when you do. And watch for the kickback. Always put the stock to your shoulder."

Nori gazed upon the gun in her hands with silent awe, clearly shocked Tracey had finally given her a firearm. But Tracey knew it was time. If the girl could handle all that had happened so far, she could handle a shotgun. The last thing Tracey wanted was for Nori to get captured again. The poor girl would be better off dying in a gunfight if it came to that.

Taking the AK47 from the rack, Tracey checked that it was fully loaded. Judging by the magazine, she guessed it held more than twenty rounds. She wasn't sure what Bart and his cronies had done with her rifle and didn't care. This upgrade would do nicely.

"We go out the back," she told Nori.

They exited into the black and frozen night, the arctic wind sounding like a distant train. At least it had stopped snowing, for now. Tracey scanned their surroundings for any other militia soldiers, just in case, but right now they were the only people at the compound that were still alive.

Tracey slung the rifle over her shoulder by the strap and drew her knife from its sheath.

"Wha-what is it?" Nori whispered.

Tracey unscrewed the bolt at the end of the knife's handle, dug inside with one finger, and removed the small device.

"Alicia," Tracey said, looking down at the receiver.

The GPS tracker had been attached to Alicia's ferrocerium rod, which was the main reason Tracey had stressed to the girl not to lose it. She would have told Alicia she'd planted the device on her, but had feared it would only frighten Alicia, that she might not want to be tracked by a madwoman like Tracey. Looking at the tiny screen, she saw the green dot indicating Alicia wasn't out of range. The device

THE OLD LADY

showed what direction to go in and how many miles away Alicia was. The girl was closer than Tracey would have expected. It was a relief to know she could still rescue Alicia, but it pained Tracey to realize the teen hadn't made it off the mountain yet. If anything, she'd lost some of the ground they'd gained. Had she gotten lost even with the compass? Had the snowstorm discombobulated her? It was concerning. Just because the tracking device was still working didn't mean it would lead Tracey to a living girl. It might already be too late for Alicia, but she had to know for sure.

"She's about a mile downhill," Tracey told Nori.

"Th-that's all?" Nori asked, seeming equally confused. "Y-you sure that th-th-thing is working?"

Tracey hadn't considered this until now. Perhaps the receiver had been busted in the snowmobile crash. Maybe Alicia had lost it. Or maybe the old thing had simply died.

"I'm not sure of anything," Tracey admitted. "But right now, this is our best shot, and we're headed downhill anyway."

She showed Nori how to read the tracking device and told her to hang on to it in case they got separated. Somehow, Tracey was sure they would. At least this way Nori could locate Alicia. Hopefully they could escape together. And if Alicia was already dead, Nori would be able to lead police to the body.

"Okay," Tracey said, looking to the treeline. "Let's move out. I know you've been through a lot, but I also know you're stronger than you look. We need to move fast, kid. No matter how deep the snow or how tired we are, we must get to Alicia as quickly as possible—for her sake as well as our own—and get off this mountain before the last of these scumbags come back and realize we're gone."

They stuck to the thin path, avoiding Harding Trail. Tracey figured it would be the first place Bart and his last remaining soldier would look for them. She'd also set several traps there, and with the snow this high and the cloudy skies making the night extra black, Tracey doubted she'd be able to spot them anymore.

It had stopped snowing, but they had to tromp through what had already fallen. It was deep enough to swallow half their shins, but they kept moving, propelling themselves down the mountainside in a steady trudge. Nori held the tracking device up so they could both watch the screen, and Tracey turned on the flashlight attached to the rifle, exposing the white forest ahead.

The thin trail grew thinner. The pain between Tracey's legs

became more apparent, and the aches of all her bruises returned as her adrenaline dropped. The cold numbed some of it, but she was beginning to realize just how injured she really was. Nori wasn't looking so good either. Though she hadn't been beaten and mutilated as Tracey had, the cold had done extensive damage to her face, leaving it purple, ashen, and waxy. Being inside for a while had eased some of Nori's muscle stiffness, but Tracey guessed the poor thing would probably lose a toe or two once this was all over. But considering all Nori had lost already, toes would be but an afterthought.

"How're you holding up?" Tracey asked her once they'd been on the trail for a while.

Nori didn't say anything. It worried Tracey until she remembered Bart had taken away the girl's hearing aid. Tracey repeated what she'd said a little louder, and Nori said she was fine through heavy breaths. Being four decades older, Tracey was breathing even heavier, her worn body threatening to give out regardless of how well she could ignore pain. The pad between her legs was soaked through with blood, and one of her eyes was so bruised it was halfway closed. When she tongued her teeth, she found one of them was loose, and she was fairly certain Bart had broken her nose.

She was battered. She was tired. She was old.

And she was insane.

The urge to just sit in the snow and freeze to death was growing stronger. After all these years of putting guns in her mouth but never having the courage to pull the trigger, Tracey now felt it would be easy. More than that, it would be right. Despite the circumstances, she'd killed seven people today. One of them had been an innocent engineer. The others she'd killed either in self-defense or on a rescue mission, but she'd ended their lives with brutal savagery. She was everything people had always said she would turn out to be—a monster.

"*You did what you had to do,*" her father said from within.

"They were your friends," she mumbled, knowing Nori couldn't hear her.

"*But they were your enemies, and you did away with them efficiently. I am proud of you, kiddo.*"

"That you're proud of me only proves just how horrible all I've done truly is."

"*No, it's praise from Caesar. You did it all just like I taught you, like a real soldier.*"

"That's what you said the last time I killed someone, and just look

THE OLD LADY

where that got me. Nine years in prison, that's where."

"Would you have been happier letting that son of a bitch get away with what he did to you? Have you forgotten how much he hurt you?"

The question infuriated her. How could she have ever forgotten the events of that night? Every time she looked in a mirror, the long scar on her neck reminded her that the man she'd killed had left scars on her body as well as her mind.

~

It happened on her fortieth birthday. Tracey had been separated from Gavin and Olivia for a couple of years, drifting so they couldn't find her, and not even calling to check on them or tell them she was okay. She'd already decided they were better off without her, and it would only be more difficult for them to move on if she kept popping back into their lives. Having surrendered to the dark embrace of drugs and alcohol again, Tracey drifted between flophouses and drug dens, sleeping in her car and camping out when she had to, and going home with men she met in bars just for a warm bed and a sexual tryst that could take her mind off her self-hatred.

But she'd had no intention of going home with Randy Duncan.

She'd been celebrating her birthday at The Brass Tap, a seedy bar in Somersworth, and Randy was just one of several male strangers who'd bought her a drink that night. Unlike the others though, Randy seemed to think buying a woman a vodka and tonic meant she owed him something. He followed Tracey around the bar half the night, continuously invading her personal space. Though not particularly threatening, he came off as overly friendly and desperate, which turned her off as much as his beer belly, curly mullet, and matching black goatee. He was a typical New Hampshire redneck with paint-stained construction boots and a Patriots hoodie, with a can of Narragansett always in hand.

It was near one in the morning. Tracey was moderately drunk. The remaining stragglers were all filing out as the lights came on and the jukebox cut ZZ Top short. Tracey had been flirting with a tall man in a lumberjack flannel all night, but he hadn't reciprocated interest when she'd asked to go home with him. This meant another cold night sleeping in her car, but while Tracey didn't prefer it, she'd grown used to it. She was walking through the parking lot when she heard footsteps behind her, and she turned around sharply to see Randy unlocking his minivan.

He spotted her and waved. "Hey, birthday girl. Want to keep this party going?"

"No, thanks." Though the man might have a warm bed at home, Tracey wasn't keen on what she'd have to do to sleep in it. "I'm pretty tired."

Randy took a few steps toward her. "I've got just the thing for that."

A Toyota Celica passed between them on its way out, leaving Tracey alone with Randy in the parking lot.

"You into blow?" he asked, grinning with one side of his mouth. "I've got some for special occasions."

The familiar yearning for cocaine tingled through Tracey then. It'd been nearly a week since she'd snorted any. She also had a booze headache and knew just how well a line of blow cured them.

"Oh yeah?" she asked, being playful even though she wasn't so sure about going anywhere with this guy. "Where's it stashed?"

"Just in my van here." He pointed back to it. "Interested?"

She crossed her arms, contemplating, still tipsy. "Okay. But just one thing—I'm not gonna sleep with you."

Randy furrowed his brow and looked away, embarrassed.

"Just want to be up front about it," Tracey said. "So there's no misunderstanding. No offense, but I'm just not interested in you that way. So don't expect even a hand job."

Randy nodded, still unable to make eye contact. "Yeah. Yeah, it's okay."

Tracey waited for more, but Randy said nothing further.

"If you want to rescind your offer, it's fine," Tracey said.

"Nah. It's cool. C'mon."

He turned back toward his minivan, waving her on to follow. Tracey hesitated. She'd had bad experiences before with men behind taverns. But it was her birthday, and she did want to keep the party going to avoid thinking about her advancing age. She was also desperate for cocaine, and addiction had a way of clouding her better judgment.

She looked at her car. Inside the glovebox was a stun gun. After her arrest for drugs, her father's pistol had been taken away from her, but she hadn't been carrying it on her at the time of her arrest and therefore wasn't charged with possession of an illegal firearm. She was tempted to get the stun gun now but knew it would frighten Randy off if he happened to see it, and her tight clothing made concealing any weapon impossible. As Randy reached the van, he slid the

THE OLD LADY

big door open and waved her toward him again.

Having just turned forty, Tracey scolded herself for being such an old lady. When she'd been in her twenties, she'd had many wild nights doing drugs with men she barely knew, partying in cheap motel rooms, apartments, and parked cars. Sometimes she slept with one of the guys and sometimes she didn't. Only once had she found herself in a dangerous situation with a group of strangers in a back alley. But she hadn't let that stop her from having a good time with others because she didn't want to live in fear. Her father had lived his life that way and it had corroded his soul and sanity. Being spontaneous, carefree, and even reckless had always been alluring to Tracey because it went against everything her miserable old man had taught her. Was she willing to let that part of her youth go now that she was approaching middle age? Was she going to let herself become just another scared old lady peeking through the blinds, or was she going to enjoy life?

No sooner was she in the back of Randy's van than Tracey realized she'd made a grievous error. Like a foolish little girl, she'd been led into a stranger's van by the promise of candy. As the door slid closed behind her, her nerves went taut, and she reached for the handle without a word.

"Don't," Randy said, taking her wrist.

Tracey tried to twist away. When Randy didn't let go, she punched him in the face. She was too drunk to land a solid blow, but still managed to hurt him. Randy's grip on her loosened, but when she pulled the handle, she realized the door was locked. She ran her hands along the door, searching for the release in the dark.

That's when the knife went to her neck.

It was a small, folding knife with a serrated blade, and Randy had pressed it against her throat hard enough that the teeth tore tiny holes in her skin.

"Don't move," he said.

She didn't listen. Tracey swung at him, writhing in her seat, and Randy dug the blade in deeper, opening her neck. He got on top of her, his weight pinning her down until she was forced to stop struggling.

"You don't understand!" Randy said, sounding almost as rattled as she was. "I didn't wanna do this. You just never gave me a chance!"

Tracey tried to get an arm free, and he squeezed his thighs tighter to lock them to her sides. She jerked and the blade cut higher, inching up her jaw just below her ear.

"Why don't women want to have sex with me?" Randy demanded. "I'm a nice guy! I bought you a drink, didn't I? Why're you all so mean?"

Again Tracey tried to get out from under him, but the man was heavier than she could handle, she was drunk, and he had a knife to her neck.

"I don't wanna hurt you," Randy said. "But I need this. If you can't be nice to me, at least be still."

He crawled down to get between her legs but kept the blade at her throat. She closed her knees together, but he managed to pry her legs apart and lift her skirt. The weight of his body pinned her, and whenever she made a move he didn't like, Randy dug the blade's teeth deeper into her neck, sawing through the flesh.

The big man took what he wanted from her, and the thing Tracey hated the most about it was that her body responded to his forced entry with natural lubrication. Later, she would learn this was merely the female body's defense mechanism against further vaginal harm, but in the moment, it filled her with a nauseating shame to think that some part of her might be enjoying getting raped.

Randy was finished within minutes, and once his hunger for sex was satiated, his face went pale, as if he was shocked by his own actions. He didn't say anything, but he slowly backed off Tracey, and as soon as the knife left her throat, she made a grab for it. Bending her leg back, she kicked Randy in the stomach and grabbed his wrist, digging her long nails into it until his grip on the knife loosened. She snatched it with her other hand and kicked him again, knocking him back against the wall of the van, and as she scooted out from under him, he raised his hands passively.

"Wait," he said. "Please, don't go…"

That he thought she was going to flee at this point baffled Tracey. Randy's wet eyes couldn't meet hers, and he put his hands to the sides of his face. He seemed to be struggling to say something—probably some weak apology, Tracey guessed. It didn't matter what he may have said. Nothing would have changed her mind.

She lunged at Randy with the knife.

He put his hands up in self-defense, and Tracey drove the knife through one of his palms and tore the blade free before he could even scream. She swung again, hacking into his forearm, and when Randy punched at her she ignored the pain and kept stabbing. Every time

THE OLD LADY

he tried to snatch the knife, he paid for it with further mutilation to his hands, and as he tried to kick his legs out from under her, she brought the knife down through his thigh, sinking the five-inch blade through the meat. Blood gushed, the backseat of the van becoming a slaughterhouse floor as Tracey continued to stab and slash at the man who had violated her. They both screamed and bled, going mad together, and even when Randy stopped fighting back, Tracey continued to drive the blade in and out of his body.

She was still stabbing him when the police arrived.

Someone had noticed the commotion in the parking lot and called 911. The police ordered her out of the vehicle with their guns drawn. Tracey finally stopped stabbing Randy, and it was as if she were seeing his corpse for the first time. The mangled man was peppered with bloody holes. Tracey would later learn they totaled eighty-seven stab wounds. His face was no longer recognizable, and his open stomach exposed his insides.

A voice called to her, snapping her out of her trance. "Get out of the van with your hands up!"

Tracey found the latch and stepped out into the glow of police lights, a blood-caked woman with a torn skirt and a sliced neck. She was ordered to drop the knife she hadn't realized she was still holding and was immediately placed under arrest and escorted to a hospital under police supervision.

The evidence acquired by the rape kit ended up being crucial to her trial. Despite the brutality of how she'd murdered Randy Duncan, Tracey's murder charges were reduced to manslaughter because of the deep wounds on her neck and the proof she'd been raped by the man. She was found guilty and, the court taking her previous criminal record into account, as well as the savagery of her violence, she was sentenced to ten years in prison, but served only nine.

While in prison, she rejected tribalism and refused to join any gangs or participate in any group activities. Gavin had tried to see her while she was serving time before her trial, but she'd refused. He continued to try to make contact while she was in prison, but now more than ever, Tracey wanted him and their daughter out of her life. Not only did she want them to move on, but she also considered herself finished with other human beings.

Tracey sunk further inward, spending the next nine years in relative silence, reading and exercising alone, eating quickly in the lunch hall to avoid small talk, allowing her misanthropy to swallow her whole. She got into a few fights while in prison, most of which she won, but she was also jumped by several groups because she refused to join one, which would have offered her protection. Tracey came to despise women almost as much as she did men, but over time the other inmates decided she was simply insane and left her alone. Even the guards seemed uncomfortable around her, but she gave them no trouble because she didn't want to interact with other people any more than she had to.

She trusted no one and believed in nothing.

Eventually, Gavin stopped trying to bring Olivia to visit her mother. And when she was finally released, no one came to pick her up. It wasn't until her father's lawyer managed to track her down that she heard from anyone at all.

Dad was dead.

He had a new home in Hell, and the cabin was hers.

THIRTY-FIVE

THE PLOWING PROVED DIFFICULT. THE old pickup truck didn't have the power it once had, and Bart had to take it slow so the engine wouldn't stall, even though he'd been plowing downhill. But he managed to clear a path down to the street, which the town's trucks would clear in the morning. The drive back up the mountain was too difficult to use the plow, so Bart drove on the wrong side of the road, which he'd already cleared. But while this struggle was annoying, Regina's cold silence was worse. Every time he glanced at her profile, the woman's face was tight and bitter, her eyes misty though no tears fell.

When they finally returned to home base, she jumped out of the truck and sprinted toward the house to check on Lance.

"Fetch Wylder and Julie while you're in there," Bart told her. "I want everything loaded before morning."

As he closed the driver's side door, Bart looked about the barn, admiring the inventory of explosives they'd amassed. Despite everything they'd gone through, the truck bomb was going to be a success, and the aftermath of the detonation a just reward. The strike would honor all who'd given their lives to the cause, especially Charlie. To quit now, as that moron Regina insisted, would be to dishonor the sacrifices made by the rest of the team. Bart couldn't let Quin and Paul's deaths be in vain. He couldn't allow Stan—the new kid who'd been hacked to pieces on the couch—to die for no reason. Even Bart's mentor Henry, who'd died of natural causes, would be paid tribute by the explosion. That Henry's daughter was going to die tonight by Bart's hand made no difference. Their plot to bomb the James C. Cleveland Federal Building and conjoined Warren B. Rudman Courthouse was coming to fruition. If all went according to plan in the Capital Business District of Concord, New Hampshire, they would immediately start prepping for the next target on their hit list. Bart had never been to Virginia before. He was looking forward to it.

He was just walking out of the barn when he heard Regina scream.

~

Bart walked into a massacre.

The house was like a scene from a horror movie. There were trails of fresh blood and red streaks on the walls, reminding him of Manson Family crime scene photos. Regina had found Lance dead in their bed and was bawling in the hallway. The door to Wylder's room was open, and his bloody corpse was flat on the floor. Bart went down to the cellar, dreading he would find exactly what he expected, but even though he'd anticipated Julie being dead, he hadn't been prepared to find her with an induction heater wedged into the back of her skull. The stench of burnt brain matter permeated the cellar, making him retch.

Glock drawn, he inspected the cellar before scrambling upstairs to search every corner of the house.

The hostages had escaped.

"Fuck!" he shouted, punching a hole in the drywall.

He punched several more, cursing until his face was as red as a stop sign.

"Bart!" Regina yelled.

He spun around to see her standing behind him. The tears she'd held in during their drive had been set free. Grief twisted her face, and her shoulders had sunk. Bart stepped toward Regina, extending a hand to console her. She slapped his hand away. Then she smacked him in the face.

"This is your fault," she said.

Bart only stared at her.

"If you'd just *listened*," Regina said. "If you'd just cared about us

THE OLD LADY

half as much as you care about that fucking bomb!"

The hairs on Bart's neck stood up.

"You selfish bastard," Regina said. "Do you realize what you've done to us? They're all dead because of you, Bart. You've killed everyone!"

Bart narrowed his eyes. "Not everyone."

He raised his Glock and put a bullet through Regina's face.

Her body collapsed on the floor. Having fired the pistol just inches from her skull, the bullet passed straight through it and imbedded in the wall behind her with a mist of blood. The wisp of smoke from the barrel gave a welcome reprieve from the stench of gore that had enveloped the house. He stepped over Regina's body and looked down at her still face and the entry wound in her forehead. Though she was obviously dead, Bart put two slugs in her chest, venting just as he had by punching holes in the wall. He shot her in the face again, breaking through one cheek, then popped rounds into her torso until the magazine was empty.

Bart tilted his head back and closed his eyes, taking long breaths through his nostrils, focusing on the rise and fall of his lungs. He was subduing it all—the anger, the grief, and the horror—pushing it down to be confronted later, after this was all over. Now was not the time to get emotional. The loss of his entire team was an unfortunate cost that often came with war. He would load their remains into the truck before leaving for Concord, so they could celebrate the explosion with him. The plan would not be altered. Bart would blow up the courthouse and federal building on his own, even if that meant he would die in the blast.

But first, he had to go hunting.

Going to the armory, he retrieved his Heckler & Koch G36.

That goddamned woman wasn't going to make it off this mountain.

THIRTY-SIX

THE COLD DARKNESS HAD BULLIED Alicia, confusing her, stunting whatever progress she could make. It'd been some time since she'd heard any gunshots, which she wanted to think was a good thing, but it didn't necessarily mean the horror was over. She might just be too deep in the woods to hear anything. Despite having a compass and doing her best to head down the mountain, she'd gotten completely lost and had been forced to backtrack up the mountain at times to avoid dangerous terrain. The beam of her flashlight was growing dim. As night fell in full, the temperature dropped considerably, and the wind at this altitude was inordinately cruel, forcing her to take breaks in places where she could hide from it behind boulders and trees. During these rests, she had difficulty staying awake, and when she caught herself dozing off, she forced herself back to her feet again.

Alicia wept often, unable to get thoughts of Dylan, Marcus, and Nori out of her head long enough to really focus on her own escape. She also grieved over Tracey, and tried not to imagine what kind of torture those terrible people were putting the woman through if they hadn't killed her already.

THE OLD LADY

Alicia had heard no police sirens, seen no red and blue lights. No forest rangers or rescue scouts had come by. No one was coming to help her because no one knew where she was. Alicia had come to believe her only hope for rescue was if people came looking for the civil engineer Tracey had shot by accident, the one whose snowmobile they'd stolen before being ambushed. It was full dark now. Surely someone expected to see or hear from him. Surely someone would report him missing. If not, Alicia was going to die out here and she knew it. This dread made her feel physically ill. There was a very real possibility that she wouldn't make it out of this. The thought of freezing to death terrified her, and that only made her feel guilty because Marcus and Dylan had died more horribly than that, and who knew what kind of suffering Nori was facing. But death was still death, and staring into her own slowly opening coffin filled her with fear. It was this that kept her moving, kept her trying, even though she was increasingly sure all was lost.

Something twinkled in the blackness, drawing her attention. She drew her Glock from her waistband with a shaky fist. At first, she thought the flicker was a trick of the brain, her duress making her see things, but as Alicia watched, the flicker became a beam of light. It landed on her before she could duck. Then she heard her name.

"Alicia!"

Recognizing the voice as Nori's, her eyes went wide.

Alicia stepped out of the brush, following the sound of her friend and the glow of the flashlight, half thinking she was trapped in a dream, that she'd passed out in the snow somewhere and was imagining all of this. But if that were the case, at least she would die believing they'd managed to escape together. She crunched through twigs and snow until she could make out the shadowy forms of Nori and a taller figure. At first, she feared the other person was one of Nori's captors, that she'd been forced to lure Alicia to them. But then she heard the person's voice.

"It's okay," Tracey said. "We've got you."

Tracey lowered her assault rifle, redirecting the beam of light to reveal who she was. Alicia almost didn't recognize her. The woman's face was bruised, bloodied, and swollen, as if she'd just finished twelve rounds of a bareknuckle boxing match. Both she and Nori had firearms.

Nori came to Alicia and wrapped her arms around her. Alicia was relieved to see she hadn't been badly beaten like Tracey had, but there was extensive frostbite damage and a haunted look about her that exposed a deep, inner pain. For all the bad things Alicia had endured, she could tell these two had experienced far worse during their time as hostages. The teenage girls held each other and cried in a combination of joyous relief and shared trauma.

"Oh my God," Alicia kept saying. "Oh my God, oh my God, oh my God."

Tracey didn't let the girls embrace for long. "C'mon. There isn't much time."

"How?" Alicia said. "How did…"

"I got lucky," Tracey said. "But there're two of them left, and I suspect they'll be on our tail soon. Keep quiet and follow me."

There were no objections. After failing in the woods on her own, Alicia was now willing to fully hand her safety over to Tracey. Before coming up on this mountain, she'd thought she'd become an adult. But now, in the face of all this blood and death, she felt more like a child than ever before, and was ready to cling to the one adult trying to protect her. She felt like a shy little girl hiding behind her mother's leg and, in a strange way, Tracey had become like a mother to her in this darkest hour. She was Alicia's unwavering defender, the only adult other than her parents who would endure pain to spare Alicia from it.

Tracey either didn't feel fear or didn't react to it. Like any mother with a child in danger, she only acted, with her own safety being an afterthought. She was violent, murderous, and mentally disturbed, but she was also Alicia's only source of security and guidance.

The golem was hope itself.

The girls followed Tracey to the thin trail she and Nori had emerged from. Then the golem gave the orders.

"Move fast but be careful. I'll distract the last of our enemies while you get away. This trail eventually leads to another path running alongside a wall of rock that will take you down to the same place on Harding Trail where the snowmobile crashed. Whatever you do, don't backtrack on the Harding Trail! Just look for the big wall of rock and you won't miss it. Then it's less than a mile to the parking lot." She put her BOB on the ground and drew out her wrinkled pack of cigarettes and Zippo, then pushed the BOB to the girls. "Take this. There are protein bars and a water bladder in here, and first aid supplies. Eat the food and drink the water as you go, even if you don't feel like it. There's also an entrenchment tool. When you get to the

THE OLD LADY

lot, go to my pickup truck, and use it to smash a window out so you can get inside. In the cab is a blanket and a toolbox with duct tape, amongst other things. Use the tape to secure the blanket to the busted window, to keep the wind out. The snow has stopped but it might start up again too. Use your body heat to keep each other warm."

"Okay," Alicia said. "Then what?"

Nori stared at Tracey. "And what about you?"

The woman's busted face made it impossible to read her expression.

"You two just get to the truck and keep warm," she said. "It must be below freezing out here—worse with the wind chill. If you try walking to town now, you'll never fucking make it, understand?"

Alicia nodded reluctantly. Nori said nothing, her sad eyes saying it all.

Tracey gently took Alicia's head in her hands, cupping her face. "I'm sorry I wasn't there for you, kiddo, but I never stopped loving you, in my own weird way. I always thought you were better off without me in your life, but maybe I was just making things easier for myself. Maybe some women just aren't cut out to be mothers."

Suddenly Alicia understood Tracey better. She realized why the woman called her Olivia and why she was telling her she loved her now.

"It's okay," Alicia told her. "It's okay… Mom."

Tracey's eyes grew wet, revealing a fragility Alicia never would have thought the woman was capable of. And when Tracey bent down to kiss Alicia on the forehead, Alicia found that it felt good, that it was reassuring.

"Now run," Tracey said. "You can't get to the police, so I'm gonna bring the police to you."

"Tracey, what're you—"

Tracey hushed Alicia. "Just go."

"But what about—"

"Shut the fuck up and do what I say!"

"I will, but I just want to—"

Tracey smacked Alicia in the mouth, stunning her into silence.

"Get moving!" Tracey said. "*Now!*"

Alicia felt a small hand grasp hers. Nori gently tugged her in the direction Tracey was pointing. Alicia started to follow, but she kept her eyes on Tracey as they walked away. As the woman watched her go, she gave Alicia a small wave goodbye that somehow felt more permanent than death itself.

Then she turned back and was gone.

THIRTY-SEVEN

WHEN TRACEY RETURNED TO THE compound, the pickup with the plow was back, parked a few yards in front of the barn. Putting out the butt of her cigarette in the snow, she crept through the trees alongside the ranch house, listening with bated breath, the fully loaded AK47 held tight in both fists like it was a ledge she was hanging from. The windows were lit but the curtains were drawn. She looked for human-shaped shadows—any sign of movement—but saw nothing on this side.

Her heart sank a little. Bart and his final soldier may have already left to hunt her down, taking Harding Trail, which could lead them to the girls before Tracey could get there to rescue them. It was possible, but Tracey doubted it. Though she and Nori had avoided Harding Trail in case they were being hunted, Tracey believed Bart would have anticipated this and used the accessory trails. He might have even split up with his last soldier. If either were so, she would have come across them on her way back, and if they had used Harding Trail, she might have heard the explosion of one of the landmines she'd planted earlier in the day or someone screaming when a spring trap was triggered. Bart knew Tracey had planted traps there, which made it more unlikely he would have taken Harding Trail at all. So while the house was silent, Tracey approached it with caution, sensing she wasn't alone here.

Her aches and pains grew fainter as adrenaline surged. She sprinted across the backyard, doing her best to stay out of the beams of the floodlights, and stared down the target of her assault rifle, pointing it at the back door of the house. The rear windows also offered light without shadows or movement. All was eerily quiet. The snowstorm had ceased. Even the wind paused.

Using the plowed path, she sprinted across the yard, heading to the pickup truck. She looked in the window but there were no keys in the ignition. Going around to the passenger side put the truck between her and the house. She looked back at the barn. The doors were closed but the old wood had bowed and warped so they didn't sit evenly, leaving a gap she could peek through. She flicked on her rifle's light and directed the beam into the barn, spotting gas cans and random auto parts. There was a closed stall with stacked bags of fertilizer rising far past the height of the stall's door.

She would have to do this carefully.

Returning her attention to the ranch house, Tracey stepped to the front of the truck just before a hail of bullets came for her.

~

As Bart was about to leave the house to search for Tracey and the girls, he checked the security cameras to make sure the yard was clear. He suspected Tracey may not have traveled far, that she was waiting in the brush, locked and loaded, ready to assassinate him the moment he stepped outside. He switched the monitor to show all the screens at once, then enlarged one image at a time. The screen cast him in a sickly, pale blue glow as he stared at the camera feeds carefully, not wanting to miss so much as a field mouse. He was itching to get out there and chase those bitches down before they could gain much ground, but he had to put defense before offense. Though he hated to give Tracey credit for anything, Bart had to admit she was highly skilled at guerilla warfare, just like her father had been. Just *who was this woman*? She was a ruthless warrior, an expert killing machine unlike any he'd encountered before. What else could he say about someone who had annihilated his entire team?

Bart even blamed Regina's death on her, for Tracey had driven him to the point of such anger that he took it out on his last soldier, with lethal results. Bart didn't mourn Regina—he'd hated the lousy

THE OLD LADY

nag too long for that—but killing her had been a mistake. She may have been mad at him, but she would have been even angrier at the woman who'd killed her husband. She would have been a sidekick in vengeance, however embittered.

Now, Bart was alone—alone and scared.

Years in law enforcement and freedom fighting had hardened him, but no one was immune to jitters when it came to this level of violence. Even the hearts of the most experienced soldiers went into overdrive when the bullets started flying. Surrounded by the bodies of your murdered friends and family would put anyone in a state of terror just as well as rage. Bart was tough, but he wasn't impervious to this level of fear.

But somehow, he knew Tracey was. He'd seen no terror in the woman's eyes, not even when she was facing torture. Even tied to a chair and whacked across the face until her nose snapped, Tracey had continued to mock and provoke him, instigating further harm against herself as if it were nothing. The only thing she seemed to worry about was the kids. It made Bart want to kill both of those little girls just so he could finally hear Tracey scream in pain, but such revenge now had to take a backseat to practical bloodshed. He had to focus on killing Tracey. No more interrogations or torture. As soon as he had the chance, he would murder her as quickly as possible. It was the only logical thing to do. But to succeed, he had to protect himself, so he flipped through screen after screen, staring and waiting until he saw a shadowy figure sprint across the backyard.

Bart's flesh pimpled. Knowing Tracey was close made him gulp even as his mouth went dry.

Okay, he thought. *You can do this.*

But when he picked up the Heckler & Koch, the assault rifle rattled in his trembling hands.

Easy, he told himself. *Do it for the mission. Do it for the team.*

Bart breathed in through his nose and out his mouth.

Do it for Charlie.

He started toward the front door.

Once outside, Bart crept toward the backyard, sticking to the shadows at the side of the house as he maneuvered around the woodchipper, chopping block, and stacked logs. He moved in a crouch, sweating despite the cold, shielding himself behind the row of ATVs with the butt of the rifle pressed against his shoulder. His finger gently touched the trigger as he scanned the yard.

He spotted Tracey near the pickup truck. She was on the passenger side, the truck between her and Bart, just like the ATVs. She'd acquired an assault rifle.

Fuck.

Bart locked on her with his rifle, but the cab of the truck was in the way. Patiently, he held his position, waiting for her to emerge from behind the cover of the truck, but then he saw her turn toward the barn, seeming to look through the crack between the doors.

"No," he whispered to himself. "Stay away from there, bitch."

He tried to get her in his crosshairs, but the truck shielded her. It wasn't parked too close to the barn—Bart could shoot at Tracey without risking hitting the barn and the explosives within it—but he wanted to get a clear shot to end this quickly and resoundingly.

Hold steady, he thought. *Come on, you psycho cunt. Get out from behind the pickup.*

Tracey moved toward the front of the truck, her lower body behind the hooded engine but her upper body exposed. Bart knew he should wait for her to get closer, to assure a hit, but seeing her moving toward him while carrying a rifle filled his heart with fear.

Panicked, Bart opened fire.

~

The windshield exploded and Tracey ducked behind the truck and shielded her feet with the front passenger tire. The crackling staccato of gunfire broke the stillness of the night, more bullets sinking into the vehicle and flying overhead. The windows burst and the truck sagged as the driver's side front tire went flat. Steadying her breathing to lower her heart rate, Tracey looked for something to throw, her gaze landing on a fallen branch as long as her arm. She waited for a break in the gunfire, then grabbed the branch and hurled it toward the tree it must have fallen from, rattling the remaining branches. This diversion drew fire to the tree, and she peeked over the hood to locate the source of the gunshots. Seeing a muzzle flash behind the assemblage of ATVs, she raised her AK47 and returned fire. Gunpowder burned. The powerful weapon blazed in her fists, riddling the ATVs and the house behind them with hot lead. She couldn't be sure if she'd hit the hidden assassin, but judging by the way the bullets were coming at her, she could tell there was but a single shooter. Was it Bart or his female soldier? If only one of them was behind the ATVs, then where was the other?

As she fired, Tracey counted every bullet she spent. Ten of her

THE OLD LADY

rounds went quickly, but her opponent was spending more. Whoever it was had taken to panic-firing, shooting in her direction with abandon. Perhaps they had plenty to spare. Or perhaps they were simply panicking. She got low as another barrage of bullets came her way, the truck popping and clanging as it was hole-punched.

Tracey looked to the barn. It now seemed miles away. But running to it would be too dangerous anyhow. With all these bullets flying, it would be like running into a ticking atomic bomb. A single bullet might provide all the gunpowder and spark needed to detonate the explosives within.

But Bart and his teammate would know that too. They didn't want to risk blowing up the barn. Not only would it spoil their mission, but the blast would be enough to kill all three of them. So maybe Tracey's best bet was to run for the barn because she wouldn't draw their fire once she was close enough.

The gunshots ceased.

Tracey waited, listening as best she could with her inner ears shocked by the consistent shooting. It seemed like a long time passed. She wondered if her trigger-happy enemy had run out of bullets. Poking the barrel of the Ak47 around the front of the plow, she squeezed the trigger, sending a few more rounds into the night.

"*Eleven rounds left,*" her father's voice echoed within her brain.

"I don't need your help," she told him, firing a few more. "I didn't need it then and I sure don't need it now."

"*The other soldier might be sneaking up behind you right this minute.*"

Tracey knew that. She'd kept her back to the truck when not firing, watching the woods around her for sneak attacks.

"I only wish you were here with your militia friends," she told her old man before firing again. "Then I could kill you too. Something I should have done a long time ago."

Her father was unphased. "*Eight rounds left.*"

Tracey drew back, waiting to see if the shooter would return fire, if they were still able to. There were no rifle cracks, no bullets whizzing by. Tracey waited still. She might have hit the shooter, or they could be out of ammo. Or they might just be playing dead, waiting for her to come out of hiding so they could get a good, clear shot at her.

But Tracey could wait too. She stayed behind her only cover, the busted pickup serving as sandbags, Tracey being the rabbit in the hole. It suddenly occurred to her that this may be her last stand. She'd known going into this that the end of her journey was drawing ever-closer. Perhaps this was as far as she could take it.

"*You're not licked yet*," Dad said.

Tracey looked toward the barn again.

She'd come here to make sure the police would be able to locate the girls. Killing Bart and the lady soldier would be a bonus, but if Tracey were to die without doing what she'd set out to do, Olivia and her friend would either freeze to death in her truck or get captured and be forced into prostitution. Tracey had let her daughter down all her life. She couldn't bear to fail Olivia now that her life was on the line. This might be her last and only chance to show her baby that Mommy loved her.

Tracey got to her feet and kept on firing at the ATVs as she darted toward the barn.

THIRTY-EIGHT

OUT OF AMMO, BART HAD curled into a ball behind one of the ATVS as Tracey continued to rain bullets upon him. He cursed himself for not bringing his Glock, which he'd placed on the kitchen table after putting most of its bullets into Regina. He'd been in too big of a hurry to catch Tracey, and he'd foolishly believed the Heckler & Koch would be enough to take her down. The magazine held thirty rounds. That he'd blown through them all already was astounding. He'd panicked and knew it.

He'd also been hit. The round had only nicked his thigh, but the cut was deep, and his blood was decorating the snow. All he could do right now was wait for Tracey to cease fire. Then he could move back through the shadows, get into the house, and go to the armory to reload. But now that Tracey knew where he was, creeping by without her spotting him would be much more difficult.

With his hearing muffled, he didn't notice the hinges creak as the barn door opened, but when the interior lights were turned on, Bart gasped and turned his head that way.

Tracey had gone inside.

"Jesus Christ, no…"

That lunatic was in there with all the flammable supplies, all the ingredients of the bomb strike he'd planned. This would be the end of everything. Not only could Tracey ruin the mission by damaging these goods, but she could also generate an explosion big enough to take out the entire compound, killing them both and setting the surrounding forest ablaze.

And she was just crazy enough to do it.

Bart got to his feet. His thigh ached but his balance held. He looked back at the house. The armory might as well have been in another country. The time it would take for him to even get to the front porch would be enough for Tracey to start a decimating fire.

"Son of a bitch!" Bart hissed.

He quickly searched the ATVs, hoping one of the men had left a pistol inside an enclosed hatch, but lifting the lids revealed no weapons. All Bart had was an empty rifle and the pocketknife clipped to his belt. Groaning in frustration, his fear blossoming into white-hot rage, Bart glanced back at the woodchipper, and the stack of logs piled beside the house.

The blade of the axe gleamed under the floodlights, sticking out of the chopping block like Excalibur.

~

Throwing the empty assault rifle to the ground, Tracey grabbed two gas cans, tore their spouts off, and held them upside-down, creating a river of fuel. When they were emptied, she flung open a stall door where canisters of nitromethane and DMSO were stacked beside crates of roofing nails. She picked up two more gas cans in the same fashion and poured a sloppy trail to the stall before throwing the cans in there. Drawing her hunting knife, she punctured the plastic of another gas can so it would bleed out on its own, creating a deluge of gasoline that soaked into the hay bales and the barn's wooden boards near the remaining can. The fumes rose around her, blurring the air.

"Tracey!" a man's voice called.

At first, she thought it was her father barking through her mind again. But then Bart called her name again from outside. Tracey looked out the open door but couldn't see him, so she backed against a stall, just in case.

"It's just you and me now!" Bart said.

This told her the female soldier was gone, or at least Bart wanted her to think that. Maybe Tracey had killed the woman in the gunfight, but she wasn't going to take Bart's word on anything.

THE OLD LADY

"I see you've thrown the AK away. Out of bullets, huh?" Bart said. "Why don't you come on out of there? I'd hate to have to shoot you."

Tracey smirked. "Bullshit. If you had a gun on you, you wouldn't have stopped shooting in the first place."

But she knew he might just be hesitating to shoot because she was surrounded by explosives.

"Just come on out," Bart said. "Enough people have died already. You know how dangerous that barn is."

"And you know how dangerous *I am*."

Silence.

Finally, Bart spoke. "If you come out now, I promise no further harm will come to those girls."

"You already told that lie, dipshit."

"I'm not lying anymore. Things have changed."

"Not for me, asshole. I'm still gonna kill you."

Tracey drew the Zippo from her pocket. If this was the end, she needed to be ready to set the world on fire. She'd never thought she'd go out as a suicide bomber. And she still wanted to survive this if she could. But Bart didn't need to know that.

"I've got an idea," she said. "Why don't you come on in?"

Silence but for the whistle of the wind.

"What's the matter, Bart? You only tough with ladies when they're tied to a chair? C'mon in, and we'll see what kind of man you really are."

It was a gamble. Tracey knew that. Bart might have a gun and was only waiting for a chance to shoot her without risking an explosion. The female soldier might be alive and the two of them might be closing in on her from both sides. As long as Tracey was in the barn, she had the advantage, but unless she wanted to blow up with him, she had to kill Bart if she were ever going to leave this compound alive.

She balanced her weapons in each hand—the hunting knife in her right hand and her Zippo in her left.

Tracey gripped her knife's handle so hard her knuckles ran white. "C'mon, chickenshit! What're you waiting for?"

"You're fuckin' crazy!" Bart shouted, sounding closer now. "Do you have any idea how insane you are?"

"Enough to send us both to Hell."

She flipped the Zippo lid, loudly clicking it back and forth in a taunting percussion.

Slowly, the barn door opened further, and a tall shadow appeared. It moved closer until the light revealed a worn, frightened, angry man with an axe. Bart's leg was bleeding, and he had a slight limp. There were other blood stains upon his coat, but at this point they could have come from any number of dead people. His arctic stare bore into Tracey, as if his eyes could drill straight through to her soul.

"This is it," he said.

And it was all that needed to be said.

Tracey raised the Zippo, putting her thumb to the flint wheel.

Bart called her bluff and charged with the axe raised high.

If not for his limp and her kickboxing training, she might not have been able to avoid the swing of the axe. The length of it gave him the reach advantage, but Tracey's reflexes were better than his and she managed to dart out of the way. The axe collided with the stall door behind her, and in the split second it was wedged in the wood, she stuck Bart in the side with her blade.

The big man took a huge intake of breath, his eyes going wide. Blood sluiced through his torn flesh and clothing, and Tracey put her weight into the knife, driving it in another inch.

Abandoning the axe, Bart swung an elbow at Tracey, hitting her in the side of the face. Stars danced across her vision, the pain of her already broken nose threatening to make her faint. She withdrew the knife and, wanting both hands free, she tucked the lighter into her pocket and gripped the knife with both hands like she was wielding a battle sword. Bart's blood on the blade dribbled over her fingers, warm and wet and wonderful. He held his wounded side, and as he struggled to regain himself, Tracey smiled at the suffering she'd inflicted upon him. Spilling his blood excited her, filling her with the sort of joy she'd long thought she was unable to feel. And while she delighted in cutting him up specifically because of all he'd done, Tracey also had to admit to herself that she'd been experiencing similar joy on and off throughout the day.

The harsh realization hit her like a kick to the stomach.

Nothing in life made Tracey happier than hurting other people.

She didn't have time to process this. Bart charged at her again. She'd thought he'd just been holding the wound at his side, but now she saw he'd taken a pocketknife from his belt. She could have ripped him apart before he even unfolded it, but Tracey found she didn't want to. Some deranged part of her enjoyed the idea of a knife fight. Bart had a standard Bowie knife, and he opened the four-inch blade,

THE OLD LADY

struggling with his blood-slick fingers. As soon as she heard it lock in place, Tracey came at Bart again with both hands on the handle of her hunting knife, attacking as if using a bayonet.

Sidestepping her, Bart slashed at Tracey and his blade caught her ear, ripping the earlobe and cutting open the area behind it where the neck meets the skull. Ignoring the pain, she dove into him. Bart backed up, so instead of the blade going into his belly, Tracey impaled his right thigh. He screamed and slashed at her again, opening the flesh of her cheek as he tried to slit her throat. Ramming him with her shoulders, Tracey drove Bart against a stall door, and he stumbled with her blade still in his thigh. She twisted it, widening the hole. Blood cascaded down his shin in a red river.

That's when Tracey felt Bart's blade enter her upper back.

She gasped and then held the breath in to steady herself, gritting her teeth against the agony, and as he stabbed her where her shoulder met her neck, Tracey tried to pull her knife from Bart's leg, but it had become wedged. She tried to stand upright but Bart leaned over her, trying to get her in a headlock, so when his neck got close enough, Tracey sank her teeth into it. Bart groaned, his face balled tight in pain, and Tracey shook her head back and forth like a dog with a dead duck, ripping at the flesh. Bart raised his knife, and Tracey grabbed his arm with both hands to keep him from stabbing her again. Her knee came up sharply and pulverized his testicles, and then she grabbed him by the collar with one fist and drove the other into his nose repeatedly, her knuckles scrapping raw as she bashed his face in.

Bart collapsed.

Tracey got on her knees beside him and gripped her knife with both hands and yanked the blade out of his leg. Blood spurted and gushed, assuring her she'd hit the femoral artery. He would be finished soon, but as he swung his knife again, Tracey realized the man wasn't through just yet. She was a little too late to block the attack, but fortunately, Bart's aim was off, so instead of his knife entering her right eye, it bounced off her skull, separating one eyebrow. Tracey backed off him and shut her eye as it was blinded by her blood. This eye was already black and swollen from a previous beating, so losing more visibility in it now wasn't too disadvantaging. Tracey stood and staggered back, watching Bart as he groaned in hay soaked through with gasoline. He was bleeding out. This brought a smile to Tracey's busted face.

"He's still alive," her father told her. *"You call that playing to win?"*

Putting her dripping knife back it its sheath, Tracey staggered to the axe imbedded in the stall door. Even with the stab wounds in her upper back, she managed to pry the axe head free. She held the axe in both hands, bouncing it a little to enjoy the weight of it as she returned to the militia leader slowly dying beneath her. Tracey stepped over Bart as if she were about to straddle him, her blood dripping all over his body.

Bart gurgled. "Who… who the fuck *are you?*"

Tracey wished she knew.

"Just some old lady," she said.

The axe rose above her just before Bart's skull was cleaved in two.

THIRTY-NINE

UNSCREWING THE SPOUT OF THE last gas can, Tracey carried it out of the barn and constructed a trail of gasoline upon a path she'd forged of hay and twigs leading to the pickup truck. If it weren't shot full of holes, she might have taken it, but the front wheels were flat, and the body was so damaged it looked as if the engine might fall out if she tried to start it. She flung the gas can in the truck bed, then looked toward the ranch house.

If that other soldier had still been alive, she would have shown herself by now. She would have tried to save her fallen leader. So it seemed Bart had told the truth for once. Confident the entire team was dead, Tracey returned to the house and opened the back door. The sewer stench of death—blood and gore, voided bladders and bowels—permeated the house. The female soldier was dead on the floor. Bart must have lost his temper with the woman. Maybe he'd blamed her for something. Tracey had no reason to care. But she still had a reason to play things safe, so she snatched a full magazine for the AK47 from the woman's belt, then located the bathroom and sterilized her stab wounds with rubbing alcohol. She did a quick patch up with bandages to keep blood loss at a minimum, grabbed a hand towel, and then made her way back outside.

Tracey considered the other truck—the big one like a U-Haul. She could search the house and the bodies for the keys, but she wasn't sure just how far Bart had plowed down the mountain, and the road leading out of the compound went in the opposite direction of Harding Trail. If Tracey got stuck halfway down and had to proceed on foot, she would have to cover more ground than if she just hiked back downhill.

"Fuck it," she said, too worn out to think things through any further.

She ventured back to the barn. Though she was in rough shape, she could still tromp through the fallen snow. But her body was a tight ball of pain, and with the adrenaline wearing off, she was struggling not to feel all her wounds and bruises.

Everything you want is on the other side of pain, she reminded herself.

After loading several canisters of nitromethane and DMSO into the bed of the pickup truck, Tracey soaked the hand towel in the gasoline puddles on the barn floor, opened the truck's gas cap, and stuffed the dripping towel into the spout.

She wasn't sure how much time she would have.

The truck would go up and the DMSO and nitromethane in the bed would explode. The trail of gas and other flammable fluids leading from the truck to the barn would catch fire, and then it would be only a matter of time before the barn full of explosives became one gigantic bomb.

But how long would it take?

Tracey picked up the AK47 she'd left in the snow and replaced the spent magazine with the one she'd taken off the dead woman. She believed all her enemies were dead, but it was always best to assume there were more hiding behind the treeline like the North Vietnamese Army. And if the truck fire failed to set the barn ablaze, she could always shoot at the stacks of nitromethane and DMSO from a distance and blow the fucker up that way.

This would be the police's homing beacon—a lighthouse to draw rescue for the girls. With the number of explosives inside the barn, the flames would light the night sky as the ultimate rescue flare. The explosion would be enormous, especially with the snowstorm having ended. She just had to hope she could get away in time.

It was a risk she was willing to take.

Tracey drew her crushed pack of cigarettes from her pocket. The

THE OLD LADY

last bent and wrinkled Marlboro was hiding in there next to the rolled-up cellophane taken off the pack. Inside the cellophane was a spare Xanax. Tracey laughed and tossed the anxiety medication in the snow, drew her lighter, and lit up her final smoke. She eyed the Zippo's flame, letting it warm her broken face, then brought it to the soaked towel sticking out of the truck's gas tank. Taking one last drag as she watched the fire catch, she flicked the butt and started running.

FORTY

ALICIA AND NORI HUDDLED CLOSE. They were finally inside Tracey's pickup truck with the blanket taped over the busted window. Breaking it was easy, and with the truck being so old, no alarm system had gone off. It wasn't exactly warm inside it, but being shielded from the aggressive wind was a huge relief. Using a small multitool from Tracey's BOB, Alicia cut the extra length of blanket free from the patch covering the window so she and Nori could spoon under it.

The hike down had been challenging, but the snow had stopped falling, increasing visibility, and making the trek easier than it had been earlier in the day. No one came after them. They didn't even hear anyone or stop to hide. The girls munched on the protein bars and granola mixes in the BOB, the high-fat snacks keeping their internal furnaces burning. They stayed hydrated with the water bladder and were surprised to find Tracey had put sugar in it. Alicia figured this was for quick energy. The old lady was an endless encyclopedia of survival tricks. Now Alicia just had to hope her golem had one last trick up her sleeve.

"*You can't get to the police,*" Tracey had told them. "*So I'm gonna bring*

THE OLD LADY

the police to you."

Alicia still wasn't sure what Tracey had meant by that. While the words implied hope, she sensed something grim beneath the surface, the sentence underlined with dark finality. Did Tracey truly have a plan, or had she only been trying to get the girls to run while they still could? Alicia didn't doubt Tracey would go back and try to kill what members of the militia remained—massacres were simply what the woman did—but how was she going to get the police? Had she discovered a phone back at the compound? If so, wouldn't Tracey have used it to call 911 already? Alicia couldn't make sense of it, but in her current state, she couldn't make much sense of anything. And besides, Tracey was obviously mentally ill, so much of what she said and did was impossible to make sense of.

Realizing Nori hadn't said anything in a while, Alicia nudged her. Nori moaned.

"Don't fall asleep," Alicia reminded her.

"I kn-kn-know. I'm trying."

"You've got to keep me awake too. Let's talk about something."

Alicia waited but Nori didn't reply.

"Nori?"

"I'm awake. I ju-just don't kn-kn-know what… what…"

Nori's words became sobs. Now that they weren't exerting themselves, the horrible events of the day were returning to the forefronts of the girls' minds. Alicia held Nori tighter and simply allowed her to cry. Better to grieve than fall asleep and freeze to death. Nori rolled over and wrapped her arms around her friend, burying her frostbitten face into Alicia's shoulder. Alicia didn't tell Nori everything was going to be okay, because she had no reason to believe that was true. At any moment, the last of the people who had tormented the girls could find them. They could still die today. They could still be raped and tortured. Though Nori and Alicia had made it to the truck, the relative safety it provided was limited. Their futures were uncertain, their lives still at risk. Unless Tracey really did have a master plan, the girls would be stuck here until daybreak, provided they made it through the night.

A strange orange glow on the mountain caught Alicia's eye. Far overhead, it flickered between the trees like moonlight on the surface of the ocean before expanding into a half globe of tangerine light. The stars vanished as the sky was illuminated in a brilliant flash, and then the sound came, an intense blast that shook the mountainside. There was a rumble as avalanches of rock and snow rolled downhill.

The ground beneath the truck vibrated.

"Oh my God," Alicia said, sitting up.

The mountaintop explosion was followed by smaller explosions, adding to the initial mushroom cloud of flame. Smoke swirled and burning debris danced like fireflies in the shadows of the night.

"Wha-what's going on?" Nori asked. "What is that?"

Tears filled Alicia's eyes. "It's a homing beacon."

She took Nori's hand in hers, and they watched the mountain become a humongous matchhead. With the snow having stopped falling, the fire would continue to burn, drawing emergency services. Harding Trail was the quickest way up the mountain, and of all of them, the parking lot the girls were in was closest to the explosion.

Now there was no way rescue workers could fail to locate the girls.

FORTY-ONE

"YOU'RE STILL ALIVE," A VOICE said.

Tracey wasn't sure if someone was really there, or if was just the ghost of her father, or if she'd said the words aloud. From behind the wall of rock, she allowed herself to unfurl from the fetal position, as if she were being reborn.

In a way, she guessed she was.

After lighting the rag in the truck's gas tank, she'd ran as fast as she could, putting the ranch house between her and the lit explosives, hoping it would shield her from the initial detonation of the truck. She didn't look back to check. Tracey only kept running, making it back to the thin trail that ran alongside the compound. Using the path through the snow made by her and Nori's earlier footsteps, she managed to move quicker than she would have through untouched snow, and when she heard the truck go up in flames, she jumped off trail into the woods and rolled down the steep incline of granite. Her body was assaulted with jagged rocks, dead thorn bushes, and fallen branches as gravity propelled her downhill, but when the barn exploded, she was shielded by the granite wall like a soldier deep in a bunker.

Tracey tucked behind a log and curled into a ball as debris from the detonation flew over the bluff edge above her, raining slush and sticks and pebbles. Then came the debris from the compound, chunks of hot metal and smoking rubber spattering through the woodland in a hail of embers. Tracey kept her hands over her ears as the blasts continued to come. The earth quaked and the air grew polluted. Even at this distance, the temperature outside rose rapidly.

It was a long time before she dared to open her eyes. Now that she had, she marveled at the tangerine sky overhead. Had she not caused it herself, she might have guessed she was hallucinating. The glow was full and bright, large enough to be seen for miles. She thought it had started snowing again but realized it was ash fluttering on the breeze.

"You did it."

Now the source of the voice was clear. Tracey was speaking aloud, but she was in unison with the inner dialogue of her father's voice, which was merely her own thoughts, and always had been. It was the voice of trauma admitting to an unexpected victory. It was madness making sense.

Rising from the ground like a zombie, Tracey covered her nose and mouth with the neck of her shirt. She slung the AK47 over her shoulder and scampered the rest of the way down the jagged slope. Though conscious, she felt lost in a fever dream, her thoughts shifting from the pressing matters of the present to the blurred nightmare of her past. Her mind was so muddied she wondered if she'd suffered a concussion or brain hemorrhage. Still, she managed to navigate the terrain. Opening the handle of her hunting knife, she used the tracking device to locate Olivia and Nori and pressed on in the direction of the girls. As she continued southwest, time seemed to distort, the glowing sky tricking her into thinking the sun was rising before she came to her senses again. Her movements were labored but her pace was steady, her determination absolute. It was not the will to live that drove her; it was the need to see the girls rescued, to know her daughter was safe. That was all that mattered anymore. It should have always been.

Her injuries had gone numb, and she was grateful to feel nothing. That had been her goal since escaping her father—to feel no pain, physical or emotional. But drugs and alcohol hadn't freed Tracey from pain, and neither had the love of a good man and the promise of a happy family. She had come to understand that there was no cure

THE OLD LADY

for pain. As with cancer, there were only temporary reprieves. Even when the body was healthy, the mind tortured itself, and the heart remained fragile no matter how much scar tissue it developed. To exist was to be in pain. Life was, and always had been, merely a vehicle for suffering.

It was impossible to know how much time had passed, but Tracey felt like she'd been struggling downhill for a lifetime. Her lungs ached from inhaling smoke. Exhaustion made every part of her feel heavier than normal. The temptation to put the rifle in her mouth was strong. It had been all her life. She wasn't sure what had kept her from doing it all these years, but now suicide had to wait. For once she was putting her daughter's needs before her own. Though it had kicked in far too late, her maternal instinct now had complete control of her. She felt like she finally understood parenthood—perhaps even craved it—because Olivia's life now mattered to Tracey in all the ways her own life never had.

When she heard sirens in the distance, Tracey smiled. It was the first time in her life she'd been happy to hear them. There was a lion's roar of fire engines and the wail of ambulances. The sound of helicopters came next, and Tracey flinched at the memory of her father's terrible war stories, and even briefly believed she was in the jungles of Vietnam. She looked at the rifle in her hands—an AK47, the same weapon used by the gooks, by Charlie.

Charlie.

The name confused her. She'd killed a Charlie, hadn't she? She remembered an Asian young man being shot in the head today but was almost positive it hadn't been her who'd killed him. Charlie was someone else. Charlie was always the enemy. It was a soldier's job to take him out. Had she been transported to that world and that war? Was she but a figment in her father's mind as he flew into Da Nang? Had she died in the explosion and landed in the same Hell that had swallowed her old man?

Sanity slipped back and forth, taking Tracey into parts of her past both real and imagined, and then abruptly dropped her back into the present. She kept getting surprised by the taste of her own blood. It hurt to spit it out. Her ears were ringing with tinnitus from all the shooting and explosions, and she could only see out of one eye.

Still she marched on.

When she finally made it to the rocky path leading down to Harding Trail, Tracey frowned seeing the wrecked snowmobile. She'd forgotten all about Jeff the Civil Engineer, an innocent man she'd fatally shot.

How many people had she killed today? She'd counted them up earlier and thought the total had been seven, but she couldn't remember when she'd done the count. Was it eight now with Bart dead? Maybe ten? She was no longer even sure about that female soldier she'd found murdered back at the ranch house. Had Tracey killed her and just forgotten? Could she trust any of her memories at all anymore? Was she truly brain damaged? Her thoughts seemed to trample over one another until nothing made sense, but one of them kept resurfacing.

Am I just sane enough to know I am crazy?

Drawing closer to the end of the trail, Tracey saw flickering red and blue lights. Checking the tracking device, she confirmed Olivia had made it here. There was movement in the parking lot ahead, and Tracey heard voices, many of them male. Headlight beams knifed through the trees. An engine grumbled along with the distinct sound of a plow pushing away mounds of snow.

Tracey stepped closer to the lot and saw the assembly of first responders. There were firefighters, police officers, rangers, paramedics, and other uniformed rescuers, all of which were scrambling into a plan of action. As Tracey exited the trail, she spotted Nori being placed into the back of an ambulance. The girl was sitting up—still alive. Tracey looked for her daughter but didn't spot her inside the ambulance. She wanted to call Olivia's name, but she was too out of breath, her throat too sore from inhaling smoke. The world around her was a confusing blur of flashing lights and rushing strangers, of loud noises and frenetic energy.

Tracey's heartbeat accelerated. Though only one of them was able to open wide, her bloodshot eyes darted. Her muscles tensed and she was suddenly acutely aware of every one of her senses.

The police were here. From the sound of sirens in the distance, more were on the way. They had come to arrest Tracey for multiple murders. There would be no reduced charges this time. No plea bargains, no time cut for good behavior, no possibility of parole. This time she'd slaughtered multiple people and blown up a national forest. Either she was going back to prison for the rest of her life, or they would lock her in a madhouse for the criminally insane.

But that was only if they didn't intend to kill her.

The police she saw were all men, and she knew what men liked to

THE OLD LADY

do. They liked to hurt women. Even when she'd dealt with female officers in the past, they'd acted like men, imitating the worst qualities of their male counterparts. Cops, corrections officers, judges—they were all part of the same sinister entity, cogs in a system designed to ruin lost people like herself.

Back at the militia's compound, a Back the Blue flag had been proudly displayed. Bart had ranted about the country's mistreatment of police and mentioned he was a certified explosives breacher. Tracey *knew* he was a cop, or at least a retired or disgraced one. How many other members of the militia were law enforcement? How wide of a reach did Bart's group have? How many of the police officers she saw right now were secretly members of this terrorist organization?

Tracey stepped back into the shadows of the overhanging trees.

Her father's voice returned to the forefront of her mind. "*Worry about the six that will kill you, not the twelve that will put you away.*"

A group of police officers and forest rangers dispersed, heading toward the mouth of Harding Trail.

"*If someone comes after you, what do you do?*" Dad asked.

Tracey bared her teeth. "Kill them."

As law enforcement drew near, Tracey opened fire.

FORTY-TWO

WHEN IT HAPPENED, ALICIA WAS sitting in the passenger seat of a police SUV with the heat vents blowing over her. The door was open, and the officer was standing next to her, getting as much information from her as possible. She told him she was the one who'd called 911 earlier, and explained the terrible events in a rush, giving the lawman the important details but omitting other things, such as Tracey's brutality, and not bothering to guess what the militia might have really been. True to her word, Alicia only told the police of Tracey's bravery, how she'd come to the rescue of children she didn't even know.

"Tracey's still out there," Alicia told the cop. "Please, you have to help her."

"We're doing all we can."

Alicia didn't like his tone of his voice. She got the sense he was only placating her. He was the officer—the adult. To him, she was just a little girl to be shielded from the world's harsh truths. Even though she'd told him what she'd been through today, he still had no real grasp of just how much she'd endured, how much she could take.

A paramedic had treated her for minor injuries and given her a

THE OLD LADY

cup of tea to warm up, and Nori had just been placed in an ambulance. Knowing her friend was going to be okay seemed surreal to Alicia, as did this whole rescue. When the first responders had arrived in the parking lot, she'd almost thought she'd fallen asleep and was dreaming it all. But now that she was wrapped in warm blankets and surrounded by police and medics, the reality of it all was sinking in.

She'd survived a day of true horror.

The nightmare was finally over.

"Just a few more questions," the officer said. "Then we'll escort you to the hospital too. We just need to know what we're dealing with here, and you're our—"

The rapid crack of gunfire startled Alicia, making her drop the cup of hot tea. She looked up through the windshield. Chaos had scattered the crowd and people were quickly retreating from the trail.

"Get down!" the officer told Alicia, pushing her onto the seat sideways.

She screamed as more gunshots rang out. She'd thought the danger was over, but the violence just kept coming. Terror was an infinite loop that refused to set Alicia free. Somehow, some members of the militia had survived, and they were coming for her, no matter the cost.

More shots fired. People screamed and cried out in pain. The hum of a distant helicopter completed the soundtrack of war. And just when Alicia dared to open her eyes, she saw the officer beside her had drawn his pistol, but he didn't get the chance to use it. His body jerked once as the bullet went into his throat, and as he crashed against the inside of the door, the cop fell halfway into the car, his pistol landing on the floorboard. He clenched Alicia's leg with both hands until they went slack.

She and Nori had surrendered their weapons to the police. As the rapid gunfire raged on, Alicia snatched the policeman's service pistol. Aside from the shot that had struck the officer, no other bullets were striking the car, so she dared to peek over the dashboard.

What she saw made her heart ache.

Tracey was on the attack. She was moving through the parking lot, shielding herself with the emergency vehicles as she fired upon the police and rangers. She'd surprised everyone, and several officers already lay still in the bloody snow. Her assault rifle was much more powerful than the police's handguns, the impact of the rounds enough to break through their soft armor, and she was able to fire more rapidly, taking down another cop as Alicia stared in shock.

Tracey must have noticed Alicia's movement in the squad car. She turned to look, and when their eyes locked, Alicia forgot to breathe. Her hands were clenched around the dead cop's pistol, but fear froze her in the brief moment Tracey was looking right at her. Tracey could have shot her dead then, but of course, the golem didn't. Instead, Tracey gave her a sad smile, saying it all without saying anything, and then returned her attention to the massacre, moving past the squad car with the rifle raised to her shoulder.

Just as the legend foretold, the golem had become a monster with an unquenchable thirst for violence.

Someone else fired, and a bullet shattered one of the squad car's back windows. Alicia slid out of the car, stumbling over the dead officer and into the bloody slush. Standing in a crouch, she used the car for cover. Tracey had moved ahead quickly but Alicia spotted her as the woman took her first bullet. An officer managed to shoot her in the upper torso, and Tracey jerked, but she kept standing and shooting as if she hadn't noticed. The policeman ducked for cover as Tracey blew holes in the ranger's jeep he was hiding behind.

From the position where she was standing, Alicia was behind Tracey but far to her right. This side of Tracey's face was so swollen, Alicia doubted the woman could even see her in the corner of her eye, but even if she could, Alicia knew Tracey wouldn't harm her no matter what she did. For much of the day she'd been uncertain about that, based on the woman's erratic behavior, but now Alicia was sure the golem would never hurt her. In the poor woman's broken mind, Alicia had come to represent something forever lost but never forgotten. She was a living reflection of something that deeply mattered to Tracey, something she had loved—perhaps the *only* thing. And though Alicia was not the golem's creator, she had awakened it, and like the rabbi in the story, this monster was her responsibility.

Alicia raised the pistol in both hands, just like Tracey had shown her.

~

When the bullet entered her back, Tracey gasped for air as her right lung instantly began filling with blood. She wobbled on her feet, the rifle slipping from her hands and swinging from the strap. A second bullet struck her in the spine. As she fell, she wondered how she could have missed spotting the sniper behind her. She thought she'd been thorough in her sweep of the area. But then again, she hadn't doubted

THE OLD LADY

things might end this way. Escaping from this had been only a fantasy. The important thing was that she wouldn't be taken in, that she wouldn't be put in a cage for the rest of her life. There were too many cops and rangers for her to kill them all, too many guns pointed in her direction. And though the pigs all ducked for cover when her assault rifle blazed, she'd already been tagged in the chest by one cop's bullet and had caught a ranger's slug in her hip even before being shot in the back.

Suicide by cop, Tracey thought as she dropped to the ground. Like all forms of suicide, she'd imagined this scenario many times. Now that it was happening, it seemed almost hallucinatory, like she was in a lucid dream. It was a welcome change. Of all the nightmares she'd lived through, she was finally in control of one.

Tracey's throat clicked as she struggled to breathe. Her punctured lung was making it impossible, but she wasn't fully aware of the damage. She heard shouting but couldn't understand the words. Even when the police swarmed over her with their guns drawn, she couldn't understand what they were saying anymore. Unable to keep her head up any longer, she turned it to one side, and the snow felt soothing against the eye that had swollen shut. Her good eye remained open, and she caught a glimpse of her daughter standing ten feet away. She wasn't sure why Olivia had tears in her eyes. Tracey was proud of her, and everything was going to be okay now.

Soon these cops would have to climb up Harding Trail to investigate everything that had happened and assist the firefighters in extinguishing the inferno raging at the compound. Knowing this made Tracey want to smile but the muscles in her face failed to respond. She had told Nori and Alicia—no, *Olivia*—not to backtrack on Harding Trail for a reason. The extra homemade landmines she'd buried on the path would make for a nasty surprise for these pigs, as would the spring spear trap and whip trap she'd set up earlier in the day, back when Tracey and all three of the kids were fleeing from their hunters. At the time, she'd been hoping to impale a member of the militia with the row of blades she'd wedged into the swinging stick, but a cop would be just as good. The thought of lawmen stepping into her wartime booby-traps pleased her.

It suddenly occurred to Tracey that she couldn't hear her father's voice anymore.

Though she was suffocating, a feeling of peace came over her. At last, the sadness would end. The world that had always hurt her was finally slipping away. She would not miss it. Now that she would soon be rid of this world, she wondered why she'd fought to stay in it for so long.

Tracey's last thought was more like a wish.

She hoped Olivia would make out better than she had.

~

Alicia watched the golem die.

A strange combination of sorrow and nausea overcame her, and she dropped the smoking pistol into the snow.

Three cops and a paramedic had gathered around Tracey, ignoring Alicia as she stepped closer to see over the crouched crowd. Even though the golem was dead, the police snatched her weapon away as if she might return to life at any moment and continue her rampage. It seemed only Alicia knew the monster was gone. All that was left now was the slack body of an old lady who had saved her life. In return, Alicia had killed her. She felt she'd had no choice, and in some ways believed Tracey had wanted her to do it.

That last, sad smile Tracey had given Alicia while walking past the squad car was all the clarification Alicia had needed. Tracey wasn't just too far gone to ever come back—she'd never been in her right mind to begin with. The torture she'd endured here was nothing compared to the torture her own mind put her through every single day. Her body had absorbed every blow ever thrown at her, but her sanity could never recover from the collective damage of a life without mercy. The only mercy left was a permanent escape.

Alicia had learned a lot from Tracey.

She'd learned that sometimes, the only answer was destruction.

Sometimes, a murder was for the greater good.

Acknowledgements

Thank you to all my readers and fans, who mean more to me than I can ever express.

Thanks to Edward Lee, Daniel J. Volpe, Chandra Claypool, Aron Beauregard, Candace Nola, Mort Stone, C.V. Hunt, Bryan Smith, Brian Keene, Ryan Harding, Gregg Kirby, Josh Doherty, John Wayne Comunale, Jonathan Butcher, Tim Lebbon, Wrath James White, Shane McKenzie, Mona Kabbani, and George Cotronis.

Special thanks to Jack Ketchum.

Extra special thanks to Bear.

And big thanks to Thomas Mumme—always.

About the Author

Kristopher Triana is the multiple award-winning author of *Gone to See the River Man, Full Brutal, They All Died Screaming, Ex-Boogeyman,* and many other terrifying books. His work has been published in seven languages and has appeared in many anthologies and magazines, drawing praise from *Rue Morgue Magazine*, *Cemetery Dance*, *Publisher's Weekly*, *Scream Magazine*, and many more.

In addition to his fiction writing, Triana is also a regular columnist for the magazines *Backwoods Survival Guide* and *Prepper Survival Guide*. He lives in New England.

Signed books and merch: TRIANAHORROR.COM
Newsletter: kristophertriana.substack.com
Instagram: Kristopher_Triana
Facebook: Kristopher Triana
TikTok: Kristophertriana

Made in the USA
Middletown, DE
24 January 2024